I0692080

THE CASE FILES OF
RODERICK MISELY,
Consultant

THE CASE FILES OF
RODERICK MISELY,
Consultant

JP RIEGER

Aventine Press

Contact the author at JPRieger1@aol.com

Published by Aventine Press
55 E Emerson Street
Chula Vista, CA 91911

ISBN: 978-1-59330-818-6

Printed in the United States of America

TABLE OF CONTENTS

CHAPTER ONE
THE SOUND CAMERA

The Sound Camera practically leapt from the shelf into Roderick Misely's hands. The oversized text on the outside of the box encouraged the user to "Take snapshots of your favorite sounds!" The happy faces depicted on the back panel guaranteed the owner boundless popularity at parties, picnics and other social occasions.

Roderick lifted the curiosity from among the half-broken appliances on the shelf. He smiled as he turned the box over in his hands, happy to be in contact with such a ludicrous fraud. It was too good to be true. He didn't think that an actual movie camera, complete with sound, could fit into such a compact package. And he certainly didn't expect to find such a treasure lying on the shelf of a thrift shop.

Roderick removed the contraption from the cardboard box. As he suspected, the Sound Camera was nothing more than a cheap, transistorized tape recorder. This "camera" had no lens and used no film; just reel to reel recording tape. Anyone expecting a jumpstart to Hollywood courtesy of the Sound Camera would be sorely disappointed.

Roderick performed a quick test, manipulating the controls with raccoon-like fingers. Predictably, the Sound Camera did not work. He suspected a dead battery, the bane of the transistorized age. But the three dollar price tag was too appealing to pass up. And Roderick always admired creative advertising.

He put the Sound Camera back into the box and headed towards the checkout counter of the Dime A' Dozen thrift shop.

Racks of donated clothing brushed against Roderick as he made his way to the cashier's counter; a siren's call. He glanced over at the men's clothing, but decided to pass. On the men's rack were no less than three, dark brown, single-breasted business suits that would have fit Roderick perfectly. He might have been interested in the suits, but he already owned eight such brown suits, seven of which were hanging in one of the two metal wardrobes at home. He was wearing the other one, now. In fact, he always wore a brown business suit every day of the week; the eighth was a spare. Of course, Roderick had other suits and sports coats: a seersucker, a few double-breasted and several loud plaids. But those were solely for costume purposes and were housed in the other metal wardrobe, the one with the door that had to be kicked closed, due to a broken latch.

Roderick's brown suit uniform served its purpose. If the term "chameleon" could ever be applied to a human, it applied to Roderick Misely. Misely - with his always buttoned brown suit, his dull shirts and neckties and his brown oxford shoes - blended innocuously into every conceivable setting. Adding to the chameleon effect were his thoroughly unremarkable physical features. He was of average height and build; a swimmer's frame, gone somewhat to pot. His hair was a nondescript brown. Roderick was not bad looking; his face simply lacked distinctive, readily identifiable features. People who met Roderick often failed to recognize him later. He generally went about unnoticed. And this was a gift of tremendous value to a person like a Roderick Misely.

Regrettably, not all men carry within their hearts the basic, moral goodness so necessary to the well-being of a civilized world. The milk of human kindness nourishes not every man's soul. The law books that Roderick had been studying, spoke of "mens rea," and "scienter," meaning the culpable state of a criminal perpetrator's mind. Sadly, Roderick's mind was swimming in mens rea and awash in scienter. Adding insult to injury was Misely's decidedly misanthropic streak. His generally asocial disposition could be summed up, succinctly: He liked people but he liked himself better.

Misely paid the three dollars to the gray-haired lady at the cash register. Walking back towards Iroquois Avenue in the early spring afternoon, he decided to drop the Sound Camera off at home before going to dinner. He had been wondering exactly where he would put the darn thing, as he already owned no less than three other tape recorders, including a Wollensak inherited from his father.

"Home" was Roderick's suite at 7 North Central, just up the street from the northeast corner of Iroquois and Central, one of the main crossroads in downtown Elk Neck. Downtown Elk Neck consisted of about four, square blocks surrounding the Courthouse. But except for the law offices, banks and a few restaurants near the Courthouse, the area was in serious decline. The building boom of the early '50's had churned forth the upscale Washington Heights subdivision, just outside of downtown Elk Neck and a mere 20 minutes north by streetcar ride from the City. The middle-class had evacuated to the new suburb, abandoning Elk Neck to the ravages of innocent neglect and the indiscriminate passage of time. Washington Heights was well within walking distance of downtown Elk Neck, but besides the fluke of geography, the two were now worlds apart.

About Roderick's suite: He was renting a two-room eyesore in what amounted to the second floor, rear, of the commercial building running up from the corner of Iroquois and Central. So positioned, it was continually assaulted by the aromas of the Greek restaurant below, County Restaurant, at 22 Iroquois. At any given time of the day, Roderick's hole in the wall reeked of feta cheese, spinach pies or singed lamb stew, but Misely never seemed to notice.

Roderick trudged up the two long flights of outdoor wooden stairs that led to his quarters. Paint bubbled and peeled from the steps and flaked from the outside wall of the building, often following Misely inside. The outside door of Roderick's quarters had no sign or other indicia of office use - just the number "7."

On entering his suite, he was met by the neat outer room used as an office. A large mahogany desk sat on a rust-colored Oriental rug, facing the entrance. Behind the desk was a worn but beautifully crafted leather chair. The chair, desk and Wollensak tape recorder were the sum total of Roderick's inheritance from his father.

A tarnished brass nameplate tacked to the inside face of the entrance door announced, "R. Misely, Consultant" to anyone in the room. But for the nameplate, it would be otherwise impossible to guess the nature of Misely's "profession."

Things had not quite turned out the way that Roderick might have expected. Roderick's father, a successful accountant, had high hopes for his son. He wanted Roderick to become apprenticed to and "read the law" with one or more of his lawyer colleagues, this being the path to Bar admission. But there had been trouble for Mr. Misely. The revered old Elk Neck law firm of Walls and De Roachbroom had found itself running startlingly short of operating capital. In response, the firm decided to favor a particular client's estate by allowing it the privilege of "lending" the law firm estate funds. This was accomplished informally, without the pointless need for consent from the heirs.

The heirs, who had been waiting patiently for their money, finally realized the situation and blew the whistle on the law firm. But old man Walls claimed no recollection of any such transaction. And De Roachbroom had become incapacitated and unable to comment. Instead, a liver-spotted finger was pointed squarely at Mr. Misely, the estate's accountant. Mr. Misely, however, had no knowledge of the ongoing misappropriation. The estate's canceled checks appeared to represent legitimate expenditures, thanks to the manipulations of the law firm of Walls and De Roachbroom.

Mr. Misely was cleared, eventually. But the publicity surrounding the investigation had stampeded Mr. Misely's clients away in droves. The business creditors took just about every-thing. Eventually, after Mr. Misely passed away, the County Solicitor made his case against the law firm. But the scandal had unfairly sullied the family name, stigmatizing Roderick and se-riously eroding his chances of obtaining an apprenticeship with any lawyer in Elk Neck.

Roderick placed the Sound Camera on the desk. Besides the uncluttered desk and leather chair, the office held two folding aluminum chairs, a neat bookcase filled mostly with legal trea-tises and a well-worn gray plaid sofa for use by Roderick's cli-ents. A framed certificate on the wall appeared to be a diploma of some sort but upon closer inspection turned out to be Roderick's Notary Public commission.

Behind and to the right of the leather chair was a second door marked with a store-bought "PRIVATE" plaque, featuring conservative black lettering against a fake gold background.

Through this door lay the complete and utter confusion of Roderick's living quarters.

A cot was located, somewhere, in the middle of the room, but the cot was covered over with layers of newspapers, books, maps, shoeboxes, a pair of binoculars and various items that comprised Roderick's current "case." Below the cot, a low slung metal footlocker housed an assortment of used theatrical com-pany garb, wigs, mustaches and beards. A small, well-bruised metal desk and cheap folding chair were covered with piles of books, a portable typewriter and several radios pulled apart for repair. An open chemistry set, complete with corked bottles, test tubes and eye droppers, performed a balancing act on the folding chair. More books were heaped into piles nearby on the floor. The piles leaned precariously against the legs of the folding chair, preventing the chair from being moved without causing an avalanche. An olive drab, flannel horse blanket was heaped onto the worn linoleum floor near the cot, making it nearly im-possible to find floor space on which to walk.

A brutally scorched electric hot plate graced the top of a homemade, ramshackle shelf. The shelf was a wooden plank, leaning on one end on top of the radiator and suspended at the other end by a bracket attached to the wall. Joining the hot plate on the shelf were tape recorders, reels of recording tape, a waffle iron, a Hammarlund shortwave radio (covered with a sheet of cheesecloth used as a dust protector) some chipped plates and cutlery, old coffee cans filled with nuts and bolts and a soldering iron. Beneath the shelf were stacks of canned goods, dry cereals, a wooden box of rusty tools and skeleton keys - and rustier, expired license plates - old paint cans, two pots, a bleached white duffel bag filled with laundry, a metal waste paper basket, galoshes, a shoe shine kit and a fabric sewing basket filled only with tea bags.

The window over the shelf would have presented an uninteresting view of the side of the Graham Independent Free Public Library building across the street. But Roderick had stuffed a pillow up against the window for additional insulation during the previous winter. He hadn't gotten around to removing it.

Two metal wardrobes held their positions, side by side, against the rear wall.

A doorless bathroom held hostage an unfortunate toilet and a dented metal shower stall. Upon flushing, the toilet coughed out a low death rattle, followed by an ear-splitting banshee wail that could be heard anywhere within the building. Roderick, having become accustomed, no longer noticed the performance. The warped, metal shower stall was of fairly recent vintage, having been added to the premises a mere eighteen years earlier. The green, plastic shower curtain was embossed with a school of uniform, open-mouthed fish, frozen mid-stream. They were swimming straight for the edge of their mildewed ocean.

Above a tiny, rust-stained sink, a skinny glass shelf - cracked in half but spliced together with masking tape - held onto the wall for dear life. The shelf held Roderick's comb, safety razor and shaving soap. A small shaving mirror glued to the particleboard wall above the sink provided the finishing touches for the bathroom decor.

Outside, the wall opposite the wooden-plank shelf held a large bulletin board, bursting with layers of papers. Among the paper thicket were several baseball schedules and no less than five calendars obtained earlier in the year from five different proprietors. Inexplicably, each calendar was marked with different dates and notes.

A respectably modern, metal filing cabinet joined the bulletin board against the wall. It was located just past the sweep of the entrance door and proved the one exception to the general rule of chaos about the room. The bottom two drawers of the cabinet were filled with carefully maintained files representing cases on which Roderick had acted as consultant.

The filing system was simple; file numbers began with either the prefix "O" or "C." "O" files were "objective" cases, meaning cases where Misely pursued some particular objective of his own. The "C" files were actual "client" cases. There were a lot more "O" files than "C" files.

The top drawer held empty file folders and a copybook that served as a file ledger. Placed immediately behind the copybook were no less than 40 separate file folders, containing sets of letterhead, envelopes and business cards, each boldly proclaiming the holder to be: a process server, bail bondsman, notary public, estate agent, title abstractor, sales specialist, insurance investigator, commodities factor, property broker, philatelist, general agent, transporter, appraiser, courier, surveyor's assistant, freelance auditor, interpreter, and on and on. And each of these diverse activities were said to be taking place at the humble confines of 7 North Central.

It was approaching 5:30 PM, so Roderick decided to stop around the corner for his usual dinner. He entered County Restaurant at 22 Iroquois and was enthusiastically greeted by Mrs. Marie Georgelus, the plump and bubbly wife of the proprietor, Simenon "Sam" Georgelus, her far less bubbly husband.

She was standing in the entrance foyer by the wooden podium, ready to greet the hungry masses.

"Good evening, sir, it is so good to see you again! Will you be joining us for dinner tonight?" Her shriek bounced around the restaurant and into Misely's ear canal.

Misely grimaced, biting back the sarcasm welling up in his throat. Mrs. Georgelus had asked this same question of Misely with every visit that he had made to the restaurant since moving into his quarters, over three years ago. Accounting for the various meals taken by Roderick at County Restaurant, Mrs. Georgelus had asked this same question of Misely, approximately 1,095 times.

"Why, yes ma'am," he smiled politely, "I will be staying for dinner this evening."

Misely picked up a random newspaper from the corner of the lunch counter and headed towards the back of the restaurant. The restaurant featured an eight-seat lunch counter, four formica-topped tables and three wooden booths in the rear. Misely took his usual spot in the last booth, farthest away from the entrance. A pay phone was installed against the back wall immediately adjacent to Roderick's booth. Misely always sat facing the back wall, partly because that side of the booth had the best light for reading. It also allowed him to avoid eye contact with Mrs. Georgelus, who would otherwise continually look over to Roderick during his meals, with her earnest eyes asking whether "everything is all right?"

The Georgelus family genuinely liked Roderick. Like many people surviving in a hostile world, they mistook Misely's displays of ordinary, common courtesy as an offer of lifetime friendship. And Roderick was very courteous.

Eleni, the Georgelus' daughter, emerged from the kitchen when she heard Roderick's voice. Like her parents, she deeply admired the neatly groomed young gentleman. She pictured Roderick as a sad but courageous young man with some secret or tragic past. Sometimes, when she thought about him, a tear or two of sorrow would fill her kind, brown eyes, as they did, now. Coincidentally, at that very moment, tears were also welling up within Roderick's eyes. He had just read a particularly maudlin Letter to the Editor in the Star Sentinel and could not help but laugh derisively to himself over its contents.

Roderick enjoyed the lamb stew special with tyro pita and read the paper from cover to cover. He marched back around the corner to his quarters. There was some time to kill before the radio broadcast of that evening's baseball game, so Misely sat at his office desk and began to fiddle with the Sound Camera. It was a clever device, built to resemble an actual movie camera.

He grabbed a screwdriver from the top desk drawer and unscrewed the stubborn screw that held down the battery compartment. Immediately, he understood the problem. Someone had attempted to install a 9-volt battery backwards by forcing the claw-end terminals of battery and battery clip, together. And when the round terminals refused to keep in contact, as the laws of physics required, the same person attempted to force the contacts together by wrapping them with layers of tightly wound cellophane tape. The wrappings had created an oozing, sticky glob that took Roderick several minutes to disassemble and clean.

He replaced the battery and opened up the top lid. A small reel of tape had already been threaded onto the take-up reel by the previous owner. Roderick hit the "play" button. From the speaker came the voice of an elderly-sounding man reciting a time-honored "Testing, one, two, three," followed by a potpourri of Sound Camera selections: some Big Band music, interrupted mid-clarinet solo by the remnants of a pipe organ recital, interrupted, again, by portions of a baseball game. All were, apparently, tape recorded from the radio.

Roderick reached into the package and pulled out a flimsy cardboard tape box marked "Addie." He removed the tiny reel of tape from the box, threaded the tape onto the machine and pressed the "play" button. After some microphone fumbling and another "Testing, one, two, three," the tenuous voice of the same man creaked through the speaker:

Addie, by the time you hear this, things should have settled down. I wanted to thank you for your many years of devoted service. You've been a kind helper and I will never forget you or your wonderful mother. Addie, as you know, besides this tape recorder and the one hundred dollars, I left you my black and green, Chinese silk smoking jacket, my favorite one. Many years ago, I had your mother cut open a seam and sew a gold coin into the jacket. You are to keep the gold coin Addie. It is very valuable. If you are ever down on your luck, you should take the coin to one of the coin shops on Konrad Street. Tell the pro-prietor that you will sell him the coin for 85 percent of its Red Book value. 85 percent is a fair price. If you don't want to go by yourself, take your Uncle Robbie with you. Tell the coin man that it is a Panama-Pacific Exposition $50 gold piece. But don't worry if you forget the name, he will know what it is. If you do as I say you'll always be able to keep food on the table.

And with that, the taped message ended and the tape flew off onto the take-up reel, which spun and spun. Roderick flicked the switch off and thought about the strange message. He re-thread and rewound the tape and played the message, again. He leaned back in his leather chair, cupping his hands behind his neck. He pictured the fortunate Addie, living high on the hog. The Panama-Pacific was a remarkable treasure. Being a com-memorative coin, very few were minted and most of those were later melted down. He knew that the $50 gold piece came in two varieties, round and octagonal, both exceedingly rare. They were minted in connection with the San Francisco Exposition of 1915 to celebrate the opening of the Panama Canal.

Distracted, he got up out of his chair and wandered back into his living quarters to look for his copy of Yeoman's Red Book. He was rummaging through a pile of books on the floor near his metal desk, when a thought crossed his mind: Suppose Addie had never heard the taped message? After all, how had the tape recorder and message wound up in the thrift shop?

He turned back into his office and jumped into his leather chair. He unbuttoned his suit jacket and unconsciously opened the top drawer of his desk, grasping the lip of the drawer with his clenched left hand. Years of this bad habit had imbedded the rim of the drawer with the sweaty impressions of his thumb and clenched fingers. He considered the possibilities and began to perspire. He clumsily re-thread the tape and played it back, again.

Addie, by the time you hear this, things should have settled down. I wanted to thank you for your many years of thoughtful, devoted service. You've been a kind helper and I will never forget you or your wonderful mother. Addie, as you know, besides this tape recorder and the one hundred dollars, I left you my black and green, Chinese silk smoking jacket, my favorite one. Many years ago, I had your mother cut open a seam and sew a gold coin into the jacket. You are to keep the gold coin Addie. It is very valuable.

Misely hunched forward in the chair. Judging from the speaker's tone, it seemed obvious that Addie had been in the speaker's employ somehow, perhaps as a maid or housekeeper. The man had given her the tape recorder, a hundred dollars and his smoking jacket with the coin. It struck him that the taped message may have been left for Addie to be played back following the man's demise - once things "settled down." That would explain why he said he had "left" her the items. Perhaps he meant for Addie to receive the items as an inheritance after he had died?

Misely sat back in his leather chair and tapped his fingertips together. Addie would have received the money, smoking jacket and tape recorder from the man - or man's estate if his theory held true - played the tape and found out about the coin. That had to be the answer.

But why had the speaker gone to such lengths to make a secret gift of the coin? If the coin was intended as an inheritance, why not just include it in a will? Did the man fear that such a valuable bequest would be challenged by grasping family members or stripped by the taxing authority?

He leaned back in his chair. It probably didn't matter. After retrieving the coin, Addie must have disposed of the Sound Camera by donating it to the thrift shop. That was the answer.

Misely got up from the desk and began to pace around the room. Yes, it was possible that Addie, as planned, had received the Sound Camera, retrieved the treasure and later discarded the Sound Camera. But wouldn't she have erased or destroyed the tape? Exposing her secret gift to the world by failing to erase the tape would have defeated her benefactor's elaborate efforts at secrecy. Wasn't it at least possible that Addie had, somehow, never received the message and that a small treasure remained hidden within the fabric of a smoking jacket?

And then in a split second, another thought crossed Roderick's mind. He glanced down at his wristwatch: the Dime A' Dozen closed at 7:00 PM, in less than five minutes!

Roderick buttoned his suit jacket and catapulted out of his quarters, his brown oxford shoes clomping noisily down the wooden stairs. He wanted desperately to run at full bore down Iroquois, but to avoid drawing attention to himself, he walked quickly up a half block to the parallel alley, turned the corner and began a mad sprint. He emerged from the alley and tried to regain a more conventional gait, but his mixture of walking and half-running gave him the appearance of a stiff marionette, engaged in a stutter step mazurka.

The sight of the panting man in the suit surprised the gray-haired lady, who was tallying-up the day's take. Misely charged up to the racks of men's clothes and quickly began an inspection, scraping the metal coat hangers along the rack, one by one. And there it was: the black and green Chinese silk smoking jacket! Misely grabbed the jacket and pounced upon the cashier's counter, interrupting the gray haired lady's third attempt at counting the bills in the cash drawer. Misely quickly fished the requisite $3.50 from his pocket, paid, and exited the store, his heart pounding. As he walked back home, he held the jacket before him, squeezing the fabric in hopes of detecting the coin.

Back at 7 North Central, he moved the Sound Camera off to the floor and spread the jacket over the desk top. He began systematically probing and pinching the fabric. He turned the jacket over and continued the massage. "Drat!" He could not detect the bulk of the coin. He opened the top desk drawer and removed a magnifying glass. He clicked on the desk lamp and moved the magnifying glass over the coat, carefully inspecting each seam, looking for the telltale signs of homemade stitching. He found none. This was not the jacket. Sadly, the forces of fate that had brought the Sound Camera to the thrift shop had not operated in a similar fashion upon the smoking jacket.

He moved the jacket off of the desk and re-entered his quarters, emerging with his copybook ledger, a legal pad and an empty manila file folder. He entered "O-59-23 Sound Camera" into the ledger and onto the border of the empty folder. He pulled out one of the pots from under his shelf, filled it with tap water from the bathroom sink faucet and placed it on the hot plate. He would make some tea.

He began to formulate a game plan. He needed to identify the speaker on the tape and the mysterious "Addie." He retrieved the Sound Camera and placed the original reel back onto the hub. The partial recordings of the Big Band music and organ recital were of no help. But the portion of the radio broadcast of the ballgame yielded a clue. In the third inning, Denny Crawford, pitcher for the Wrens, walked in three runs, giving the visiting Zephyrs a five run lead. Roderick thought that he remembered this game from almost exactly a year ago, near the beginning of last year's Wrens' season. He could double-check this tomorrow by reviewing the box scores from the collection of Star Sentinels archived at the library across the street. But, presuming for now that he was correct, this particular tape was likely made about one year earlier.

Over the next few hours, had a disinterested person observed the scene at 7 North Central, such an observer would have noted Misely: pacing around the office, adding notes to the legal pad, drinking cups of tea, sitting at his desk, adding more notes, pacing some more and finally, yawning.

Tired, Misely entered his chaotic living quarters, changed out of his suit and grabbed the horse blanket. As he often did, he decided to sleep on the floor. There were too many items currently "under study" on the cot.

The next morning, Misely was back at the Dime A' Dozen, promptly at opening time. He polled the ladies working in the shop but they recalled receiving no other smoking jackets as donations in recent months, save the one.

Roderick went to work in another direction. He believed that the Sound Camera was intended to pass as an inheritance and that, barring some earlier interception, the Sound Camera, money and jacket would be part of the speaker's estate. And, judging from the taping of the Wren's game, if Roderick's assumption was correct, the man's passing would have occurred within the last year or so.

Roderick also believed that the man was likely a coin collector and fairly well off. He had mentioned the Red Book and the coin shops on Konrad Street, in the City. And a citizen of average income would not own a Panama-Pacific Exposition gold piece. He would check probate filings for decedents dying in Elk Neck County Township and in the City. Both had significant populations of middle and upper class residents. He would avoid the probate records of the more rural counties for the time being. Roderick decided to check the local Elk Neck probate records, first. The Courthouse, after all, was his home turf, located just three blocks away.

He entered the Register of Wills Office and was immediately greeted by several of the familiar staff. The staff were fond of Roderick. After Mr. Misely died, Roderick had tried to take on any sort of job that would place him in close proximity to the legal profession. Early on, Roderick had worked for "Tip" Paradiso, who sold Executor's bonds from the high-backed stool in the hallway outside of the Wills office. Tip was known to abandon his post in the afternoons during the racing season, occasionally assisting a few of the Orphans Court judges with "proxy" selections. Misely manned the stool in his absence earning a two dollar commission on each bond sold.

Roderick also ran odd jobs for the clerks and staff; sneaking illicit sodas and sandwiches into the Courthouse to those who could not stomach the cafeteria cuisine. And, occasionally, a cold beer in a lidded paper cup was smuggled in at the request of a particular Orphans Court judge.

Being a decent typist, he often assisted overwhelmed Orphans Court clerks, who would pay Roderick, quietly, through the office's petty cash.

Misely had proven himself particularly useful when Stu Bogden retired. Stu was the last of the clerks trained to enter Administration Accounts by hand in the oversized Accounts book. Stu had been carefully tutored by his predecessor in the traditional, florid cursive that had graced the handwritten Accounts book since before the turn of the century. But, the transition to the handier typewritten account pages meant that only accounts for the older, ongoing estates were still entered in the handwritten book. To the surprise of the staff, Roderick demonstrated his ability to precisely imitate Bogden's handwriting and was often called upon to enter accounts in the old book in return for a modest payment through petty cash.

Most importantly, Roderick was always happy to dispense what he called "practical advice" to the staff. Art Green, Chief Orphans Court Appraiser, was one of Roderick's biggest fans. Over the years, Art had recommended Misely to many of his friends and acquaintances, including repeat customers such as Ralph Martin and Chazzy Plink.

Art Green heard Roderick's voice, so he stopped into the record room. Art had a funeral director's quiet tone and a paternal bearing that most found comforting. Art understood Roderick's "consulting" talents and was always impressed with Roderick's unorthodox methods for solving problems. Subconsciously, though, Art wrestled with the notion that there might be a significant magnetic variation in the true north of Roderick's moral compass.

"Mr. Misely, when you get the opportunity could you stop by my office?" Art's request would have been barely audible to outsiders but was heard clearly by Misely.

"Yes Mr. Green!"

Being addressed as "Mr. Misely" meant only one thing; Art had some business for Roderick - possibly a new client.

Misely rapped on the outside doorframe of Art's cramped office and was beckoned in by Art. He took a seat in one of the two high backed stools facing Art's desk.

"Rod, I just wanted to let you know that I ran into Dusty Blackwell yesterday. Dusty was very pleased with the way you handled that matter with the Warrentons." But before Misely could respond with a "thank you," Art continued. "Now that I have swelled your head, Tip mentioned he had a man with a missing bike - presuming you still would handle that kind of thing." Art smiled, knowing Roderick would.

On the way out of Art's office, Misely nearly bumped into Appraiser Meg O'Callanan. But before she could say a word, Roderick jumped in.

"Meg, I'm just about done your radio. I'm missing one tube, but I know where to get it." Roderick had been cannibalizing junked radios looking for just the right part. Meg had long ago abandoned hope of ever seeing her radio again.

"OK Roderick. Just before I'm old and gray."

Roderick mused that such would be an impossibility, but bit his tongue. "You bet, Meg."

Roderick took a table in the record room and helped himself to the probate files. He began with a stack representing estates of decedents who had died during the preceding year. It was an enormous stack. He winnowed the stack down by eliminating the files where the decedent had died without a will.

Roderick first turned to the property listing for each file. He was looking for coin collections, on the theory that the speaker on the tape probably owned a significant coin collection. A few of the inventories contained collectible coins, but the collections seemed pedestrian: silver dollars, Buffalo Nickels, Indian Head pennies. Nothing too esoteric. He noted those files on his legal pad and moved on.

It was nearly Noon, but Misely didn't want to break for lunch. He decided to stop into the hallway to take a drink from the water fountain, though. Tip, stationed the hallway, caught his attention.

"Hey Buck-O. I've got a live one for you. Skip Ferris - his kid lost his bike or it was stolen - not sure. He's got the number here and might give us a call."

"Thanks Tip. I appreciate the lead, as usual."

Misely drank thirstily from the white enameled water fountain. He was thinking about other missing bike cases. There had been two or three - maybe four? Of course, he had never actually found one of the missing bikes. He had never bothered to look. Finding a lost bike was a near impossibility. Mass-produced bicycles were too fungible. The thieves were usually kids who would strip the bike of any identifying features. But Roderick could usually turn a few dollars by finding a similar model for a bargain price at the swap meet or a thrift shop. He'd clean it up and offer to sell it to the "client" for the same price as the reward money. It had worked every time. The clients were delighted to see a virtual duplicate of the missing bike, now clean and ready for immediate use by the nagging child.

Roderick went back to work in the record room. Near closing time, he hit pay dirt. One Philip Harwall Jackson had died in the preceding October with a will. His inventory included some incredibly rare Colonial era coins and currency, as well as a collection of U.S. gold pieces of varying denominations. There was no mention of the Panama-Pacific $50 gold piece - good news. If this were the speaker's probate estate, it meant that the Executor of the estate and heirs were likely unaware of the existence of the coin.

His palms now sweating, Misely pulled the will from the probate file. After noting the usual but highly unenforceable devise of the decedent's "immortal soul to the Almighty," Roderick scanned the balance of the "Last Will and Testament of Philip Harwall Jackson." Jackson devised his home in Elk Neck to a daughter and a commercial building in the City to a son. He gave an exercise bike to a nephew and in Item 6, devised his "elephant leg umbrella stand," to one Robert Watson, who, it was stated, "often admired" the object. In Item 7, he devised his automobile, coin and art collections and library of books to his two children, share and share alike.

But Roderick's heart leapt as he read Item 8. *"I give, devise, and bequeath to my longtime housekeeper, Adelaide Burke, the sum of $100, my portable tape recorder and my black and green Chinese silk smoking jacket."* Roderick had now identified the speaker and the intended recipient of his secret treasure.

By item 9, Philip Harwall Jackson devised the rest and residue of his personal property and effects "to the charitable organizations chosen by my Executor." Item 10 identified the executor as none other than P. Wendell Brighton.

Misely knew of Brighton. Brighton was an estate lawyer who admired the law almost as much as himself. Brighton carried himself with an air of indignant propriety, much like the nouveaux riche clients he served. A thin man with spindly legs, he prided himself on his straw-textured mustache, which overwhelmed his otherwise pinched facial features. Regrettably, the line of demarcation between facial and nostril hairs had become blurred over time without Brighton ever noticing.

Brighton maintained an office in the stylish Highgrove Building on Equity Row, just off of Courthouse Square. Brighton was universally despised by his fellow tenants. He was known for disabling the automatic elevator in the building by using a metal office chair to prop open the door when moving estate items in and out of his office, habitually burning out the motorized door. Seems he had never considered pressing the bakelite knob marked "open."

Art Green had put Roderick onto Brighton, years ago. Brighton specialized in the craft of "estate planning" for the wealthy. "Estate planning" for most attorneys, meant the process of developing a legally enforceable strategy, through wills, trusts and gifts, by which well-to-do clients could avoid probate taxes. For Brighton, it meant finding the most efficient means to exploit and profit from the wealth of his unwary clients.

One of Brighton's favorite techniques was to inveigle himself into the confidences of the family and have himself, rather than a family member, appointed as executor of the estate. This was presented as a means by which the family could secure his maximum attention to their needs. In reality, as Art Green had explained to Roderick years before, it provided another means of exploiting the estate, because the executor was paid a percentage of the estate value as a commission. To avoid conflicts of interest, most attorneys disavowed such commissions, taking only legal fees for their services. Not so Wendell Brighton.

And Brighton never discouraged his clients from making bequests to their new "best friend," P. Wendell Brighton, Esquire. This, too, was universally condemned by the legal profession.

Roderick continued his examination of the probate file, taking down copious notes. The smoking jacket was inventoried along with other personal effects and money; but no tape recorder was listed. However, a "camera" was listed, leading Roderick to believe that Brighton may not have realized that the Sound Camera was actually a tape recorder.

Brighton indicated that all assets had been distributed to the heirs. But, the account mentioned a distribution to Adelaide Burke of only the $100 and the smoking jacket. Not the tape recorder or "camera." Misely sat back in his chair at stared up at the ceiling. The Sound Camera's appearance in the thrift shop could be explained, perhaps, as a mistaken effort on Brighton's part to donate the "camera" pursuant to the will. Had he realized the "camera" was the "portable tape recorder" he would or should have distributed it to Adelaide Burke. That made it all the more likely that Adelaide Burke had never heard the message.

More surprising was the inked-in notation of "deceased" next to Adelaide Burke's neatly typed name in the Account. 'So,' Misely thought, Adelaide Burke had probably died after Jackson, sometime during the administration of his estate.

Roderick walked over to the countertop that held the large index book of decedents' estates. But he found nothing in the index for Adelaide Burke. This was not surprising. The families of persons of modest means often handled the division of a loved one's property, informally, ignoring the technical requirements of estate administration and tax payment.

Misely returned to the probate file. According Brighton's account, Adelaide Burke had never received the Sound Camera. But Roderick was more concerned about the ultimate destination of the smoking jacket. The account stated that the jacket had been distributed to Adelaide Burke. But because she had died with no probate opened, there was no way to confirm which, if any, of Adelaide Burke's heirs received the smoking jacket from Brighton.

Roderick had another concern. He knew of Brighton's reputation for playing fast and loose with estate assets. The Probate Code gave discretion to the executor to "abandon" any property deemed "inconsequential or burdensome" to the estate. Brighton once bragged about furnishing his home with a brand-new, but "fully depreciated" washing machine that he, in his discretion, had "abandoned," deeming the machine "burdensome" to the particular client's estate. Misely would put nothing past him.

Roderick finished up with the probate file just as the staff was about to flick the switch and plunge him into darkness on their way out the door. He headed over to County Restaurant for supper. Marie and Eleni Georgelus were delighted to see their honored guest who, it was determined, would be staying for dinner that evening.

After dining and reading the paper, Roderick caught himself nodding off in his booth, so he quickly headed back around the corner. He re-filed File O-59-23 in the filing cabinet and carefully hung up his brown suit in the metal wardrobe. Clad in his long underwear, he fell asleep on the floor wrapped in his horse blanket.

Next morning, Roderick poured out a bowl of dry cereal, devouring the cereal without the benefit of milk. Misely's suite lacked the modern convenience of refrigeration. He pulled File O-59-23 from the filing cabinet and reviewed his file notes at his office desk. He thought some more about the smoking jacket.

He needed to find out more about the heirs of Adelaide Burke. The Jackson Estate was not too helpful. But Roderick remembered there was a mention on the tape about an "Uncle Robbie."

If you don't want to go by yourself, take your Uncle Robbie with you.

Roderick saw that Jackson had devised the "elephant leg umbrella stand" to one Robert Watson and that Watson had a mailing address of 62 1/2 Hampson Street. Roderick knew that this address was located in Eastside, one of the less glamorous sections of the City. Since the names of most of the other heirs included the "Jackson" surname and listed mailing addresses out of state or in better-off sections of Elk Neck, Roderick figured that "Robert Watson" was probably not related to the decedent. But, could he be the "Uncle Robbie" mentioned on the tape?

Roderick thought that it was about time that he drop-in on his own Uncle Tack. "Tack" Misely was his father's brother, a lifelong bachelor and the closest thing that the family had to a black sheep. Tack did not particularly subscribe to the virtues of holding a steady job, which he believed stifled a man's opportunities in life. Doing freelance work as a surveyor's assistant and selling tip sheets at the racetrack was sufficient for his current financial needs. Tack had gotten himself into a number of scrapes throughout his life. He occasionally mentioned an arrest for being a "rovin' vagabond," which Roderick later understood to mean a charge as a "rogue and vagabond."

While Roderick's mother was alive, Tack was barred from the family home. Mr. Misely remedied this miscarriage of justice by bringing Roderick along to meet up with his uncle at the Wrens' games, where Tack boisterously held court in the bleacher section. To his credit, he was seldom thrown out of the park. Mrs. Misely lived in mortal fear of exposing young Roderick to a lifelong loafer like Tack; but it was for naught. Roderick had been born with the genetic predisposition.

Tack owned a Nash Rambler station wagon, which was the object of Roderick's visit. Tack won the Rambler a few years earlier, by purchasing a one-dollar chance at a church raffle. This unlikely event caused Tack to vow to turn over a new leaf, which he would do, soon. Tack never bothered to get a driver's license as he seldom drove. Roderick, on the other hand, held a driver's license, courtesy of the state-of-the-art photographic reproduction equipment installed in the Rare Book Room of the Graham Independent Free Public Library.

Roderick took the streetcar down to Tack's place, southeast of the City. Tack was living in an old fishing and trapping hut on Blackstrap Cove, modernized by a coal stove. Tack, as usual, gladly lent Roderick the car. It was now time to implement the next phase of Roderick's plan.

Robert Watson was just finishing lunch when he heard the bell ring. He opened the door to a man wearing a brown suit and holding a clipboard. The man introduced himself as "R. Mise, Independent Estate Auditor." The man handed over his business card which declared the same, thus satisfying Mr. Watson of the authenticity of the claim.

"Mr. Watson, I hate to trouble you, but I had a few questions relative to the Estate of Philip Harwall Jackson. Had you received the elephant leg umbrella stand that you inherited from the Estate, yet?"

"Me? Was I supposed to get that thing?"

"Why, yes sir. Had you or your niece Adelaide received anything from the Estate? Had the lawyer contacted you?"

Robert Watson looked puzzled. "I've never gotten anything from Mr. Jackson's Estate or heard from a lawyer or anybody. I don't know anything about an inheritance."

"How about your niece, Adelaide?"

"She didn't get anything, either. I'd have known if she did. She was boarding with me after Mr. Jackson passed away. She took ill, you know. I paid for the burial, myself. I've still got Adelaide's worldly possessions. It's mostly her clothes."

"Did your niece happen to own a man's green and black silk smoking jacket?"

"A man's jacket? Green and black? No sir. And Adelaide never smoked. You can thank my sister for that."

The Independent Auditor, quickly jotted down a "power of attorney" document on the sheet on the clipboard, authorizing R. Mise to "assert any and all claims, on behalf of the undersigned, to the umbrella stand devised to the undersigned pursuant to the Last Will and Testament of Philip Harwall Jackson."

Mr. Watson looked on blankly. "You know, I really don't want that ugly, old thing." But, Mr. Mise nodded so encouragingly and approvingly as he handed over the pen, that Watson shrugged and signed the handwritten direction on the clipboard, anyway.

Roderick was now convinced that Brighton was up to his usual handiwork.

Later that afternoon, a disinterested observer might have noticed a Rambler station wagon pull up to the front curb of an exquisite home in northern Washington Heights. The detached Colonial, with metal shutters, conformed to the builder's plans for the "Blenheim," model, which, along with the "Seville" and "Roma" models constituted the only permissible house plans for that particular subdivision in Washington Heights. The brown-suited man exited the Rambler, just in time to meet P. Wendell Brighton, Esquire, as he was walking up the last step of the short front porch stoop and placing his house key in the door lock.

"Excuse me, sir. My name is J. R. Milessi, a Book and Magazine Retailer. I would like a mere moment of your valuable time to inform you of a remarkable offer."

Startled at the sight of the strange man thrusting forth a business card, Brighton pushed open his front door.

"I'm not interested."

"Sir, if you knew of remarkable publications my company has available for your entertainment, your interest in patronizing my company would be guaranteed. Now, if I could simply describe these to you for just one moment..." Milessi was now practically inside the "Blenheim."

"No thank you, now get out of here, immediately!"

The door closed, nearly taking off Mr. Milessi's nose, but not before Mr. Milessi had poked his head around the corner into the living room and set his eyes upon one incredibly ugly Victorian era, elephant leg umbrella stand.

That evening, following a dinner of stuffed grape leaves and prassorizo at County Restaurant, Roderick sat at his office desk at 7 North Central. He'd made remarkable progress on file O-59-23. Roderick now believed that Brighton had simply taken the bequests of Adelaide Burke and Robert Watson for himself. After all, who would be heard to complain? Adelaide Burke had passed away and her uncle had known nothing of his own inheritance, let alone hers. Who would be the wiser? The Sound Camera had been surrendered to the thrift shop, possibly in accordance with the will, but more probably because Brighton couldn't get it to work and didn't think it worthy of keeping for himself. The cellophane-taped battery clip had all the earmarks of Brighton's general level of technical incompetence. That meant that there was a very good chance that Brighton had never managed to play the "Addie" tape before ditching the Sound Camera at the thrift shop.

As for the smoking jacket, it could very well have been consigned by Brighton, somewhere, for a few dollars. Or, Brighton may have decided to keep the jacket for himself.

Roderick leaned over his desk top, opening and grasping the top drawer with his left hand. In his younger, more brazen days, he would have simply entered Brighton's home at an appropriate hour and exercised his legal right to "self help." The law books he had studied allowed a creditor to repossess collateral as long as the creditor did not "breach the peace." But Roderick was not a creditor. He held the power of attorney for Robert Watson, but it didn't help much. He could arguably seize the umbrella stand for Watson, but not the smoking jacket, if, indeed it was even in Brighton's possession. And Roderick, of course, had been precluded from informing Robert Watson of his possible legal rights, if any, to the jacket and coin. Giving such advice would have constituted the practice of law, which Roderick, as a layperson, of course, would never do.

But, ultimately, the prospect of having a "breaking and entering" on his record eliminated any serious interest on Misely's part in effecting a clandestine search and seizure inside Brighton's home. That sort of thing was part of the past. He had come fairly close to finding an apprenticeship (Mr. Friedman would have probably taken him on, but for retirement) and he didn't want to make a stupid mistake. A criminal record would forever preclude his admission to the Bar. No, there would have to be another way to lay his hands upon the smoking jacket, wherever it was.

During the weeks that followed, a disinterested observer might have noticed a man wearing a brown suit, with a legal pad, leaving 7 North Central early in the morning and driving a Rambler station wagon to a particular Washington Heights neighborhood. The driver would have been seen staked-out in front of a particular house, noting on the legal pad, the bushy-faced occupant's first appearance at his front door in the morning and later departure for work.

Typically, the pajama-clad subject would be observed just after 7:00 AM, retrieving his daily newspaper. But the routine varied slightly on Mondays and Thursdays, milk days, thus providing welcome comic relief for the brown-suited man. On those days, the subject would have been seen gathering up his two quarts of freshly delivered milk, swooping up the bottles against his chest with one arm while simultaneously stooping down to grab his newspaper with his other hand, temporarily securing the rolled paper in his clenched teeth as he reopened his front door. The subject's bushy mustache and nicotine-stained incisors over the newspaper gave him the look of a snarling Pekinese, going fiercely at a bone.

Thereafter, the subject would be observed in business attire, departing from the home in his turquoise Chevrolet Bel Air around 7:50 AM and arriving at his Elk Neck office on Equity Row by 8:00 AM

The trip back from the office to the Washington Heights home in the evening would, similarly, have been observed and logged. Visits by the bristly-faced subject to the grocery store, hardware store, dry cleaner's, laundry, and other shops would, likewise, have been noted on the legal pad of the brown-suited man, as to time of arrival, purchases made and departure times.

It was soon determined, that there were substantial "safe times" when the subject was buttoned up in his office, usually in the mornings from 8 AM to 11 AM. During these times, the brown-suited man would have been observed visiting coin shops on Konrad Street, inquiring about commemorative coins, and visiting thrift and consignment shops located throughout Elk Neck and the City, pinching and poking at certain clothing.

Coincidently, back at the "Blenheim," Brighton's evenings were beginning to follow an unfortunate pattern. Invariably, in the middle of his supper, Brighton would be interrupted, mid-chew, by his ringing doorbell. He would wrest himself from his dinner table to answer the front door, only to be met by some salesman or another, offering a bewildering array of goods and services, from encyclopedias, to life insurance, to household appliances to magazine subscriptions, and on and on. Each annoying salesman would make every effort to gain a toehold into the residence, just before Brighton would abruptly slam the door shut. Brighton was beginning to believe that suburban life in Washington Heights was its own brand of hell.

Day after day continued to pass for Misely, frustratingly, with no sign of the smoking jacket. Not on the skinny frame of Brighton as he retrieved his milk and paper from his front porch stoop in the mornings, nor as he answered his door to the parade of salesmen in the evenings. And Roderick had fully exhausted each and every thrift and consignment shop in the area, sadly, without success.

Back at County Restaurant, the Georgelus family huddled around one of the formica-topped tables. It was a slow night and they had been wondering about the absence of their honored patron. Misely had not dined at County Restaurant in over a week. They presumed that Roderick was off on important business, perhaps out of state, or, more likely, in London or Europe. They pictured their neatly dressed friend dining on gourmet meals, perhaps in a luxurious Viennese hotel or maybe in a Parisian café. Coincidentally, at that same moment, Roderick was sitting on the edge of his cot, hunkered down over his long wooden shelf in his room, just over the restaurant. He was dining, miserably, from an open can of congealed beef stew, warmed by the hot plate. His devotion to file O-59-23 had caused a serious reduction in his liquid assets. As usual, he was short of funds. He had been "hot plating" it for the past week or so to save money and was unable to grace County Restaurant with his presence or his customarily generous 6.2% gratuity.

But the serendipitous arrival of a late spring cold snap in Elk Neck changed Misely's fortunes for the better. One chilly Thursday morning, a disinterested observer would have noted the brown-suited man, again, at the Blenheim, viewing the milk and paper balancing theatrics. But this time Brighton would have been observed wearing one pleasantly warm, black and green Chinese silk smoking jacket over his pajamas.

Misely swung into action. He collected articles of clothing very similar to the clothing worn by Brighton. The Rambler soon held neatly organized stacks of shirts, pants, suits and ties, piled into the back of the station wagon and covered over with towels. One of the clothing items was the black and green Chinese silk smoking jacket that Misely had originally purchased from the Dime A' Dozen, early on in case No. O-59-23.

Early the following Monday morning found Misely busily preparing a mixture of dried milk powder, water and granulated "instant" tapioca pudding in a rusty coffee can. The concoction was swirled and slopped about in the can by a forlorn and withered paintbrush. The coffee can and brush had found their way onto the floor of the passenger's side of the Rambler station wagon, which now sat quietly in the early morning darkness just in front of the Washington Heights address of P. Wendell Brighton, Esquire.

The newspaper had been delivered earlier, but Misely had arrived in time to watch the milkman drop off two bottles of fresh milk onto the front porch stoop. As soon as the milk truck departed, Misely quickly exited the Rambler with coffee can and brush in hand. He slathered generous helpings of the emulsified mess onto the milk bottles, already glistening from condensation.

At 7:00 AM, Brighton emerged from the Blenheim attired in pajamas and a black and green Chinese silk smoking jacket. He dutifully performed his ritual, gathering up the milk bottles in one arm, clutching them to his chest as he grasped the newspaper with his free hand. He hadn't noticed that the bottles were particularly dewy that morning. As he wrapped his jaws around the rolled newspaper he felt the moisture from the bottles permeate beyond the jacket and onto his favorite pajamas. Once inside, he placed the annoying and apparently leaking milk bottles on the kitchen table. Irritated, he quickly removed his smoking jacket to inspect the milky-looking Rorschach splotches, which threatened to ruin his recent acquisition.

On the following Wednesday morning, a disinterested observer might have noted the movement of a Rambler station wagon following close behind Brighton's Bel Air on the way to Atwell's Dry Cleaners. Brighton emerged from his car holding what appeared to be three white dress shirts, one gray suit, a yellow tie, and one black and green Chinese silk smoking jacket. As Brighton climbed up the dozen concrete stairs to the establishment, a brown-suited man quickly darted to the rear of the Rambler station wagon and grabbed, from beneath the towels, three dress shirts, one suit, a gold tie and one black and green Chinese silk smoking jacket.

Brighton was in the process of describing, meticulously, the proper amount of starch for his shirts and his grave concerns over the apparent milk stains on his smoking jacket, to Madeleine, the middle-aged clerk, when the brown-suited man entered and plopped his clothing with the second of the two clerks at the counter. The brown-suited man quietly gave his name as "Breiton," which he pronounced as "bray ton." He received his receipt, bearing the number 1187. He was informed by the teenaged clerk, Suzanne, that his order would be ready at 4:30 PM on the following Tuesday afternoon. In fact, the middle-aged lady and teenaged clerk practically gave the same direction, in unison, to both the brown-suited man and P. Wendell Brighton. The two men then left the establishment, receipts in hand, with the brown-suited man, politely holding open the door for the esteemed attorney.

At 4:20 PM on the following Tuesday, "Mr. Breiton" appeared at the Atwell's Dry Cleaners. When asked "Can I help you" by the teenaged clerk, Mr. Breiton announced, "Yes, please, I'm picking up my order for 'Brighton,' ticket No. 1186, three shirts, one tie, one suit and one smoking jacket, cost: $3.20." "Breiton" pulled the cash and change from his pocket and plunked down the money and his dry cleaning receipt onto the counter, the dollar bills obscuring the receipt number on the ticket.

Not that it made a difference. Suzanne emerged from behind the curtains holding Brighton's order No. 1186, and handed the dry cleaning bags over to the polite gentleman. "Breiton" gratefully accepted the order and receipt, now stamped "paid," and trotted down the stairs to his waiting Rambler.

Roderick quickly laid the plastic dry cleaning bags over the towel-covered piles in the back of the Rambler station wagon. Now sweating, his hands trembled as he pushed the plastic bag off of the smoking jacket. His raccoon fingers probed the fabric of the jacket. He felt a surge of excitement when he unmistakably detected a round, solid object in the hem of the jacket, just below the right hand pocket! He grabbed a razor blade from where it had been placed, in advance, underneath one of the towels. He quickly cut open the stitching of the seam. He gently rustled the garment, and into his hand plopped one round, Panama-Pacific $50 gold piece.

Misely's heart nearly pounded out of his chest and with trembling hands, he wrapped the gold coin in a piece of green felt and then placed the coin into a waiting coin envelope. He placed the envelope in his pants pocket and quickly smoothed out the fabric of the smoking jacket, repositioning it in the plastic dry cleaning bag. He grabbed the entire dry cleaning order and raced back up the concrete stairs.

"Excuse me," said the polite, somewhat winded young man. "There seems to have been some mistake. This does not appear to be my order. Could you check this, please? My name is 'Breiton' spelled 'B r e i t o n' and I seem to have received an order for a 'Brighton.' Here's my ticket."

Suzanne jumped to attention, happy to assist the kind man. "Hang on." She took the ticket back behind the curtain and emerged with Breiton's correct order.

"Oh yes. Well. Look at this Madeleine! This man is 1187 not 1186. But his order is exactly the same!" Madeleine pushed her reading glasses down on her nose.

"How about that. Sorry sir," said Madeleine. "I don't know how that happened!"

The gracious man replied, "Do I owe you anything extra?" The dry cleaning orders were exchanged over the counter.

"No, no, you won't believe it, but the other man had the same exact same order, three shirts, one suit, one tie and one jacket, so the price is the same." Madeleine doubted herself as she spoke the words.

"Thank you, ma'am and I'm sorry to have troubled you."

Madeleine responded, cheerfully, "Oh, no trouble at all, sir, please come back again soon."

As Misely descended down the concrete stairs he passed Brighton, working his way up. Brighton was a few minutes early but he figured his order would be ready by now. Like Lot's wife, Misely could not help but look back up the stairs and into the shop to see Suzanne and Madeleine, in pantomime, describing the incredible coincidence to an utterly uninterested P. Wendell Brighton.

Back at 7 North Central, Roderick took stock of the situation as he examined the coin, thick with gold, between his thumb and forefinger. He placed the coin on the green felt sheet, sat back in his office chair and considered the legal status of his newly found property. He knew from his legal studies that his ownership of the coin was good, as against anyone in the world but the "true owner."

And just who was the "true owner" in a case like this? Certainly not Brighton. His jurisdiction over the coin as Executor of Jackson's estate ended when he "de facto" declared the smoking jacket, and hence the coin, to be "abandoned" by taking possession of the jacket for his personal use. And Brighton's own, personal interest in the coin, if any, ended when Roderick took possession of such abandoned property.

And, certainly, the coin could not be said to be the property of Adelaide Burke, now deceased, nor her uncle and likely heir, Robert Watson. Neither she nor Robert Watson had ever taken delivery of Jackson's attempted gift, which was nothing more than an invalid effort by Jackson to circumvent the duly enacted tax and probate laws of the state.

'No,' thought Misely, the law would not and should not countenance or encourage such a demonstration of bad faith on Jackson's part. That left Misely as the true, rightful owner of the coin.

Roderick then stepped into the chaos of his living quarters and pulled some plain bond typing paper, a sheet of carbon paper, one envelope and a stamp, from out of his filing cabinet. He excavated his portable Royal typewriter from among the papers and books strewn over the metal desk. In Robert Watson's name, he typed a letter addressed to P. Wendell Brighton, Esq., Executor of the Estate of Philip Harwall Jackson:

Dear Sir:
It is come to my attention that you have not yet distributed to me, the elephant leg umbrella stand specifically bequeathed to

me pursuant to item 6 of the Last Will and Testament of Phillip Harwall Jackson. Presuming that this is a mere oversight, please, immediately, deliver this bequest to me at my home at 62 1/2 Hampson Street. Your failure to promptly attend to this matter shall result in my filing an appropriate report with the Chief Judge of the Orphans Court for Elk Neck County Township. Thank you for your consideration in this matter.

Sincerely,
Robert Watson

Dining at County Restaurant was particularly satisfying that evening. Misely smiled to himself, picturing the bumbling Brighton, hastily making his way into the City's Eastside to deliver the umbrella stand. Following his rice pudding dessert and second cup of coffee, Misely happily deposited the letter into the mailbox at the corner of Iroquois and Franklin and retired to his quarters. He filed the carbon copy of the letter along with the coin envelope containing the Panama-Pacific $50 gold piece, in file No. 0-59-23, and marked the case "closed" in the copybook ledger.

The file and ledger can both be found residing in the metal filing cabinet in the living quarters of Roderick Misely, Consultant, just beyond the office anteroom, at 7 North Central, just up the street from the northeast corner of Iroquois and Central.

CHAPTER TWO
THE MAILBOX RULE

Things had been fairly quiet for Misely of late. He had been occupying himself with a few "inquiries," but these had not resulted in actual cases. During these calmer times, Roderick undertook the study of the Law. But unlike an apprenticed student, Roderick was not "reading the law" with an attorney mentor. He was on his own. Lacking appropriate supervision for his studies, Roderick seized upon whatever topic happened to suit his fancy at the time. He had come across a casebook on contract law at Culpepper's used bookstore in the City.

Misely was enjoying his giouvetsi and stuffed grape leaves at County Restaurant, absorbed in an 1818 English case about a dispute between a wool dealer and a manufacturer. He hadn't noticed Marie and Eleni Georgelus hovering around his booth, refilling his water glass, trying to glimpse the title of the impressive volume.

The wool dealer in the old case had sent a letter to the manufacturer, offering to sell a large quantity of wool. Although no specific deadline for acceptance was stated, the dealer presumed that he would hear back from the manufacturer through the mails by the week's end. When the acceptance letter did not arrive, the dealer went ahead and sold the wool to someone else. The dealer didn't know that his offer had been misdirected in the mails for several days and that the manufacturer had, in fact, sent a letter of acceptance to the dealer. But the acceptance letter had arrived after the dealer had already resold the wool.

The English Court held the wool dealer to his offer, anyway, because of the "mailbox rule." This seeming injustice fascinated Misely and he read further. According to the "mailbox rule," a party making an offer will become bound if the recipient posts an acceptance letter in the mail prior to any stated deadline, or otherwise, within a reasonable time period. Posting the letter is sufficient. Whether the offering party actually receives the response is immaterial. Having a "rule" based upon the foibles of the postal service bolstered Misely's already strong desire to join the legal profession.

Misely glanced down at his wristwatch. He had taken an early dinner at County Restaurant in anticipation of his meeting with Art Green, Chief Orphans Court Appraiser. He needed to drop the book back to his "suite," and walk over to the Courthouse in time. Misely knew that something was up because he had been invited to Art's office at 6:30 PM, an hour and a half after scheduled business hours.

Art Green, like a few other senior personnel, held the keys to the Courthouse and Orphans Court offices. But he seldom used his tiny office after hours. Art sat behind his desk and explained to his visitor that the name of the other invitee was "Misely, pronounced and spelled just like 'miserly,' but without the 'r'." Art's visitor sat on one of the two standard issue, high-backed stools that faced Art's desk. The stools had been placed against the wall on opposite sides of Art's bulletin board. The wall also held a framed, Colonial era will, complete with sealing wax and ribbons. This particular display had been inherited by every occupant of that office as a permanent part of the decor and was now, virtually invisible to anyone but a new visitor.

Roderick tapped lightly on Art's closed door and was beckoned in by Art's familiar, soothing tone. Roderick entered and saw the gray-haired, mustachioed, gentleman, decidedly beyond middle age, wearing a blue, vested business suit. The man's considerable paunch protruded from his sitting position on the high-backed stool, causing anguish to the buttons of his vest. A once-white, now yellowed, silk handkerchief squeezed forward from the breast pocket of the man's suit coat. Misely recognized the gentleman but could not place a name with the face. He thought he'd seen him, before, around the Courthouse or maybe in the County Council Office Building.

"Roderick, I'd like to introduce you to Mr. Grayson Porter. Mr. Porter is the Deputy Chief Land Planning Officer for the Elk Neck County Council." The two shook hands.

"Mr. Porter, I'm pleased to meet you."

"Mr. Misely," croaked the old gent, "Arthur Green tells me that you're a problem solver, perhaps even a miracle worker and, most importantly, that you can be trusted, completely."

"Well, I've had some luck in helping others with their problems, but I'm certainly no miracle worker." Misely hoisted himself up onto the other stool. "But as far as your trust is concerned, you can depend upon that. Anything that you say here will be kept in strict confidence."

Porter was pleased. "Arthur said that you're a man of your word and I trust him, absolutely. Art and I go way back, to when I brought him into the lodge - you know, the Beneficent Cavaliers' Lodge, Elk Neck Chapter."

Art quickly broke in when he saw the formation of a long and sentimental story passing over the old gentleman's face. Art knew from past experience that a certain glazing-over of his friend's eyes signified the beginnings of such a ponderous narrative.

"Rod, Mr. Porter has an interesting problem - the kind that you're good at." Art smiled, confidently on Misely's behalf. "Grayson, tell Rod about what happened."

Mr. Porter blushed and squirmed on the office stool as Misely repositioned himself, attentively, on his. "Well young man, sometimes an old fellow can get himself into trouble. As you know, I work for the County Administrator, Jim Bynam, a fine man... but, not that it matters, I had been a bit more supportive of his opponent in the primary election, Gene Langhorn. You remember our old Administrator, Gene Langhorn?"

"Of course." Langhorn had been the County Administrator for many years until unseated in the election by Bynam, who was, fundamentally, a younger political version of Langhorn.

"Anyway, there was a woman, you see, a fine young lady.... well it turned out she wasn't, really quite so fine…"

Misely was beginning to get the picture.

"So, we had a friendly relationship and I had written her several letters, which, I'm embarrassed to admit, could be called 'love letters'- well, really just the foolish ramblings of an infatuated old man. But, worse yet, in one particular letter I did a very stupid thing. I revealed to the young lady, a certain piece of information that could be thought of as being, perhaps, restricted County government information."

Misely spoke up. "Confidential information?"

"Well I hate call it 'confidential' but you could say it was highly restricted. But, call it what you like, my mentioning this information to the young lady, along with the fact of the stupid thing being a 'love letter,' was a big mistake. And then, of course, just to make matters worse, I went and said a few bad things about Bynam in the letter."

A look of hopelessness came over Porter's face.

"If Bynam ever read that stupid letter, my career would be over. It's a nightmare."

"You need to get the letter back - I understand."

"Well, it gets worse. Did I mention my 'rival?' His name is Thomas von Gunton. You may have heard of him. He's also in the Administration. He heads up the County Highways Division. He's a close friend of Jim Bynam. Anyway, von Gunton now has the letter. My old sweetheart did me in. Well, she didn't mean me any harm, but von Gunton squeezed it out of her. She works with von Gunton's bunch over at County Highways, too."

Porter took a deep breath. "So, as it turns out, I'm being blackmailed." His face went scorched red with embarrassment.

"Yes, hard to believe, but that's what it is. I pay von Gunton a 'consulting fee' once a month by check. It's $300. 'Consultant' he calls himself! What a nerve!"

Misely winced and shifted his position on the metal stool. "So how long have you been paying the $300?"

"It's been going on for about two and a half years."

Misely began doing the math, formulating his fee demand.

"The paying is bad enough; but it's getting worse. The young devil taunts me. If I pass by him in the hall or see him at meetings, he never fails to mutter some comment, just something to rub in my face. Or he'll smile and give me the fisheye if, at our meetings, certain matters are discussed that touch upon the information in that letter. He treats me badly in front of my peers. He's a bully. I've had enough, really."

Misely noticed that the old gent's eyes were welling up with tears, so he did some more math, escalating the fee demand upward.

Art, in a gentle, soothing, voice consoled his friend. "Now, now Grayson. Cheer up. Rod's on the case, right Rod?"

Roderick replied respectfully. "Well, there will be certain terms and conditions. But first, do you have any idea where he keeps the letter?"

Porter composed himself. "Well, now. That's the tricky part. I have no idea. I do know that he has it. He showed it to me in his office in the beginning, about two and a half years ago. He was very casual about it. He walked me into his office, like an old friend and said, 'Guess what I found?' And then he laid out his terms. $300 a month or the letter would be sent to Bynam or maybe even the Star Sentinel. And then I'm finished."

Misely nodded sympathetically. "O.K. Where does von Gunton live?"

Porter shifted on his stool. "Well, he's a bachelor and he lives in one of those expensive cooperative apartments on Stanton Row, you know in Washington Heights. Thanks, no doubt, to my paying his 'consulting fees.' By the way, did you know that I helped plan the public utilities for Stanton Row? An interesting project..."

Roderick quickly fended-off the detour. "So he could be hiding the letter in his apartment?"

Porter had begun shaking his head in the negative, before Roderick had finished his question. "Don't think so Mr. Misely. That would be too easy. Let's just say that I don't think so," he smiled, knowingly.

"Are you saying that you've been in his apartment?"

The old gent chortled. "Hmm... well anything is possible. It wouldn't be that hard, right? They've got both a maid and concierge service and people sometimes will take money in return for a favor."

'So,' Misely mused to himself, bribery was part of the old goat's vocabulary.

"OK. Well, if you had 'hypothetically' taken a look around, would you have seen a safe or a desk with locking drawers?"

"Oh no, definitely no safe and no locked drawers in the desk. And with that maid service in and out all the time, you'd have to figure that the letter simply was not there."

Misely leaned back in the stool and gazed up at the ceiling. "The Purloined Letter."

Porter looked on, puzzled. "Pardon?"

"The Purloined Letter - the Edgar Allen Poe story?"

"Can't say I've ever heard of it. What about it?" Porter looked over to Art for help.

"Well, the Poe story featured a stolen letter, which was being kept on the thief's premises. But rather than hiding it in a clever hiding place, the thief simply stored it out in the open, in a letter rack of sorts. The Parisian police tore the place apart, but failed to check the most obvious place to look for a letter."

Porter looked over to Art Green, again, still puzzled. He was thinking that the Poe story about police who couldn't find something in plain sight didn't sound like much of a plot and that's why he'd never heard of it.

"Well, I don't remember any sort of letter rack and I'm pretty sure I'd have seen my letter if it was just lying around." He rolled his eyes for Art's benefit.

"OK, what about his office? Any locked drawers or filing cabinets?"

"Well, that's even easier. He's an Administrative official like me. By law, all administrative files are public even the ones in his filing cabinet. The desk drawers and filing cabinets have locks, but are not locked. The offices all have glass partitions, so it's kind of like working out of a fishbowl. There's no privacy. With the public and everyone else coming in and out of our offices, there is really no safe place to hide a letter in an Administrative office."

"Does he own a car?"

"No siree. Checked into that, too. He walks to work. It's easy enough from Washington Heights. Besides, the parking is no good over there."

Porter paused, temporarily flustered, sensing an inadvertent admission. He quickly corrected the record. "But that was not my department!"

"So," said Roderick, leaning back against the corner of Art's bulletin board momentarily, until he felt the pinned-on papers rustle against the back of his neck, "you've got quite a doozy here."

"You bet, son. So, can you get me back that letter?"

"I believe that there is a significant probability that I can get you your letter back."

"Great!" exclaimed Porter, while mentally considering exactly what Misely meant by "significant probability."

Porter then sat upright on his stool. "Now, you're not going to do anything that would get me into trouble with the law or anything, right?"

Art Green spoke up from his chair: "Oh, no. Mr. Misely uses only legal means to accomplish his objectives, right Rod?"

Misely reassured, "Of course, only legal or legally defensible means."

Porter, again, mulled momentarily over exactly what "legally defensible" meant, but he let it pass.

"OK, so far, so good. Now, what about those terms and conditions?"

"First, everything that we discuss and do must be kept completely confidential."

"Of course," Porter replied.

There was a pause as Misely gave the old gent a sidelong glance.

"Well, yes, yes," said the blushing Porter. "I know I blabbed in that letter, but that was before I learned my lesson. Please don't worry Mr. Misely. I can keep my mouth shut."

Roderick continued. "Next, you'll have to be extremely patient. Something like this will take some time."

"Yes, yes," said Porter, earnestly. "I've been waiting patiently this long. I can wait as long as it takes!"

"Fine," said Misely clearing his throat. "Now, my financial terms are as follows: If I retrieve your letter for you, you'll pay me $3,000. I require no advance funds. You'll only pay me if I get your letter. If not, you owe me nothing."

Porter interrupted. "But you said you could get me my letter?"

Roderick shook his head and waved off the assertion. "I said that there was a significant probability of success. Nothing is guaranteed in life."

Porter, saddened, dropped his head to his chest, creating several double-chins. He pulled the yellowing handkerchief out of his breast pocket to mop his forehead. "OK, that's true, nothing is guaranteed in life. I know it." He puffed out his cheeks and exhaled. "Whew. $3,000. That's a piece of change. Almost a year's worth of payments, but I can scrape it up. Fair enough."

The two shook hands. Art jumped up from behind his desk and patted each firmly on the shoulder, a quarterback in his huddle. "Don't worry, Grayson. Rod's your man. You'll see."

Roderick broke in, eager to get to work. "Now, Mr. Porter, I'll need you to produce the kind of writing paper and envelope that you used in writing the letter."

"Oh, that's easy," said a now enthusiastic Porter. "I've still got the writing paper and envelopes."

The two arranged to meet the next day at 9 AM at Roderick's "office suite" to go over details.

Walking back in the twilight, Misely was excited about his new case. He did not place much stock in Porter's searches of the home and office. He really couldn't picture the old goat even dropping down to his knees to check under the bed, let alone perform a real search of von Gunton's apartment. Roderick would have to take a look for himself. But Porter's information about the maid service and the County Council Office Building policy was helpful.

Roderick clomped up the stairs to his office suite at 7 North Central. He entered the office anteroom, kicking a few paint chips back outside, behind him. He went to his living quarters and pulled out the copybook ledger and a fresh file folder from the top drawer of his metal filing cabinet. He marked the ledger and margin of the file folder with "C-58-31 G. P. Letter." He sat at his office desk in his leather chair and began to make a mental list of activities for the new case. But he soon became drowsy and repaired to his living quarters.

Except for tubes from a superheterodyne radio and a soldering iron, the cot was clear. He moved the items onto the floor, away from the striking distance of his feet. As he lay down on the cot, the mattress puffed out a small dust cloud of pulverized yellow foam rubber particles. The particles were atomized through some slashes in the side of the skimpy mattress, causing Misely to sneeze a few times before falling asleep.

9:00 AM the next morning found Mr. Porter ever so slowly working his way up the two flights of wooden stairs outside 7 North Central. He had suffered from gout off and on for years and his legs were shot. After completing the first, impossible flight, he wiped his brow with his handkerchief and rested for a spell at the landing, preparing for the next agony. As the exhausted hulk finally entered the outer office, he stared blankly at Misely.

"Gee Whiz, Mr. Misely. Just what the heck kind of office is this?"

Roderick sat Porter down on the sofa and went to fetch him a glass of water. He opened the door to his "private" living quarters by just a hair, wrapping himself around the mostly closed door, hoping to expose as little of the view of his room as possible. Porter got a small peek of the chaos, though, as Misely reentered with the water glass, performing another impromptu tango with the door. Having viewed the horror inside, Porter wondered what he'd gotten himself into. Roderick handed him the glass of water.

"No ice?" scowled Porter.

But Misely and Porter soon got down to business. Porter had samples of the writing paper and envelope. He remembered that the letter was one sheet, a page and a half long, but did not remember the number of paragraphs. He had folded the letter, twice, as would be customary for a business letter. He always used a cartridge pen, but couldn't remember if he had used blue or black ink. The letter's salutation was: "My Dearest Bunny," which was short for "Bonnie De Sonto," his Mata Hari.

Roderick confirmed specifics about von Gunton's home address and office number and tried to figure out a polite way to throw the old gentleman out of his office. Seems as though Mr. Porter had gone off on several nostalgic tangents. With a misty glaze to his eyes, Porter talked, ad nauseam, about the "good old days" in Elk Neck. His lengthy discussion of the processes and procedures of the old Planning Department interested Misely, not one bit.

Roderick finally seized upon a way to get rid of Porter by retreating into his living quarters to fetch another glass of water. He turned his hot plate on "high" and placed a half-eaten can of beef stew, left over from earlier that morning, on the plate. Following a discussion of the land subdivision process for the early stages of Washington Heights, the acrid stench of heated tin and burning beef drifted into the office anteroom. Porter's nostrils twitched.

"Do you smell that?"

Roderick sniffed too and yelled "Fire!"

He quickly swooped the old gent out the door and down the wooden stairs for "his own safety." Roderick, then, darted across Central and hid behind the library building, watching as the somewhat confused Porter glanced around for Roderick, yelling, "Son, son?" Porter eventually gave up and drove home. He would have chosen anything over another ascent up the wooden stairs.

The next morning found Mrs. Libby Dashield opening the office door of the Stanton Arms to the stylish young man. He was dressed in black slacks and a maroon, double-breasted sports coat, featuring epaulets. The polished brown oxford shoes were an unexpected selection, though. Mr. "R. J. Milstead" had telephoned earlier that morning to make an appointment to look at a cooperative unit.

She immediately judged him to be a suitable prospect. His clothes betrayed a decidedly stylish bent that telegraphed adequate wealth and sophistication. In fact, she had purchased an identical maroon sports coat for her husband just the year before from "L'Enfant Terrible," her favorite men's clothing boutique.

She would make him wear it again, since the young prospect was adequate proof that the coat was stylish, notwithstanding her husband's protests to the contrary. But then she remembered how her husband had confessed to sneaking the coat into the bundle of clothes donated to the Dime A' Dozen for the Ladies' Auxiliary's clothing drive. "Not to worry." She would purchase him a similar jacket, again, as soon as possible.

After exchanging pleasantries, Mr. Milstead described his current housing needs. He politely insisted to Mrs. Dashield that he be allowed to see an apartment "as truly lived in." He needed a perspective on how his art and furnishings would fit into the rooms. Mrs. Dashield was only too happy to grant the wish of the courteous young man. She summoned Mrs. Layton from the maid staff to accompany Mr. Milstead to a particular apartment unit, owned by an understanding tenant and friend, and occasionally utilized for just such purposes. But Milstead's modest gratuity placed in the hands of Mrs. Layton, gave rise to a detour and assured him of uninterrupted access to the apartment of Thomas von Gunton.

Once inside, Misely quickly went to work and discovered that the old gent was absolutely correct. There were no safes or locking drawers of any kind in von Gunton's apartment. He undertook a thorough search of each room, methodically checking for possible hiding places for the letter. He searched in likely and unlikely places; in and under cabinets and drawers, under throw rugs, behind curtains and even under the ironing board lining. When searching the pantry, he carefully lifted up canned goods and other items from the shelves, making certain that the letter could not be hidden between containers or underneath the shelf paper lining. The underside of each and every flat surface in the apartment was probed, even the underside of the toilet tank lid. He looked behind each painting and mirror adorning the walls. Photographs were temporarily removed from, and replaced back to, their frames. Furniture was carefully inspected for unusual alterations. Slipcovers over the sofa cushions and pillows were unzipped and inspected. Chair legs were tapped for hidden cavities.

He searched under von Gunton's bed, mattress, and box spring. He carefully went through his dresser, probing through layers of clothing. He patted-down the clothes hanging in von Gunton's closet. He noticed that, although von Gunton had several belts, he was apparently fond of belt-less slacks. And blazers and loafers were obviously preferred to business suits and proper shoes.

In the living room, Misely pulled each book from out of the bookcase and carefully flipped through the pages. Afterwards, he took the same book, turned it upside down and flipped through the pages in the reverse direction. He even checked inside each of the pages of a two-week pile of recently delivered, but apparently unread, Star Sentinels.

When he went through von Gunton's papers in his desk drawers he came across both his check book and pass book for accounts he held at Second State Bank. Misely scanned the check register. He found routine entries for groceries, utilities and rent payments to Stanton Arms; but he was looking for payments to any safe deposit box company. He found none. The pass book indicated that von Gunton often made deposits towards the end of the month. He could see the likely deposit of his County Council salary check as well as the $300 blackmail payment, usually on the same day. There appeared to be contemporaneous withdrawals of lesser amounts, probably for spending cash. 'Von Gunton was doing just fine,' thought Misely when he spied the significant amount of cash that Porter's rival had stashed away at Second State.

The search continued and took nearly three hours. But by the time Misely was finished, he knew that Porter was correct. The letter was not in the apartment.

Misely was tired and hungry and his fingertips were sore, so he quit von Gunton's place and headed over to Bertram's Deli, just south of Washington Heights. He seldom ate lunch there. He found the lunchtime business crowd oppressive and annoying. But arriving at 3:00 PM assured a patron of plenty of room for undisturbed dining. Roderick disliked crowded, noisy restaurants and particularly abhorred "social dining," preferring his own company. After a lunch of chili with pumpernickel slices, he stopped into the County Council Office Building and checked the hearing schedule. He was pleased to see that von Gunton and several staff people would be out from 10 AM until noon on the following day at hearings.

By 10:00 AM the next morning, the Highways Division was down to a skeleton crew. Division Chief von Gunton and his two assistants were busy at hearings. The Repair and Maintenance Chief had been called over to a Budget meeting. The few remaining secretarial and clerical workers barely noticed the appearance of the Building Inspector. He had introduced himself as "R. T. Mossly." His starched, white lab coat and clipboard were sufficient proof of his identity and mission. After performing cursory, visual inspections of two offices, the Inspector made markings on the clipboard and entered von Gunton's office.

In plain view of the disinterested staff, he checked the desk and filing cabinet drawers, carefully sifting through each paper and file. He lifted a dusty pile of papers from the top of the filing cabinet and after stifling a sneeze, examined each. He then checked behind a framed diploma and several awards hanging on the partition behind the desk. The back of the diploma frame was completely intact. But the "Public Service Citation" awarded for von Gunton's involvement in a blood drive looked suspicious. Producing a small screwdriver from his lab coat, the Inspector quickly dismantled the award. He laughed to himself when he saw that von Gunton had altered the award, originally granted to von Gunton and three others, by carefully folding the paper over to exclude the names of the other recipients.

He dismantled von Gunton's desk lamp when a light tap with the screwdriver seemed suspicious; but this turned out to be a false alarm. He dropped down to the floor and meticulously checked the undersides of the desk and desk drawers. He then rocked the filing cabinet out of the corner sufficiently to check underneath by probing the undersides with a wooden ruler.

He had dropped onto his back and was checking the undersides of each file cabinet drawer, when he noticed two horrifically swollen ankles in black, flat pumps standing next to the cabinet, close to his head. "What are you doing?" asked a female voice, from above. "Ball-bearing test," the Inspector immediately replied, moving the drawer in and out to demonstrate the physical principle. "Oh," said the voice, in retreat.

"Mossly" concluded his inspection, making additional markings on his clipboard. He passed through the secretarial and clerical pool and walked past the desk of none other than the infamous Bonnie De Sonto. He was surprised to find that Mrs. De Sonto was the unhappy owner of the grossly swollen ankles. Gazing upon the face of the medusa, he discovered that, besides needing a good shave, Mrs. De Sonto was no spring chicken.

On the way out of the Highways Division, the Inspector passed von Gunton and his entourage returning from their hearings. Misely had seen von Gunton's picture in the Star Sentinel, but was glad to get a closer look at his prey. Von Gunton was nattily dressed in an expensive blue blazer with grey wool slacks and a new pair of tassel loafers. His monogrammed shirt, gold cufflinks and jeweled tie pin, spoke to his elevated standard of living, thanks, no doubt, to the involuntary benevolence of Grayson Porter. Von Gunton led his parade of sycophants back to the office, his hyenas cackling obediently and loudly at each of his sarcastic quips.

Following the search, Misely's neck was sore. His fingertips were still numb and throbbing from the day before. He stopped for a hot dog from the vendor at the Courthouse Square and reviewed his thoughts from a Courtyard park bench. He didn't like to admit it, but the old goat was right again. Von Gunton's office was simply too open to provide a safe haven for a letter worth an extra year's salary to the holder.

Following a leisurely walk back home, Misely hung the lab coat next to the maroon sports coat and other Dime A' Dozen treasures housed in the other metal wardrobe in his quarters. The door popped open following an initial absent-minded attempt at closing, so Misely administered an effective and well rehearsed kick to the bottom part of the door. He pulled File C-58-31 from his metal filing cabinet and walked the slender file over to his desk in his office anteroom. He pulled a legal pad from his top desk drawer, and sat back in his leather chair, musing over his game plan.

Misely knew, unmistakably, that the letter was being held somewhere other than in von Gunton's home or office. He believed that two possibilities were likely: either von Gunton was carrying the letter on his person, continually, or he was keeping it in a rented safe deposit box or locker of some sort.

Keeping the letter on his person seemed the less likely possibility. But if von Gunton were to do so, the simplest place to hold the letter would be in the breast pocket of a suit or sports coat. Keeping the letter in the shorter side pockets or even in a pants pocket would mean that the letter would have to suffer additional folds. Too many creases could wear upon the ink, injuring legibility and decreasing or destroying the value of the letter. Additionally, von Gunton would have to constantly remember to move the letter from one suit or sports coat to another, or from one pants pocket to another.

Keeping the letter in a money belt would simplify its movement. But, Roderick had checked the belts in von Gunton's closet and had found no such belts. And a belt would cause even more destructive creases to the letter. A body pouch also seemed unlikely. Roderick couldn't picture a casual dresser like von

Gunton putting up with the irritation and constraint of having a body pouch around his chest or waist all day long. As Misely saw it, von Gunton could barely put up with wearing a standard business suit.

No, Roderick concluded that it was more likely that von Gunton was holding the letter in a locked box of some sort. A nearby safe deposit box would make the most sense. Roderick understood enough about human nature to know that most people hid or stored their most prized possessions close by, so that the particular item could be easily retrieved and observed. A person with a safe deposit box often accessed the box, just for the assurance of seeing the valuable with the person's own eyes. Misely also knew that he would always be able to find a way of moving a treasure from behind the security of a locked box and into his own hands.

Roderick would be trailing von Gunton over the weeks to follow, so he decided to pay a visit to his uncle, Tack Misely. He needed to borrow Tack's "one dollar" Nash Rambler station wagon, which always made the job of tracking a lot easier. Roderick took the streetcar down to Barrick Alley where Tack held a two room row house under a "lease with option to buy." Certain parts of the City were enjoying a renaissance, of sorts, complete with coffee shops, museums, antique stores and artist colonies. Barrick Alley was not such a place.

Tack met his nephew with his usual broad smile, revealing a missing molar, courtesy of some prior, forgotten, disagreement with a fellow citizen. As it turned out, Roderick's unexpected arrival was propitious; Tack was planning a move to a new residence and could use Roderick's help. He had decided to not exercise his option, after all. Roderick knew from past experience, that Tack's moves were customarily made under cover of darkness and that there would be some time to kill that afternoon. Tack recommended a walk over to Wrens Park, where they could enjoy the balance of the afternoon's baseball game, first from the sidewalk outside the gate, and later from the stands following the seventh inning, when the gates were opened, free of charge, to all.

After the game, the two packed Tack's few furnishings into the Rambler and drove down to Blackstrap Cove in the southeast part of the City. Tack had worked an excellent deal on a "lease with option to buy" one of the old fishing and trapping huts off of the river. Moving Tack's stuff in under the moonlight, Roderick noticed that the place seemed to lack indoor plumbing and electricity, which apparently explained the very favorable rent.

During the weeks that followed, Roderick carefully trailed von Gunton, taking copious notes on his legal pad. Von Gunton was a creature of habit. He stopped off at Wilkon's Laundry on Mondays and Fridays before work. He often ran errands during his lunch hour; he visited the Post Office on Tuesdays and Fridays and took a swim at the YMCA on Mondays. He usually ate lunch at O'Reilly's on Equity Row, a popular place with the political crowd. He stopped at Prentiss Bros. Grocers, on the south side of Washington Heights, usually on Monday evenings and Saturday mornings.

Misely was encouraged when he trailed von Gunton to the Second State Bank. Second State was the only bank in Elk Neck that had safe deposit boxes, although several banks in the City provided the service. Von Gunton openly flirted with the young teller, Cindy Fosgate, who seemed somewhat in awe of the well-dressed, middle-aged bachelor. Vacuous banter followed, but Misely was disappointed when no trip to the safe deposit box vault was undertaken.

Later that afternoon, Cindy Fosgate was surprised when her supervisor, Mrs. Newell, mentioned that there was a call for her, on line two - "Your Mr. von Gunton," she smirked, her eyes cast upwards. Cindy Fosgate anxiously clicked line two to find that it was Mr. von Gunton and responded, "Yes," she'd be happy to assist him. He had forgotten to ask her earlier, whether the bank planned to increase the rates for his safe deposit box and would they be billing him? Miss Fosgate, quickly, double-checked her favorite customer's account. After a few tense moments, she returned to the line and apologized that she "couldn't find any safe deposit box account" for him at the bank. Whereupon, von Gunton, remembered that, "Yes," she was absolutely correct. He had gotten his banks mixed up. He apologized, humbly and profusely, asking her to forgive his absent-mindedness and to please let the whole mistake be "their little secret."

Miss Fosgate was tickled at the opportunity and anxiously responded, "Yes, no trouble at all, it will be our secret!" Pleased with how things worked out, she now felt a special bond with her favorite customer. She couldn't wait to see him again; she'd give him a wink to let him know that his secret was safe with her. In fact she would practice just the right kind of wink, later that evening in front of her dresser mirror.

Misely racked the handset of the phone back to its cradle and crossed the name "Second State Bank" from the list on his legal pad. He was sitting in the phone booth located on the first floor next to the rear stairwell of the Graham Independent Free Public Library. Members of the public seldom used the rear stairwell or the phone booth there. He had no phone service inside his "office" across the street, preferring to use the one next to his booth at County Restaurant or this one, his favorite.

His legal pad also listed the names and phone numbers of the banks and safe deposit box companies located in the City. He systematically called each number, identifying himself as von Gunton and angrily demanding the manager. After some delay, the stilted tone of the particular manager would invariably be heard over the phone requesting how the manager might help the caller. There would follow a caustic diatribe by von Gunton, demanding to know why his safe deposit box rental fees had been increased and wanting to know just who had perpetrated the outrage. Invariably, Mr. von Gunton would be placed on hold, while quick research was accomplished.

Soon, poor Mr. von Gunton would be greeted with tones ranging from saccharine, to smarmy, to downright course, depending on the particular school of management attended by the speaker. But, unfortunately for Mr. von Gunton, the message was universally the same: that von Gunton did "not have an account" with the particular institution; that perhaps he should "call elsewhere" followed, in some cases, by an abrupt "good day," a click and a dial tone.

Unabated, Misely continued his tracking efforts over the weeks that followed. Because the check register information found at von Gunton's apartment was inconclusive, he undertook to follow von Gunton into the Elk Neck Central Post Office on his Tuesday and Friday lunch hour visits. He wanted to spy the names of the addressees of von Gunton's correspondence, looking for leads.

On one Tuesday, Misely followed von Gunton over to the cramped customers' table across from the wall of Post Office boxes and joined him across the table, pretending to address some envelopes. Von Gunton, like Misely, held a post office box there, where he received his mail. As von Gunton finished licking and applying postage stamps to his letters, he left the letters, momentarily, on the table, turning his back to Misely as he unlocked his post office box. Seizing the opportunity, Misely, quickly, craned his head around and took a good look at the addressees on the three pieces of correspondence, just in time before von Gunton performed an about-face back to the table. Von Gunton then sifted through his received mail, tossing some "junk mail" into the rubbish can next to the table. He closed up his box and headed over to the main counter to post his letters, tossing one more piece of "junk mail" into the can as he left.

As soon as von Gunton turned the corner towards the counter, Misely swooped down into the rubbish can and pulled out the abandoned correspondence, looking for more leads. Regrettably, there were none. The discarded mail was pure "junk mail" the same kind that Misely received all the time in his own box. And the posted letters he did observe, appeared to be routine payments for rent, the grocer and presumably, von Gunton's membership at the Greater Elk Neck Country Club. But Misely, undeterred, went through the same drill several times in the ensuing weeks, desperate for leads.

And Misely had not forgotten the less likely possibility that von Gunton was carrying the letter on his person. He had been following von Gunton to his favorite lunchtime destination, O'Reilly's just off Equity Row. Following several failed attempts, one afternoon, luck intervened. Misely was finally able to grab a booth, back-to-back with von Gunton's, in the always crowded restaurant. The booths shared a single coat hook. After von Gunton and his two office lackeys hung their suit and sports coat jackets over the hook, Misely nonchalantly placed his brown suit jacket immediately over the three. Quickly and unobtrusively, Misely's raccoon fingers probed the pockets and lining of von Gunton's sports coat. Sadly, Roderick detected no tell-tale rustling or crackling of paper. Disappointed, Roderick ordered a cup of the chicken soup and a glass of water.

More disappointed, however, was the waiter who realized that a busy booth had been wasted on a cup of soup and a remarkably frugal tip.

Misely regrouped back at 7 North Central. He sat at his office desk, scanning the contents of File C-58-31. Clutching the lip of the top desk drawer with his clenched left hand, he reviewed pages and pages of notes, carefully organizing his thoughts. He leaned back in his leather chair, hands behind his neck. He knew, now, that von Gunton was not carrying the letter with him, or at least, not in the most likely place, his jacket. And he did not have to go through a jacket search again because, under his theory, von Gunton would have to consistently keep the letter with him in his jacket at all times. One search was enough. He was certain that von Gunton was storing the letter in a locker or locked box, somewhere. And he firmly believed that "somewhere" would be relatively close by.

He thought about von Gunton's other activities. Von Gunton visited the YMCA at least weekly. But there were no permanent lockers available there. One simply brought along a padlock or combination lock and used any available locker during the visit. And presuming that von Gunton held a membership at the Greater Elk Neck Country Club, Roderick already knew, due to one disastrous summer episode as a caddy, that permanent lockers, likewise, were not available at the club. No, he would have to be patient and step up his surveillance. Something would break.

He continued his efforts to check on von Gunton's mail recipients and trailed him into the Post Office more frequently. He utilized the simple disguise of a pasted on mustache and "costume" clothing such as his corduroy and hounds tooth suits to avert suspicion. Sadly, no leads developed.

Once, during lunch hour, Misely held his breath as he followed von Gunton from the County Council Office building, unmistakably, towards the bus station. Misely had felt all along that the bus station lockers were a distinct possibility. The station took cash, only. Identification was not required and the holder of a locker would be difficult to trace. The lockers were usually paid for week to week, but von Gunton could have paid for several months in advance. Misely's pulse began to race as von Gunton approached the station. But his hopes were crushed when von Gunton turned in to the tobacconist's shop, just a half block short of the bus station. He purchased pipe tobacco, which he had gift wrapped.

Predictably, as a third month approached, Porter was becoming impatient. "Not complaining, mind you, just wondering what was going on." He had relayed his concerns by phone to Art Green one afternoon. He wanted Art to arrange another meeting, but as Art Green later relayed to Misely, "I told him to hold his horses."

Misely had his own problems. He was beginning to run out of money for normal living expenses. His concentration on this one case had taken time from other revenue producing activities, such as selling tip sheets with Tack. And Roderick hated the idea of selling any of his "investments," many of which could be found in the closed files in his metal filing cabinet in his living quarters. He would be "hot plating" it for the time being to conserve funds.

On one particularly sunny, spring day, von Gunton enjoyed a stroll through the Courtyard gardens. The flowers were in bloom and the park lawn had come in particularly rich and green. As he passed along the park benches he noticed, out of the corner of his eye, an elderly gentleman in a seersucker suit who had stood up from his park bench, perhaps too quickly. In a flash, von Gunton realized that he was on an inescapable collision course with the elderly gentleman. He tried desperately to avoid the old man, but, as though in a nightmare, he felt himself and the man tumble to the grassy lawn, together. He struggled, almost hopelessly entangled with the man, who rolled over him several times in a desperate effort to upright himself. Finally, after the bizarre wrestling match ended, both men stood, the old gentleman profusely apologizing to the young stranger. Von Gunton, waved off his apologies, dazed. After von Gunton had regained his composure, he had the distinct impression that he had just been tickled.

The old gentleman blended into the scenery and headed slowly towards 7 North Central. Back in his living quarters, Misely removed the seersucker suit and the remainder of the disguise. The body search of von Gunton was necessary to eliminate any possibility that he was keeping the letter in a body pouch or other similar device. He was not.

Misely was now in danger of becoming obsessed with his mission. Surveillance was extended to 24 hours a day. He caught necessary cat naps in the back of the Rambler station wagon, covered with his horse blanket. Misely was beginning to believe that he had hit an absolute dead end. He would hate to admit it to Porter but even more so to Art Green, his biggest fan: he could not even find the letter, much less extract it.

Resigning himself to the possibility of failure and tired of "hot plating" it, Misely took a break from case C-58-31. He grabbed his book on contract law from the bookcase and dined, with some of his remaining available funds, at County Restaurant. He tried to re-read the chapter on the "mailbox rule," but he was too distracted to absorb anything new. After dining on youvetsi and baklava, his exhausting schedule caught up with him. He nodded-off in his booth, but slept fitfully.

Misely was having a nightmare. In his dream, he saw Porter as the wool dealer in the old case, dressed up in a rough country gentleman's suit circa 1817. And there was von Gunton as the manufacturer wearing a high collared shirt, typical of the period, but, inexplicably with a blue blazer sports jacket worn over top. They were in some sort of English courtroom that turned out to be the Elk Neck Central Post Office. They were in a wild contest; each man was racing around mailing and then receiving offer and acceptance letters. One would race to the front counter to post a letter while the other would open up his post office box to receive the letter. In turn, the recipient would race to the front counter to mail the letter as an acceptance, with the other man racing wildly over to his post office box to receive the response, and on and on, at a frightful pace. The English judge was none other than Elk Neck Postmaster, who wore a judge's wig and robe. He was holding a stopwatch behind the counter yelling "Go!" and "Now!" Roderick was trying to make sense of the chaos and was standing behind the customers' table, trying to get a glimpse of the letter. Finally, he came to understand that the letter being mailed was the blackmail letter.

He awoke with a start and in a cold sweat, trembling. He composed himself, paid his check and slunk back to his quarters. He hung up his brown suit in the metal wardrobe and tried to fall asleep on his cot. After lying on the cot for a moment, Misely bolted upright and charged into the office anteroom. He jumped into his leather chair and grabbed a legal pad from the top desk drawer. He began writing notes, furiously.

A disinterested observer, looking over Roderick's shoulder throughout the night, would have seen page after page of Roderick's hastily scribbled notes along with a drawing, which appeared to be a mechanical arm of some sort. But the drawing was soon stricken out, fiercely, by several dark pencil strokes. Misely would have also been seen jumping up from his chair in his long underwear to retrieve a chemistry textbook from his office bookcase. Later in the evening, the notes on the legal pad would have revealed a list of chemicals, along with a list of more common items such as oranges, tea, onions and vinegar.

The next morning, that same disinterested observer might have also seen Misely, binoculars in tow, pulling the Rambler station wagon up onto the hilly part of the parking lot in the rear of the Elk Neck Central Post Office. The binoculars afforded a view through the glass windows in the rear of the Post Office, into the activities going on behind the counter. In the afternoon, following a brief trip to the grocer's, Misely's presence might have also been noted in the Rare Book Room at the Graham Independent Free Public Library. He would have been observed taking notes from a chemistry book while sitting at the partner's desk, across from "Dad" Graham. Misely might also have been seen utilizing the Rare Book Room's state-of-the-art photographic reproduction equipment.

The following day would have found Misely back in his quarters at his wood plank shelf, surrounded by bottles of chemicals from his chemistry set. Paper cups containing freshly squeezed lemon juice, onion juice, vinegar and tea would have also been observed on the shelf. A disinterested observer, viewing the scene, would have also noticed Misely applying the chemicals and natural substances from the vials and paper cups, by eye-dropper, onto a variety of different papers. The papers would have been seen, lined up on Misely's cot underneath the sole window. An elaborate handwritten grid, listing various types of papers and weights, certain chemical substances and some sort of numerical information, would have been noted on Misely's office desk.

That afternoon, Porter received the phone call that he had been waiting for.

"Mr. Porter, I believe that I have potentially good news. I've located your letter, and believe that it can now be retrieved."

Over the phone, Roderick heard Porter exclaim, "Good golly! Go to it lad!" Porter then wondered exactly what "potentially" good news meant.

Roderick continued: "I have an additional proposition to discuss. Would you like to stop by my office?"

Within minutes, Porter had excused himself from work and driven over to Misely's. He was, again, making his way up the wooden staircase outside of 7 North Central, but this time, with a decided spring in his step. As he entered the office he said, "Son, let's hear all the details. I want the works!"

Roderick settled him down. "Mr. Porter, let me first say that I'm not at liberty to give you details, yet. I still have a long way to go. But I'm almost there." Before Porter could question him further, Misely began his windup: "Now, would you like to hear of my additional proposition?"

Porter practically yelled back, "You betcha!"

Misely continued: "Would it in any way be worth your while to turn the tables on your rival?"

"Good golly Mr. Misely, spill the beans, please man!"

Misely delivered the pitch: "How would you like it if, instead of holding your letter, von Gunton wound up with a substitute letter that bore the same general appearance of your letter. But the substitute letter would, of course, be of your own design and would contain information that, if revealed to Bynam, the newspaper, or whomever, would cause embarrassment to von Gunton, while presenting you in a favorable light? How would you feel in refusing to pay, knowing full well that von Gunton might produce the substituted letter, instead?"

"Yes, yes, yes!" the old gent growled, "Full speed ahead!"

Roderick watched the pitch head straight towards the plate: "Because there would be a significant additional amount of work involved, I would have to charge an extra $1,000, bringing the total to $4,000." The fastball sailed right over the plate and into the catcher's mitt.

"Son, if you can pull that off, I can find you another $1,000!"

The two shook hands and went to work.

Misely and Porter sat on the sofa in the office anteroom, composing Porter's "wish list" letter. It would be addressed to his "Dear Aunt," not his "Bunny." It would dote upon the excellent work being performed by the Bynam Administration. It would reveal no secrets of any kind. At Roderick's suggestion, it would even "throw a bone" to von Gunton. It would faintly praise some routine and mindless function with which von Gunton was involved. Roderick keenly understood that a little mild praise for von Gunton would paint Porter as an even-handed person, with no axe to grind. Porter liked the suggestion.

The two had finished up the text, but Roderick was having a little trouble expelling his guest. The afternoon's creative activities had enlivened Porter, sending him off into newly found nostalgic territories. Roderick should have known better, but he thought that the old gent would have had to return to his office at some point that afternoon. Apparently, steady working hours were not required of County Council employees.

Remembering his former trick, Misely excused himself to visit his restroom, but he first opened a can of pork and beans and placed it on the hot plate, set for "high." After washing-up, he returned to his office anteroom, only to find Porter, saucer-eyed, and in an apparent state of shock.

"What in blazes is that?"

Puzzled, Misely looked around, not knowing what he meant. "What's what?"

"That siren, that alarm, man!"

Roderick then realized that the old gent was hearing the sound of the toilet flushing, which he barely noticed anymore. Seizing the opportunity, Misely yelled, "Alarm!" and proceeded to trot Porter, quickly, down the wooden stairs and out to the street.

Once outside, he told Porter that he would contact him soon and to be patient. He then got into the station wagon and drove off, leaving a confused Grayson Porter, again, on the sidewalk in front of 7 North Central.

A few weeks later, at Misely's request, a meeting was arranged with Porter and Art Green, in Art Green's office, at 6:30 PM. Without fanfare, Roderick produced a crisp, white business envelope, opened it and handed the letter over to a thunderstruck Porter.

"Would this, by chance, be the letter?"

Porter unfolded the letter and tried to choke back his tears. "Yes, yes, you did it!" After his sobs subsided he asked, "And did you pull the switcheroo?"

Roderick nodded in the affirmative, humbly.

"So, do I refuse to pay next month?"

"Absolutely, and let the fun begin!"

Right on the spot, Porter produced his check book and wrote out a check to Misely for $4,000, easily the equivalent of a year's pay. Roderick politely thanked Porter, shook hands all around, and with check in hand, quickly exited Art Green's office, leaving Art to fend for himself.

With the excitement over, Grayson settled back in the high-backed stool to savor his victory with his friend. Before long, he had recounted for Art's benefit, some of the early history of the Orphan's Court. Of particular interest were the proceedings of the old Chancery docket in the early days of Elk Neck. Desperate, Art opened his door, keeping an eye out for the nighttime security guard, Flip Needles. Flip walked by once and waved a friendly "hello" to Art, but didn't notice Art making a subtle slashing motion with his right hand across his neck, the universal "cut" symbol. Fortunately, as Porter gazed off into the distance, Flip came by for a second pass, this time noticing Art's entirely overt and desperately dramatic rendition of the "cut" sign. Catching on, Flip came by, knocked gently on the doorframe and informed the two that it was time to lock up the building.

The next morning, Roderick headed over to the Greater Elk Neck Savings Association to deposit Porter's check. Afterwards, he thought he'd better stop over to say "hello" to Art Green, hoping Art wasn't too put out about his abrupt departure the night before.

"Now, Rod, I know you don't usually like to give details, but please, I would like to know just how you pulled this one off."

Roderick pulled up one of the stools and began. "Well, the hardest part was figuring out where von Gunton was keeping the letter. It took me a while, but I finally figured out that he was using his post office box as a substitute safe deposit box. Like many residents of Elk Neck - present company included - von Gunton maintains his mail delivery through his post office box. Now, I'm speculating, but I think that von Gunton originally had the idea of hiding the letter by mailing it to himself, over and over again. That way, the letter would be out of circulation and not recoverable by third parties. So he would mail the letter to himself from the Elk Neck Post Office, where it would arrive the next day in his post office box. Of course, once a letter is in a post office box, only the postal workers and the key holders have access to the box.

"But I think that at some point, he got tired of re-mailing the letter to himself. After all, following delivery, the letter would simply be sitting in his post office box with his other mail. So, rather than mailing the letter to himself, why not simply keep the letter in the post office box? But von Gunton didn't want to get in trouble with the Postmaster for using the box for storage - which is not allowed - so he needed to disguise what he was doing by placing the letter in different envelopes, moving the letter around, from envelope to envelope received in the ordinary course. So, von Gunton would, for example, receive a piece of "junk mail" or other mail and dispose of the contents, while retaining the envelope. He would then insert Porter's letter into the retained envelope and then place that envelope back into his post office box. 'Junk mail' envelopes were particularly useful because they were usually mailed at the cheaper rate with the envelope flap simply folded in and not sealed."

"Now, wait a minute. Even if he did that, wouldn't there be a risk that the Post Office would treat the letter as a piece of uncollected mail and return it to the sender?"

"Exactly. Under postal regulations, a piece of mail delivered to a post office box, but uncollected, is treated as refused and is returned to the sender after 14 days, unless an earlier return is indicated. To avoid the problem, von Gunton was constantly moving the letter to a new envelope with a more recent postmark. So, ordinarily, because von Gunton routinely checked his box on Tuesdays and Fridays, there was virtually no risk of the plan backfiring. Von Gunton always appeared in plenty of time within the 14 days to make the switch. Once I understood what von Gunton was doing, I knew I could solve the problem. As you may be aware, I have access to a considerable printing resource."

Art Green, actually, was not aware, but he let Misely continue.

"I was able to design some very simple 'junk mail' letters and envelopes addressed to the 'occupant' of von Gunton's post office box. Of course, the 'junk mail' letters were simple ruses, advertising nonexistent products and services. I knew from observation that von Gunton would not even read those letters. I also knew that I could mail a significant number of envelopes into von Gunton's post office box, each a potential holder of Porter's letter. In fact, one day, the plan succeeded. Von Gunton chose my 'junk mail' envelope, placed Porter's letter inside and returned it to his post office box."

"I'm following you so far Rod, but what good would that do? Wouldn't von Gunton simply return to his box the next time, remove Grayson's letter from your envelope and replace it in, yet, another envelope?" Art leaned back in his chair, trying to concentrate.

"You're right, but I realized that the trick would be in disguising a contrary postal instruction on the outside of my envelope that would not be seen by von Gunton when he placed the Porter letter into the envelope, but would be seen by a postal worker at a later date. So, I began experimenting with several forms of invisible ink. I remembered reading how our Founding Fathers often used invisible inks to transmit secret messages during the American Revolution. A particular favorite was a mixture of ferrous sulfate and water. Another was cobalt chloride, glycerin and water. Even lemon, orange and onion juices can be used. All of these require a significant amount of heat, though, because the secret writing is revealed only when the paper is exposed to a heat source. The sun pouring into the back of the Post Office and into the rear of the exposed post office boxes produced some heat, but not enough to do the trick.

"I found that silver nitrate - used in photography - was a better bet. Light, alone, would trigger the reaction and cause the writing to appear on the envelope. Luckily, I was able to find a particularly effective combination of silver nitrate and other buffers that, when used with the right kind of paper, would gradually appear on the paper in about three days after exposure to sunlight. So I began my weekly mailing campaign, sending several items of 'junk mail' every Wednesday."

Art Green knew a little about chemistry and his head was beginning to spin, but he let Roderick continue.

"Last Friday, von Gunton placed the Porter letter into my envelope, which I had previously mailed and was postmarked two days earlier on that Wednesday. By the following Monday morning, the instruction: 'After three days return to sender' became visible on the outside of the envelope just above the return address. When the postman delivered Monday's mail into von Gunton's box, he checked on the unaccepted mailings in the box and saw and acted upon my 'return to sender' direction, because three days had passed. The return address on the envelope just happened to be my own post office box. The postman simply rubber-stamped the mailing as undelivered and moved it to my box, just a few yards away. Like any crabber, checking his lines, I had been routinely checking my post office box, hoping for a catch. And this past Monday, there was my catch."

Art Green was still confused. "But, wait a minute, what was Grayson saying about switching letters?"

"Well, I realized that an opportunity to plant a false letter had also arisen. All I needed to do was, using an identical version of my false, 'junk mail' envelope, enclose a substitute letter and mail the false letter back into von Gunton's post office box before Tuesday, when von Gunton would arrive to switch envelopes again. I had already received instructions from Porter on what to include in a false letter. When I received the 'real' Porter letter that Monday, I used Porter's stationary and transcribed Porter's revised text onto a blank sheet. But I had to do so in such away that the written text would appear, if casually observed by von Gunton, to be the same text as in the original letter. Obviously, the text of the two letters would be entirely different. But I knew I could replicate the general appearance of the letter - the length of the paragraphs, the spaces between lines, and the general 'look' of the letter itself. As you know, I have a fairly decent talent for penmanship."

Art Green knew this to be true from Roderick's assistance with the handwritten Administration Accounts; but his subconscious was simultaneously struggling with the word "penmanship," thinking that there was a better word to describe when a person is able to mimic another's handwriting to their own ends. He put the thought aside.

"So then, what happened?"

"Well, after transcribing the text, I 'played with' the appearance of the paper, duplicating the folds and the approximate extent of the wear and tear of the paper. I then inserted the false letter into my 'junk mail' envelope and mailed the false letter to the 'occupant' of von Gunton's post office box, just as the other had been addressed. It arrived in von Gunton's box the next day, on Tuesday morning. Von Gunton dropped by the Post Office at lunchtime on that Tuesday to retrieve what he believed to be the Porter letter from the envelope, and without observing the letter closely, or examining the postmark of the envelope, he simply placed the false letter into some other envelope, just as he had been doing all along. He then returned the false letter back to the safety of his post office box.

"So, Mr. Porter will soon stand up to von Gunton and refuse to pay the blackmail. Although it is not certain, there's a strong possibility that von Gunton will not even read the letter, again, before acting on his longstanding threat to make the letter public. If he does read it, he'll know that he's been duped by his old rival. But if he doesn't, he may wind up embarrassing himself by revealing the rather innocuous replacement letter to Bynam or the newspaper, expecting some fireworks."

Art Green sat back in his chair. "OK, wow, I get it, now, … yes."

The two shook hands and Roderick parted, ready to enjoy the first "calm" day in months.

That evening at County Restaurant, Roderick savored his victory, enjoying the lamb stew special. He was always glad when a case broke and he could finally enjoy the fruits of his labor. He didn't really mind sharing information on his cases with Art Green. Art knew how to keep a secret. And telling the story gave an opportunity to edit out the unpleasant or difficult parts of the case.

For example, he would never admit to Art that his nightmare over the "mailbox rule" led him to the solution. He had been so preoccupied with getting a look at the names of the addressees on von Gunton's letters that he never noticed what von Gunton was actually doing, right under his nose. Von Gunton's leaving the box open and then always dropping one final piece of junk mail into the rubbish can before going to the counter should have been an obvious tip off. Von Gunton had been extracting all but the Porter letter from his box, reviewing his "junk mail" and other correspondence and then selecting one, necessary, envelope. He'd walk the one envelope back to his box, quickly move the Porter letter into the new envelope, and then throw out the unnecessary envelope on the way to the front counter.

Additionally embarrassing was Misely's original idea of extracting Porter's letter by means of a mechanical arm extended through the front of Misely's box and into the rear of von Gunton's. Such an action would, arguably, not be legally defensible, unlike all of Misely's other actions in Case C-58-31.

And he couldn't really take full credit for the idea of switching the letters. That idea was straight from Poe's story, which Porter had obviously never read. But, in the story, Poe's character performed the letter switch as a "throw-in." Misely, on the other hand, operated strictly on an "a la carte" basis.

A month later, Misely was, again, sitting in his booth at County Restaurant, enjoying French bread and tzaziki. He was reading through the Star Sentinel when he noticed a short column buried inside the paper, announcing the retirement of County Highways Chief Thomas von Gunton. There was a tiny picture of a youngish looking man next to the column, whom Roderick did not recognize. The column also reported that Deputy Land Planning Chief Grayson Porter would become acting head of von Gunton's old Highways Division, with a full County Council promotion. As it turned out, the picture next to the column was a file photo of Porter taken thirty-five years earlier. Misely had not gotten around to officially "closing" his file, so he carefully tore out the column, which would make a fitting postscript.

When he returned to his quarters after dinner, he pulled file C-58-31 and his copybook ledger from the metal filing cabinet. He was about to drop the newspaper clipping into the file jacket, when he came across the photographic reproduction that he had made of the Porter blackmail letter, courtesy of the state-of-the-art equipment in the library's Rare Book Room. He had almost forgotten about it; but Porter's check had cleared long ago, so Misely retrieved the metal trash basket from his quarters, grabbed a book of matches from his office desk and set the copy ablaze in the trash basket.

The file and ledger can still be found in the metal filing cabinet in the living quarters of Roderick Misely, Consultant, at 7 North Central, just up the street from the northeast corner of Iroquois and Central.

CHAPTER THREE
LOST AND FOUND

Tack and Roderick had maneuvered the plank up to the short landing between the two flights of wooden stairs. Tack was leaning the plank against the handrail, taking a breather. His sunburned face looked up towards Roderick, his eyes squinting in the glare of the late afternoon sun. Tack wiped his brow, driving back the mass of reddish blonde hair that had fallen into his eyes. It had been a long day. Tack had hired-on to a survey team checking for property lines along Railroad Canyon, just north of the Marigold Branch. As was often the case, Tack was able to secure a spot on the crew for Roderick, his favorite and only nephew. Roderick never passed-up the opportunity; the pay was decent and there was always the chance of finding a "treasure" such as the wooden plank.

The crew members of the Hudson Surveying and Engineering Company were always pleased to work with Roderick. Dressed in his brown suit, tie and galoshes, Roderick was presumed by the other workers to be one of the proprietor's sons. No one else would have worn a coat and tie out into the field. The bramble cut on his face, just below his left eye, evidenced Roderick's willingness to share in the lowliest burdens of the survey party: clearing thorny areas with a machete, digging out rocks and mud to find buried survey markers and cleaning up the truck. He took orders from the crew chief without griping. This placed him in good stead with the other men. Someday, they would enjoy working for such a fair-minded egalitarian.

The plank was not heavy, just bulky. Roderick had spied the object lying along the side of the gorge, leading down to the creek bed. It might just solve his pressing storage problem. His living quarters had become a shambles. Boxes, books, cans and containers, once stacked one upon the other, were now scattered about the worn linoleum floor. The urgency of the storage situation had been brought home to bear just a few days earlier, as Misely was wrapping up case O-57-24.

As usual, Roderick had been scouring the Lost and Found section of the classified ads in the Star Sentinel. Following his move into his office suite, Roderick found himself with plenty of time, but few clients. He had resorted to combing the newspaper for opportunities. The Lost and Found section was particularly fertile ground. Roderick made a habit of scanning the truncated and often incomprehensible text of the Lost and Found ads, seeking that all important word: "reward." Finding and returning lost pets had become something of a sub-specialty within Misely's "consulting" practice.

For Misely, an intelligent Lost and Found ad would describe, in detail, the particular kind of pet that had gone missing, including the pet's name, breed, age, size and any identifiable coloration or markings. The ad would mention the area or neighborhood where the pet was last seen and include the date of the disappearance. A phone number for contacting the owner was vital. Most importantly, the ad would clearly articulate whether a reward was offered and the amount. Misely was amazed at the number of ads that failed to provide this basic information.

The ad in case O-57-24 was fairly well done. The white, long-haired Persian had gone missing about a week earlier. The Whitelakes had offered a reward, but no amount was stated. "Snowflake" had last been seen near the family's home in the Castlemoor section of Washington Heights.

Misely first read the ad on Monday evening, as he dined on soutzoukakia at County Restaurant. On Tuesday morning, he walked over to the Castlemoor neighborhood, getting the lay of the land. But there was little of interest there for a renegade house cat. The neighborhood was immaculately maintained - there were no back alleys with hiding places and trash receptacles. So Misely doubled back towards downtown Elk Neck, checking the rear of the few retail stores on the border with Washington Heights. But he soon ran out of time. He had agreed to stop into the Register of Wills Office that afternoon to help the clerks type the particularly onerous administration account of a wealthy decedent.

Misely had better luck on Wednesday morning. Behind Bertram's Deli, he thought for sure that he saw a flash of white darting from behind a gaggle of trash cans and into the hedgerow surrounding the parking lot. Misely cornered the cat and attempted to coax it closer by extending his open arms while calling, "Here Snowflake, come here!" But the cat took off, again, cutting through an opening in the hedgerow. Misely would have to return with some appropriate bait.

That afternoon, after finishing-up more typing, Misely stopped into Bertram's Deli for a can of tuna. Borrowing a can opener, he pried opened up the lid about half way and headed back towards the rear of the building. In a flash, he saw the cat dart through the grass back towards the hedgerow. Misely took pieces of tuna from the can and dropped them along the hedge, forming a food trail. He sat cross-legged on the edge of the sidewalk, holding the half-opened can in one hand, pretending to be uninterested.

Snowflake eventually took the bait. Ever so slowly, the cat advanced, moving from morsel to morsel, devouring all the way towards the waiting arms of Misely. After a seemingly endless ritual of self-cleaning, grooming and sniffing, the cat finally came to Misely, meowing as it rubbed up against Misely's kneecap. Misely petted the cat, gently, as it nestled into his arms, its nose and tongue mining the fish from the half-opened can. He checked the tag around its neck: "Snowflake." He was in business. Misely wrapped his arms around the cat, lifting it up, while the cat continued feeding from the can. He then walked slowly back towards 7 North Central, allowing the cat to feed from the can along the way.

By the time they made it back to the office suite, Misely's arms were getting sore. The cat had finished the tuna and was beginning to get restless, writhing in Misely's arms. Misely quickly walked up the two long flights of wooden stairs as the cat licked Misely's fingers, looking for more morsels. He somehow managed to juggle the restless cat and empty tuna can as he unlocked his front door. As he entered, he felt his right foot step on something on the floor; but he caught himself just as his foot began to slide out from under his leg. Performing an awkward balancing act, he quickly passed through his office anteroom and opened the door to his living quarters, releasing Snowflake into the room, just in the nick of time.

He closed the door of his living quarters to Snowflake and walked back to the front door to see what he had nearly slipped on. Written on a stale racetrack tip sheet were the words "6 AM, Tack." This was Tack's way of communicating that a survey job had turned up for the following morning. Roderick lacked a telephone and Tack lacked writing paper. But the tip sheet was an improvement over the matchbook that had nearly sent Roderick flying, last time. Roderick would have to work quickly to finalize the exchange of Snowflake for reward. He didn't want to leave the cat unattended for an entire day.

The noise from the vacuum cleaner was bad enough, but Henrietta had turned up the volume on the TV set, to boot. Eleanor Whitelake answered the ringing phone.

"Hello, Whitelake residence" She cupped her hand over the mouthpiece and yelled "Dearie, please turn down the sound for Mommy!"

'Good news,' thought Misely. The whining and nagging of a child gave him a strong bargaining advantage in negotiating a reward. After all, the Whitelakes had been unwilling to state the amount of the reward in the ad. Such a decision had its consequences.

Roderick opened negotiations: "Good afternoon Mrs. Whitelake. This is Ron Meisel. I'm pleased to report that I found your cat, Snowflake. I'd be delighted to return your cat and, of course, claim the reward."

Mrs. Whitelake hoisted the handset to her shoulder, squeezing it with her chin as she freed both hands to straighten-up Henrietta's hair. "Oh that's wonderful. But I'm not sure about the reward. My husband, Buck, isn't home from work yet. He gets in around 5 o'clock, so could you call back then?"

Roderick was disappointed. He knew that "Buck" Whitelake would probably turn out to be the cheapskate who placed the ad without naming the amount of the reward. Misely responded politely, "Certainly Mrs. Whitelake. I'll call back later. Thank you."

At least he could get rid of the cat that evening. He wouldn't even need to put out a saucer of cream.

It was only 4 PM so Misely repaired to County Restaurant to kill some time and take an early dinner. His early arrival confused Mrs. Georgelus who had lost track of the afternoon and thought that Misely had made a rare lunchtime appearance. Misely grabbed a copy of that morning's Star Sentinel lying on the lunch counter near the cash register. He took up his usual spot in the last booth and sat facing away from the front door and the rest of the goings-on in the restaurant.

As he dined on a gyro and chunks of feta, he turned, again, to the Lost and Found column. He found the Whitelakes' ad, of course. But there it was. Another ad for a "found" Skye Terrier. This had to be about the third or fourth ad for a Skye Terrier in the last 12 months. He recalled that the ad would usually run for four or five days. In fact, he remembered that he had actually opened an "O" file the last time he had seen the ad run. But he had other matters to handle, for now. He would get back to it later.

Terence "Buck" Whitelake was irritated. The drive home from the City was ordinarily difficult during rush hour. But a broken-down car, partially blocking the right lane of Carlton Highway, was making the trip downright impossible. The car was a junker and the driver, a man in overalls, apparently had no jack, or maybe no spare tire. To make matters worse, he was attempting to wave-down passersby for help. This was slowing down traffic even more. Mr. Whitelake scowled to himself, angry that such an inconsiderate person would interfere with his efforts to get home to family and supper. Commuting to the City was bad enough without having to put up with people so easily willing to inconvenience everyone else because of their own laziness or stupidity. If such people could not afford to properly maintain a car, they should not be allowed to drive. It was that simple.

Mr. Whitelake was still fuming when he finally arrived home. Eleanor hugged her husband and related the good news about Snowflake. Buck's annoyance increased, though, when his wife relayed the part of the message about Mr. Meisel's decided interest in the reward. Mr. Whitelake hit the roof.

"Typical, typical. Everybody wants their pound of flesh. Where are all the Good Samaritans?"

The phone rang, interrupting "Buck" in the middle of his fury. He picked up the handset, anxious to put the money grubbing reward-seeker in his place. A cheery voice spoke. "Is this Mr. Whitelake? My name is Ron Meisel. I'm pleased to report that I found your missing cat and would like the opportunity to return Snowflake to you as soon as possible. Could you please tell me the amount of the reward?"

Buck choked back his fierce animosity. "Well Mr. Meisel, we'll keep it simple. You bring the cat over here immediately and I'll provide you with the reward."

The voice became less cheery. "That's wonderful, sir. But I would like to know the amount of the reward before making the trip to your home."

"I'm offering three dollars. Take it or leave it."

"Mr. Whitelake, I don't mean to sound rude, but my time has some value, too, and it might be a lot easier for me to drop Snowflake off at the pound, tonight. That way, you could pick him up, tomorrow, or whenever you want and save yourself the three dollars."

Terence went for the jugular. "Oh, so I see you're resorting to blackmail now? Is that the way you always do business?"

Misely bit his tongue. "Well, I think calling me a blackmailer is a bit harsh. Frankly, I wouldn't have bothered rescuing your cat if I had thought that the reward would be so insubstantial."

Buck responded in mock umbrage. "Oh my heavens. I've insulted you? I didn't think a three dollar reward was 'insubstantial.'" He spoke the word "insubstantial" in a mocking pseudo-intellectual tone. "And, friend, I can go to the pound anytime I want and get myself a stray; no charge at all."

Roderick heard Mrs. Whitelake in the background saying, "Oh Buck, Buck. We don't want a stray." Little Henrietta could be heard crying, "Tell him to bring Snowflake back!" Roderick then heard the muffled sound of Buck's hand over the mouthpiece. "Shh! Be quiet you two!"

"Okay, Meisler or whatever your name is. What do you think an appropriate reward should be?"

"That's Meisel and I'm thinking that twenty dollars would be reasonable."

Buck Whitelake adopted a saccharinely sweet tone. "Well that's fine, Mr. Meisel. Just bring my cat over here, now and I'll take care of it."

Roderick, a bit puzzled, reconfirmed. "Now, that's twenty dollars, cash, right Mr. Whitelake?"

"You bet, friend. Cash on the barrel head."

Misely hung up the phone, concerned. He presumed that the twenty dollar offer would be negotiated down to something like eight dollars. The sudden change of attitude meant only one thing: "Buck" was going to renege, somehow. He would have to play this one by ear.

Misely trudged back across the street and entered into his living quarters. He looked around the room, horrified. Snowflake had gone on a wild rampage. The cat was darting around the cramped room, frolicking among the canned goods and boxes once stacked against the wall, but now lying haphazardly on the floor. Roderick heard a clattering sound and saw the cat sliding around on his treasured collection of out of state, expired license plates.

"Snowflake!" Misely yelled. But the cat failed to respond. Misely, instinctively, began to pick up the canned goods, some still rolling around on the linoleum floor.

Then he noticed that Snowflake was swatting at something with his paw, spinning it around like a top. It was the second-hand Kodak Brownie camera that he had picked up from Ralston's Thrift Emporium just the week before. He had barely even tried it out. He grabbed the Brownie from off of the floor, stuffing it into his left suit coat pocket.

But before he could get back to the canned goods he looked over his left shoulder to see Snowflake standing on his hind legs against the cot. Snowflake was slashing away at the thin mattress on the cot with his exposed claws; a harpist mid-concerto. And if Roderick hadn't known better, he would have sworn that the cat was smiling at him.

"Snowflake, no!" And Snowflake was off again, underneath the cot.

Roderick now realized that getting the cat out of his premises was going to be tricky. He wished he had another can of tuna to distract the cat for the long walk back. Then he remembered the dusty can of sardines that he'd come across from time to time, in his quarters, never being quite desperate enough to partake. He searched around the chaos on the floor and spotted the tin of sardines where it had been flung underneath his cot. He wasn't sure how old it was, but he didn't think Snowflake would be all that choosy.

He plucked the metal key from the can and partially peeled back the lid. The pungent aroma soon did the trick. Snowflake approached, gingerly, sniffing at the can in Misely's hand and began to bite hungrily into the sardines. Misely carefully scooped Snowflake up with one arm, balancing the feeding cat and can with the other hand. He slipped out the door and headed down the wooden stairs as quickly as possible. The sardines would not last forever.

He was walking, briskly, towards Washington Heights, but after a block he began to notice the gentle rustling of the Brownie camera that he had stuffed into his suit pocket. His walking motion was causing the camera to sway in his suit coat pocket, at first, gently tapping against his side. But the camera was now picking up momentum with each stride, swinging like a pendulum, kidney-punching him first in his gut and then in his back. Roderick was trying desperately to adjust his stride and repositioned his arms around Snowflake, doing anything he could to stop the pounding attack of the camera against his now bruised left side. But shifting his arms made the cat restless, so he had to endure the agony for the entire trip.

As he passed the halfway point, he noticed that Snowflake had eaten most of the sardines and was poking his nose further and further into the can. He tried to squeeze the can lid down just a bit, to stop the cat from eating all of the sardines. Snowflake did not appreciate the effort. With a quick flick of his paw, Snowflake slashed at Misely's face, cutting him just below his left eye socket, causing tiny droplets of blood to form at the cut.

Misely quickly gave up all efforts at restraining Snowflake's appetite. As Snowflake bit greedily into the rest of the can, Misely watched drops of blood fall onto the bright white fur of the cat. While still holding the cat, he instinctively wiped at his bleeding face with the back of his left hand, inadvertently rubbing more blood onto the cat's fur. He worried that the sight of the blood on the cat might concern the family and didn't want to provide any excuses for the Whitelakes to welch on their deal.

He finally made it to the front yard of the home to find the Whitelakes standing outside, waiting for the arrival of their precious family member. Eleanor and Henrietta were clapping and cheering, "Yay! Welcome back, Snowflake!" "Buck" stood by, smiling, checkbook in hand.

"Well Mr. Meisel, it looks from your face like you've had a little run-in with Snowflake? Are you sure you wouldn't like to keep him little longer?"

Misely grimaced, "No, that's quite all right Mr. Whitelake. I'm sure he's happy to be back home."

He handed Snowflake off to Henrietta, rubbing the cat's fur with his hands to brush away the streak of blood. He pulled a handkerchief from his breast pocket and dabbed the cut on his face. "Now, if it's okay with you, I'll just collect that twenty dollars in cash and be on my way."

"Yes sir," said Terence, opening up his checkbook and pulling a pen out of his shirt pocket. "Now, how do you spell 'Meisel'?"

Roderick scowled. "Mr. Whitelake, you agreed to cash on the barrel, right? I have a policy against accepting checks."

Whitelake responded, cynically, "Oh, you have a policy do you? I have a policy too. My check is every bit as good as cash. And my word is my bond."

Seeing that he was losing the battle, Misely relinquished, "Okay. Make the check payable to 'cash.'" Whitelake nodded, gravely, and handed the check for $20 over to Misely.

Roderick looked the check over. "You'll need to endorse on the back, please. And also, please add on the memo line 'payment for reward earned.'"

Whitelake scowled. "Sure enough, 'offer of reward.'"

Misely was becoming perturbed. "No, Mr. Whitelake, it should say 'for reward earned' not 'offer of reward.'" Roderick was pretty sure that Whitelake was planning to bounce the check.

He had capitulated too quickly on the amount of the reward. The more proof that Roderick could muster that he had performed his part of the deal, meant the less likely that Whitelake would try to bounce the check.

Roderick's left side was still throbbing, reminding him of an opportunity to improvise. He pulled the Brownie camera out of this suit jacket pocket. "How about a picture of the family, reunited?"

He lined up the shot with sourpuss "Buck" standing between his happy wife and daughter, who was still holding Snowflake. "Say cheese," said Roderick as he snapped-off a shot.

"Now, Mrs. Whitelake, could you please take a picture of me with your family?" The two traded places with Misely buddying-up next to "Terence." Misely held the reward check against his chest while Mrs. Whitelake snapped a photo. Misely figured that having a photograph documenting the harmonious reunion of cat and family might just give "Buck" Whitelake second thoughts about bouncing the check. After all, a photograph like that would hold up pretty well as evidence before the Elk Neck Magistrate's Court. Of course, Roderick knew that the Brownie had no film. But Whitelake didn't.

The wooden plank was bulky, not heavy. The two maneuvered the plank through the office anteroom and back into Roderick's living quarters. Items were still strewn about the floor, higgledy-piggledy. Roderick hadn't had time to rearrange things following his episode with Snowflake. Tack volunteered to help his nephew bracket-up the plank as a shelf, but Roderick waved him on. Tack would want to get going to that evening's Wrens game. And Roderick wasn't even sure he could lay his hands on the shelf brackets that he had come across when first moving in to 7 North Central. He'd fool with it tomorrow, after finishing that typing job at the Register of Wills Office.

Art Green, Chief Appraiser of the Elk Neck Orphans Court, thought he had seen Roderick walk past his partially opened office door earlier that Friday morning. Ralph Martin sat across from Art on one of the two high-backed metal stools in Art's cramped office.

Ralph Martin, a short, squat man, had a salmon-toned bald head that grew proportionately more crimson as his blood pressure rose. A dark, pencil-thin mustache paralleled his thin upper lip and contrasted suspiciously with his powder white sideburns. Like Art, Ralph was a member of the Beneficent Cavaliers' Lodge, Elk Neck Chapter; but Ralph had gone on to become an elected officer of the organization. He was currently serving as "Associate Vice President and Acting Treasurer." In the "old days" this position would have been called the "Exalted Office of the Chief Booma Rang," but Martin and several others had coaxed the group to adopt more "dignified" titles for their leadership positions several years earlier. Ralph Martin was also the only man that Art knew who had regular manicures. Art wasn't so sure about the pedicure situation.

Ralph Martin was angry. His white sideburns looked as though they would burst from his swollen red face. "She's done me in, but good, Art. Her and her fancy pants lawyer, Samuel Stuart."

Art sat behind his desk and gazed over at the paperwork that Martin had handed over. "This says it's your Will, Ralph. But the other thing you say is a will contract?"

Martin growled. "Yes. That second thing is the contract. You can see I already signed it. I hadn't realized what was going on."

Art laid the documents back down onto his desktop. "So what did she do, exactly?"

"Well, it's obvious to me, now," Ralph fumed. "You see, in the contract, I'm required to leave her one-half of my real estate holdings owned at the time of my death. That's no problem. We agreed to that before she filed for divorce. But in the small print, it requires that I make out my Will in the same form as the one attached as exhibit 'A' that you have, there. If you read the Will closely, it says that I name Samuel Stuart as my executor."

Art understood. "Oh, he's going to get commissions based on the value of all of your estate. I get it now."

"Yes," steamed Martin. "I get it now, too! Tommy Blanchford told me about how that works at lunch yesterday and reminded me that you were the head cheese over here. He said you might have some suggestions. So, what can I do, Art? She's hell bent to divorce me, take half of my property and then deplete my estate with her attorney's commissions. What if I remarry and have more kids? There may not be all that much left for them after paying the taxes and his commissions."

Art was still piecing the story together when he remembered Roderick. "Ralph, what say I get you a bottle of ginger ale or glass of cold water? Hang on, let me get some help." Art slipped around the corner and popped his head into the main office of the Register of Wills. He spotted Roderick sitting behind a typewriter.

"Mr. Misely, could you come here a moment, please?" In Art's mind, he had virtually yelled the request; but, being soft-spoken it had actually risen only to the level of a decisive whisper. Roderick heard Art address him as "Mr. Misely" and knew that something good was up, quite possibly a new case.

"Yes, Mr. Green?" spoke Roderick as he entered Art's office.

"Rod, run down to the 'caf' and fetch Mr. Martin here some ice water or soda pop - Ralph, what will you have?"

Martin barely noticed Roderick. "Just a ginger ale or sarsaparilla will do." Martin handed Roderick two bits. "Here, keep the change."

Roderick nodded a polite "Yes sir," and scooted out of the office.

"That's a smart one, that Mr. Misely," spoke Art, softly. "In fact, he's quite a marvel of practical knowledge. You might want to let him have a look at those papers."

Martin looked on, blandly. "Oh, is he some kind of lawyer?"

"Oh no, Ralph. He's a problem solver, of sorts. He's helped several of my friends, including a few of our mutual acquaintances, who shall remain nameless, of course."

"Of course," stated Martin, dryly. "Well, if he can be trusted to keep everything under his hat, perhaps I will."

"Oh, absolutely. Rod's very discreet and completely trustworthy."

A few minutes later, Misely returned with the ginger ale. He had also obtained a paper cup filled with ice since the bottle didn't feel all that cold when he removed the cap.

After introductions, Ralph Martin repeated his tale of woe. He reported that his wife, Lenore, had become fed up with him. She unfairly viewed him as the proverbial leopard, unable to change his spots. To her, he had become a penurious, penny-pinching miser, accumulating wealth hand over fist, but too cheap to allow a proper vacation or the simple luxuries that other couples took for granted. According to her, he never bought her anything: no gifts, not even modern appliances. Martin explained to Art and Misely that such, of course, was simply incorrect. He had been a model husband and very generous. Lenore was the unreasonable spouse, determined on spending them both into the poorhouse.

She had filed for divorce and had reached an amicable settlement with Ralph Martin, thanks to the adroit intervention of her learned counsel, Samuel Stuart, Esquire. Lawyer Stuart was nothing if not an opportunist. He had explained to Mrs. Martin that he could provide legal representation for her at a reduced price, because he could structure her settlement to allow him to earn acceptable commissions from the estate of her soon-to-be-former husband. And Stuart, still a young man, figured that he would out-last Ralph Martin. Ralph Martin had been remarkably successful in real estate and Stuart was betting on his continued success. The arrangement was a wise, long-term investment for Stuart.

Lenore agreed wholeheartedly, delighted with the clever means by which Stuart would fleece her husband's estate to their mutual advantage. She also guessed that her husband would be too cheap to hire his own lawyer and too impulsive to read anything all that closely before signing on the dotted line. She was right.

Misely glanced over the will contract and Will. "Mr. Martin, by chance did you have an attorney look at these before you signed them?"

Martin's face grew red, despite the cold ginger ale. "Of course not. That would be ridiculous, right? That's kind of like going to the doctor's before you're actually sick, right Art?"

Art, wincing, looked up from his desk. "Quite possibly, Ralph."

Martin continued. "Well, what do you make of those Mr. Misely? Do you have any brainstorms?"

Roderick leaned back in the other high-backed stool, absorbed, in particular, in the will contract. He placed the documents on this lap, while stretching his arms behind his head and cupping his hands behind his neck, in thought. His cupped hands tapped up against Art's cramped bulletin board, knocking free something that had been tacked-up. He hopped off of the stool to retrieve the item. It was a carry-out menu from a Chinese restaurant that opened five years ago and then closed two years later.

Misely re-tacked it back in place on the bulletin board and sat back down. "Well, I have an idea of sorts if you'd like to hear it."

"Of course," said an impatient Martin, now chewing on the ice from his paper cup. "Let's hear it."

Roderick re-situated himself on the metal stool. "Well, the will contract calls for you to make a 'disposition' to Mrs. Martin of one-half of the real estate holdings that you own at the time of your death. It then references the Will attached as schedule 'A' as the means to accomplish such." Roderick, concentrating, looked off into space.

"But suppose you chose another means to accomplish the spirit of the contract. For example, what if you created a series of deeds that would allow you to hold the designated properties for your lifetime, but with the properties passing to Mrs. Martin upon your death. You see, that way, those properties would not pass through your probate estate and Samuel Stuart would earn no commissions on the value of those properties. In fact, you could place all of your real estate in similar deeds - the other half of your real estate holdings could be set up to pass to your children, or a new spouse, upon your death. That way, Stuart would receive virtually no commissions because most of your assets would not pass through your estate."

Art Green spoke up. "Is there such a deed, Rod?"

"Well, yes," Misely explained. "I see them all the time in the land records in the Courthouse. They are called 'life estate' deeds."

Ralph Martin beamed, "Now you're talking! But couldn't Stuart do something to contest this when I die?"

Misely pulled himself upright, proudly. "That's the good part. Only Mrs. Martin could sue to enforce the will contract. Samuel Stuart would have no standing to do anything. So the key thing is to give Mrs. Martin an extra incentive to prefer inheriting under your deeds as opposed to the Will. You could, for example, throw in an extra property or two in your deeds so that Mrs. Martin would receive, say, 51 or 52 percent of your real estate. No one in their right mind would start a legal action to enforce their right to receive less property. And, nothing in the Will guarantees that Samuel Stuart would receive a dime. He's only entitled to commissions, whatever they will be."

Ralph Martin slapped his knee, joyously. "Bingo! Good thinking young man! Now, can you do-up those deeds for me? There are a lot of properties involved."

Roderick had already begun calculating his "consulting" fees. "Well, Mr. Martin, as you know, I'm no lawyer and cannot practice law by drafting those deeds. However, like anyone else,

I can purchase appropriate form deeds from the stationers. Then, I would only be typing in the blanks and notarizing your signature. That's typing work, not legal work. And I am a qualified Notary Public."

"Perfect!" exclaimed Martin, as Art Green nodded, approvingly. The two agreed to meet the next day, Saturday afternoon, at Roderick's office "suite."

The next morning, Misely pulled file O-57-14, the Skye Terrier file, from his metal filing cabinet. He would fiddle with bracketing-up the wooden plank later on. He had torn out the Lost and Found column with the Sky Terrier ad from yesterday's Star Sentinel, after dining, as usual, at County Restaurant the night before. He spread the file folder open on his desk in his office anteroom. He had torn out three other similar ads and had been careful to preserve the publication dates for the file. The current advertisement had run for four days. Typically, the ads ran for four or five days. The ad read:

Found, grey Skye Terrier, N. E. corner 6th and O'Donnell. Inquire box holder P.O. Box 41218, Main Branch.

Misely examined each of the other ads. The format was identical. But, in each case the location where the dog was said to have been found and the post office box number for the reply, were different. Roderick had suspected that the ads were not all that they appeared to be. He had planned to spend the afternoon on the file but his appointment with Mr. Martin would take him away from his inquiry.

Before he could put the file away, he heard a tap at his outer door. He quickly placed the file on top of his cot in his living quarters and carefully closed the door marked "private" behind him. He didn't want the client to have a look at the sorry state of his living arrangements, fearing it may not inspire confidence.

Mr. Martin had barely crossed the threshold when he complained, "Egads, man. I drove by this place three times before I decided that this had to be 7 North Central."

"Sorry about that Mr. Martin. I know it's little hard to see the '7' from down below.

"I'll say!" laughed Martin.

Ralph Martin's nostrils flared widely as he inhaled, deeply.

"Smells like you've made yourself a delicious lamb roast, Mr. Misely. You must be quite a chef? I pride myself on being something of a decent cook, too. Perhaps you'll show me your kitchen, later?"

Confused, Misely didn't realize that Martin was smelling the ubiquitous aroma of roasting lamb that permeated his suite, courtesy of County Restaurant, below. Misely no longer noticed the cooking smells.

"Oh, probably just some beef stew that I warmed up for breakfast."

Martin sniffed. "Beef? I could have sworn that was lamb."

Martin looked around the carefully organized office. "Nice, Mr. Misely, very nice. Shows an organized mind. I appreciate an organized mind."

Roderick instinctively looked back towards his living quarters, relieved that he had remembered to close the door. He sincerely hoped that Ralph Martin would indefinitely postpone his interest in Misely's "kitchen."

Misely beckoned Martin over to have a seat on the sofa. As Martin sat down he took a close look at Misely's face. "What happened, there? A razor cut?" he was pointing to a spot just below his own left eye.

"Oh, just a run-in with a hungry cat."

The comment reminded Misely that he still needed to deposit "Buck" Whitelake's check. He hadn't had a chance to get to the bank, yet, since he had spent all day Thursday with the survey crew and all of Friday at the Register of Wills. He was running short on cash and would have to try to negotiate some "up-front" money from Ralph Martin.

Martin had brought a catalog case full of his property deeds. Before too long, Martin was sitting on an aluminum chair facing the sofa, dealing-out deeds into piles; a croupier at a poker table. He made three piles. He picked out enough properties to equal about 52 percent of the value of all of his real estate for one pile. He directed Misely to place the properties in those deeds in the appropriate "life estate" deeds, to satisfy the settlement with his wife. The other two piles were allotted to deeds for his two sons. If he remarried, he would have Misely change those deeds, as necessary.

As Misely went through the piles, he noticed that several of the older deeds had been titled in the name "Raoul Martines" or "Raoul Martinez." Roderick made no comment, but thought to himself that one never knew just what one might learn about people when acting as a consultant.

He worked out a deal with Martin. Martin would pay him 5 dollars a property. Misely counted 38 properties. Part of the money would reimburse Roderick for the stationery store form deeds; the balance was compensation for typing and providing notarial services. By Misely's calculation, he stood to make nearly $130 from the job.

Martin was a tough negotiator. Misely tried to get a cash advance, but Martin was only willing to cough-up $20. This would all go towards the purchase the first group of form deeds. No work, no money.

Lacking an imminent monetary incentive to begin the arduous typing project, Misely decided to do some preliminary work on the Skye Terrier case. He walked over to the Graham Independent Free Public Library, file in hand.

He hoisted himself over the red velvet rope suspended between the two shiny gold plated posts stationed in front of the entrance to the Rare Book Room. From the middle of the velvet rope hung a placard: "Rare Book Room - Entrance by Appointment Only." The prohibition was perpetually ignored by Misely. "Dad" Graham was not in attendance in the Rare Book Room, it being late on a Saturday afternoon, so Misely was able to utilize the entire surface of the partner's desk for his work.

Roderick grabbed the massive City Atlas from the reference section. The Atlas was preferable to an ordinary street map, because it showed property lines and buildings and was reproduced at a much larger scale than an ordinary map.

He opened the book to locate each of the intersecting streets where the dog was said to have been found: 4th and Prescott; Alvey and Barrick Alley; 3rd and Guy and, most recently, 6th and O'Donnell. Misely knew from past experience that those intersections were located in the City's rough "Eastside," an industrial area interrupted by strips of hardscrabble housing. This was not the kind of place where one would expect to find a Skye Terrier; a junkyard dog, possibly, but not a Skye Terrier.

He sat back in the comfortable, upholstered chair, provided courtesy of the Rare Book Room. He read through each of the four ads:

Found, grey Skye Terrier, N. W. corner 4th and Prescott. Inquire box holder P.O. Box 23122, Main Branch.

Found, grey Skye Terrier, N. E. corner Alvey and Barrick Alley. Inquire box holder P.O. Box 15219, Main Branch.

Found, grey Skye Terrier, S. W. corner 3rd and Guy. Inquire box holder P.O. Box 32130, Main Branch.

Found, grey Skye Terrier, N. E. corner 6th and O'Donnell. Inquire box holder P.O. Box 41218, Main Branch.

He cupped his hands behind his neck. How likely would it be for the same kind of dog to be repeatedly found by a person or persons who would then place the same kind of ad in the Lost and Founds each time? And directing a reply to a post office box made no sense at all. A person who found a dog would want to provide a phone number for a fast response, not a mailing address.

He looked more closely at the post office box numbers. Impossible. The numbers were obviously faked. The box numbers in the City's Main Branch only ran to the hundreds, not the tens of thousands. The post office boxes had three digits or less, not five.

And the oddest thing about the ads was the reference in each case to the precise corner where the dog was said to have been found. Whether the dog was found on the north side or south side of any given corner wouldn't really matter to the person who lost the dog. A mention of the general area where the dog was found would suffice.

Roderick believed that the ads were meant as communications of some sort between the party placing the ad and some, particular recipient or recipients. Providing deliberately incorrect box numbers meant that no ordinary member of the public would even be able to respond to the ad. Running the ads for just four or five successive days every 3 or 4 months would provide just enough opportunity for the intended recipient to receive the communication, but without enough repetition to draw unwanted attention.

Roderick also surmised that the newspaper ads were meant as one-way communications; he recalled seeing no unusual "reply" ads following the publication of any of the Skye Terrier ads. Once the intended recipient received the message, perhaps some preordained response would follow, such as a meeting. If such were the case, the ads would have to provide enough information to allow the targeted recipient to take the required action.

Roderick brought the upholstered chair closer to the desk. He absentmindedly reached forward to pull out the top desk drawer, his raccoon fingers grasping eagerly at the desk drawer handle. But all of the drawers in the partner's desk had been permanently sealed shut by the library to prevent excessive wear and tear on the antique.

Roderick leaned back in the chair and continued his musings. Perhaps the intersecting streets represented places where a prearranged meeting or exchange would take place? The fact that the ads included the specific corner of the named intersection seemed to bolster his theory. Misely took another look at the four sets of intersecting streets in the Atlas. He didn't know the area that well, but felt that none of the intersections would make particularly promising meeting places. He'd take a look at those intersections tomorrow afternoon, while the streetcars were still running.

Misely walked the Atlas and his file over to the glassed-in area marked "Technical Staff Only," and fired-up the recently installed Photostat copying machine, situated next to the four color offset printer. The machine hadn't been used since the last time Roderick made a copy.

He made photostatic copies of the pages from the Atlas that showed the four intersections. Although using the Rare Book Room's equipment was restricted to "Technical Staff Only," other than the head librarian, no current member of the library staff had the faintest idea on how to operate the machinery.

Misely finished up and carried his file and photostatic copies over to County Restaurant for an early dinner. Eleni, the Georgelus' daughter, showed Roderick to his usual booth, which meant that Mrs. Georgelus was busy helping her husband with something in the kitchen. He could hear Mr. and Mrs. Georgelus in the back shouting something in Greek. Misely thought that they might be having an argument, but then within a few seconds, he heard them both laughing. It was hard to tell.

Eleni stood beside the wooden podium in the reception alcove and watched the back of Misely's head as he sifted through the newspaper clippings in his file folder. She felt both curiosity and an abiding sorrow for the solitary young man.

Roderick, on the other hand, felt hunger. He quickly lost interest in file O-57-14 and attacked his meal, voraciously. He'd been so busy with Ralph Martin and his Skye Terrier file that he hadn't gotten around to eating lunch.

After the meal, he decided to put the Wrens game on the radio and look for those shelf brackets. It was late in the season and the Wrens were in a pennant race. He scoured through the piles of chaos and found the wooden box of rusted tools and hardware that he had "inherited" from the prior tenant. Sure enough, he found one shelf bracket. It fit the plank width, adequately; but its mate was nowhere to be found.

He decided to improvise by placing one end of the plank on the top of the radiator; it was about the right height for a shelf. He held the other end of the plank flush against the wall, eye-balling the approximate spot where the bracket would have to be installed in order to make the plank level. He held the position against the wall with one hand, while reaching into the wooden box for a hammer and a wood screw. But the distraction of looking for the hammer in the box caused him to lose his "spot" against the wall, so he eyeballed it afresh and let the hammer fly.

Of course, this would be a temporary arrangement. He'd find a matching bracket and reposition the shelf, hopefully, before the onset of winter, when the radiator would fire-up. He didn't think it would be such a good idea to allow a wooden plank to sit on top of a steaming radiator.

It took a transfer to get to the City's Eastside, but the streetcar dropped Misely off only two blocks from his first destination, 3rd Avenue at Guy Street. He removed the folded photostatic copies of the Atlas pages from his suit coat pocket and glanced down at the first sheet.

As he walked down 3rd towards Guy, he kept up his guard. Even on a Sunday afternoon, the rough-and-tumble Eastside was not the safest place to be. Misely kept an eye out for bad actors, never realizing that at any given time and on any given street, he was actually the person with the strongest predisposition towards crime.

The southwest corner of 3rd and Guy was not much of a meeting place. A filling station took up the entire corner. And another gas station was located cattycorner across the intersection. The northeast corner was a vacant, overgrown lot. The southwest corner was a parking lot for an adjacent pawnshop. As Misely moved onto the next stop, 6th Avenue and O'Donnell, he marked the Atlas sheets with information, particularly noting the locations of places such as restaurants, taverns and motels; places where people could meet without much public scrutiny.

He took his time marking-up the copies with landmarks after checking each intersection. None of the designated corners were particularly promising. At best, the corner of Alrey and Barrick Alley made some sense. A small produce stand was located on the lot adjacent to the corner. But the corner lot, itself, was the apron for a driveway leading back to a cemetery monument manufacturer.

Misely checked his watch and circled back to the streetcar stop, adding a few more notes to his Atlas copies. He dropped his token into the fare box and found an empty seat about two-thirds back. There were only a few other people on the streetcar, which gave Misely a chance to stretch out in his seat.

Misely stared down at the folded copies of the Lost and Found ads he had made the day before. He pulled his mechanical pencil from his breast pocket and made a list of the post office boxes on the back of one of the sheets:

23122

15219

32130

41218

Misely believed that each 5-digit number represented a code. He didn't think the code would be all that difficult to break, as it was apparent that not too much thought had been placed in writing the ads. Using the overly-long post office box numbers was a glaringly obvious error. Keeping things simple, Misely figured that the date and time for a possible meeting or exchange would be communicated by the digits. He scoured the sequences, looking for numbers that could represent months, days and hours. Misely recognized that a sophisticated code could present the digits in a complex manner, using non-adjacent numbers or running them backwards, from right to left. But he thought it more likely that the scrivener of these ads had not gone to such extremes.

The most recent ad was placed in the present month of September, so he looked for the numbers "9" or possibly "10," for October. Neither "9" nor "10" appeared, nor "11," for that matter. The number "12" occurred in the second and third digits, but Misely felt that the ad would not likely direct action three months later, in December. It seemed too far into the future. Several of the ads had been placed within a three-month period of one another, indicating a greater likelihood that a response would have to follow promptly after publication of the ad.

Abandoning the question of the month for the time being, Misely directed his attention to digits that could represent the particular day in the month. Looking at the first two digits in each series convinced him that those two digits could not represent dates in the month:

23
15
32
41

There was no 32nd or 41st day of the month. The second and third numbers, as a pair, were also ruled out:

31
52
21
12

There was no 52nd of the month. That left either the third and fourth digit pairs, or the fourth and fifth pairs:

12, 22
21, 19
13, 30
21, 18

Either of those series could work.

He thought, some more, about the month designation. It was possible that the designated month could simply be the month in which the ads were placed. He checked the photostatic copies of the ads for publication dates. Sure, enough, the ads had run early in each month, with the last publication ending by the 15th of each month. This being the case, he needed to find two-digit sequences representing dates beginning on at least the 16th of the month and on.

23122

15219

32130

41218

The third and fourth digit pairs in each box number would have to be eliminated, because a "12" and a "13" appeared. But the fourth and fifth digit pairs of the box numbers would work. Each of those sets of digits would represent dates occurring after the 15th of the month, thus allowing sufficient time for the recipient to receive, and act upon, the message.

Misely began to perspire, believing that he had cracked at least part of the code. He unbuttoned his suit jacket and repositioned himself in his seat.

Turning his attention to the remaining, first 3 digits of each number, he noticed that the third digit in each box number consistently came up as either a one or two:

1

2

1

2

He "guessed" that the numbers 1 and 2 could represent the hour of the day for the meeting or exchange. Misely surmised that persons conducting periodic meetings or exchanges would probably tend to schedule them at predictable times. He would hold that thought for the time being.

Cecil Twigmore was glad to see the streetcar coming his way. Sunday was his favorite day, because he worked the 5 AM to 3 PM shift at Anderson's Sheet Metal Fabricators. Leonard Watkins spelled him for the dreary 3 PM to midnight shift. Not much was happening on Sundays and he seldom faced any trouble as security guard. His favorite part of the day was the ride back home. He placed his dentures in his lunch pail along with his cheese sandwich on white bread and hard-boiled egg. He hadn't gotten used to his new dentures, yet. They were torture.

He liked to hold-off from eating lunch at the shop, so that he could enjoy his lunch on the streetcar where he could continue working on the Star Sentinel's Sunday crossword, his favorite. He'd been working on it all morning and was about half way finished. He always liked getting help from people on the streetcar. He always picked out the most intelligent looking person to sit next to.

Misely was staring down at the folded sheets of City Atlas pages that he had annotated earlier. He'd given up, temporarily, on figuring-out the significance of the first two digits of the box numbers. Misely looked up to see the blue-uniformed man with a lunch pail boarding the streetcar and walking back in his direction. The man seemed to be looking straight at him. He slid down in his seat and looked out the window to divert his gaze away from the new passenger. The last thing he wanted was pointless conversation with a stranger.

Sadly, his efforts were shattered when the man plopped himself down in the seat next Misely, causing Misely to recoil back to his corner.

"You look like a bright young man."

Roderick was having a hard time understanding him. And then he noticed his toothless grin.

The man held out his right hand, with Misely returning the handshake, tepidly. "I'm Cecil Twigmore. I bet we could crack this thing wide-open!"

The statement confused Misely, momentarily, until he saw that the man was carrying the "B" Section of the Sunday Star Sentinel, folded to expose the crossword puzzle, his least favorite. Crossword puzzles generally annoyed Misely, particularly the one in the Sunday Star Sentinel, where the overly clever clues never seemed to match up to the answers.

Cecil pulled the hard-boiled egg from the lunch pail. "Care for a bite before I dig in?"

The notion of a shared hard-boiled egg did not particularly appeal to Roderick, who waved-off the offer with a polite "No, thank you."

Undeterred, Cecil advised that he would "start with the cheese sandwich," in case Roderick changed his mind. As Cecil massaged bites of the sandwich, he continued working his cross-word puzzle.

"3 across, a three letter word: 'Punches holes in your theory.'"

Misely had diverted his attention back to his Atlas copies, but found himself distracted by the man's conversation.

"Awl," he replied.

Cecil looked over at Misely. "Aw what, son? Is something wrong?"

Misely replied, politely, "No, that's 'awl' 'a-w-l.'"

Cecil hooted "Oh, I get it. Good!" He wrote the word in and continued.

"Now, number 4 down: 6 letters. I've got the last two letters as 'k' and 's:' 'Removes a husky friend's jacket.'"

The man's conversation was interfering with Roderick's musings. Misely unconsciously tapped his pencil against the Atlas sheet, thinking of the crossword grid and "four down and six letters."

And then it occurred to him. Could the digits in the box numbers relate to the street intersections? He grabbed the photostatic copies of the ads from his suit coat pocket and compared them to the Atlas sheets.

41218

He started with the first two digits from the most recent ad, 4 and 1. That ad stated that the dog was found at the Northeast corner of 6th and O'Donnell. If one were to begin at the corner of 6th and O'Donnell and travel 4 blocks north and then travel in an easterly direction for 1 more block, one would come to the Continental Motel, at the corner of 2nd and Craydon.

32130

He rifled through his copies and found the Atlas sheet for the Southwest corner of 3rd and Guy. If one began at the corner of 3rd and Guy and traveled in a southerly direction for 3 blocks and then in a westerly direction for 2 blocks, one would find the Blue-Belle Motel, just about at the corner of Hazel and Carlton Highway.

15219

The same applied to the Northeast corner of Alvey and Barrick Alley. If one traveled north 1 block and then easterly for 5 blocks, one would find the Thunderbird Motor Lodge.

23122

And traveling north 2 blocks from the corner of 4th and Prescott, and then westerly for 3 blocks, brought one to the Continental Motel, again. Using the first two digits of the box numbers in this manner always led to a particular Eastside motel.

Misely now believed he had cracked the code.

Misely looked up to notice that his transfer point was one-stop ahead, so he stood up and collected his papers. Cecil Twigmore was lazily finishing his cheese sandwich.

"Shucks," replied Roderick.

Cecil watched Misely scoot by him in the seat. "What's wrong, son?" But Roderick had already slipped out the rear exit of the streetcar.

Monday afternoon at 7 North Central found Misely busy at work on Martin's deeds. He had been occupied that morning depositing the Whitelake's check and purchasing a couple of form deeds from Watson's stationers. He realized that he could pocket a portion of the $20 advance money by purchasing a few necessary deeds and making photostatic copies from those forms. Misely could make all of the photostatic copies that he needed, free of charge, courtesy of the Rare Book Room.

There were still several days to go before the 18th, the likely date for the assignation at the Continental Motel.

The remaining days flew by thanks to Martin's ongoing typing job and a few visits to see Art Green at the Register of Wills Office.

On Tuesday, he stopped into the Elk Neck Central Post Office to retrieve his mail from his post office box. It was bad news. Misely didn't even have to open the envelope from the Greater Elk Neck Savings Association. But he did anyway. "Buck" Whitelake had stopped payment on the check. The Savings Association "regretted to inform" Misely that it was required to rescind its "provisional credit" of the $20.00. It was being deducted from his account. The news was particularly bad because Misely was running desperately low on spending cash and had already run through the money he had earned from the recent survey job.

He was walking back to his quarters at 7 North Central, still thinking about the check, when he thought he noticed a car, motor idling, stopped at the curb in front of his premises. As he walked towards the outside wooden stairway, he saw the driver's side window roll down. It was Ralph Martin. He was scowling.

"Mr. Misely, as it turns out, I won't be needing your services, after all. Just return my deeds to me along with whatever part of my $20.00 you haven't spent yet, at your earliest convenience. And let me say for the record, that your kind of clever treachery is not the means by which people in a civilized society resolve their difficulties and is certainly not becoming to a true gentleman. A word to the wise is sufficient."

He began to roll up the window, but then rolled it back down. "Of course, feel free to provide your bill for services rendered if, and to the extent, you feel it appropriate." The car rumbled away.

Misely stood on the sidewalk, stunned. He wasn't sure exactly what had happened to change the plan so abruptly. Martin's words had stung him like a sharp slap across his face. Not the part about his "treachery"; that was water off a duck's back. The part that wounded him was the comment about his sending the bill "if and to the extent appropriate." This meant that he would not be paid.

He decided right on the spot to return the entire $20.00, along with a note thanking Martin for his advice. He would mention how he had enjoyed working with Martin and that should he ever need Misely's services, not to hesitate to contact him. Roderick wanted to make sure that Martin knew that he had not burned any bridges behind him. There was a good chance that Ralph Martin would be back. Impulsive people with money often were.

As it turned out, and as Art Green explained to Misely, later, Martin had disclosed to his wife that he intended to actually provide her with 52 percent of his real estate holdings, not 50 percent. Those words were manna from heaven for poor Lenore Martin. The generous overture was the sign that she had long been waiting for. The old leopard could change his spots, after all. The two reconciled, immediately.

At noon on Wednesday, September 18th, a disinterested observer, tracking the occupant at 7 North Central, might have witnessed several interesting activities. A man dressed in a white guayabera shirt and black slacks, touting an oily black mustache, would have been seen bounding down the two flights of wooden stairs and over to the streetcar line. The guayabera shirt gave the man the appearance of a deposed South American dictator, or possibly a barber.

The man would have later been seen walking into the area that passed for the "lobby" of the Continental Motel.

The white-shirted man took a seat on one of the three green naugahyde upholstered chairs that faced the knotty pine counter serving as a front desk. The seat corners of the three chairs had split open from wear and tear and were leaking yellow upholstery.

The white-shirted man nonchalantly grabbed a coffee-stained magazine from the top of the air conditioning unit that hummed away in the window next to the chairs. The manager barely glanced up from his newspaper.

"Mister, I have to tell you that you can't loiter here in the lobby unless you're paying for a room."

"Oh, sorry sir." The white-shirted man stood up. "How about I take a room for the afternoon? But let me wait here and I'll pick which room, later."

The white-shirted man handed the manager the required 3 dollars, plus an extra 3 dollars as a "tip."

"Sure thing, pal. Thanks."

The white-shirted man settled back down into his chair and began reading the magazine. It was a Popular Mechanics, about two years old.

The manager looked up, again, from his newspaper. "Friend, shall I sign you into the register?"

"Sure. That's John Smith," said the white-shirted man, thumbing through his magazine.

The manager chuckled. "We've already got you in Room 9. How about John Jones?"

The white-shirted man beckoned an 'O.K.' hand signal without looking up.

At 1 PM, the white-shirted man glanced over the top of his magazine to watch a very tall, burley man enter the "lobby." The man was dressed in a pair of khaki pants and maroon blazer. He was carrying what appeared to be a standard issue, black book bag, the kind commonly sold at any five and dime store.

"I'd like a room for the afternoon," said the gravely voice.

"You bet. That's three bucks."

The man pulled out a gold-plated money clip and placed the 3 dollars onto the counter, one bill next to the other, as though doing so somehow amplified the importance of the transaction.

"Room 3, down the hall." The manager handed the man a key. "What's the name, for the register?"

"Skye, John Skye. Another man may be coming by to see me. Show him back." And with that, "John Skye" plunked a quarter down onto the counter and headed down the hall.

A moment passed and both the white-shirted man and manager glanced up at each other, both scowling in mutual acknowledgement. Two bits was way too small a "tip" with which to expect any special courtesies from the staff of the Continental Motel.

The white-shirted man waited for a couple of minutes and then went over to inspect the hallway. Room 6, just across the hall from Room 3, presented the best vantage point. He informed the manager of his room selection, received the key, and took a look around his room.

It was a grim affair. The bedspread was threadbare and layers of dust had settled on every surface of the room. He locked his door behind him and took up his post again in the lobby.

At about 1:50 PM, another man entered the lobby. The cramped area had grown incredibly hot in the midday sun, notwithstanding the noisy window air conditioner. The new arrival was a young man with wire-framed glasses. He was dressed in a gray plaid sports shirt and black slacks. He carried a black book bag, virtually identical to the one carried by the occupant of Room 3.

"I'm here to see Mr. Skye. Which room is he in?" The manager looked up from his newspaper, very slowly.

"That would be Room 3, friend." Neither noticed that the white-shirted man had gotten up from his chair and had left the lobby.

Misely peeked out of Room 6, keeping the door opened by just a crack. But it was enough to get full view of the activities immediately across the hall. The younger man tapped lightly at the door. Misely could hear the bolt and the safety latch being pulled back from the door. "Mr. Skye" stuck his head out from behind his partially closed door. "Yes?" The two men looked at each other, as though for the first time. The young man with the glasses asked, "Did you lose a dog?" Mr. Skye opened the door further and craned his neck up and down the hallway. "Yes," and let the younger man enter the room.

After the door had closed behind, Misely crept across the hallway and listened attentively. It was hard to pick up the conversation, because the room radio had been turned on. Big Band music was being forced out of the tiny speaker in the radio.

Misely placed his ear flush against the door, being careful not to bump the door against its frame. Misely concentrated, but it was still difficult to hear. It sounded as though "Skye" was pacing around the room. Misely was picking-up more of the conversation as Skye paced closer to the door. He heard the word "prints" several times and thought for sure that he heard the words "schematic" or "schematic works." He definitely heard the voice of "Skye" saying the word "political." He heard the younger man talking about a "modest proposal" and then say something about the "middle of March," several times. The older man definitely talked about "swift work."

After a few minutes, the front desk manager came walking down the hallway. He could not have missed Mr. Jones standing there with his head up against the door, but he averted his eyes. Misely ignored him.

The conversation was becoming clearer because the two men had moved closer to the door. The meeting was ending. He heard "Skye" say the words, "Get me whatever you can" and "ready to pay." Misely quickly removed his ear from the door and slipped back into his own room, leaving his own door open, just a crack. First, the younger man left, book bag in hand. A minute later, Mr. Skye left, carrying his newly acquired bag.

Back at 7 North Central, Misely returned the guayabera shirt and black slacks back to his metal dresser, the one with the door that had to be kicked closed at the bottom in order to shut. He carefully replaced the wax mustache back into its case along with the other theatrical garb in his metal footlocker. He pushed the footlocker back against the cot.

The surveillance had been successful. He now possessed sufficient information with which to implement his plan. He felt certain that the parties were exchanging cash for blueprints or plans of some sort. The reference to "prints" and "schematics" and the reference to "political," made him believe that blueprints or specifications were being purchased for some ulterior political purpose. It sounded as though something was being planned for mid-March as a consequence of the ongoing barters and that the two would have to work swiftly.

Misely figured that Mr. Skye was the money man. He was "looking" and paying for lost items. He had encouraged the younger man to "get me whatever you can." Misely guessed that the younger man's job was to "find" the requested plans and specifications and then inform Mr. Skye or his associates by placing the Lost and Found advertisements. But he couldn't be 100 percent sure. The best part of the scouting mission was finding out that the two men did not seem to recognize one another. It was highly likely that either a different "Mr. Skye" appeared each time; or possibly a different "finder" of the lost dog. In either case, this would greatly benefit Misely's plan.

September came and went leaving Misely, as usual, short of cash. He handled a few more typing jobs for the Register of Wills Office but his "lost pet" services had hit a dry spell. He was getting anxious to implement his plan.

On Friday October 4th, a disinterested observer would have noted a brown-suited man entering the main office of the Star Sentinel and placing a Lost and Found ad, using cash. The ad was scheduled to run for five consecutive days beginning on Monday October 7th and running through Friday October 11th. The ad read as follows:

Found, grey Skye Terrier, S. E. corner 5th and Comstock. Inquire box holder P.O. Box 21223, Main Branch.

After leaving the Star Sentinel building, the same brown-suited man would have been seen at the Lewis & Clark Five and Dime store, purchasing a standard black book bag. A disinterested observer would have also seen the brown-suited man back in Elk Neck, first in the Reference Section of the Graham Independent Free Public Library and then, later, carrying several reference texts past the velvet rope guarding the Rare Book Room. The same observer could have also seen the brown-suited man using the state-of-the-art photographic reproduction equipment to make copies from those texts. Schematic diagrams for transistor radios, televisions and x-ray machines were being reproduced along with plans and blueprints for well pumps, bookcases and even a steam shovel.

On the morning of Tuesday, October 22nd, Roderick took the streetcar down to Tack's place. His uncle had been rooming at "Matilda's Room and Board," a rooming house only two blocks away from the racetrack. The arrangement had worked well; Tack could easily walk to the track to sell tip sheets. And Wrens Park was right on the streetcar line which stopped just a few doors down from the rooming house. Roderick was visiting Tack in order to borrow Tack's "one dollar" Nash Rambler station wagon, recently won courtesy of a church raffle. Tack seldom drove, generally preferring the more reliable public transportation. Roderick could use the Rambler for his upcoming activities.

On the morning of Wednesday, October 23rd, a disinterested observer would have seen a man with black plastic framed glasses, dressed in a beige turtleneck shirt, corduroy slacks and brown oxford shoes, bound down the wooden stairs at 7 North Central. The man would have been seen carrying a black book bag as he entered the Nash Rambler station wagon parked at the curb.

Horst Lungren was glad to see the ad placed in the Star Sentinel so soon after the last exchange. His people would be pleased, as there was a real hunger for the product. He drove his Ford Fairlane into the gravel parking lot in front of the Thunderbird Motor Lodge. The gravel crunched and gave off a grey cloud of dust as the tires turned and then came to rest.

He entered the "lobby" with a black book bag in his hand and registered as "John Skye." He told the innkeeper to expect a caller and showed himself to his room, No. 5, just down the slender hallway. The hall, smelling of knotty pine and mildew, featured one payphone midway between the lobby exit and the screen door at the end of the hall. The screen door was the back entrance to the motel. It led to a gravel pathway in the back, overgrown with weeds. Two disheveled hedgerows flanked the sides of the motel building and gravel parking lot. The hedgerow paralleling the north side of the building had begun its life is a chain link fence; but locust saplings and other scrub had overtaken the fence, creating an ersatz, patchwork hedge.

Lungren paid the $3.00 afternoon room charge and dropped a quarter on the manager's counter. He entered his room and clicked on the dusty table radio, but not too loud. He locked the front door and slid the safety chain across. Lungren closed the window drapes and flicked on the ceiling lamp after feeling around for the light switch on the wall near the bedpost.

He sat on the corner of the bed and waited. He unclasped and peered into his bag, counting the packets of cash bound in rubber bands. He wondered to himself just what sort of pipsqueak would be sent over this time. He didn't like that part of it. It seemed to him that there were too many people involved and too many chances for someone to turn coat, or maybe mention the wrong thing to the wrong person. But it didn't really matter to him. A job was a job. Pretty soon, they'd be moving him South, anyway.

He checked his watch when he heard a light tap at the door. It was about 1 PM. He slid back the safety chain latch and poked his head out the door, looking up and down the hallway. He didn't recognize this one, either. The man with the black framed glasses asked, "Did you lose a dog?" "Yes," he replied allowing the man to enter.

"Here you are," said the visitor, handing over his black book bag. Lungren reached for the bag, noticing that the man's right hand had a black smudge along his thumb and the heel of his palm.

"Fine," he said handing over his own black book bag to the man. "Just keep 'em coming."

Lungren unclasped the latch to the book bag he had received. The younger man with the black glasses spoke, "Thank you and good day," and began to walk towards the door.

Lungren began pulling out the contents from the bag, leafing through the reproductions of the schematic diagrams and blueprints. Confused, he put his beefy hand back into the bag, feeling around for other contents.

"Just what is this supposed to be?" he growled, sounding angry.

"Pardon?" asked the bespectacled man, one hand on the doorknob.

"This! This stuff! Is this some kind of a joke?"

He stuffed the blueprints back into the bag and tossed the bag onto the floor at the feet of the younger man.

Lungren then reached into his sports coat, pulled a snub nosed revolver out of his breast pocket and pointed it straight at his visitor: "Give me back my bag!"

The younger man quickly handed back the bag.

"Has there been some mistake?"

The huge man's face grew red with anger: "Mistake! Yes, you've made a very big mistake, whoever you are!"

The younger man responded, calmly, "Look, this is obviously a misunderstanding. I think I was looking for Room 4 - is this Room 4?"

Lungren was considering the comment, momentarily, but before he could respond the younger man continued: "I'm very sorry. I'll be out of your way. I've got some business to attend to elsewhere."

He was backing his way to the door, with his own bag in hand. He then quickly opened the door, closing it behind him. Lungren didn't know exactly what to make of it. And then he realized that the story of the mistaken room number was a lie, because the man had asked about the lost dog.

He ran out into the hallway, revolver in hand, looking first towards the front lobby entrance and then quickly to the rear. He saw the rear screen door swing slightly on its hinge and figured that the young twerp had run out the rear exit.

He collected himself and walked back down the hallway and out through the front lobby. He realized that someone must have talked too much to someone else; just enough to allow some fool to attempt an impossible scam. He would report it to his people. He'd be heading South for sure, now.

He dropped his black book bag of cash onto the backseat of the Ford and walked around to the driver-side. He was about to enter the car, when he noticed that both the front and rear, drivers-side tires were flat. Someone had slashed his tires! And then he remembered seeing the black smudges on the pipsqueak's hand.

Enraged, he slammed the car door shut and felt for the gun in his breast pocket. He stormed back in the hotel bursting through the lobby and into the hallway. He ran down the length of the hall cursing under his breath. He slammed open the rear screen door, nearly taking it off its hinges, and looked around for the young turk. He was nowhere to be found.

Lungren padded back down the hallway and out to his car to view the damage. He had one spare, but not two. He'd have to phone his people for help.

Misely's hands were still trembling as he wheeled Tack's Nash Rambler wagon from out of its parking space. Roderick had parked it on a side street a block north of the intersection of Corona and Welton. He hadn't expected to come face-to-face with a loaded pistol. He had obviously miscalculated badly. Very, very badly. As he drove back towards Elk Neck, he tried to figure out what had gone wrong.

He had made too many suppositions. His plan was far from airtight. He obviously must have misunderstood the conversation at the Continental. He thought for sure that some kinds of plans or specifications were involved. He didn't think that the Skye character would know one sort of schematic diagram from another. But he must have really missed the mark, somehow. And when he heard the word "political" being mentioned, he should have realized that the plan was dangerous. The thought that he would be exposed to real danger had not even occurred to him.

Fortunately, his decision to improvise, slashing the man's tires before attending the meeting, had worked in his favor. He wouldn't need to check the rearview mirror, continually, on the drive back home. But he had been checking, instinctively, anyway.

As Misely drove on, he began to calm down. In fact, a mood of righteous indignation had taken the place of his earlier anxiety. 'How dare the man pull a gun?' Misely had, in good faith, simply offered an exchange of his wares for whatever was in the corresponding bag. The man had every right to reject such offer, of course. Business was business. But pulling a gun was not the way that business was transacted in the civilized world. In fact, the law books that Roderick had been studying would have defined Mr. Skye's actions as a criminal assault, possibly a felony.

Fully indignant, Roderick decided to improvise, again. He spotted the phone booth as he drove by the parking lot of the used car dealer at Alhambra and Carlton. He made a quick turn into the lot, pulling the Rambler up close to the phone booth. He dialed the Metropolitan Branch of the City's Police Department. He knew the number by heart.

"Police, can I help you?" said the dispatcher's voice.

"Yes, please. There's a man with a broken down car and he..."

But the dispatcher interrupted. "That's Traffic. Let me connect you." A second later another voice came on the line: "Traffic Division. Can I help you?"

Misely tried again. "Yes, there's a man in the parking lot of the Thunderbird Motor Lodge. He's waving a gun around and looks very dangerous."

The voice replied, "You said a gun, sir?" Misely responded, "That's correct, officer, a dangerous-looking man with a gun at the Thunderbird."

The voice continued, "And what is your name sir?"

"Raoul Martinez." He slapped the handset back into the cradle. He was getting tired of "John Smith."

By the time he arrived back at 7 North Central, Misely was feeling more of his old self. He dropped the book bag next to his desk in his office anteroom and went, immediately, back into the doorless bathroom inside his living quarters. He was anxious to remove the plastic glasses which had been pinching the bridge of his nose. He splashed his face with lukewarm water and dried himself.

He stepped back into his office and emptied the contents of the book bag out onto his desk top. It was cash; seven packets of bills in red rubber bands. He removed the rubber band from one of the packets and made a quick count. It was $200.00 in $5's, $10's and $20's, about $1,400.00, total, in the bag. The bills looked well-circulated. If extraordinary circumstances presented themselves, he could begin utilizing portions of the cash, immediately.

Misely had long ago learned that organization and good planning were essential to the success of every file. But he had also learned that, where required, improvisation was equally important. After he had run down the hallway of the Thunderbird Motor Lodge and out through the back screen door, he had darted behind the south hedgerow, taking cover. Crouching down, he had moved as close to Welton as he could while remaining out of sight behind the hedge. He would have simply waited for Mr. Skye to drive away before making his getaway to his own car; but he had slashed Skye's tires as a precaution and had to wait for an opportunity to make a run for it when Skye wasn't looking.

When he saw Skye toss the book bag onto the backseat of the Ford and then head back inside the motel, he knew it was time to vanish. He hadn't planned on exchanging the bags. He was simply making his escape. But Skye's car was directly between Misely and his route to Tack's Rambler. So as he approached Skye's car, it only made sense to improvise and switch the bags.

Misely cleaned up, returned the turtleneck shirt and corduroy slacks back to his metal wardrobe and donned a much more comfortable brown suit and tie.

He was sitting at his mahogany desk in his office anteroom, contemplating the contents of the bag. Exchanging the bags was the right thing for a citizen to do. Clearly, he had succeeded in interrupting some criminal enterprise. Most likely, some news about the crime would hit the newspaper. And he would be ready to claim, or suggest, an appropriate reward for turning-over the contraband cash to the authorities. And contraband it almost certainly was. The law books that Misely had studied, discussed how "fruits of the crime" were contraband and not the property of the criminal. Contraband evidence could always be seized and disposed of by the authorities; the criminal had no say in a matter.

Of course, Roderick was running painfully low on cash and began to consider the feasibility of taking an advancement of his reward money from the contraband funds. After all, the cash, itself, was circulated and nondescript. He decided that he could preserve the evidentiary value of the contraband by making a list of the serial numbers of the few bills that he would allot to himself as a preliminary reward. His testimony, along with the balance of the cash and listing of serial numbers, would be more than sufficient in any criminal prosecution. He would keep his eye out, as usual, for any newspaper story or published request for citizen assistance from the Police Department.

And if he heard nothing more about the case in the months to come, it seemed that he would be entitled to receive the balance of the cash on the basis of "finders keepers." After all, the contraband cash was, technically, probably owned by no one; and certainly not the criminal enterprise. Misely thought that the same rules that applied to abandoned property, would, likely, apply to the contraband. He would have to check this out in one of his law books later on. But for now, it seemed a reasonable premise.

Several months passed and Misely, as usual, continued to check the Star Sentinel, not only for new clients, human or animal, but for any news items relating to the cash he had come across in the book bag. He wondered, from time to time, about Mr. Skye and his criminal operation. There had certainly been no more Lost and Found ads for Skye Terriers; Roderick suspected there would be none in the future.

One evening, a few weeks later, while dining at County Restaurant, Roderick was perusing the Police Blotter column in the Star Sentinel. There were the usual reports of petty crimes: a burglary, a purse snatching, some vandalism on a streetcar. But the lead item mentioned how the Metropolitan Police force had foiled a theft ring that traded in rare books. Seems that some local college students had been dealing with a book theft ring operating along the coast. The students had brazenly stolen several valuable first editions from the Normal College library. One signed first edition had even been taken from a display case and replaced with another ordinary, unsigned, copy, published 60 years later. No one had even noticed.

The article included a quote from Benjamin Wainscott Graham, scion of the Graham family, the founders of the Graham Independent Free Public Library. Graham was "happy to report that, due to the implementation of appropriate security measures at the Rare Book Room, none of the library's rare books were stolen or missing." He applauded the work of his son, Wylands Wainscott Graham, Curator of the Rare Book Room. Roderick thought to himself that he had never actually known "Dad" Graham's name until now.

The theft ring had specialized in stealing thematic works with political and social subject matter. They had stolen an extremely rare first edition of Machiavelli's "The Prince," as well as a collection of signed first editions of the works of George Eliot and Jonathan Swift. The article reported that the ring was connected to a group of collectors from Eastern Europe. Credit was given to the Traffic Division of the Metropolitan Police force for cracking the case. Several suspects were now in custody.

Misely sat back in his booth. "Drat!" That was just the kind of case that he would have loved to have sunk his teeth into. He could have easily inveigled himself into the investigation and suggested an appropriate reward. He only wished that something had hit the newspaper before the crime was solved.

He folded up the newspaper, dropping it back onto the lunch counter on his way out the door. Eleni, drying a cast-iron skillet with a rust-stained dishtowel, watched the mysterious young man leave the paper on the counter and walk out of the restaurant.

She was still drying the pan when, a few moments later, she saw him burst back into the restaurant and virtually lunge at the newspaper on the counter. He left, again, unfolding and re-reading the newspaper on his way out the door.

File No. 0-57-14, containing only Lost and Found ads, a newspaper clipping about a book theft ring and a sheet of paper with a lengthy list of serial numbers, can still be found in the metal filing cabinet inside the living quarters of Roderick Misely, Consultant, located at 7 North Central, just up the street from the northeast corner of Iroquois and Central.

CHAPTER FOUR
CONSIDER OTHO PRAMM

Aloysius Friedman's conference room also served as his library. Saturday afternoons were fairly quiet in the City and the streetcar from Elk Neck had delivered Misely to Friedman's office in record time.

Misely was the first to arrive. He killed some time by leafing through Friedman's collection of old law books. He was surprised to find a volume from Blackstone's Commentaries; he had certainly heard of Blackstone's famous treatise, but he had never actually seen a volume before. Misely opened the book. The yellowed pages from "Book the Second, The Rights of Things" came loose from the binding, so he put the book back in the bookcase, immediately. He glanced around. There were no witnesses.

He looked up to the top of the bookcase. He saw several of Friedman's award trophies, representing a variety of civic and legal accomplishments. He spotted a framed photograph of Friedman shaking hands with surveyor Davey Evans, both holding a plaque. The frame was inscribed "N.A.A.C.P. Awards Banquet 1955."

Before long, Malcolm Hudson and Davey Evans arrived and took their places at the conference room table. Attorney Friedman didn't ordinarily maintain Saturday office hours, so there must have been some urgency in getting the group together. Although he had never met Malcolm Hudson before, Roderick had previously worked under Davey Evans, one of the crew chiefs for the Hudson Surveying and Engineering Company.

Roderick's Uncle Tack had also been invited to meeting, but Tack declined, preferring to avoid the near occasion of attorneys and law offices. Tack was partly responsible for Roderick's presence at the meeting, though. Malcolm Hudson had mentioned to his crew chiefs that Mr. Friedman was looking for a title abstractor who could "drop everything" to quickly assist on a case. Tack suggested Roderick to Davey, describing his nephew as a "crackerjack" title abstractor.

The three waited around the conference table for only a few minutes before Aloysius Friedman entered the room with a painfully thick file folder.

"Gentlemen, I'm sorry for the delay. That was the client just now on the phone."

The three stood up and shook hands all around. Davey Evans spoke up, "Mr. Friedman, this is Mr. Roderick Misely, the title abstractor."

"It's a pleasure to meet you Mr. Misely." Aloysius Friedman deftly eyed Misely up and down quickly judging Misely's suitability as a witness for the defense. He was immediately impressed by Misely's professional demeanor; a neatly groomed young man in a proper suit and tie, with a firm handshake.

"Mr. Friedman, I'm, likewise, pleased to meet you and glad to be of service."

"I presume, Mr. Misely, that you do not know anything about this case, so let me bring you up to speed. My clients are the Principio Brothers. No doubt you've heard of them. They specialize in land development and building."

'Heard of them' was an understatement, thought Misely. The Principio Brothers were the dominant land developers in the region. "Yes sir, Mr. Friedman, I've certainly heard of them," he nodded.

"Now, Mr. Misely, the Principio's own a 63 acre tract out along the Marigold Branch. They're planning a major housing development and have put in for County approvals. About 8 or 9 months ago, they received word of an adverse claim to their title to the land. Out of the blue comes the Appalachian-Atlantic Railroad Company, or, I should say the purported modern day owners of the Appalachian-Atlantic. These supposed owners claim title to roughly a third of the Principio land by virtue of their alleged right of way. Now, we all know that the Appalachian-Atlantic ceased operations around the turn of the century. And there has never been any evidence that they so much as laid a single track anywhere near the Principio property. But their Quiet Title suit asserts that sometime in the 1890's, the Railroad planned a branch line to travel off from the main line near Bay Acres all the way west towards Cliff Rapids at Marigold Falls. They point to an old valuation map found in the Company's archives which shows the line generally running westerly, between those points. But the val map does not give any particular indication of which lands would have been crossed, nor does it give the Railroad good title to anything. It is just a general depiction, without obviously traceable monuments. Here, take a look."

Friedman opened the file and pulled out a copy of the map, a series of photostatic copies pieced together with cellophane tape. Misely, Evans and Hudson stood up and huddled around the opened map. It was even less clear, seeing it. Davey Evans ran his finger over the line of the right of way on the map, encountering several cellophane tape splices: "This could be anywhere." Malcolm Hudson retrieved a pocket magnifier from his breast pocket and pointed it over the east side of the map, working the magnifier up and down over the map. "We thought we could find this set of monuments down here, but no dice. We don't even have a point from which to project this thing westerly." Davey chimed in again: "It's crazy. Any one of these unmarked curves could throw the thing off by miles, not just feet!"

Friedman nodded. "That's the problem. They have conveniently figured it to cross directly over our client's property. Shockingly, the plaintiffs are looking for damages in return for dropping the suit." He pulled the bill of complaint from the file and read in a mocking, overly formal tone, "'Plaintiff herewith demands the immediate cessation of all unauthorized activities by defendant upon plaintiff's land and further, requests compensation for damages suffered by plaintiff for such unlawful trespass and wrongful occupation of plaintiff's land.'"

Friedman continued. "Now, the best part of this fable is the identity of the Directors of the Appalachian-Atlantic. It would appear that one D. Ronald Ganst holds the honor as Chairman of the newly constituted Board of Directors. Have you heard of him Mr. Misely?"

"Would he be any relation to the Gansts that developed some of the Washington Heights land?"

"Congratulations, Mr. Misely!" he chuckled. "Yes, it looks as though Ganst had somehow gotten control of the stock of the defunct railroad. How, exactly, is unclear, but it will all come out in the wash. Now, it gets better. After being served with the suit, the Principios hired Mr. Hudson to check the property lines, to look for any evidence that the railroad had ever occupied any of the land. If it had laid and removed tracks in the past, something would turn up out in the field; sections of track, old railroad spikes or ties, something to prove possession. This becomes very important in the context of the legal challenge to title. If a railroad acquires a right of way, but does not exercise rights of possession, the railroad's title will disappear if and when the line is abandoned. But if the railroad exercises provable rights of possession, the later abandonment of the line would not necessarily terminate the railroad's title. Do you follow me, Roderick?"

"Yes sir. I'm with you."

"Now, when Hudson Surveying went out they, in fact, did find numerous railroad spikes and ties. Mr. Evans' crew took down positions for each 'find,' but on my advice, did not remove or disturb the spikes and railroad ties." Roderick remembered that he had actually assisted on one such mission with Tack, just 3 months or so, earlier.

"So, of course, things began to look bad for the Principios. But there were some odd things about the finds. Mr. Hudson's men retraced the property line from east to west, beginning, logically, at the public road and moving towards the more rugged terrain to the west. Mr. Evans, do you want to pick up the story from here?"

Davey Evans cleared his throat. "Yes, like Mr. Friedman said, we started at the road and began to find occasional railroad spikes as we moved westerly. They appeared to be spaced apart in a random manner, but were placed very close to our property lines. This struck me as odd. Almost as if bread crumbs were being dropped along the line as bait. Occasional railroad ties were found too, in a similar fashion. We couldn't miss them. We would have stumbled over them. Then, as the terrain got more rugged, we noticed that things looked a little less careful. Instead of just one tie being found in the underbrush, two or three would be found together. This is not the way ties are spaced along a railroad, obviously. The best find was at the west end of the property near the horseshoe bend in the Marigold Falls. It's very rugged and swampy there. We cleared back some brush from off the site and, low and behold, we found about five or six ties just heaved into the swamp. As though the men who placed them there had grown tired and did not want to lug the extra ties all the way back to the road. I wish we could have taken a picture."

"Pictures we shall have!" laughed Friedman. "That's one of the next steps, sending out our photographer with Malcolm. You can bet that Ganst's people have their own witnesses lined up to testify about the trackage. But, Davey, tell him the rest of it."

"Sure. One of my men happened to mention that some of the railroad ties looked familiar to him. He remembered that Streeper Construction Supply Company had bought up an odd lot of surplus railroad materials when the Southwest Municipal line was re-routed around the Floral Valley development, south of the City. Apparently, Streeper had a whole back lot of bins filled with old railroad ties and spikes. Streeper would sometimes sell the ties to landscapers and farmers. I'm not sure what he was planning for the rest of the stuff. But, we are pretty sure that Ganst bought a bunch of the Southwest surplus and had his men dump it, strategically, more or less, along Principio's line. That way, it would look like the Appalachian-Atlantic had actually laid track."

Friedman joined in: "Which would greatly help them in proving their title to the land. Amazing, huh? We're going to speak with and eventually subpoena John Streeper to get his testimony on selling the ties and spikes to Ganst. And as I said, we'll get photos of the suspicious way the ties and spikes were found. But, Mr. Misely, we need you to do some fast, accurate title work to see if the Appalachian-Atlantic ever took any recorded easements in the area. If we do, the Principios may be in trouble. But if we find no easements, it leaves the Gansts with their questionable val map and railroad ties. Can you start, immediately? And, ultimately, I see you as my expert witness, testifying as to what the land records actually show. Can you handle it?"

Roderick looked off into the distance, solemnly. He tapped his fingertips together, pretending to give the matter great consideration. In fact, as usual, he was out of spending money and would jump at the chance to take on the work. "Well, Mr. Friedman, I maintain a busy schedule and would have to rearrange some of my other work - but I think the case has some remarkable aspects and is worth shuffling my schedule around. I would only ask for reasonable compensation in light of such."

"Good, then. I'll need a full report in a week - ten days maximum, but I would like you to call-in every couple days to let me know what you've found. If you find anything, we'll need to quickly get an abstract to Malcolm to plot it out. Time is truly of the essence. As it turns out, trial is set in about four weeks. The client has authorized me to offer you $150.00 for the title search and $100.00 for your testimony at trial if needed."

Roderick generously waved away the later suggestion. "Mr. Friedman, tell your client that I would not charge anything for appearing as an expert at trial. I've been very interested in reading the law, someday, and trial experience would be great. I would simply ask that your client pay the $150.00 for the title, but also reimburse me for my out-of-pocket expenses, such as phone calls, postage, car fare, etc."

"I'm sure that will be fine." Friedman thought the response interesting and wondered about Misely's prospects for reading the law. If Friedman were a younger man, he could have used someone like Roderick as an apprentice. But retirement loomed ahead. He could almost see the finish line. His wife, Ruthann, wanted him to slack off the pace and enjoy life. Maybe do some traveling.

The men shook hands and Friedman arranged with his secretary, Mrs. Blaine, to tape another map together for Roderick, in case it would help. She'd get it delivered to his office "suite" at 7 North Central in Elk Neck.

It was nearly dusk and Roderick was about to hop onto the streetcar out in front of Mr. Friedman's office when he saw a remarkable headline glare at him from the stack of Star Sentinels at the newsboy's corner:

MUSEUM THEFT! PRECIOUS RUBIES GONE!

Roderick usually read the leftover remnants of the Star Sentinel over at County Restaurant with dinner. But this was too important a story, far too interesting a reward-earning opportunity, to put off until dinner. Consequently, Roderick did something almost unheard of: he paid 4 cents for a newspaper.

He took his seat in the back row of the streetcar and began reading the story.

Reliable sources report that the Guild-Municipal Museum was recently the victim of a remarkable crime, perpetrated by particularly brazen thieves. The thieves stole the ruby "eyes" from the 'Jaguar in White Onyx,' which had been on loan to the Museum as part of the Bolivian Folklore Exhibit. Sources indicate that the thieves managed to remove the priceless ruby eyes from the statue and switch the rubies with worthless, red glass pieces. The switch only came to light when the Curator for Bolivia's National Museum inspected the various collection pieces prior to their shipment back home. The Bolivian authorities were said to be furious with the Guild-Municipal and shocked that something as obvious as the glass jewelry switch would go unnoticed by professionals on the Museum's staff. The same sources indicated the Guild-Municipal's insurance carrier, Trans Global Indemnity, would be conducting its own investigation in cooperation with the police.

And that was all for the story. Misely sat back and thought about the crime. The newspaper story didn't say, but obviously, the thieves must have made the switch when no one was around. Which meant that, besides stealing the gems, the perpetrators had managed to break into an otherwise secure museum.

Misely disembarked the streetcar at Franklin and High Streets, not far from his quarters at 7 North Central. Evening approached so he decided to stop into County Restaurant for an early dinner. As he entered, he saw that the normally ebullient Mrs. Georgelus seemed distraught, almost near panic. "Sir, sir, I hope you decide to stay with us for dinner this evening; but look!" She pointed back towards Roderick's booth. Three people were seated in his booth, a middle aged married couple with a small child, probably their granddaughter. Roderick was horrified at the sight, but composed himself, immediately. "That's fine, ma'am. I'll just take a seat at the end of the counter."

He brushed crumbs from the seat of the counter stool with his newspaper and perched himself facing the kitchen, out of eye contact with Mrs. Georgelus. This sort of thing happened from time to time. There was no way for the Georgelus' to prevent a customer from sliding into his booth, even though Misely was cognizant that the proprietors made every effort to prevent such a disaster. He had already read the paper, anyway.

The keftedes and olive bread were up to the usual standard and as he ate he mulled-over the interesting events of the day. He was delighted to have a new case that could potentially take him to the witness stand of the City's Superior Court. 'Potentially,' because he knew that not all cases made it to trial. And he had made sure that Mr. Friedman knew of his desire to read the law. He would certainly have jumped at the opportunity to study with an attorney as respected as Mr. Friedman. The deal he had made for the title work was not great; but he didn't want to make a bad impression by seeming overly mercenary. And out-of-pocket expenses were a "bird in the hand." Testifying as an expert was a more speculative venture. He'd have to remember to mention to Mr. Friedman that he was registered as a private process server with the Elk Neck Superior Court. Elk Neck had reciprocity with the City. He might be able to pick up a few more dollars by serving that Streeper subpoena.

As he sipped coffee his thoughts turned to the Museum theft. This was the second disaster to befall the Museum in the past 3 or 4 months. He remembered reading about the Museum patron who was found dead in a basement storeroom. It was a sad story. An out-of-town visitor had gone downstairs to the men's lavatory and had made the fatal mistake of turning into a storage room, instead, somehow getting himself locked in. The poor guy never made it out. The janitorial staff eventually found the man's body when somebody opened up the room to get to the floor wax and mops. According to the newspaper story, the man had been dead for several weeks. The Coroner's Office reported that the man had died of heart failure, probably brought on by the stress of his situation. The newspaper later reported that the victim's family had filed a "wrongful death" action against the Guild-Municipal, claiming that the Museum's negligence caused the death of their loved one. Trans Global Indemnity was defending the suit.

Misely found the theft of the rubies a lot more interesting than the Principio case and wanted desperately to spend some time at the Museum to observe the goings on, keeping an ear out for any offer of a reward. But he had to get the Principio work completed as fast as possible.

As he headed back around the corner to his office "suite" he saw a few snow flurries blow around the windy corner. Misely had been hoping for a snowy January. Shoveling snow for reasonable compensation was another Misely specialty. The weather did not disappoint. He spent the better part of Sunday shoveling snow and, later, hijacking a few rides with the kids sledding down the hill at Montcroix Estates.

Monday morning came and Misely roused himself from sleep. Pushing aside his olive drab horse blanket, he hoisted his legs over the side of his metal cot. As he stood up, he felt a cold, clammy object underneath his right foot. It was a tropical fish - a red Sword Tail to be precise. Misely jumped up, nearly out of his skin. He hopped around on his left leg; a dancing man with a Charley Horse. As he bounced around, he bumped into his metal desk, causing a cache of books to slide from on top of his Royal typewriter and onto the floor below. After regaining his composure, he looked around on the floor. There was no tropical fish. He had stepped on a cylindrical superheterodyne vacuum tube. He hadn't owned an aquarium since he was a teenager. But the memory of waking up as a boy and accidentally stepping on his favorite tropical fish had never, fully, been dispelled.

After dressing in his brown suit, white button-down shirt and blue tie, he absent-mindedly pulled two manila file folders and his note book ledger from the metal file cabinet which was located just beyond the sweep of the door of his quarters. He entered his office anteroom and sat at his mahogany desk, making entries into the ledger and onto the file folders.

The Principio case was entered as "C-58-3 Principio Bros. - Title." He entered the jewel theft case as "O-58-6 Guild-Municipal." After re-filing the folders, he threw on his winter overcoat, grabbed his legal pad and a few pencils and bounded down the outside stairs. His brown oxfords clapped dully against the water-saturated wood of the stairs.

Misely walked the three short blocks to the Land Records, located within the Courthouse, and began the tedious job of searching the railroad title. There were voluminous docket entries on the Appalachian-Atlantic Railroad. He spent the better part of the day hand-copying the index to conveyances. He skipped lunch and spent the balance of the afternoon pulling the Land Record books, reviewing each document. He was able to eliminate many of the entries. They represented acquisitions of land near the old Cyprus One Hundreds: the railroad supply yard, the Cyprus spur line, and the actual station. But many of the documents could not be specifically eliminated thus requiring Roderick to abstract by hand, the lengthy railroad indentures. Copying the railroad indentures was difficult, to say the least. Extreme care had to be taken. One missing course or distance would make it impossible for Hudson Surveying to plot-up the description and locate the land in the field. Although photostatic copying machines were available in the Docket Clerk's Office, the title abstractors had teamed up to keep the machines out of the Land Records, fearing the loss of their jobs.

Famished, Misely ventured over to County Restaurant for an early dinner. He grabbed the Star Sentinel from the counter and took his usual spot in the back booth. The headline told the story: "Guild Comes Clean Over Clean-Out." The story had now broken and Museum was "on the record" in describing its humiliating loss. The official press release was short and formal:

Recently, the Guild-Municipal Museum learned that it had suffered a serious theft. Officials from the Bolivian government's Ministry of Culture informed the Museum that the red diamond eyes of its 'Jaguar in White Onyx,' on loan from the Bolivian National Museum, had been replaced with counterfeit gemstones. The Guild-Municipal Museum can only presume that the real gems were removed while the objet d'art was in the

Museum's custody, notwithstanding the Museum's around-the-clock security. The Museum deeply regrets these unavoidable events and, with the cooperation and assistance of our insurer, Trans Global Indemnity, will fully compensate the Bolivian Ministry of Culture for its loss. At the suggestion of Trans Global Indemnity, the Guild-Municipal will be seeking the assistance of Otho Pramm, the renowned private investigator, in order to track down the red diamonds and bring the perpetrators to justice.

An impromptu press conference had also been held at the main entrance to the Museum, at the top of the long flight of marble stairs leading to the impressive glass and metal entrance doors. A couple of local reporters had snagged Chief Curator Ronald Sanderford as he was going off to meet with the Museum's attorneys. The Star Sentinel reporter had summarized Mr. Sanderford's comments in a brief news item. Sanderford explained to the reporters that the gems were actually red diamonds, not rubies as had first been reported. There was no question that the red diamonds were stolen while the object was on loan to the Guild-Municipal. The entire Bolivian collection had been inspected and photographed upon arrival in United States. The Bolivian officials had, likewise, inspected the collection on-site, before it was packed for shipping for its return.

The initial photograph of the Jaguar did not do the work justice, but even average, industrial grade photography could not mask the sculpture's unquestionable beauty. The creature's eyes blazed from its glacially white onyx head and torso. Comparing the photograph of the Jaguar's eyes in its original state to the Jaguar in the "after" photograph indicated that the Jaguar's glass eyes were about 10 percent larger than its original diamond ones. And a closer inspection showed that the junk jewelry eyes were glued back into the eye sockets in a less than artful manner. The poor creature looked a little cross-eyed.

Mr. Sanderford also explained that the suggestion for seeking out Otho Pramm had come from counsel for Trans Global

Indemnity. One of the reporters had asked whether the suggestion was due to the McCausey lawsuit. Sanderford declined to comment. But it was surmised by the writer that officials of Trans Global were less than enthused over the second, major loss to occur on the Museum's premises within the last four months.

How often does a museum kill a visitor? Roy Botkin McCausey had been accidentally locked in one of the museum's abandoned storage vaults and never made it out. His family members, from Atchaflaka County, two states over, filed a wrongful death lawsuit in the Elk Neck Superior Court, locus of Mr. McCausey's domicile at the time of his final feed at the cultural trough. The family members were inconsolable. Roy Botkin was the family patriarch, said to be only 45 years old, but looking more like 70 at the time of his death. The family's attorney, Byron Cradley, estimated their sorrow at $178,000, representing the loss of Roy Botkin's future income-earning potential, as well as compensation for the family's emotional pain and suffering.

The theft of the red diamonds, being the Museum's second foul-up, would almost certainly take the Guild-Municipal beyond policy limits, exposing it to potentially dire financial consequences. The Guild-Municipal had been grossly under-insured. The Museum had calculated the value of the Bolivian 'Jaguar' believing the eyes to be rubies, which would certainly have added great value to the work. But the Museum had not realized that the gemstones were actually red diamonds - those gems being a nearly priceless endowment made to the Bolivian government from a wealthy family from La Paz. For this reason, Trans Global suggested that the Guild-Municipal consider Otho Pramm in attempting to recover the stolen red diamonds.

Misely was completely absorbed in the Star Sentinel stories and had not realized that he had finished his dinner, lamb souvlakia with stuffed grape leaves. His plate had been cleared right from underneath his nose by Eleni, who went about her business, unnoticed.

There was yet a third story in the newspaper, this one a short piece on the distinguished private investigator, Otho Pramm. Pramm ran his investigation services, "Oxford Investigations," from an office on 5th Avenue in New York City. His business card also mentioned a second, London address, which was followed by the phrase "Off Oxford Circus" in italics below the address. But the London office was actually a dingy second story walkup, well "Off Oxford Circus," all the way down to Berwick Street in Soho, in fact, a lot further down Berwick than most refined people were willing to travel. Pramm seldom visited his London office, but felt it important to maintain a presence there.

But back in Manhattan, Pramm ran his decidedly well-appointed office suite like a king. His razor-sharp intellect and decisive methods brought many seemingly hopeless cases to successful conclusions. He specialized in insurance fraud cases and recoveries. Sophisticated legal adversaries knew and feared Otho Pramm.

Physically, Pramm was heavyset, borderline obese, but earnestly believed himself to be merely "husky." In the New York office, his loyal staff quietly referred to him behind his back as "Mycroft," because of Pramm's superior intellect. Believing himself to be descended from British aristocracy, Pramm dressed the part and was often seen about town wearing a black bowler hat and a black-vested suit. His bowler masked his somewhat thinning, stringy black hair and provided shade for his bushy, walrus-like mustache. He traveled at all times with an ornate-handled umbrella, rain or shine, which he referred to as his "bumbershoot." A photograph of the rotund Pramm, complete with bowler and umbrella, accompanied the article.

Pramm was of English descent, but, regrettably, would not have been able to trace his ancestry to British royalty had he tried. Rather, Pramm was the direct descendent of a humble, particularly hard-working Pramm who came to the New World indentured as a servant to his own brother. The newspaper account mentioned Pramm's interest in his British background in describing his eccentric affectations of dress and manner.

The story also mentioned Pramm's considerable interest in the philosophy of personal motivation and self-improvement. Pramm was a fan of Dr. Norman Vincent Peale and, like Peale, often wrote and lectured on such topics. Pramm was particularly pleased with a monograph he published entitled "Overcoming Arrogance… With Pride," which was made available, gratis, to fraternal and charitable organizations. The pamphlet also served as the basis for his lectures. In his publication, Pramm described his journey to self-awareness and how he was able to conquer his personal demon, a perceived "arrogant" attitude towards the world at large. The fortunate recipient of the monograph would have read:

Having a sense of superiority is a stumbling block in today's world. The homogenous American culture (if you care to use the word 'culture') fails to recognize that there will always be select intellectuals, scholars, people without peers, who, due to their skill, tenacity and superior intellect, must lead and must do so decisively. (How soon we forget our Founding Fathers, the new nobility of a new nation?) But a leader must not dwell upon the characteristics that separate him from the common rabble of the streets, because in a nation of equals, no man considers himself inferior to the next, irrespective of his lack of intelligence, skills or breeding.

The monograph continued with a few more paragraphs describing the "average" people that make up American society and the value of leadership and then continued:

For these reasons I found that the misperception on the part of others, that I was "arrogant," was having a deleterious effect on my personal and working relationships. This impercipience I would have to overcome. After a great deal of soul-searching and logical reasoning, I concluded that, because all men are created equal, truly equal, to those within their social station,

I should, forthwith, make every effort to recognize that my own talent and intellect should never be the source of misunderstandings with my fellow man. To that end I have entirely changed my attitude and demeanor. I am no longer bound by past constraints and have embarked upon my personal journey to excellence, now overcoming "arrogance," with pride.

The monograph concluded with the suggestion that further copies could be obtained by qualified organizations from Pramm's charitable foundation for what was described as a "nominal" fee representing the cost of postage, handling, copying, and reasonable author's royalties.

Misely lingered, reading the newspaper accounts several times. It was getting late, so he folded the paper under his arm on the way out the front door of County Restaurant. No one else would be dining at the restaurant at this late hour and the newspaper would not be missed. When he had climbed the wooden stairs leading to his "suite" he saw a package leaning against his outside door. Mr. Friedman had delivered a copy of the valuation map, as promised.

Roderick's second day at the Land Records was almost as tedious as his first. Again, Misely painstakingly abstracted the remaining railroad indentures. Towards the end of the day, he finished-up and headed over to the pay phone just outside of the Docket Clerk's office. He tried to call Mr. Friedman to arrange for delivery of the abstracts to Davey Evans. But Mrs. Blaine informed him that Mr. Friedman was attending a court appearance. Roderick left the message that he would call back again, tomorrow.

Misely was now nearly free of the Principio case. He was looking forward to diving into the Museum theft case, head first. Tuesday night meant that County Restaurant would feature their lamb stew special, always one of Roderick's favorites. Misely was further rewarded by yet more news items in that day's Star Sentinel.

One story covered the Bolivian collection, describing the origins of the art treasures and their significance to Bolivian culture. The piece included a discussion on several up-and-coming artists, including Marina Nunez del Prado. More ink had been spent on the Bolivian collection following the theft and after the items had been shipped back home, than before or during the actual Exhibition. But the most important information was delivered by Chief Curator Sanderford to a Star Sentinel reporter. Mr. Sanderford confirmed that Otho Pramm, himself, had taken the case and would be arriving at the Museum on Friday at 10:00 AM to undertake the investigation. Sanderford declined to comment further on the terms of Pramm's employment, but did say that "Should Mr. Pramm succeed, everyone will be quite happy."

Misely smiled to himself. Knowing Pramm's reputation and excellent clientele, his significant asking price was probably met with little haggling on the part of the Museum. This gave Misely just two more days to corral something useful to offer to Pramm. He'd always wanted to meet the man ever since reading accounts of the brilliant eccentric's successes. Misely had an idea - a long shot - but possibly something to parlay into an introduction with Pramm: Was the McCausey death in any way connected to the theft of the red diamonds? After all, how does a person of ordinary intelligence mistake a storage vault for the men's restroom? What had McCausey been up to on that fateful day four months ago?

On Wednesday morning, Roderick headed back to the Courthouse, this time to visit the Docket Clerk in Elk Neck Superior Court. He would pull the wrongful death case filed by the McCausey family. But first, he detoured to the public phone booth located just inside the Docket Clerk's office.

Aloysius Friedman and just arrived at his office with his beaten-up brown leather briefcase in tow. His secretary announced that "Mr. Misely" was on the line. Mr. Friedman had the call transferred into his office.

"Mr. Friedman, I've completed the title abstract on the railroad and have five 'possibles' to deliver to Davey Evans. I say 'possible,' but I think 'not likely' is a better description. The five seem to be associated with the spur line leading to the old serpentine mine out at Minebank Run."

Friedman was pleasantly surprised to hear of the quick results provided by Misely. "That's great Mr. Misely. Can you get those abstracts over to Davey this afternoon or maybe tomorrow, preferably before noon?"

"Yes, sir. By the way, did you need any help in serving the Streeper subpoena? I forgot to mention that I'm qualified as a private process server for Elk Neck Superior Court and can also serve process out of the City courts."

Friedman sighed to himself. He hadn't wanted to burst Misely's bubble, but the practice of law had its difficulties. And Misely needed to understand that simple fact of life. "Well, I didn't want to dampen your enthusiasm Roderick, but I'm afraid I have some bad news: serving Streeper is no longer in the picture." Friedman felt the silence from the other end of the line and empathized with Misely's obvious puzzlement. He continued:

"Roderick, as attorneys, we must always place the wishes of our clients first, even if doing so seems illogical or contrary to client's best interests. The Principio's have instructed me that we are not to involve Streeper. Apparently, the Principios deal with Streeper all the time and are very dependent upon him for supplies. They don't want to do anything to jeopardize their business relationship with him. Streeper, apparently, would not look too fondly upon being forced to produce records and testify about selling the railroad supplies to another good customer. You see, Streeper deals mostly in cash..."

There was another brief pause but Friedman heard Misely on the other end of the line give a knowing "Ahh, understood."

"So, my problem is that there will be only circumstantial evidence available to prove that the railroad supplies were dumped by Ganst. A jury will have to infer the skullduggery based solely upon our photographic evidence and the testimony of Davey Evans. We can suggest that the materials are not those of the Appalachian-Atlantic. But we will not be able to mention Streeper as the source of materials from the Southwest Municipal line. It's what we call a 'conundrum.'"

"Well Mr. Friedman, if you don't mind, I will put on my thinking cap for this one."

Friedman admired the young man's attitude. "Excellent, Mr. Misely. Let me know if you come up with anything. And I would appreciate your dropping those abstracts off as soon as possible."

Back in the phone booth, Misely clinked the handset back to the cradle. He wasn't surprised that Streeper was operating on a "cash" basis. But he was surprised and pleased that Friedman confided in him freely about the case. He would mull-over Friedman's "conundrum" but for now, the Museum case was beckoning.

In the file room, the Docket Clerk handed Misely the wrongful death file. From the bill of complaint, Misely learned a great deal of useful information. The grieving family alleged that Roy Botkin McCausey had visited the Museum "on or about September 6, 1957." Allegedly, McCausey had followed the signage downstairs to the men's lavatory located in the basement area. But rather than enter the restroom, he somehow wandered into a room across the hall, which had once been a vault room, complete with a combination door lock. The room once held stored museum pieces not currently on display. But a larger warehouse equipped with thermostats and a humidity regulator had been built, later, courtesy of a capital improvements drive held by the Guild Museum prior to its merger with the City's Municipal Museum of Art.

The suit alleged that, in an obvious attempt at modesty, Mr. McCausey closed the vault room door behind him and found himself locked in the pitch black chamber. McCausey's death must have been horrific. He must have cried out to the Museum guards, but the vault doors may have been too thick to transmit his desperate pleas for help. The bill of complaint alleged that the Guild-Municipal "knew or should have known," of the danger that the open vaults door posed to Mr. McCausey and the public at large.

The suit also included a copy of the police report. The police report indicated the Museum had contacted the Police on September 21st. One of the janitors had unlocked the vault door to retrieve some mops and floor wax and stumbled upon McCausey's prone body. The janitor explained in the witness transcript that the vault room was used solely for storage of janitorial supplies. The janitors never intentionally locked the door; it was ordinarily left fully ajar. But if and when the door was closed, occasionally the door would "freeze-up" requiring the janitor to "move the dial a hair towards 3" on the combination.

Sadly, for McCausey, the tumbler must have slipped when the door closed behind him, forever sealing his fate.

The police report included the coroner's findings - that McCausey had died of acute heart failure. The police report also provided an inventory of McCausey's personal effects, recovered at the scene. Besides the clothes on his back, McCausey's pockets contained some loose change, cigarettes, a lighter, a packet of chewing gum, a wallet with identification and $7 in cash. The police also recovered a paper bag near the body. The paper bag was from the Museum's gift shop and contained a 1957 color calendar and cash register receipt for eighty-five cents. Misely figured that the calendar's price must have been heavily discounted due to the lateness of the year. Eighty-five cents for a color calendar was a bargain. The report indicated that the gift shop's cash register receipt was dated August 31st, 1957, which Misely thought may have been a more accurate means of establishing the date of the incident, rather than the plaintiff's general assertion that the incident occurred "on or about September 6, 1957."

But, alas, there was nothing else particularly helpful in the wrongful death file. What had he expected? To find the diamonds inventoried among the personal effects of McCausey in the police report? Not likely. But could McCausey's clothing or wallet have contained a secret compartment? Certainly, yes, if only the diamonds were being hidden. But what about burglary tools? The thief would have needed some means, mechanical or chemical, to extract the diamonds from the settings in the Jaguar's eye sockets, and some other means to glue the glass pieces back in. Could all of these be hidden in McCausey's meager personal effects?

Misely dropped another dime into the payphone. Sarah Golden, of the Central District Precinct's Property Control, cupped her hands over the mouthpiece of the phone. "Are we allowed to talk about the stuff in the Property Room? I think it's a lawyer." Officer Rothbard took over the handset. "Rothbard. Can I help you?" The voice on the other end of the line spoke up. "Yes, Officer. I'm following up on the McCausey wrongful death lawsuit. Could you tell me whether Mr. Roy McCausey's personal effects have been claimed by the family?" Rothbard grumbled "hang on." A half minute later Rothbard returned to his desk. "No sir. Everything is still here. Tell a family member to come over and sign for this stuff. The Department will otherwise dispose of it if unclaimed for six months." And with that, Officer Rothbard heard a quick "Thank you," followed by a dial tone.

Misely slumped back against flat wall of the phone booth. His imagination was running rampant. He was picturing McCausey's shoes. He imagined a hidden compartment in the heels, hiding the gems. He pictured McCausey's belt, which could be hiding a collection of jeweler's tools. The police would have never looked that closely at those items - they would never have associated the death of McCausey, four months earlier, with the presently publicized the Museum theft. After all, the theft, although recently discovered, could have taken place at any time during the Bolivian Exhibition, which ran from August through December. Neither the art-loving public nor the Curator had ever noticed the switch. This could be just the sort of information that could earn Misely an introduction with Otho Pramm.

Misely emptied his pockets of his coins, lining up a row of dimes and nickels on the metal tray below the pay phone.

Robert 'L.B.' Bartin, Junior was reading that morning's Atchaflaka County Dispatch while sipping on a cup of hot, black coffee from a stained porcelain mug. The Dispatch also served the independent townships of Wittenburg and Runyon Ridge.

"I'm not sure who you mean by 'Deputy Clerk,' sir. Bobby Barton is off hunting."

L.B.'s ears perked up. He began waving his arms frantically, trying to get Lara Robesby's attention, desperate to have a call, any call, forwarded to his desk. At least it would give him something to do.

Lara saw L.B. waving and adopted a more official sounding tone: "Oh, one minute, sir. I'll connect you to Deputy Clerk L.B., I mean Robert, Bartin. Robert Junior, that is." She looked over at L.B. and gave him a huge, knowing wink. "L.B." - "Little Barton" was Clerk Robert Barton's son. L.B. had finished up high school just a year before and ventured into the Clerk's office to "hold down the fort" on days when his father was out hunting or fishing. But there was never a whole lot for the Clerk of the Court for Atchaflaka County to do on any given day, anyway.

Little Barton heard a friendly voice through the handset. "Mr. Clerk, I'm calling from the Elk Neck Superior Court and thought I might ask your assistance on a particular matter."

L.B. had never been addressed as "Mr. Clerk," and snapped to attention, eager to serve a fellow clerk from Elk Neck, wherever the heck that was.

"Yes Mr. Clerk. What can I do for you?"

The friendly voice chimed back. "Here's the question: do you have access to the criminal docket from your office?"

L.B. glanced up, over to docket counter. "I'm looking at it now!"

"Excellent. Now, Mr. Clerk, could you please take a look and see if any folks by the last name of McCausey are listed as defendants in that docket?"

L.B. sat upright in his chair. "McCausey? I don't even need to leave my seat. The McCauseys are all over that docket. Everyone here knows the McCauseys. That bunch has been in the hoosegow more times than they've been out over all kinds of things, including some well-documented trespasses and poaching on... certain land with which I am personally familiar." He had caught himself before blurting out "my Dad's land." After all, a professional demeanor was required of public officials.

"That's very helpful Mr. Clerk. Now, does the name Roy Botkin McCausey ever come up?" L.B. practically jumped out of his seat.

"The Weasel? Everyone here knows Weasel McCausey. Or should I say, knew Weasel McCausey. He went missing about a year ago much to the distress of his common law wife and the County D.A. He's up on federal charges now and will get himself locked away but good this time if he ever turns up to face the music. Burglary and bad checks were his modus operandi." He thought that was the right phrase. Lara Robesby shot him a questioning glance. She hadn't realized that Junior had taken French.

"Anyway, the whole bunch are no good in my opinion. Did you need anything else, sir?"

As he was speaking, L.B. thought he heard the telltale signs of a coin being dropped into a pay phone on the other end of the line. He quietly sympathized with the Elk Neck Clerk. Their office, too, had to use the public pay phone in order to make long distance calls.

"No, Mr. Clerk. That tells me exactly what I need to know. Thank you for your kind assistance."

"My pleasure, Mr. Clerk. Call me if you need anything else. That's Robert Bartin, Jr. Deputy Clerk, Atchaflaka County." L.B. handed the phone back to Mrs. Robesby, proud to have helped out a friendly fellow-clerk.

Misely sprung from the phone booth. That was it. He was compiling some very useful information to share with Mr. Pramm. He wasn't exactly sure where it would lead, but at this point he was more interested in providing salable information, not solving someone else's problem. He headed back to 7 North Central. There was still a lot of work to be done between now and Mr. Pramm's arrival on Friday morning.

Back in 7 North Central, Misely sat at his mahogany desk in his office anteroom and prepared the packet of abstracts, including a short note to Davey Evans. He suggested in the note that the various abstracted property descriptions could concern the Minebank Run spur line, but that he wasn't entirely sure. He also noted that in his abstracts the abbreviation "I. Sp." meant "iron spike" and "I.P." meant "iron pin" and not the usual "iron pipe." This made perfect sense as the railroad's surveyors would simply have used available iron railroad spikes or "pins" to mark the property corners rather than the typical iron pipes that surveyors often used. And then an idea flashed across his mind.

Later that afternoon, a disinterested observer viewing the activities at 7 North Central would have noticed a brown-suited man bounding down the wooden stairs and over to the streetcar line on Franklin, disembarking downtown in the City. The same brown-suited man could have been observed in the Municipal Archives building, perusing the Public Service Commission records for common carriers. Later, he might have been seen dining at a greasy spoon on Eucalyptus Avenue and later, up the street at the Guild-Municipal Museum, where he may have been noticed taking a quick tour of the Main Gallery followed by a short visit to the men's lavatory in the basement.

The same brown-suited man may have later been observed at the Central District Police Precinct, requesting review of the personal effects of Roy Botkin McCausey. A disinterested observer would have noted the brown-suited man hand over his business card to the Desk Sergeant with the Sergeant inquiring whether the man's insurance company "was involved in the wrongful death action?" The observer may have then heard the brown-suited man respond that, "in fact," he "had presently been handling the file." The brown-suited man would have then been seen seated at a table in the Property Room, carefully examining, first, Roy Botkin McCausey's wallet and loose items and later his clothing. He would have been seen poking and prodding the clothing fabric and then examining the decedent's shoes, tapping the heels with a cartridge pen and feeling inside the shoes with his fingers, mining to no avail. The man would have also been observed examining the decedent's belt, twisting and prodding the cheap cowhide material, but without any particular result.

Later, the brown-suited man would have been observed, back on the streetcar, disembarking in Elk Neck near the Graham Independent Free Public Library. Inside the library, the man could have been seen seated across from "Dad" Graham at the partner's desk located inside the Rare Book Room, reading from a science text on mass spectography.

The next morning, Roderick readied himself. He was making substantial progress on both files O-58-6 and C-58-3. He still had one day left before the arrival of Otho Pramm and there was much to be accomplished.

But, unbeknownst to nearly everyone, Pramm arrived at the Guild-Municipal exactly one day early, on that very Thursday at 10:00 AM. And so it was that the huge, hulk of a man could be seen, slowly ascending the long white marble stairs of the Museum. It was a sight that no City resident had ever witnessed before: the great, mustachioed man in English bowler hat and plastic mackintosh raincoat, carrying an attaché case and using his black umbrella as a cane. He was taking a step at a time in a deliberate and highly dignified manner.

He pushed through the glass entrance doors of the Museum and reviewed the directory in the foyer, which indicated that the Curator's office was down the Main Gallery hall, to the right. But Pramm had another destination in mind. He noted the direction to the Museum's coffee shop, "La Café" and trudged down the East Wing, in that direction.

Pramm burst through the doors of La Café, announcing in a stentorian tone: "I am Otho Pramm. I shall require a proper tea this afternoon at 3 PM. Can you provide that courtesy?"

Surprised, the counter clerk, Emma Tolton, responded "we serve tea here all day long, sir. You can have some tea whenever you like."

Pramm was not satisfied with the response. He smiled, sweetly. "Then, Madam, do you have an actual tea room where high tea is served?"

Confused, Mrs. Tolton responded. "This is where we sell the tea, sir. And we'll be open at 3:00, PM, too."

Resigning himself to the inevitable, Pramm looked down through the glass counter window, perusing the available baked goods. The display case still held yesterday's leftovers. It was too early for the day's delivery of fresh pastries. There were two grisly-looking croissants and a blueberry scone. The scone looked like someone had taken a bite out of it. "Very well. If this is it, please reserve these 3 items or their hopefully fresher equivalents for me for my tea at 3:00 PM Clotted cream and strawberry preserves are preferred." He turned his back and was nearly out the door when Mrs. Tolton spoke up: "We have cream cheese and jelly?"

Several of the Museum staff had witnessed the dramatic entrance of Pramm. Mrs. Druscilla Romney had dialed over to Louise Travers, Chief Administrative Assistant, who held down the Administration Desk situated in the Main Gallery. "Mr. Pramm is already here, a day early!"

As though shot from a cannon, Mrs. Travers practically flew across the Main Gallery floor to the office of Chief Curator Ronald Sanderford. She rapped sharply at his closed door, until she remembered that Sanderford had arranged to take the day off to catch up on household matters. With Sanderford out, she scurried down the Main Gallery and tapped on the open door of Assistant Curator, Dorsey Prescott.

"Dorsey, you won't believe it. Mr. Pramm is here, now!"

Prescott's eyes bulged. "What?"

They quickly decided that Sanderford was needed, pronto, vacation day or not. Prescott picked up the phone and dialed him.

Pramm only had to cool his heels for a few minutes. Mrs. Travers had unlocked Sanderford's office and directed Pramm to "Take a load off," and 'what a load it was' she thought. Pramm squeezed himself into Sanderford's plush, upholstered desk chair. The springs of the chair made an unhappy, squeaking metallic sound as Pramm settled himself in.

Sanderford burst into his office, out of breath. Pramm stood. His prodigious belly swayed as he rose, a tidal flux at full moon. Further introductions were made. Pramm began, humbly. "I must apologize for my early arrival. I sensed that this case would not require a great deal of my time, as I intend to recover the diamonds, post haste. Now, it is appropriate that I review with you, the terms and conditions of my engagement with your institution."

Sanderford looked at Prescott, befuddled. Prescott opened Sanderford's wooden filing cabinet, pulled a manila folder from the top drawer and, with great ceremony, handed the file folder over to Sanderford. Sanderford opened the file jacket and withdrew the telegram that Pramm had sent just two days earlier.

"Yes Mr. Pramm. The terms and conditions are fully summarized in your telegram."

Pramm sat back down behind Sanderford's desk and received the manila folder marked "O. Pramm Contract." Pramm opened the manila folder and looked over the telegram.

"Piffle." Pramm flung the telegram back into the file jacket.

The two were thunderstruck. Sanderford spoke up, meekly. "Are you suggesting some revision to these terms Mr. Pramm?"

"Yes, of course. The terms in the telegram are mere pro forma; just the ordinary boilerplate copied off by my well-intentioned assistant in Manhattan. The terms call for employment on a daily basis with a minimum payment of $5,000. plus expenses. But fortunately for this institution, I have had a chance to ruminate on this matter and would like to propose a modification, of course, with the institution's approval. However, I must insist that these terms and conditions be held strictly confidential, for the eyes and ears of Officers and Board members, only."

Louise Travers had been hovering around Sanderford's office door, intending to offer assistance as needed. She now looked positively wounded. She was neither an Officer nor a Board member. She scurried back to her desk on the Main Gallery floor. Prescott closed the office door behind her.

Pramm retrieved the telegram from the file folder and began to slowly crumple it into an indistinguishable wad of paper. Sanderford's and Prescott's jaws dropped. "Let's forget about this and get down to business. You want fast results and I can provide them. I would like to submit the following: I believe that I can locate and return the missing diamonds to you within 24 hours. If I am able to produce such a result, that is, the diamonds in your hands by 10:00 AM tomorrow morning, in this very office, you will deliver a cashier's check to me made payable to 'bearer' in the sum of $10,000. If for any reason I fail to recover and deliver the diamonds to you by 10:00 o'clock tomorrow morning, we shall revert to the original terms outlined in the telegram."

The office went silent for several palpably long moments. Sanderford finally responded. "Well Mr. Pramm, I would like, of course, to place this before the Board of Directors since this matter would require their approval. Unfortunately, the Board only convenes for regular meetings on a monthly basis, although the Chairman has discretion to call for emergency meetings as necessary. But even an emergency meeting could take several days to arrange." Sanderford was beginning to sweat and sincerely hoped that that Pramm would see the wisdom in the Museum's highly rational organizational structure.

Pramm smiled sweetly. "Ah, then, regrettably, I will have to forego your offer of employment at this time. I bid you good day, gentlemen." And with that, Pramm rose to his feet and moved his hulking frame out from behind the desk and towards the closed door. Sanderford all but fainted. If Pramm left, the Museum would have no chance at recovering the stolen diamonds. Prescott quickly pulled Sanderford aside. "Uncle Ronnie, come on now, we've got to authorize this as Officers of the Museum. The Board will back us up." He whispered hoarsely in Sanderford's ear: "We can temporarily pull the $10,000 from the South Wing campaign. We can't break ground until spring, anyway. Besides, he's promising us the diamonds in 24 hours. If he doesn't meet his own deadline, he'll be back to the approved engagement. Either way, we'll be fine."

Sanderford rallied. "Yes, of course, Dorsey. You're right. The Board would have our hides if we let Mr. Pramm walk out of here just because he requested a slight modification to his engagement."

Pramm had been working his way over to the office door, almost in slow motion, as though repelled by some irresistible force that prevented him from clutching the doorknob and exiting the office. But he had left his hat, coat and umbrella hanging on Sanderford's teak coat rack and he hadn't retrieved his briefcase. Sanderford and Prescott reached him, in the nick of time.

"Yes, Mr. Pramm. Your terms are acceptable. Will you need anything in writing from the Museum?"

"Absolutely not. Your handshake and cashier's check in the amount of $10,000, tomorrow morning, at 10:00 AM, will be quite sufficient. Can you manage it?" Pramm had now adopted a gentle and forgiving tone.

"Most certainly, Mr. Pramm. Dorsey?"

Prescott chimed in. "I'll take care of it, immediately."

Sanderford and Pramm quickly shook hands. Pramm smiled pleasantly. But the smile made his bushy mustache crinkle, inadvertently producing a menacing grimace.

Pramm continued in a soft tone, engendering a sense of confidentiality. "Now, gentlemen, as Officers of this institution, you no doubt have realized that there is at least a possibility that the theft was orchestrated by, or with the help of, someone inside the Museum's employ." Pramm was being polite. It was almost a certainty that the theft was an "inside job." The fact that the burglars had so successfully gotten into the Museum, defeated its alarm system, and did so without any sign of tampering, made the conclusion nearly inevitable.

Sanderford and Prescott were astonished. Prescott piped up. "Really?"

"Regrettably, yes. For that reason, I shall need to review the personnel files on all of your staff, as I plan to interrogate key employees. In particular I will need to review, post haste, the personnel files of the guards who had been on duty throughout the Bolivian Exhibition."

Sanderford was beginning to relax. "Well, that will be easy. There are only three guards. Their shifts are staggered so that there is always at least one guard on duty at any given time, 24 hours a day."

"Excellent. After you have fetched the personnel files, I shall begin the interview process with the guards." Sanderford realized that Pramm's requested would mean that one of the three guards would have to be summoned from home, immediately. He swung open the office door to look for Mrs. Travers, who, coincidently, happened to be hovering near the doorway.

"Oh, Mrs. Travers, Mr. Pramm needs to interview all three of our guards, immediately, if not sooner. Later, he'll be talking to some of the staff and will need access to all personnel files. Could you do whatever needs to be done?"

Mrs. Travers snapped to attention. "Yes sir." Under the watchful eyes of her co-workers, she strutted officiously through the Main Gallery and marched up the marble steps that led to the second floor Gallery which housed the Etruscan Collection, along with the American Indian Folk Arts and Colonial Crafts exhibit. The American Indian Folk Arts and Colonial Crafts exhibit were holdovers from the Guild Museum days.

Both day shift guards in the "Office of Security" were sitting with their feet up on Stan Holt's desk, sipping on hot coffee courtesy of the office's electric percolator. They were on break. The door flew open: "Stan, Smed - call Bill at home, immediately. He's got to get down here on the double. Mr. Pramm is here a day early and wants to question all three of you, pronto!" The two nearly fell out of their chairs. "Yes, ma'am!" Stan Holt grabbed the phone off the hook and began dialing.

Bill Needles was dreaming. He was at a smorgasbord, carefully placing slices from a steamship round of beef onto his large plate. He was about to stab at a deviled egg on a pewter serving tray when the phone rang, jarring him awake. "What? You mean 'now' as in 'right now?'"

Sanderford laid the stack of personnel files on the desk before Pramm, with the personnel files for the three guards on top, as requested. But Sanderford could not help but mention, "Mr. Pramm, I know what you are saying makes sense, but I just don't see the possibility of any of our own staff having stolen the diamonds. Most of us came over from the Guild." This information was thought by Sanderford to cinch the fact that the staff was beyond reproach. Pramm looked up from the stack in a kind and forgiving matter. "Thank you Mr. Sanderford. That will be all for now." Sanderford retreated back to Dorsey Prescott's office.

Pramm began reading through the personnel files. He kept Sanderford's office door open, purposefully, so that he could glower, icily, at any curiosity seeker foolish enough to look through the door. There were a few unfortunates. Those who peered in quickly shriveled and blew away; dust clusters on a hardwood floor. Withering intimidation was part of Pramm's psychological warfare.

In reviewing the files, Pramm was looking for recent hires, persons with poor attendance records and employees with other blemishes on their records that could indicate disloyalty. Experience taught that older employees with proven, long-term track records were less likely to conspire against their own masters, barring some personal or financial catastrophe. And people in the midst of such catastrophes tended to have a greater incidence of absenteeism and other episodes of antisocial behavior. Pramm was surprised to see that the most recent hire, Thelma Gottschalk, had been with the Museum for seven years. Some had been in the employ of the Museum or one of its predecessors for over twenty years. And he was equally surprised to find that the staff members had impeccable attendance records, much better than he had expected. Perhaps there was something to what Sanderford had said? No. Pramm was still convinced that this was an inside job, in whole or in part, somehow.

It was 11:30 AM and the all-important luncheon hour was fast approaching. But Pramm decided to first make a surprise visit to the Office of Security. It took a while, but he eventually worked his way up the winding marble staircase from the Main Gallery to the Museum's second floor.

He rapped gently at the door of the Office of Security, located in the East corner. Stan Holt, the senior member of the guard staff, was alone. He had been occupying himself with several half-hearted efforts to "clean the place up" in anticipation of the inevitable visit from Pramm. Holt had gathered up an armful of old newspapers, more accurately the Sports sections from countless past Star Sentinels, planning to relocate the unsightly pile from their spot in the corner of the office to somewhere less obtrusive. But there was no place better to put the mess, so he dumped the dusty pile back into the same corner. In a desperate effort to "dust," he grabbed his handkerchief from his pants pocket and swatted randomly at various dust piles; a horsetail going at flies. Pramm rapped again, this time a little harder and Stan opened the door to his unexpected guest.

"I am Otho Pramm."

Stan Holt introduced himself and shook Pramm's hand. Stan was the oldest member of the guard staff and his thick gray hair and matching mustache made him look more like a college professor than a museum guard. His seniority made him the de facto captain of the guard staff. He apologized for the absence of the other two guards and explained that Mr. Phillips had gone out to pick up Mr. Needles. Pramm seated himself, gently, in a tiny metal folding chair in front of Holt's desk. Once seated, the tiny chair became nearly invisible. Pramm announced that he merely had a few preliminary questions.

"Mr. Holt, how is the Museum secured at night. How is it locked-up?"

"Very simple, Mr. Pramm. Closing time is at 6 PM. Mrs. Travers, or whoever is manning the Administration desk in the Main Gallery, will get on the public address microphone around 5:40 and announce that the Museum is closing in 20 minutes. Then, the assigned day guard will make a quick sweep of the building, basement and two floors, looking for stragglers. We wait a few more minutes for employees to get out and for the night shift guard to show-up around 6:00. Then, usually by around 6:15 we lock up for the night. That is, the guard pulling the night shift locks himself in and everyone else out."

Pramm looked pleased. "Excellent Mr. Holt." Do you keep a log of the guards assigned to the various shifts on a daily basis?"

"We switch the shifts around weekly, Mr. Pramm. And, yes, we maintain a log for the guard shifts, vacations, days off for illness, etc. And, to keep the record straight, we occasionally enlist the help of Bill Needle's brother Flip, er Phillip, that is, to cover in the event of an illness or vacation."

"Do the janitors work at nights?"

"Just two nights out of the year, for floor waxing. They clean-up throughout the day and dry mop after we make the 5:40 announcement."

"Did they work at night during the Bolivian Exhibition?"

"No. We schedule the waxing once in June after the schools let out and then once just before Christmas."

"Do the janitors have an office or place where they keep their things?"

"Right over there." Stan Holt made a hitchhiking motion behind his back, pointing to a rusty-looking metal wardrobe in the back of the office. "They keep their smocks and dust brooms in there. Their detergents and wax are kept in the basement vault." Pramm saw that the wardrobe was open and had no lock. A couple of dingy white smocks were hanging from wire clothes hangers. There was nothing else in the wardrobe.

"Is the Museum open seven days a week?"

"Yes sir. With the exception of a few holidays, such as Christmas, Good Friday, Easter, Independence Day and the couple others."

"Very good. Now, I take it you carefully inspected the entrance door lock after the theft was discovered. I saw it has a double-key system. Had the door or lock been tampered with in any way?"

"No. Not a scratch. No sign of anyone breaking open or jamming the lock or anything like that. The doors and windows are alarmed, too. Anyone tampering with the lock or windows would set off the alarm. We did replace the lock system just this past Tuesday, though, out of precaution. We believe that the thieves must have gotten their hands on the keys, somehow because of the fact that the locks looked untouched and the alarm never went off."

Pramm looked on gravely. "And now for the obvious question: Who has access to the keys?"

"Yes, sir. I knew that one was coming. Only the guard staff - the three of us each has a set, plus a master set is maintained by the Board of Directors in a safe deposit box at their bank - although I'm not sure which bank they use. Mr. Sanderford would know."

"Very, good sir. Now, obviously, a person needs the keys to get into the Museum; but what about a person trying to leave the Museum after closing hours - they are locked in, are they not?"

"Yes, Mr. Pramm. Once everyone is cleared out, anyone left behind would be locked in. We've had a few close calls where someone lingered too long and nearly got themselves locked in. But we've never locked anyone in past closing time. We would have found out about it pretty fast when the person tried to get out." Holt corrected himself. "Oh, I'm not including that Mr. McCausey who had locked himself in downstairs - but technically you could say that he was locked in here, I suppose."

"Yes. One could. Now, my preliminary inspection indicates that the Museum has only one set of entrance doors - the doors leading to the foyer in the Main Gallery and that the windows are barred. Are there any other means of entrance; any service entrances or windows that can be opened and are not secured by bars or the alarm system?"

"No sir. There is only the one way in and out. Only about half the windows can even be opened and they are barred. We've checked all windows and all bars are intact and solid. No tampering."

"Now, Mr. Holt, you said there are three guards. How are the shifts divided among the guards?"

"We have two day shifts and one night shift. The day shifts overlap in part because it helps to have two guards here at the Museum during peak visitor hours. Most of our visitors come here in the morning or in the early afternoon, such as busloads of school kids. So, one guard handles a shift from 6 AM to 2 PM; another guard comes at 10 AM and works until 6 PM. The night shift guard works from 6 PM to 6 AM. The night shift is the worst because you're by yourself for 12 full hours. On the plus side, your duties are minimal at night. We switch the shifts around so that the guard handling night shift for a week will follow that up with two 'good' weeks handling day shifts. And, we're pretty flexible with each others' schedules. We try to help each other out."

"So, all three of you handled night shifts during the months of July through September?"

"Yes. I can pull the log if you need to know about any particular week."

"That would be helpful, Mr. Holt. In particular, I would like to know which guards handled the night shifts for the weeks of September 1st and September 8th."

Stan Holt eased-out his office chair just far enough said that he could turn to open up a suspension file drawer from the right side of his desk. He quickly laid his hands upon a spiral notebook. He found the page and reported. "I handled the week of September 1st and Bill Needles handled the 8th."

"Tell me about a typical patrol during the night shift. How often do you make rounds?

"The night guard logs three 'sweeps'; the first at 9 PM, the second at midnight and the last at 3 AM. The day guard coming in at 6 AM makes his own sweep shortly after settling in. The rest of the time is spent in the office."

"How long does a typical sweep of the Museum take?"

"About 45 minutes. Sometimes an hour at night. We take our time. Every gallery is checked. We walk around every piece of art; the run the flashlight over everything in the room. We check every office door to make sure that each door is locked. If anything is awry, we log it in and report it to the Curator the next morning."

"Are the galleries pitch black at night?"

"No, they keep auxiliary lighting on for nights. You can see your way around, but the flashlight helps."

"The basement, too?"

"No, actually, it is pretty dark down there and you do need a flashlight. Sorry. I was thinking more of the main two floors."

"Quite alright, Mr. Holt. Now, around what hours during the night would a guard patrol the Main Gallery, near the area where the Jaguar in White Onyx had been displayed?"

Holt leaned back in his office chair making some quick calculations. "Depending on the guard, probably around, say, 9:30 PM, 12:30 AM and 3:30 AM. The Main Gallery is usually the first one checked."

"When does a guard get a break to go to the lavatory?"

"The basement area is included in a sweep, so a guard is allowed a five-minute break to use the rest room. No dawdling. Five minutes only."

"That still leaves on an awful lot of time stuck in the office. What does the night guard do with all that time?"

Holt chuckled. "The radio. It's the only friend you have at night. But only in the office; portable radios are not allowed. And, we are not allowed to read books but, thankfully, it's considered okay to read the newspaper."

"Sounds like a tough shift! Now, Mr. Holt, during your night shifts of the week of September 1st, did you see or encounter anything suspicious, whatsoever?"

"No, not a thing."

"Was the Museum closed on Labor Day?"

"No, open. In fact it was supposed to have been a pretty busy day."

"Thank you, Mr. Holt. No doubt we'll talk some more, later." And with that, Pramm hoisted himself from the folding chair and unceremoniously exited the "Office of Security."

It was a few minutes before Noon. Pramm closed Sanderford's office door behind him. He decided to take a walk down Eucalyptus to visit the "All Day Diner" for lunch. As he strolled through the Main Gallery of the Museum, he felt the piercing eyes of the Museum staff pressing against him. An air of hostility had descended upon the place. Those employees who greeted him did so perfunctorily. News of Pramm's suspicions about the staff and his interest in the employee records had spread like wildfire. "Good," he thought. "All the better." He looked over towards Mrs. Travers' desk as he passed through the Main Gallery and noticed her busily stuffing program guides into envelopes to mail to Museum patrons. Mrs. Travers shot Pramm a sour look as he passed by.

After Pramm exited the Museum, several of the staff congregated in the foyer by the glass doors to watch the hulking frame, complete with bowler, briefcase and "bumbershoot," jiggle his way down the marble stairs. A couple of the staffers dared to stick their heads outside the entrance doors and watch. Pramm eventually disappeared from view as he entered the "All Day Diner" down the street. "Figures," sniped Matilda Mayhew. "He's going over to that trough they call a diner." The others nodded in agreement. Someone said, "I don't care how smart he is, he looks like a big old pig to me." Mrs. Parkins whispered, "And did you notice his enormous gut? It hangs over his belt like blubber." And then one of the ladies whispered, "Yes, but he's got that remarkably small backside, somehow." Hearing this, several of the women began cackling, loudly, and then the group quickly dispersed.

Pramm took a seat at the counter and ordered a ginger ale and a cup of tomato soup.

The law office of Aloysius Friedman was having another busy day. Mr. Friedman had attended several depositions in a child custody case and had consulted with a business client over a tax matter. But when Mrs. Blaine mentioned that the "young man doing the abstracts" was on the telephone, Friedman emphatically signaled that he would take the call.

"Mr. Misely, glad you called. Malcolm called-in a few minutes ago to let me know that he had received your abstracts. He said that he agreed with your preliminary thoughts - that none of the indentures seem to have anything to do with the Principio land. He said that you had done fine work."

"Thanks, Mr. Friedman. But I was really calling to let you know that I had an idea - a possible solution to your conundrum."

"Great! Let's hear your brainstorm." Friedman was trying to sound enthusiastic.

"Well, I wouldn't put it that strongly but I would say that it at least falls into the 'idea' category. Now, your problem is that you need to prove that the railroad materials dumped on the Principio land did not originate from the Appalachian-Atlantic, but from some other source. Here's my idea: I took the liberty of checking the Public Service Commission records over in Municipal Archives. I was able to locate the bound volumes of corporate minutes for the Appalachian-Atlantic dating from the late 1800's. There are a number of entries indicating corporate approval for accounts and inventory. The inventories are voluminous. As you can imagine, the railroad used a lot of materials. But, whenever railroad spikes are listed, they are always described as being "wrought iron" spikes. Thus, any railroad spikes found on the Principio land should be made of wrought iron -that's the only kind of railroad spikes ever used during the short history of the Appalachian-Atlantic. Consistent with that, is the fact that the railroad indentures I abstracted always referenced 'iron pins' or 'iron spikes' for marking the corners."

Misely continued. "Now, the Southwest Municipal line was originally established in 1926. I also found corporate books for the Southwest. Its inventory always listed steel railroad spikes, not wrought iron spikes. Thus, we know that the railroad spikes found on the Principio property will almost certainly turn out to be made of steel, not wrought iron. So, picture if you will

- you could enlist the assistance of an expert witness, a scientist familiar with metallurgy. An example would be someone like Dr. Neil Trainer from the Physics Department of the Normal College. I happened to know that the school has a mass spectrograph in its Physics lab. You could have someone like Dr. Trainer run a test on those dumped railroad spikes. He could explain how the spectrograph works and demonstrate to the jury that the railroad spikes found on Principio's land were made of steel. I could then testify as to the contents of the Public Service Commission records - that the only kind of railroad spikes used by the Appalachian-Atlantic were wrought iron. The Doctor could even provide the jury with the tests to show the difference between a spectrograph for steel and one for wrought iron. Voila! You will have proven that the railroad materials were dumped, without mentioning Streeper."

Friedman had been sitting back in his office chair, quietly taking it all in. He sighed to himself. He really hated to throw cold water, but the idea was simply too far-fetched, too much like the plots of those trashy "mystery" stories that his wife read and repeated to him, night after night, torturing him as he lay in bed, trying, desperately, to get some sleep. No, the juries he knew would not know what to make of a physicist and his laboratory evidence.

"Well, Mr. Misely, those are some fine ideas. But I think that a jury may find that kind of evidence a little too complex. Most probably never went to college and the spectrographic evidence could be a little over their heads. But I truly appreciate your trying."

Misely sat back against the wall of the phone booth. A second or two passed as he did some quick re-thinking. "What about a blacksmith? You could have a blacksmith come in and testify as to the difference between a steel spike and a wrought iron spike. He could even show the jury how wrought iron looks when a spike is split open. It would look a lot different than steel."

Friedman was impressed with Misely's quick thinking, but it was time to spill the beans.

"Roderick, you probably sensed from our earlier discussions that being a lawyer has its difficulties. Well, the client informed me yesterday that I am to make every effort to settle the case out of court. So, there is almost no chance that this will actually get before a jury. The client simply cannot tolerate a delay - every lost day results in a significant reduction in income. I know settling an interesting case like this doesn't sound like much fun. But such is the practice of law. We have to follow the instructions of our clients, even if we feel our clients' decisions are not necessarily in their best interests. But, I like your idea about the metals and the blacksmith and it just may come in handy in my efforts to get the case settled."

There was a brief pause, but Misely eventually chimed back in, cheerily. "I understand Mr. Friedman. I'm glad that my ideas might help out in the long run. If there's anything else that you need me to handle, please let me know."

Friedman was impressed with the young man's mature attitude. If he were not already in his mid-60's and if the practice of law were more like it was 20 years earlier, he'd stay around to tutor a young man like Misely. But he was and it wasn't. "Yes, Roderick. I'll let you know how it all works out. I'll also make sure you get your fees. And I want to thank you, again, for the prompt work and solid brainwork that you've provided for this case."

Bill Needles made it back to the Museum by 12:30, only because Smedley Phillips had stopped by to pick him up. The bus would not have brought him to the Museum until 1:30 or 2 PM. Pramm returned from lunch just a few minutes after Needles.

On arrival, Pramm delivered his heavy frame downstairs, to visit the men's lavatory. Stan Holt's confirmation that patrons would be locked-in after closing time significantly narrowed his focus.

It was simple. There were two basic scenarios. Someone with access to the keys could have stolen the jewels. Having the keys would allow the perpetrator access to the Museum at critical times, such as at night, between sweeps, when the Jaguar in White Onyx would be left unguarded. A key holder could simply unlock the door on the way in and re-lock on the way out. The guards or the persons with access to the Board's safe deposit box would make perfect suspects.

Alternatively, a thief without keys could enter the building during normal business hours, hide, and then steal the jewels at night at an opportune time. The thief could sneak out the next day after the Museum re-opened. McCausey could fit that bill. Except for the fact that his body was recovered from the locked vault without the jewels and without the "tools of the trade" necessary to extract and replace the gems from their settings. Where had they gone?

Nevertheless, Pramm was leaning towards the McCausey scenario. Conspiracy was not an impossibility. McCausey could have plotted with one of the Museum staff members to steal the jewels and then hide-out in the vault until the next morning, only to be betrayed by a murderous partner. It wouldn't be the first time.

But was it really likely that anyone in this group would commit a murder? His instincts told him "no." The employee records were too strong.

But the question remained: Where had McCausey stashed the loot and burglary tools? The thief would have needed a penknife, a razor blade or screwdriver, or some other tool for prying the jewels out of their settings. Maybe a dental pick. Possibly even a small hammer. And, presuming the jewels had been cemented into the settings, some sort of solvent would be necessary to loosen-up the chemical bonds holding the diamonds in place. And then there was the small matter of the glue and applicator needed to set the glass pieces back in the settings. Had an inside accomplice spirited away these items or were they still on the premises?

While in the men's room, Pramm investigated thoroughly, poking around at fixtures, looking for places where a burglar could hide the jewels and the tools of his trade. He slowly and carefully sat down on the lavatory floor and inspected underneath the men's room sink. He was hoping to find something; anything jammed or taped up into the undersides of the sink. He inspected the two wire-reinforced windows, which communicated at ground level along the West side of the Museum. The windows were permanently sealed shut. The toilet and other lavatory fixtures yielded no hiding places and no secrets as proven by the layers of dust and grime that Pramm later washed from his fingers at the rust-stained sink.

Pramm also took a look into the basement storage room, which was catty corner, and just a few yards away, from the men's lavatory. To prevent further tragedy, the Museum had removed the entrance door from its hinges. The door was now lying face-up on the floor of the storeroom. It looked exactly like an old door to a bank vault, complete with fist-sized combination lock. The room was dark, but Pramm's eyes had adjusted to the dimness of the basement. He noted that the room was now empty, save a dozen folding chairs, an assortment of mops, brooms and buckets and cans of cleaning detergents and floor wax. Pramm poked around in the room and behind the cans but he found no sign of burglary tools. He picked-up the cans and shook them, listening for foreign objects. He heard nothing unusual.

As Pramm puffed his way up the stairs from the basement, he again, passed by the desk of Louise Travers in the Main Gallery. He seemed to catch her off guard with his "Good afternoon, Mrs. Travers." She jumped to attention in her chair, startled. Her eyes quickly darted over to the left-hand corner of her desktop, towards her outgoing mail tray, now filled with Museum correspondence. Quickly composing herself, she looked up and returned the greeting. "Good afternoon to you, Mr. Pramm."

Back in Sanderford's office, Pramm found a typed-up Museum telephone directory and dialed the extension for the "Office of Security."

Holt picked up the phone on the very first ring. "Yes sir, Mr. Pramm. I'll send him down, right now." Hanging up the phone, he looked up at Smedley Phillips. "You're next, Smed. Mr. Pramm will probably ask you about your day shift duties in early September. Bill, he'll definitely ask you about your night shift, the week of September 8."

"Aye aye, Chief." And Phillips was out the door. Needles slumped down in the office chair. He had turned pale.

In Sanderford's office, Pramm confirmed Phillips' day shift duties during the weeks of September 1st and 8th. When questioned about how the guards performed the "sweeps," Phillips confirmed the procedures outlined by Holt.

Phillips spoke up: "Mr. Pramm, there has never been a break-in during the entire 10 years that I have worked, first for the Municipal, and now for the Guild-Municipal. In fact, in all those years, I've never even heard the alarm go off, except for the scheduled testing we do every six months."

"Was there anything unusual worth reporting during either of those two weeks?"

"No, nothing. Although I'm happy to report that the Wrens won the playoff series during the week of the eighth. You probably heard that they didn't win the Championship the following week, though."

Pramm feigned bored amusement at the comment. "Ah, yes, baseball. The 'National Pastime.'" He scowled, derisively, and dismissed Phillips.

After Phillips hurried out, Pramm eased himself out of the office chair and poked his head out the opened door, scowling menacingly at a handful of innocent Museum visitors who happened by. A baby cried.

He looked over at Mrs. Travers desk, catching her eye. Once again, he thought, for sure, that he had caught her nervously glancing over at her outgoing mail tray on the corner of her desk. He walked over in her direction, trying to get a reaction. But Louise Travers kept her head down and busied herself at her desk. Pramm made a quick left turn and availed himself of the water cooler. He trudged back towards Sanderford's office, but when he saw Sanderford and Prescott sitting in Prescott's office, he decided to pay a visit.

"Gentlemen, I am given to understand that the Board of Directors maintains Museum door keys in a safe-deposit box. Who has access to that box?"

Sanderford responded: "I do, Mr. Pramm. And after the theft was discovered, I went to our box and confirmed that that the keys were still there. I also had the bank pull the records for our box and found that no one tried to access the box since my last visit nearly a year ago. There is simply no way to even imagine that any of the Directors would be involved."

"Very good, Mr. Sanderford." Pramm had actually been thinking more in terms of Sanderford as a suspect rather than the other Directors. If the Guild-Municipal was anything like other museum institutions, the other Directors were wealthy men of high repute who needed stolen jewelry like a hole in the head. "Besides yourself, is it true that only the guards have sets of keys?"

"That's correct Mr. Pramm. Each of the full-time guards has a set of keys. There's a part-time guard, Mr. Needles' brother, who does not have a set of keys."

Pramm closed Prescott's office door. "Do either of you have any suspicions about the guards? It is time to be brutally frank."

Prescott chimed in, "Mr. Pramm, those men are completely honest. They have been with us for years. I'd stake my own reputation on it."

Sanderford added: "I agree. They can be trusted, completely."

Pramm rubbed his chin and then crinkled his mustache, inadvertently producing a malevolent-looking leer. "Very well, gentlemen. Thank you."

Pramm marched back to Sanderford's office and closed the door behind him. He paced around the room. It was now 1 PM. He believed Sanderford. There would be no profit in a Director stealing the red diamonds. If the Corporation had to reimburse the Bolivian government for the value of the diamonds, each Director would be potentially exposed to personal financial liability. The cash value of the "hot" diamonds coughed-up by a friendly fence might not even equal a Director's share of the financial liability.

And, so far, the guards looked blameless, too. That left the McCausey theory as the likely crime scenario. But how did the diamonds and burglary tools become separated from McCausey?

'And then, sometimes there's the obvious solution,' he thought. Pramm, again, left Sanderford's office and headed up the long marble staircase, back to the Office of Security. The door was open. Both Holt and Phillips stood at attention as Pramm entered the room.

"At ease, gentlemen. A simple question: do you maintain a Lost and Found department?"

Stan Holt responded. "Yes, Mr. Pramm. It's not much of a 'department.' We keep the lost and found items over here."

And with that, Holt walked over to the top of the file cabinet and lifted down a large cardboard box marked "Elston's Eggs." Inside the box was a hardbound ledger and one lady's black purse. Holt brought the box over and laid it on his desktop. Pramm reached in and pulled out the lady's pocketbook.

"Can you tell when this purse got reported to Lost and Found?"

Holt reached in and opened the ledger. The last entry was marked "September 10, 1957- Matilda Mayhew - lady's black purse next to M.M.'s desk chair."

"Yes, Mr. Pramm. Mrs. Mayhew reported this back on September 10th. Looks like some lady must've left her purse sitting next to Mrs. Mayhew's desk. Mrs. Mayhew's desk is the Information Desk, the one just after you pass by the foyer. She gives out flyers on the exhibits."

Pramm stood over Holt's desk, removed the white handkerchief from his breast pocket and carefully plucked out the contents of the purse, one item at a time, handling each one with the help of his handkerchief, so as to avoid contaminating possible fingerprints. The two men looked on in awe.

Pramm carefully placed on the desk blotter, a lipstick, a makeup compact, a ladies handkerchief, tweezers, a small bottle of perfume with an atomizer, a nail file, nail polish and a small bottle of nail polish remover. He held up the compact first. Opening the lid, he removed the powder puff. The makeup, itself, looked barely used. He tamped the powder puff against the makeup. He picked up the lipstick, unswirling the lipstick and watching the red cone rise and then return into the gold tube. He opened the bottle of red nail polish and saw that it was mostly full. He removed the silver top from the perfume bottle and sniffed at the atomizer. He made a sour face and his walrus mustache twitched. He noticed that the perfume bottle appeared to be nearly empty. He tried to open the bottle of nail polish remover. The lid was held tight by dried-up polish remover crystals. He was able to wrench the tiny lid open, growing red-faced with the strain of the exertion. He tapped the applicator attached to the lid down into the bottle. The bottle was dry.

Smed Phillips piped-up. "Mr. Pramm, I know you're being very careful with those things for fingerprints and all, but I've already handled all those things myself with my fingers. I hope I didn't mess up."

"No, that's fine, Mr. Phillips. It's a precaution born out of habit for me." And at that moment, Smedley Phillips knew that he would never again handle another Lost and Found object without a handkerchief. No. Better, he would ask Mrs. Travers if she could requisition some sort of silk glove for the Office of Security just for such purpose. And thinking about Mrs. Travers reminded him...

"I wouldn't have even touched anything, but Mrs. Travers had asked me to remove the various items and open each of them up for her, just like you are doing now."

"Pardon me? Did you say Mrs. Travers had a look at these items?"

"Yes sir. She stopped in a couple weeks after the purse was found, wanting to see it. I assume she may have gotten a call from somebody and she was trying to see if the purse matched their description, I guess. But no one ever claimed it."

"I see. Would that be the normal procedure for something like this - Mrs. Travers letting you open up the contents of the purse, etc.?"

"I think so. Administration is separate from Security. Mrs. Travers probably just didn't want to step on our toes, I guess. Security has always been 'Municipal' while Administration is 'Guild.'"

"Ahh. That explains everything," said Pramm with a cynical smirk. "Now, please continue to maintain this purse and its contents under your ordinary high standards."

As Pramm was turning to leave, he saw Bill Needles enter the office, having finished-up a round.

"Ah, Mr. Needles. I request your presence in Mr. Sanderford's office in exactly five minutes." Bill Needles had a panicked look in his eyes. "Yes sir!"

After descending back down the marble staircase, Pramm shot a glance over towards the desk of Louise Travers. She was on the phone. But she had the presence of mind to offer him a quick scowl before she turned her back to him and continued her conversation.

Bill Needles walked sullenly to Sanderford's office. He tapped on the open door and was beckoned in by Pramm.

Bill Needles knew that the jig was up. He closed the door behind him, sat down and began sobbing quietly. "I did it Mr. Pramm. I didn't mean to. It's my fault."

Needles was now fully in tears, sobbing loudly into his open hands. Outside, one of the staff members just happened to be passing by Sanderford's office door. Within a few minutes the word had spread that Mr. Pramm "was bullying poor Bill Needles - he's got him in tears!" Dislike of Pramm grew even deeper.

Pramm was taken aback. Having sized-up Needles, initially, he didn't think that Needles had the brains or brazenness to pull-off a caper like the jewel theft. Something was not quite right with the picture.

"Now, calm down Mr. Needles. What are you trying to say?"

"I think I killed that man they found in the storage room." Needles was now sobbing louder than ever.

"Please, explain Mr. Needles."

Needles reached in to his pants pocket, pulled out of hand-kerchief and blew his nose, loudly. "Well, it was that Monday night and the Wrens were in the last games of the season. They could get into the championship game. The game was tied, but I had to make my 9 PM sweep. So I had brought along a transistor radio. We're not supposed to." Needles began sobbing again, but quickly regained composure. "I didn't want to miss anything. And we're allowed five minutes in the lavatory, but I wound up staying there, listening, until the end of the game. I probably stayed in there about a half-hour. I knew I shouldn't have stayed down there so long and when I was heading out of the lavatory and towards the stairs, I thought I heard a mouse or something in the storage room. So, because I was running so late I didn't bother to do anything, except close the storage room door so that the mouse wouldn't get loose anywhere else." Needles began sobbing again, loudly. "I didn't know that there was a man inside there!"

Needles' sobbing sounds could now be clearly heard by anyone within several yards of the closed office door, inciting terror in some and touching off yet another round of vitriolic commentary among the Museum staff.

Pramm stood up and walked around the front of the desk and stood behind Needles, giving him a firm pat on the back of his quivering shoulders. "Now, now. Be of good cheer, Mr. Needles. You didn't kill the man, he died of a heart attack."

But Needles was quick to add: "Caused by me, though!"

Pramm gave another firm pat on Needle's shoulder. "No. It's very simple. Caused by him, not you!"

Needles looked up at Pramm, eyes swollen. "How is that, Mr. Pramm?"

"What I'm about to tell you must be kept in strictest confidence. Can I trust you in that regard?"

Needles composed himself, quickly. "Yes, Mr. Pramm. You bet."

"Now listen. That man McCausey was the jewel thief. I now have the proof that I need."

Needles looked up, shocked. "Really? But how? He was just an old man. Stan Holt and I were there when the police came and had the body removed. The man only had normal things with them, like a wallet and some change?"

Pramm nodded, "Yes, that's right. But there's more to the story which I shall reveal in the entirety tomorrow morning. The important thing for you to understand is that Mr. McCausey died because he decided to rob a museum. He, alone, is responsible for hiding himself in the basement storeroom. He alone took a chance which turned fatal, trading his life for the opportunity to steal those jewels. And, by the way, the jewels will be recovered. So, rather than looking upon yourself as being responsible for an innocent man's life, you should find some solace in the fact that your entirely innocent and reasonable actions ultimately foiled a felon's efforts to do a great harm to this fine institution."

Needle's demeanor had changed. He took a deep breath. "Oh, thank you Mr. Pramm, thank you! That makes me feel a lot better!" Needles stood and the two men shook hands, quickly and gently; a father consoling a son.

"Good Mr. Needles. Now, please continue your ordinary and routine duties here. And Godspeed."

As Needles swung open the office door, at least three other staff members were hovering nearby pretending to look busy. All of them were shocked to hear a joyous Bill Needles declare loudly, "You're a saint Mr. Pramm an absolute saint!" Needles bounded away with a happy gait.

The word spread like wildfire: "Mr. Pramm may not be that bad after all. Did you see Bill Needles? We heard him crying like a baby and next thing you know he's happy as a lark! Needles said he was a saint!"

It was nearly 3 o'clock and time for Mr. Pramm's high tea in "La Café." As he waddled out of Sanderford's office, he, again, saw Mrs. Travers glaring at him from behind her desk. He noticed that her previous pile of outgoing mail had been emptied but, sure enough, he thought he saw her glancing over at the empty tray. As he approached her desk, he addressed her. "After my tea, you and I shall have a talk."

He could tell that this statement perturbed Mrs. Travers, as she blinked her eyes, involuntarily, several times. But she rallied and responded with a cheery demeanor, "Wonderful!"

As Pramm headed down the corridor to La Café, several people huddled around the water cooler. They gossiped about the great man each sharing tidbits of information. The veil of hostility had lifted from the premises.

But Pramm took a short detour and first stopped into the Museum gift shop.

Mrs. Tamara Ricci snapped to attention behind the counter. "Hello Mr. Pramm. Can I help you?"

Pramm nodded, courteously. "Yes you can. Please show me the various bags that you use for sales."

Mrs. Ricci immediately pulled three sizes of paper bags from behind the counter. "There you go, Mr. Pramm, small, medium and large." She handed the bags over to Pramm.

Pramm fingered each, nimbly. "Ma'am, where do you carry the calendars that you sell?"

Mrs. Ricci hurried from around the counter to the display a few yards away. She gestured towards the wooden rack. "Over here, Mr. Pramm."

Pramm looked over the various calendars. "These are all from 1958, of course. Do you have any of the 1957's leftover from last year?"

Mrs. Ricci looked puzzled. "We stopped selling them back in October. At that point, we can't even give them away."

"Do you have any left, though?"

Mrs. Ricci went back behind the counter. "Here's one. It's mine, actually. I've been using it to put my coffee mug on the back here." She handed the calendar over to Pramm. The corner was swollen from spilled coffee and Pramm could see the multiple indentations from the Ricci coffee mug.

Pramm smiled sweetly. "Thank you, ma'am."

The calendar fit nicely into the largest bag. "These calendars are probably some of the largest items you sell here?"

"Probably so, Mr. Pramm."

Pramm handed the calendar back to Mrs. Ricci. "May I keep this large bag?"

"Certainly, Mr. Pramm."

And with that, Pramm left, gift shop bag in hand. 'He's not all that bad' thought Mrs. Ricci. 'And so very polite.'

Pramm continued down the hallway towards La Café. Inside La Café, Pramm sat under the watchful eye of Emma Tolton. Pramm seemed to be enjoying his scone and croissants. Fresh items had, fortunately, been delivered. A few curiosity seekers stopped by and poked their heads through the door, hoping to catch a glimpse of the big man at his tea.

He almost had it solved. It was McCausey, of course. He knew where the burglary tools had been stashed and how they had been smuggled into the Museum. And he knew that the jewels were not with the burglary tools.

Pramm was so preoccupied with his thoughts that he failed to notice the large flake of croissant now occupying his greasy mustache. He bid "Good day" to Mrs. Tolton, who kept pointing to her own upper lip in an effort to inform Pramm of his new cargo, which eventually fluttered away; an autumn leaf on a windy day.

He walked past Mrs. Travers empty desk and noticed that there were now a few more pieces of mail in her outgoing mail tray. Mrs. Travers was on her break.

Back inside Sanderford's office, Pramm picked up the phone and dialed the Office of Security. Bill Needles picked up the phone.

"Mr. Needles, tell me, who picks up the outgoing mail?"

"Well, usually Drucilla Romney or her assistant. They usually try to work-in one or two runs over to the Post Office every day. But, rain or shine, there's always a pickup by around 4:30 in the afternoon."

"What happens to the outgoing mail that doesn't make the final pick-up?"

"It usually just sits around in the person's mail tray until the next day. It's safe. Everything is locked up at night of course."

"Thank you Mr. Needles."

That was the answer. He had finally figured out how McCausey had disposed of the jewels. It was time to confront Mrs. Travers.

Pramm looked out from Sanderford's office. He noticed that Mrs. Travers was still on her break. Taking advantage of the opportunity, he walked around behind her desk to take a closer look. He didn't like what he saw. All of the desk drawers had locks. He tested each. They were all locked, now. And if Mrs. Travers locked her desk drawers just to go on break, it was a certainty that she locked her desk drawers every night before leaving. That ruined the theory.

Pramm was starting to worry. It was approaching 4 PM and he had not figured out what happened to the jewels. But he knew that it must be something about that outgoing mail tray. Why had Mrs. Travers been staring at that corner of her desk? And then Pramm had yet another idea.

He sidled around behind the desk, pulled out the chair and had a seat. He engaged in a short wrestling match with Mrs. Travers' chair, trying to replicate her line of sight. He looked over the corner of the desk towards the outgoing mail tray. Just beyond the tray and across the desk, his line of sight took him out into the Main Gallery. More specifically, to the marble bench in the Main Gallery in front of the Whistler.

Extricating himself from the chair, he lumbered off and sat himself down on the cold marble bench. A few of the staff members had been keeping an eye on his explorations, so Pramm tried to be subtle. The staff members were impressed that Pramm would take a few moments of his valuable time to relax and enjoy the wonderful art of the Museum.

While peering up at the Whistler painting, Pramm quietly moved his hands along the undersides of the marble bench, tapping and exploring. He started at one end of the bench and slowly worked his way along, rubbing his palms, and tapping his facile fingertips along the bench's underside.

And then he found it. An unmistakable tackiness. He had felt it many times before, at countless greasy spoons. Chewing gum. The tiny remnants of someone's chewing gum tacked onto the underside of the marble bench. There were two spots, one next to the other. One spot was simply tacky to the touch; the other revealed a tiny bit of dried chewing gum. He now had the answer.

Louise Travers had spent her break chatting with her friend Matilda Mayhew in the foyer. She was telling Matilda that she shouldn't be so quick to consider Otho Pramm as 'okay.' She didn't trust him.

Mrs. Travers had barely sat back down at her desk when she received Pramm's phone call. It was time for her interview.

Pramm open the office door and beckoned Mrs. Travers to enter. She closed the door behind her and took the seat in front of Sanderford's desk as Pramm made himself comfortable behind the desk in Sanderford's chair.

Pramm began cheerily. "Mrs. Travers, I would greatly appreciate your handing over the diamonds to me, immediately." He smiled, humbly.

Mrs. Travers expressed shock. "Excuse me? Mr. Pramm, are you implying that I stole those diamonds?"

Pramm leaned back in his chair, tapping his fingertips together. "Implying Mrs. Travers? I think not. There is no need to resort to implication when one has facts. And the fact is that you have the diamonds and that I shall soon have them back." He continued tapping his fingertips together, gently, peering intently at Mrs. Travers.

Mrs. Travers exploded. "How dare you accuse me of such a thing, Mr. Pramm, I will hold you accountable for such slander unless you recant those comments, immediately!"

Pramm chuckled out loud. "Piffle! You play a great part Mrs. Travers. But in the words of the immortal bard, 'the lady doth protest too much.' Now, please, hand over the diamonds or tell me where you are hiding them."

Flabbergasted at his cavalier attitude, Mrs. Travers continued her protests. "Again, I warn you Mr. Pramm, I take great umbrage of those remarks and will consult my lawyer, today, to prosecute an action against you. How dare you!"

Pramm hunched forward over the desk, sounding like a parent trying to soothe a churlish child. "Now, now Mrs. Travers. The game is over. Otho Pramm knows all. I've been busy today.

I've been in contact with Detective Rothbard at the Central Precinct. He has a patrol car at this very moment sitting in front of your home. I need only pick up this telephone and direct the police to enter your home to search every nook and cranny for those diamonds. If you'd like, why don't you call one of your neighbors and ask them to have a peek out their window for the squad car. You'll see."

Pramm pushed the telephone across the desk. He lifted the handset from the receiver and laid it on the desk before her.

Louise Travers continued her protests, but her tone was softening. "This is nonsense, Mr. Pramm. I'm not willing to have you traipse through my beautiful home with your henchmen. And I doubt you have a warrant, anyway."

Pramm chuckled, again. "You think not? Very well." He grabbed the phone and handset back from the desktop and began to dial.

Suddenly, he felt Mrs. Travers hand reach across the desk, stopping his hand mid-dial. "No, wait." She began to sob, quietly. She slumped down in her chair and ducked her head into her crossed arms in shame. "You win, Mr. Pramm. The diamonds are home. But I swear to you that I didn't steal them Mr. Pramm. You've got to believe me!" She sobbed louder and reached her open arms across the desk as though begging to be understood.

"Finally," Pramm said. "Now we can move forward."

"You've got to believe me!" She pleaded again.

Pramm sat back in his chair. "Of course I believe you. I realize that you did not extract and replace the diamonds from the sculpture. But you found them, didn't you? One day, you happened to notice those odd little things stuck on the undersides of that marble bench. Curiosity is a virtue and you soon discovered the two wads of chewing gum, each holding a red diamond, stuck to the bench."

"How did you know that?" She was startled to think that someone may have seen her.

"How I know that is unimportant. But what is important is that I believe that you never planned to steal the jewels. At first you were not entirely sure what you had. You probably took the gems home for 'safekeeping'. Am I correct?"

Louise Travers nodded earnestly in agreement.

"But after thinking about it, you eventually realized that the gems where the notorious 'ruby' eyes of the Jaguar in White Onyx. When McCausey's body was discovered a few weeks later, you realized that he must have stolen, and replaced, the jewels. At that point, your curiosity got the better of you. You knew that he was found without any tools for extracting the gems. So you checked the Lost and Found. You realized that everything needed to extract and replace the gems could be found among the routine items in that black purse."

Louise Travers realized that Pramm had that part wrong; she didn't think that those items in the purse could have been used to do the job. But she kept that information to herself.

Pramm continued. "The problem, however, is your behavior after finding the diamonds. Even after the theft was reported, you continued to conceal the jewels in your home. You ignored your duty to the Museum and maintained your silence. That is called 'larceny,' a most serious felony. When you are convicted, you will spend at least ten years in prison."

At the sound of the word "felony" Mrs. Travers began sobbing again, despairingly. "Help me, Mr. Pramm, help me! I'll return the diamonds; just don't let them put me in jail." She was now sobbing uncontrollably.

Pramm sat back in his chair. "I'm sorry, but there's really nothing I can do. This is a local police matter, well out of my hands."

This drove Mrs. Travers to cry out much louder, now hysterically. Outside in the Main Gallery, the huddling staff members were surprised to hear Mrs. Travers' laughter. She wasn't known as a person with a particularly strong sense of humor. Mr. Pramm was truly an exceptional man to elicit such a response.

Pramm pulled himself back up to the desk leaning over towards the sobbing Mrs. Travers. He adopted a quiet, confidential tone of voice. "Very well, Mrs. Travers, very well. Against my better judgment I can conceive of one possible option to keep you out of jail. I, personally, believe that you are a 'good' person. In fact, I have addressed the notion of moral goodness in my monograph, 'How Good is Good?' Have you read it by chance?"

Mrs. Travers was still trying to regain her composure. She shook her head "no."

"Very well. On a few rare, very rare, instances I have offered certain alternatives to felons who I believe are worthy of redemption. As you know, I maintain an eleemosynary foundation, dedicated to the welfare and education of Today's economically disadvantaged young men. I believe that the Social Contract can withstand your breach, if you are willing to repair the harm done. Tell me, Mrs. Travers, what would you be willing to give to avoid imprisonment?"

"Anything, Mr. Pramm, everything!"

Pramm rubbed his hands together, briskly. "Very well. This is your opportunity. If you are willing to donate, significantly, of your worldly goods to assist those young men, I would see no reason to report your involvement in this unfortunate matter to the Museum or to local authorities. Tell me, Mrs. Travers, how much, precisely, do you have in your savings and bank accounts?"

Mrs. Travers straightened up, soberly. "Well - it's about $750, and with the checking account, probably closer to about $792."

"I presume you bank at a local institution?"

"Yes, Mr. Pramm. At Occident Savings Bank, two blocks from here, on 9th."

"Very well, Madam. Here's what we will do. Tomorrow morning at 9 AM, sharp, I'll meet you at your bank. Please bring the diamonds and both your passbook and checkbook. At the bank, you will request a cashier's check, payable to "cash" in the amount of $792. When I file my report, I will make no mention, whatsoever, of your culpability in this matter."

Mrs. Travers had gone silent. She was thinking about the $792. Her tone soured. "Mr. Pramm, that $792 is everything we have. It's our life savings."

Pramm looked on, nonchalantly. "Is it, now Mrs. Travers? Do you have a roof over your head, clothes in your closets and shoes on your feet?"

She nodded, grudgingly.

"Well, then. I believe you have much more than many of the unfortunate young men who benefit from my foundation. But, never mind. If the money is so important, I can simplify things by calling-in the police so that they can execute that search warrant."

Mrs. Travers straightened up in her chair. "No, no Mr. Pramm I was not complaining! Please, forgive me for mentioning it."

"Very well, Madam." He stood up to dismiss her. "I will meet you at the Occident Savings Bank, tomorrow, at 9 AM sharp. Good day."

By now, Mrs. Travers had composed herself, adopting her usual façade of cheery professionalism. Her co-workers were dying of curiosity. How had Mr. Pramm broken down the ever-serious Mrs. Travers and gotten her to laugh so? He was a good egg, that Mr. Pramm.

A bit later, Pramm walked down the Gallery to Prescott's office and announced to anyone within earshot that he had concluded his day's work and would "reconvene these proceedings on or about 9:20 AM tomorrow morning."

As he slowly made his way down the long marble steps, the Museum staff quickly assembled at the entrance door, watching as the mysterious man headed, again, in the direction of the "All Day Diner" on Eucalyptus. But Pramm did not go to the diner, directly. He stopped, first, at Franklin Pharmacy, a drug store and sundries shop. Inside, he looked over a wide variety of ladies' makeup compacts. He inquired about one in particular. After making his purchase, he headed back around the corner and up Eucalyptus to the All Day Diner. He stopped into the men's restroom. He opened the makeup compact over the sink and temporarily removed the powder puff. He fished for a paperclip from his pants pocket and, using the paperclip as a digging tool, carefully dug two round holes into the makeup, tapping the excess flakes of makeup into the sink.

Things were working out quite well. Pramm was glad to have finally figured out where the jewels had been squirreled away. McCausey had hidden himself in the basement after the Museum closed. He had probably done so on other occasions, as well. During his earlier forays, he would have observed the habits of the night guard; how often the guard patrolled near the Jaguar in White Onyx; when, and how long the guard would linger in the basement, and how much time would be available for extracting the jewels. Once McCausey had removed the jewels, he wanted to make sure that, if apprehended, he would not be caught with the diamonds and burglary tools on his person. Trespassing was a simple misdemeanor; but, with his prior record, a conviction for a felony would have sent him up the river for a long, long time. He obviously succeeded in removing the diamonds. But before he returned to the basement to hide-out until the Museum reopened, he needed to "dump" the burglary tools and deposit the diamonds in a place that would guarantee their returned to his possession as soon as possible. He could simply jettison the lady's purse anywhere. It would become an innocuous "lost and found" item, permanently unclaimed. But stashing away the diamonds for future pick-up was a trickier proposition.

Pramm had initially believed that McCausey had the idea of mailing the diamonds to himself. He could have walked the diamonds over to Mrs. Travers' desk, and, utilizing the Museum's envelopes and brochures, simply enclosed the diamonds in a mailing addressed to 'Roy B. McCausey' at his local address. He would have added postage and placed the envelope in the outgoing mail tray, along with any other mailings that had not made the last mail run. Pramm thought that such would explain why Mrs. Travers had been nervously looking over in the direction of her mail tray. Under this theory, Mrs. Travers might have noticed the extra envelope in her outgoing mail tray the morning following the theft and intercepted the jewels. But that theory was demolished once Pramm saw that Mrs. Travers habitually locked-up all of the desk drawers. The desk drawers would have housed the envelopes, brochures and postage stamps.

'Simpler is better' was an adage that often made sense thought Pramm. McCausey had used chewing gum to stick to diamonds to the undersides of the marble bench. After the Museum had re-opened, he would simply have wandered up from the basement to the Main Gallery, taken a seat on the marble bench and quietly removed the chewing gum and diamonds. He would have then departed from the Museum, no one the wiser. But the passage of time and the force of gravity stretched the chewing gum down far enough to eventually meet Mrs. Travers' line of sight.

The next morning, Pramm arrived at the Occident Savings Bank just as the branch director was unlocking the door for business at 8:57 AM. Mrs. Travers arrived precisely at 9 AM tightly clutching her handbag. They met on the stairs in front of the door. "I'm here, Mr. Pramm. I've got the … 'items.'" She sounded sour. She handed over an unsealed envelope to Pramm, which he opened and inspected. Inside the white envelope, two red diamonds blazed in the morning sunlight.

"Very good, Mrs. Travers. Now, let's conclude this transaction inside."

They stood together at the customer's table as Mrs. Travers fished around in her handbag for her passbook and checkbook. She pulled a withdrawal slip from the pigeonhole rack on the table. "Now, please remember to inform the bank teller to have the cashier's check made payable to 'cash.'"

Mrs. Travers looked up, suspiciously. "Not in the name of your foundation?" There was a caustic tone to her voice.

Pramm looked down his nose, smugly. "Madam, which do you think is preferable for your situation and would arouse less suspicion in the event of further inquiries; a routine check that you drew made payable to 'cash' or a check inexplicably made payable to some charitable foundation with which you have no past association and which includes the name 'Pramm?' Again, the choice is yours to make."

She was quickly humbled. "Yes, Mr. Pramm. How stupid of me. I must strive to become less suspicious and accept the generosity of others."

"Excellent. And in that regard, may I recommend to you my monograph written on the topic of the suspicious, human personality. It is entitled 'The Personal Personality… a Study.' Have you, by chance, read it before?"

Mrs. Travers wasn't really listening. She was thinking about how her savings were being decimated. She completed the transaction at the counter. She handed him the cashier's check, less than gleefully. Pramm placed it deftly in his breast pocket; a surgeon cutting flesh with a scalpel.

"Very well, Mrs. Travers. Now, you toddle off to the Museum. I'll be right behind you, bringing up the rear."

The thought of Pramm doing so, with his unique physical characteristics and proportions tickled her and she could not stifle a loud and obvious cackle, which Pramm heard but did not understand.

Pramm entered the Museum at approximately 9:20 AM. The staff members were trying hard to feign disinterest, but they were falling all over themselves, abuzz with gossip. Word about Pramm's deal to deliver the diamonds in 24 hours had leaked-out.

Sanderford and Prescott were standing by Sanderford's office door, awaiting the arrival of Pramm. The three entered Sanderford's office. Sanderford spoke first. "So, Mr. Pramm have you recovered the diamonds?"

Pramm smiled, gently. He sat himself behind Sanderford's desk. "More importantly, do you have the cashier's check for $10,000?"

Prescott handed the manila file folder over to Pramm. "There it is Mr. Pramm, and just as you requested."

Pramm unconsciously opened Sanderford's top desk drawer by just a crack and grasped the rim of the desk drawer with his left hand, clutching the lip of the drawer in his thumb and fore-fingers. He hunched foreword and opened the file folder. Placed on top of his telegram, which had been carefully un-wadded and ironed out by Prescott, was the cashier's check for $10,000 made payable to "bearer." Pramm carefully grasped the cashier's check with raccoon fingers, looking it over.

"Excellent. Then my answer is 'yes' I have recovered the diamonds."

Sanderford and Prescott were elated. Prescott could not contain a loud "Hurrah!" while Sanderford broke into applause. Prescott joined in and, soon, other staff members could be heard applauding outside in the Main Gallery.

"Now, it is time for me to place the diamonds back in your custody. To do so, I will require the assistance of one of your Museum guards and a few moments of quiet."

Prescott jumped in. "Yes, Mr. Pramm. We're sorry for the ruckus. What would you have us do?"

"Allow me to telephone up to the guard on duty. I would also ask that you leave me alone in this office so that I may conclude my efforts, efficiently."

At that the two men answered, "Yes sir!" and shut the door behind them on the way out.

A few moments later they witnessed Smed Phillips walking down the marble staircase briskly towards Sanderford's office. He was, inexplicably, wearing a grass-stained gardener's glove. He held the black purse in his gloved hand before him, stiff-armed in a formal and dignified manner. One of the staff members gasped, overtaken by the sense of unfolding drama. Phillips rapped sharply at Sanderford's closed door. Pramm opened the door and received the purse, thanking Phillips, who made a quick bow and a hasty but dignified retreat to his post.

Inside Sanderford's office, Pramm removed the makeup compact from the black purse and placed it inside his breast pocket. He retrieved the compact that he had purchased the day before from his suit coat pocket. He removed the diamonds from the white envelope, carefully placing each diamond in its miniature trench dug from the surface of the makeup. He then massaged the surface of the makeup, hiding the diamonds beneath a powdery layer. He replaced the powder puff, snapped the compact closed and returned it to the purse.

He took a look at his watch. It was almost 9:30 AM. He would have to wrap things up, quickly. He emerged, victorious, from Sanderford's office and called Prescott and Sanderford back in. Once the three had reassembled, he began his demonstration.

"Gentlemen, allow me to explain how the diamonds were stolen and recovered. First, I'm pleased to announce that, today, you have received a substantial bargain, courtesy of Otho Pramm. Besides solving the diamond theft, I will provide you with information that will lead this institution to victory against the plaintiffs in the wrongful death action of McCausey vs. Guild-Municipal that Trans Global Indemnity is defending." Prescott and Sanderford sat forward in their chairs, on pins and needles, absorbed in Pramm's elocution. "Consider it a 'two for the price of one' deal." Pramm chuckled, but the other two were too absorbed in the moment to respond to humor.

"McCausey - the unfortunate man who passed away in your storage room, was your jewel thief." Prescott and Sanderford looked shocked.

Pramm continued. "McCausey was not an innocent Museum patron. He had a substantial criminal record in another state. He 'cased' the Museum and found an ingenious way to steal the diamonds. On the afternoon of Monday, September 9th, McCausey entered the Museum as an ordinary visitor. But he carried with him, a Museum bag containing this black purse, as well as a 1957 calender that he purchased from the gift shop a few weeks before. He didn't need a calendar; he needed a Museum bag large enough to hold this ladies purse."

Pramm produced the large gift bag that he received the day before and demonstrated how the ladies purse would fit into the bag along with a calendar. Prescott and Sanderford looked on, spellbound.

"At some point, prior to closing time, McCausey found his way down to the basement where he planned to hide out, overnight. He had probably done that several times during the previous weeks. He discovered those times when the night guard would patrol near the Jaguar in White Onyx and those when the guard would take a lavatory break. McCausey probably avoided detection during the 'closing time' sweep, by standing on top of the toilet seat or possibly slipping behind the door of your storage vault room. When the time for action arrived, he used his cigarette lighter as a light source and worked his way up the stairs to the sculpture. He removed the diamond eyes of the Jaguar by using these tools."

With that, Pramm dramatically emptied the contents of the purse onto the desktop.

He held up the tweezers and nail file. "McCausey used these tools to loosen and extract the diamonds from their settings. But he also needed something to loosen-up the cement bond." Pramm then held up the perfume bottle and bottle of fingernail polish remover. "Smell this fingernail polish remover." He opened the tight lid and passed the bottle to Sanderford who sniffed eagerly and passed the bottle over to Prescott.

"As you can see, that bottle did, in fact, contain nail polish remover. Now, smell the tip of this perfume bottle atomizer." He passed the perfume bottle along to the others.

"It smells the same, doesn't it? That's because the perfume bottle was also filled with nail polish remover. 'Why?' Because nail polish remover is made of acetone, a solvent that is effective in breaking down the chemical bonds of cement. McCausey needed a substantial amount of acetone and, first, sprayed the nail polish remover onto the diamond eyes with the atomizer. Later, he used the bottle of nail polish remover and brush to dab even more of the acetone onto the setting. As you can see, there's nothing left in these bottles."

Pramm continued. "Once the gems were loosened from their settings, McCausey pried them out with the nail file and tweezers." Pramm held up the bottle of red fingernail polish. "As for the glass pieces, he used a few dabs of this fingernail polish to glue the fake gems back into the eye sockets. The fingernail polish, of course, has cement properties."

Prescott and Sanderford continued to look on, wide-eyed.

"'And where are the diamonds?' you ask. If my surmise is correct, right here, gentlemen." And with that, Pramm opened up the makeup compact, holding it closely to his right ear, while slowly tapping at the surface of the makeup bed. He glanced over at the spellbound Prescott and Sanderford and, pretending to find just the right spot, dug with this fingernail into the makeup bed to produce two makeup-covered red diamonds for inspection.

Sanderford gasped. Prescott stood up and looked at the jewels in the palm of Pramm's hand. "Remarkable!"

Pramm extracted his white, silk handkerchief from his breast pocket and cleaned off the red diamonds, which now glistened, brightly. "McCausey had hidden the fakes in the compact, made the switch, and replaced the red diamonds back into the makeup compact, along with the other ladies' items, which he placed back into the purse. Now, because McCausey was a wanted man in his home state, he did not want to take the chance of being caught with the purse during any of the subsequent sweeps. So, before retreating to the basement, he left the purse next to the desk at the foyer. He knew that it would be turned-in to the Lost and Found. He likely planned to enlist the aid of a lady accomplice, as yet unknown, who would visit the Museum, later that day to reclaim the 'lost' purse. When he retreated to the basement, he took with him a few paltry personal possessions such as a cigarette lighter, cigarettes and chewing gum, along with the Museum's gift shop bag which held a completely unsuspicious calendar, complete with sales receipt."

Sanderford looked to Prescott and shook his head in disbelief. "Incredible!" Prescott nodded his head in agreement.

"So, gentlemen as you can see, the jewels have been under the jurisdiction of the Museum, the entire time. Much credit should be placed with your Office of Security for the excellent job that they did in preserving this, otherwise, uninteresting item." He held up the ladies purse in the air, waving it for effect. "It is, of course, not my job to dictate this institution's policies, but I highly recommend that each of the guards receive commendations for the excellent work they have done. In addition, I recommend the same for Mrs. Louise Travers who had, also, taken care to see that this Lost and Found item was properly maintained."

"Absolutely, Mr. Pramm. I will move the Board of Directors to do so at the next scheduled meeting. That is a wonderful idea!" Sanderford felt some pride. His decision to modify Mr. Pramm's engagement contract would be applauded at the next Board meeting. He could see himself at the table in the Boardroom, making the formal motion. He would review the transcription, with pride, in the corporate minute books.

Pramm looked at his wristwatch. It was approaching 9:50 AM. He picked up the bank's check for $10,000 and placed it in his breast pocket next to Mrs. Travers' cashiers check. "Gentlemen, my work is concluded here. I must take my leave.

I bid you good day. With respect to the McCausey lawsuit, you should have your attorneys confer with the Clerk of Court for Atchaflaka County, the domicile of the plaintiffs." Prescott quickly scribbled down the information on the corner of Sanderford's desk blotter. He wasn't exactly sure how to spell "Atchaflaka" but he figured the attorneys would know what to do.

And with that, Pramm removed himself from the chair and dressed himself in his raincoat. He plucked his bowler hat and bumbershoot from Sanderford's coat rack, and with attaché case in hand, walked out, into the Main Gallery. Sanderford and Prescott followed right behind him and broke into applause. Suddenly, all of the staff members, likewise, began applauding. Shouts of "Three cheers for Mr. Pramm!" rang out in the gallery and reverberated against the marble floors.

The Museum staff followed Mr. Pramm out through the foyer and large glass entrance doors. There were several more impromptu cheers. Bill Needles could be heard declaring, loudly, "The man is a saint! A true saint!"

As Pramm worked his way towards the bottom of the long, marble stairs to the sidewalk he noticed that a black 'for hire' limousine had pulled up at the sidewalk, in front of the Museum. As he hustled his way down Eucalyptus towards the All Day Diner he couldn't help but notice the large man with a black bowler hat and bumbershoot exiting the rear, passenger side of the limousine.

Once inside the All Day Diner, Misely headed for the men's lavatory. The Pramm get-up was murderously hot and he couldn't wait to get out of costume. He locked the lavatory door behind him. He opened up the attaché case and extracted 3 large cloth shopping bags. He carefully removed the false mustache, putting it aside on the sink counter. He removed the bowler and suit coat and hung the coat over a stall. He pulled up his oversized white shirt to reveal two large hot water bottles. The bottles were secured against his belly with a combination of cloth bandages and masking tape. He carefully removed the tape and emptied each of the hot water bottles into the sink, flapping out the last drops of moisture. He removed one of his own dress shirts and a tie from the attaché case. He quickly changed, and placed the attaché, umbrella, bowler and overcoat in the three shopping bags. The suit coat was quite baggy, but it would have to do. He didn't want to catch cold. He reassembled himself and took stock of his appearance in the mirror. No one would ever be able to identify him as "Pramm."

He walked back towards the Museum up Eucalyptus, but on the sidewalk opposite the Museum building. The streetcar stop for the ride back to Elk Neck was located directly opposite the Museum.

As he stood waiting for the streetcar, he noticed the arrival of a Central District Precinct police car. Its dome light was flashing although the officer had not used the siren. Two officers left the squad car and hustled, quickly, up the long marble steps. One of the two had placed his hand, instinctively, on his holstered pistol as though ready to draw.

The streetcar finally arrived and Misely took his usual place in the back row. He would have a little more room there to manage the shopping bags. As the streetcar was pulling away, he was surprised to see the two policemen escorting the real Otho Pramm out the door and down the marble steps. A large crowd of Museum employees had huddled together just outside the glass doors to watch the miserable fraud being escorted away, efficiently, by the local police. Pramm was not going peaceably. He was handcuffed, with his hands behind his back. Misely could see Pramm writhing, wrenching his head back towards the Museum entrance, yelling something back to the onlooking crowd, a hooked bass on a fisherman's line. Misely thought he saw Sanderford in the crowd, shaking his head, in quiet disapproval.

Misely wasn't too surprised to see that they had mistaken the real Pramm for a fake. After all, a museum that mistook glass pieces for diamonds would not likely be able to tell the difference between a real Pramm and a false one.

As the streetcar moved along the route, Misely took stock of the situation. He didn't think that any harm had been done. "Pramm" had solved the crime and recovered the diamonds. Misely had initially planned to sell the information to Pramm; but it occurred to him that he could just as well handle the matter himself. After all, did it really make a difference which "Pramm" handled the job? The victory would find its way into the Pramm win column, so why should the real Pramm care? And certainly, the real Pramm could afford to let a well-meaning surrogate take a crack at earning one of his famous "reasonable" fees once in a while. Misely's consulting fees in case O-58-6 were some of the best he had ever earned.

A week had passed and Misely had successfully nego-tiated the two instruments at a check-cashing establishment in the City's Eastside. The check-cashing operation took in a five percent premium and asked no questions. Presentation of identification was optional, purely at the customer's discretion. Misely had become a little worried about his gambit and wanted to cover his tracks. A five percent commission was a small price to pay for anonymity.

There had been a few follow-up stories in the Star Sentinel. The first set of stories told of the remarkable recovery of the red diamonds by Otho Pramm. Curator Ronald Sanderford recount-ed, in glorious detail, the ingenious methods utilized by Pramm to solve the mystery within 24 hours. There were other short articles, again, about Otho Pramm and his remarkable career. The police incident involving the arrest of the fake Pramm did not even make the front page. It became a "Police Blotter" item. But, the reporter had noted the impostor's belligerence and, in particular, his arrogance in the face of police detention.

A few days later, the Star Sentinel reported on how the real Pramm had been mistakenly arrested and finally released from police custody. Groveling apologies were offered by the Central District Precinct Sergeant as well as the Police Commissioner, himself. The apologies were carefully scripted and repeated, verbatim, in the Star Sentinel. Oddly enough, despite the unimpeachable evidence that the Guild-Municipal's Pramm was actually the fake Pramm, the Officers and Board of Directors offered only mild, provisional apologies. Sanderford was quoted as stating that, "If, and to the extent that the individual with whom we dealt was not, in fact, the real Otho Pramm, we then extend our humblest apologies to the gentleman arrested by the police for trespass on the morning of January 10th."

Back in Manhattan, the real Pramm was frustrated, unable to focus his wrath against the Museum. Trans Global Indemnity had quietly advised Pramm of its strong preference that Pramm not seek legal action against the Museum. Doing so would have meant that Trans Global Indemnity would have had to defend yet another lawsuit, this one brought by its favorite contractor. Denied an outlet, the real Pramm took a swipe at the Star Sentinel.

Tuesday evening at County Restaurant meant that lamb stew would be the evening's special. Misely had finished his meal and was engrossed in yet another item in the Star Sentinel dealing with Otho Pramm. This time, it was a formal retraction. As such, it was relegated to a spot just below the Obituary section in the distant reaches of the newspaper. The "Errata" read as follows:

The Editors of the Star Sentinel wish to correct a statement provided in the January 14, 1958 'Police Blotter' column of this publication. In a story entitled 'Johnny Come Fakely' the Star Sentinel referred to Mr. Otho Pramm as having exhibited an arrogant disposition towards police authorities at the time of his inadvertent arrest. This information was inaccurate. The report should have indicated that Mr. Pramm had exhibited an attitude of sincere concern with police policies and procedures. We regret this error.

Misely instinctively tore the short piece out of the Star Sentinel to add to the other clippings in file O-58-6.

Attorney Friedman was putting together a package to courier over to Misely in Elk Neck. He had purchased a small memento for Roderick. He didn't like to "fib" but he indicated in his note that the "client" was forwarding the gift in appreciation for Roderick's work on the case. Such was not true. Aloysius Friedman had settled the case, as instructed. But he was now having enough trouble getting his own client to "settle up."

He was fed up with the Principio Brothers. He would not represent them, ever again. Seems that in discussing the terms of settlement, Ganst's counsel had mentioned, casually, that the Principios had "started the whole thing" by stealing Ganst's most popular house design. The trespass suit was simply an effort to force the Principios to the bargaining table. In fact, the Principios had never mentioned to Friedman that they had "somehow" laid hands upon Ganst's house plans for his "Berkshire" home design. The Principios had been using the same architectural design, which they referred to as their "Barronshire" model for several sections of their most recent housing development. They hadn't thought to compensate Ganst. Ultimately, a settlement was reached whereby Ganst and the Principios would form a partnership to build-out two sections of the proposed "Marigold Branch Estates."

When Friedman reminded the Principios to forward the checks to pay for surveying and abstracting work, young Bobby Principio questioned whether "paying them is really necessary since we've settled the case?" Friedman reminded him that it was, indeed, "Quite necessary."

Misely was sitting at his mahogany desk in his office anteroom. He was reviewing the newspaper clippings from case O-58-6 "Guild Municipal." He found the most recent clipping somewhat disturbing. Shortly after the Star Sentinel's retraction,

Otho Pramm sent a Letter to the Editor, which was immediately published. In the Letter, Pramm, courteously, thanked the Star Sentinel for correcting its previous error. Pramm also mentioned that "as a general rule" he did "not care for imposters." The Letter went on to warn that he considered "the masquerade to be a most serious crime against my person," and that he would "bring the full force of my investigative offices in New York and London to bear in hunting down the particular individual possessing the gall and audacity to attempt such an outrageous charade." It was the last part that gave rise to Misely's concern. He didn't like the way it sounded.

He decided that it was probably best to destroy any and all references to his involvement in the recovery of the stolen jewels. He was very glad that he had taken his payments in un-traceable cash equivalents. He grabbed the metal trash can from his living quarters and picked up a pack of matches from his desktop drawer. He emptied the newspaper clippings from the file into the metal can. He took the can with him outside to the landing at the top of the wooden stairs, just outside his door. He set the clippings ablaze and watched as the ashes blew away in the winter wind.

As he was dumping out the last few ashes over the landing to the yard below, he saw a motorcycle, complete with sidecar, pulling up in front of 7 North Central. The sidecar was embla-zoned with the words "Elite Courier Services."

"Are you 'R. Misely?'" Roderick nodded, cautiously. He placed the metal waste can down on the landing and bounded down the wooden stairs to receive the package.

Back inside, he sat at his office desk and opened up the par-cel, wrapped in brown paper. It was a check from Principio Brothers, Builders "for services rendered" for his abstracting work. There was also an envelope from Aloysius Friedman, Esquire, marked "Mr. Misely." But Roderick was surprised to see that the package included a beautiful, leather-bound Black's

Law Dictionary. The lower right corner of the book was monogrammed, in gold with "R.M." Misely opened the envelope and read Friedman's note.

Dear Roderick,

The client asked that I forward this Black's Law Dictionary as a token of their appreciation for the fine work that you performed. I would also like to thank you, personally, for your promptness and professionalism. As you know, I am near retirement age; but if I were younger man, I would have considered it a privilege to have read the law with you and watched you develop a successful law career. But I have every confidence that you will, in fact, someday become a successful lawyer. You have a bright future, Roderick, and I wish you every success.

Sincerely,

Aloysius Friedman.

Misely was disappointed. It was a tragedy. No, not the missed opportunity to read the law with Mr. Friedman; rather, Misely had been mentally preoccupied, unconsciously rubbing his thumb over the gold monogram on the leather bound law dictionary. He already owned a slightly beaten-up edition of Black's. He didn't need another one. He was thinking that the leather bound edition was worth at least $50 new and that he could have ordinarily gotten, perhaps, a good $35 for the book from Culpepper's used book store. But the gold monogram with his initials would greatly reduce its value. He would be lucky to get $10 to $12 for it.

Case file C-58-3 "Principio Bros. - Title" can still be found in the metal filing cabinet located in the living quarters of Roderick Misely, Consultant, at 7 North Central, just up the street from the northeast corner of Iroquois and Central.

Chapter Five
The Perplexed Executor

Salathiel Persky was in hot water. Everything had been fine on Friday. It was now Tuesday and Persky had to see Art Green, right away. He didn't want to face the Baird brothers alone. Persky was clattering down the corridor of the Elk Neck Superior Court heading straight for Art's office. Peering down at his shoes, he was too absorbed in his worries to notice Tip Paradiso and Roderick Misely standing just outside the Register of Wills Office.

Art Green heard the sharp knock at his office door. Art really didn't want to go knee deep into Persky's quagmire, but he sensed the inevitable pull of quicksand. Art knew Persky to be the nervous type, but he had been shocked by the degree of panic in Persky's voice over the phone, just a half-hour earlier. Persky had barely been able to catch his breath between phrases and had babbled something about a burglary and a key. He had begged Art to help him.

Art beckoned Persky into his office. Persky was in horrible shape. His black suit hung from his bony, stooped shoulders like a wet dishrag. He was sweating and fidgeting nearly out of his overly starched shirt. Premature baldness was not helping the picture. Persky was 34 years old.

Art motioned Persky over to the high-backed stools facing the desk. Persky attempted to hoist himself onto one, but slipped off, his arm flailing against the overstuffed bulletin board on the wall behind him. A tickertape parade of aged business cards, leaflets and yellowing newspaper clippings fell to Art's floor. Persky stooped down to pick up the papers, but Art called him off.

"Don't worry about those Salathiel, just have a seat."

"Arthur, I have a problem."

As Persky positioned himself on the stool, he crossed one bony leg over the other, his gangly limb sailing over the corner of Art's desk, just missing Art's coffee cup by inches. Art quickly withdrew the cup from harm's way and did a quick audit of other endangered items on his desktop, pulling them each back a few inches.

"The Bairds are furious with me. I tried to get the insurance on Friday afternoon but Mr. Nelson's office was closed. So Mr. Nelson came out with me yesterday morning and we found that everything was gone!"

"Slow down, Salathiel!" Art Green's missive barely rose above the sound of an audible whisper. "Are you talking about the Baird Estate?" As Chief Appraiser, Art Green had a pretty good handle on the various estates under his jurisdiction.

"Yes, yes! The swords are gone! And most of the better stuff!"

Art knew enough about the Baird Estate. Appraiser Meg O'Callanan had filled him in on the details following her 'on-site' on Friday afternoon. She had declared it one of the worst family feuds she had ever witnessed on the job.

According to Meg, Robert Baird, Sr., had passed away two months earlier, leaving behind two sons, Robert, Jr. and Brendan. Robert Sr. had apparently tried to treat his boys fairly. The Will devised his estate to each equally, share and share alike. But Robert Sr.'s treatment of the family heirloom, a Civil War era sword memorial, had heated up the boys' sibling rivalry.

The Civil War sabers had been handed down through generations. The trophy consisted of the two crossed swords, one a Confederate Cavalry Officer's saber, the other a Union Foot Officer's sword. The sabers were mounted on an elaborate wooden frame featuring a gold plated plaque below the swords. The crossed swords represented a tragic fact of the Baird's family history. Like many families, loyalties became divided during the War Between the States. One branch of the Bairds sympathized with the Confederate cause, while the other firmly supported the Union. Both sides lost sons to the War. This bitter and tragic piece of family history was celebrated on the memorial with a quote engraved onto the plaque below the swords: "Where is Your Brother Abel?"

Robert Baird, Sr. had always disliked the morbid celebration of family dissention and violence represented by the crossed swords. He was particularly sickened by the reference to Cain and Abel. His Will called for his Executor to dismantle the heirloom, allowing Robert the first choice of sabers, with Brendan receiving the other. The Executor was then required, in the presence of both sons, to burn the wood mounting "to ashes."

According to Meg, Robert Jr. had been trying to convince Brendan to keep the memorial intact. And, because Robert was the older son and given first choice of swords, Robert felt that he should receive the entire trophy and that Brendan could choose some other property from the Estate, instead. But Brendan had insisted on following his father's desires. And Persky, as Executor, was duty bound to follow the father's direction in the Will. It was an unpleasant scene.

"Have you called the police?"

"Yes, yes, they came over yesterday afternoon. They took a report on everything missing. But that's it. They said there's nothing much more they can do."

"Nothing?"

"They said 'call your insurance company.' My insurance company. Hah! That's the problem. There isn't one!"

At that, Persky began wringing his hands and absent-mindedly wiping them on the front of his already sweat-soaked suit jacket.

"You were saying something about a key. Did they use a key to get in?"

"No, no. Just the opposite. Let me explain. On Friday, I met the Bairds at Sr.'s apartment so that your Meg O'Callanan could take the property appraisal. Well, the brothers started bickering almost immediately, mostly over the swords. And then it got worse. I thought that Robert was going to lay Brendan out. Meg saw all that."

"She filled me in."

"She probably told you that the Will says that I have to dismantle the crossed swords and burn up the rest. It's very dramatic. I don't even know where I'm supposed to do that - I don't have a fireplace in my office... that mahogany mounting would probably take forever to burn... Anyway, Robert is in the wrong."

Persky began staring off into space thinking about the fireplace in the Beneficent Cavalier's dining room, and whether it was big enough. Then he quickly remembered that he no longer had anything to burn in the fireplace, anyway. He squirmed in his seat.

"So, how did they break in?"

"It's a complete mystery. We were wrapping things up, but the two were still going at it, this time arguing about which one would keep the second key. You see, there are only two keys to the apartment door. I keep one and the boys had been sharing the other. But Robert didn't want to give Brendan his turn with the key. It was very silly. I offered to keep both, but Robert finally settled the matter, his way, of course. As I was getting ready to close the door behind us, he grabbed the key out of Brendan's hand and chucked it into the living room. He then slammed the door shut behind us, saying 'there, now neither of us have it,' which would just be a further inconvenience to me as they would have to drag me out if they wanted to get over to the place."

Persky scowled and patted down his pants pocket, confirming the reality of the bulging key ring that was his constant companion. He re-crossed his other leg, first banging it against the corner of Art's desk.

"Sorry Arthur."

"So, did they break in through a window?"

"No. Baird's apartment is on the fourth floor of the building. That's the top floor. The windows and balcony door were locked tight, same as the front door, just as we left them on Friday. And when Mr. Nelson and I came back yesterday to get the insurance, we saw the key sitting on the floor of the living room, right where Robert threw it. And then we saw that the property had been stolen. Art, it's as though the thieves walked through the walls. It's impossible!"

Art was trying to remember whether he had seen Roderick Misely outside earlier. He thought he had.

"Salathiel, there's a young man that's good with these kinds of puzzles. Mr. Misely. He works around here part time. Do you want me to see if he's around to take a listen to this?"

"Well, if you think it would do any good?"

"Hang on. Let me see if I can snag him."

Roderick had been out in the corridor talking with Tip. Tip sold fidelity bonds to executors from his informal office in the hallway. The 'office' was a borrowed high-backed stool, a clipboard and an old catalog case.

Tip was telling Roderick about a potential "live one."

"I think you could help the guy, Roderick. He said he might stop by, later, around 3 or 4."

"Well I've never tried to track down a stolen car, but I can give it a whirl. What was the man's name?"

"Buscomb. Harold Buscomb. Goes by 'Harry.' He's one of Chazzy Plink's friends. Great guy - a real cut-up!"

Just then, Art Green peered around the corner.

"Ah, Mr. Misely. Are you available, presently, to join me for a consultation?"

Roderick knew from past experience that the formal tone of Art's address indicated the possibility of a new client.

"Yes, sir."

Roderick entered Art's cramped office to find the disheveled frame of Salathiel Persky splayed about the high-backed stool. Roderick was thinking that he'd seen better-looking stale laundry flung against a dorm room chair.

Persky stood. Art made the introductions.

"Salathiel, this is Rod Misely - my colleague."

"Mr. Persky, pleased to meet you."

The two shook hands. Misely could have sworn he was handling a live, wet eel. Instinctively, he looked around for a towel, but of course, there was no towel.

"Nice to make your acquaintance, Mr. Misely."

Salathiel tried to hop back onto his stool, but it gave way, nearly sending him onto the floor. But he rallied, regained his footing and wrestled his way back.

Misely decided to stand at the doorway, just next to Art's desk. There was no profit in doing otherwise.

As Persky recounted the facts for Roderick, Art looked on. He was thinking that Salathiel was something of an odd duck. He had known him for over ten years, courtesy of their association with the Beneficent Cavaliers - Elk Neck Chapter. He knew that Salathiel desired greatly to fit in with his colleagues at the bank and Cavaliers. But he inadvertently made it difficult. For instance, he always insisted on being called "Salathiel" and eschewed the nickname "Sal" - which would have been a natural. Of course, Art also knew that, behind his back, Salathiel was referred to as "Cyclone Sal" because wherever he went, destruction followed.

Salathiel finished up his narrative.

"All told, the thieves got away with the swords, two oil paintings, two table radios, a stamp collection and coin books containing a set of silver dollars and seven $20.00 gold pieces."

Persky had unfolded a handwritten list of items. "I cross-checked the list against Meg O'Callanan's. She sent me her preliminary write-up yesterday. They didn't take everything of value, though - they didn't realize that the two large lithographs in the dining area were a lot more valuable than the smaller oil paintings taken from the living room - at least according to Meg. And they didn't take the television set or the portable hi fi."

Roderick was more interested in the break-in. "Mr. Persky - you said that the windows and doors were intact - no sign of a breaking and entering?"

"No sign at all - all windows were locked tight, including the sliding glass balcony door."

"And you said you were certain that there are only two keys - you have one and the other is locked in the apartment?"

"That's right. I left it on the apartment floor. I wanted to keep things just as I found them to show the Bairds."

Persky began more fidgeting and sweat was beginning to streak his forehead. In a few short hours he would be confronted by the Bairds. His stomach ulcer flared, nearly doubling him over as he sat.

"Could someone have stolen your copy of the key?"

"Absolutely not - my key ring never leaves my side." He patted down the fat bulge of his left pants pocket. As a trust officer for a bank, the keys were a constant and indispensible part of his life.

"So Mr. Misely - what do you think? Does any of this make sense?"

Misely was taking it all in. There had to be a third key. Maybe given out in the past by Robert, Sr. or copied-off by someone within the building management. And Misely wanted to take a look at the so-called impenetrable windows and door.

"Mr. Persky, it may not make sense to us, now, but I feel confident that I can solve this puzzle for you - and more importantly, retrieve the stolen property."

It was a bold pronouncement. But Roderick was angling for a paying consulting job and Persky was waiting to be reeled-in.

"Are you serious? That's music to my ears! Obviously, you'll need to be paid and if I can get the Bairds to approve your fee, you can get on the trail, immediately. Did you say what you would charge?"

Roderick had been leaning up against the doorframe, thinking about the puzzle but snapped to attention when the topic of conversation turned to his fees.

"Well, I have to give the matter further consideration. I'll have a better idea once I take a look around the place. Just so you know, I work on a contingency basis. If I don't get results, I don't receive payment."

Persky was very impressed. "Even better!"

Art smiled agreeably from his desk chair. "I can vouch for Mr. Misely. He's helped a number of our mutual colleagues and charges at agreeable rates."

"Well, this is a relief. We just need the Bairds to sign-off. In fact I could really use your help this afternoon. I have to meet with the Bairds at the apartment at 2 PM. They, or shall I say, Robert, is demanding a full explanation as to how the theft took place and why I failed to get insurance."

Misely was certain he saw drops of sweat fall onto Persky's lap.

Misely looked over to Art. "I'm available." And Art nodded his head in the affirmative.

Roderick reluctantly shook hands all around and got the information on the meet from Persky.

Salathiel offered to pick Art and Roderick up at around 1:30 PM to drive the group to the Sorrento Mews, the Baird's cooperative building. Getting a lift was golden because the parking was hell over in that part of Washington Heights. Art gladly accepted. But Roderick agreed to meet them in the lobby. His walk over from Elk Neck would only take 10 minutes and he wanted to attend to an important task before going out. The sole of his right shoe had come loose again. He had been saving money by using a "do it yourself" shoe repair kit. Someday he would be able to afford several pairs of shoes and the services of a shoe-maker. But for now, he would have to re-rubber cement the sole of his shoe back into place.

Back at 7 North Central, Misely took stock of his living quarters. He had come a long way, but there was still a lot of work to be done. The bank was nice about giving him the extra two weeks to clear out of the family home. He had stumbled upon his "suite" through serendipity.

He had been checking the Star Sentinel classifieds for rooming opportunities, as he saw no chance of affording his own apartment. He had just finished making a few unsuccessful calls from the payphone in the library when he decided to take a lunch break before resuming his search. He knew he could find a rooming house in the City. And Tack had generously invited him to bunk with him in his present quarters, but Roderick preferred to stay in Elk Neck if at all possible. He had decided to grab a bite at County Restaurant just up the street, when he noticed a rusted, virtually unreadable "for rent" sign just above the entrance door on the side of the building. There was a phone number, too.

Before the day was out, he made arrangements to meet with the landlord at the premises. The landlord was a tough customer but desperate to unload the white elephant. The worst selling point was the box upon box of abandoned junk, courtesy of a former tenant. Roderick picked about the rubbish and his heart leapt. There was an entire box of expired license plates - and from a variety of States. And in another box, rusted but usable tools - hammers, screwdrivers and wrenches - along with a smattering of rusty nails, screws and skeleton keys. This was the jackpot. And the rough, leftover army cot would certainly fulfill his sleeping needs.

Being rational, the landlord presumed the deadpan review of the premises by Misely meant another futile effort. But he rallied to make the deal.

"It's a bit of a mess here Mr. Misely, but because you would be stuck with the job of cleaning up the place, I will give you a month's free rent and knock the rent down from $50 to $30 bucks a month for the first year. And, by the way, if you find anything worth keeping in this mess, it's yours."

Roderick sniffed, shrugged his shoulders and started making his way back to the front door. The desperate landlord made a final pitch, trying to get the cart back on the rails.

"How about $25 bucks a month and two free months?" And the deal was done.

Thus began Roderick's treasure trove. Tack lent a hand at moving the leather chair from the house. They were able to roll it for the short trek on two pairs of borrowed roller skates. The Wollensack tape recorder was strapped into the seat with rags. Tack was quite impressed with the quality of the new digs, although he chastised Roderick about his failure to secure an option to purchase with the lease.

The piles of boxes were now whittled down to a mere dozen or so. That was progress. But there was still an awful lot of stuff strewn around on the worn-out linoleum floor.

Misely sat down in his leather chair and looked over his right shoe. He grabbed the rubber cement from the top drawer of his desk and with great effort, unscrewed the applicator lid. He brushed a generous amount onto the sole and pushed the sole back into place. He knew that rubber cement would typically take 24 hours to set, but he had many other matters to attend to. It would have to do.

Misely was first to arrive at the Sorrento Mews. He saw that the building had a 24-hour concierge service and that someone would man the lobby desk at all times. It was a pretty fancy place and he figured the rents would be astronomical. He took the opportunity to chat with the concierge, Sid Stempel. Sid had been notified of the break-in and mentioned that it was the first reported theft at the building. Sid confirmed that, besides his own passkey, each cooperative unit owner was entitled to two keys. There were no spares.

"Can an owner get a copy of their key made?"

"Not these keys. They are 'do not copy' keys and a locksmith can only make a spare at the direction of the Sorrento Mews management."

"Did Mr. Baird ever request a spare key?"

"No. I've been here from before Baird moved in and he only received the two keys."

Just then, Art and Salathiel entered the lobby.

"You beat us here. Art and I had to ride around for almost 10 minutes looking for a parking space."

Roderick attempted to introduce Stempel to Art and Persky but Art intercepted the effort.

"Oh - we are all good friends from way back" - which Roderick understood to mean that Sid was undoubtedly a member in good standing of the Beneficent Cavaliers.

"Sid was mentioning that Mr. Baird only had two keys and that only a specific locksmith can duplicate copies, at the direction of Sorrento Mews. By the way, Mr. Stempel, who is that locksmith?"

"Garland Greer."

Art chimed in: "He's near your office, Rod. Just down from the library."

"Well, this may seem like a stupid question, but can he be trusted?"

Art, Sid and Salathiel looked at each other in horror.

"Rod, Greer was our 'Ocelot' for over five years so, of course he can be trusted."

Roderick shrugged inquisitively; a tourist struggling with foreign dialect.

"Sergeant at arms."

It was almost 2 PM, so Persky led the three into the elevator and up to the top floor. As they stood in front of the door to unit

405, Persky unlocked the door and demonstrated how Robert had tossed the key into the room.

"He grabbed the key from Brendan's hand ..." And with that, Persky feigned an underhand toss of the key into the room. The actual key was already sitting in the middle of the living room floor, about 5 feet in.

"And then he pulled the door shut." Salathiel slammed the door shut, demonstrating the effect dramatically, including Robert's clapping of his hands together - as though to brush them clean.

Misely took a look at the lock in the door and saw that it was set to lock automatically when closed. He fidgeted with a lock for a few moments before finding the switch that would defeat the automatic lock function.

"Salathiel, is there any way that the automatic lock feature could have been defeated without your knowing it?"

"No - and I gave the door a good, solid grab to make sure it was locked as we were leaving, just to make sure."

They walked into the main living area of the cooperative unit.

"There's the key right where I found it when I came by on Monday. And every window and the balcony door were closed tight."

"I'm going to look at the key, ok?"

Salathiel shrugged. "Sure, but could you put it back, as Robert will want to see it."

Misely took the key outside into the hall and tried the front door. It turned the lock as expected. Misely placed the key back onto the living room's 'wall to wall' carpeting at about the spot where it had been found.

He re-joined Art and took a look around. The living space was cramped by an overly large sofa against the wall perpendicular to the hall, across from the windows. The balcony was located directly across from the front door - about 5 paces in.

A tiny dinette set was slung along the wall just below the two windows that opened from the dining room area. The sole bedroom was located just off from the living area. Not all that much room.

Two large lithographs overshadowed the two adjacent windows and took up most of the wall space in the dining room. Misely sized them up: two horrifically desolate landscapes of the American Southwest, all purple cacti and pueblos.

The living room wall stood in stark contrast. Persky stood staring at the wall.

"That's where the swords were mounted." Persky was looking at a space just above the large sofa. He pointed out the holes where the mounting hardware had been drilled. He moved further along the wall and pointed out the places where the two smaller oils had been hung.

Roderick touched the mounting brackets. He noticed how the paint had faded around the two small oil paintings, leaving behind two rectangular swaths of slightly more vivid color.

"These were original oil paintings?"

"Yes, but they were just an artist's rendering of two Monet paintings - no Manet - I always get them confused. Not the real thing."

A sharp rap at the front door caused Persky to stand at attention.

"Oh well, my day of reckoning is here."

Persky opened the door to Robert who charged in, followed meekly by Brendan. Roderick thought that the two were obviously brothers. Although Robert domineered over his physically smaller and younger brother, besides their weight and height differential, the men looked remarkably similar.

Robert, nearly bald, sported a tiny handlebar mustache. His large gut hung over his belt and when he spoke he had the habit of lunging forward, aggressively, at his unfortunate prey. He was a big man. Robert wore a short-sleeve safari jacket over an army surplus shirt and canvas safari pants. The short sleeves revealed two purple-black tattoos, one on each arm. Although he hadn't been on a horse in over two decades, he kept a chokehold on a short riding crop, his constant companion.

Brendan was the miniaturized version of Robert, replete with a somewhat less successful mustache, a bit more hair and a bit less gut. But Brendan lacked the aggressive personality of Robert. Years of being beaten down by his brother had made Brendan a milder and more reasonable version of Robert.

"Who are these people - police?"

Robert's bark caused Persky's shoulders to hunch involuntarily.

"No, Robert. I brought along Art Green, the Chief Orphan's Appraiser and his assistant, Mr. Roderick Misely. I thought they may be of some help to us."

Art and Misely extended their hands while Misely attempted to correct the record.

"Actually, I'm not technically Mr. Green's assistant. I'm more of an independent contractor - just in case you need some assistance."

"Why do we need assistance? Mr. Persky is responsible for this and will pay all the damages - right Mr. Persky?"

Salathiel went pale. "Robert, I told you I tried my best to get the insurance but Mr. Nelson was out. I've filed the police report."

Robert sneered and waved Persky away, dismissively, as though doing so negated Persky's response.

The brothers took a tour of their father's quarters, pointing at the walls where the missing art and swords had hung. Robert pushed into his father's bedroom and announced: "They've taken father's table radio!"

Soon, Robert had made a list of missing items on his notepad. It was an unnecessary act - Persky had already provided a list of the missing items to Robert over the phone.

"This is a fine way to administer my father's estate, Mr. Persky. We hold you accountable. Have you figured out how you will find or replace our property?"

Salathiel began to choke-up, so Misely took the floor.

"Mr. Baird, I've had some luck in tracking down stolen property. I'm familiar with a few establishments in town where people exchange property for cash with few questions asked. I'd be willing to take a crack at it?"

"Oh, really? Is that supposed to inspire confidence? Good for you. You know some crooks in crooked places." Robert was tapping the riding crop against his left palm.

With that Brendan broke his silence.

"Robert, wait, let's hear him out. We have to get the swords back, somehow."

Robert grimaced, causing his powder-white mustache to writhe atop his upper lip; a white cap breaking at high tide.

"Ok, Mr. Miserly. Tell us what you'd plan to do?"

"That's 'Misely,' thanks. Well, I would poke around the building, looking for witnesses. And I would search for the stolen property, keeping a lookout on certain suspect pawnshops and second hand shops."

Misely sensed that the water buffalo was about to bellow so he quickly continued.

"I want to propose a simple fee arrangement. Give me 30 days. If I return your stolen swords, you and Brendan will pay me a total of $700.00, that's $350.00 each. If I don't find your property, you will owe me nothing."

Robert slapped his riding crop against his left palm.

"Ridiculous! You expect us to pay you to do something that your friend, Mr. Persky, should be doing, gratis? Forget it!"

Persky had grown white again. Brendan edged forward and stood between Misely and Robert.

"Mr. Misely, don't listen to that. We need help." He turned and faced Robert.

"Robert, we have nothing to lose in hiring this man. You heard what he said. If he doesn't find the swords, we don't have to pay. How does that hurt us?"

"$350.00 hurts me. Does it hurt you?"

Art quietly broke the deadlock.

"Mr. Baird, there's only so much the police can do. And I have to say that I've been around the barn here in Elk Neck and can assure you that Mr. Persky has discharged his legal duty to the Estate. You have to consider the fact that your father did not have insurance on the property to begin with. Mr. Persky pursued obtaining the insurance as diligently as humanly possible. Why not ease off a bit on Mr. Persky and let Mr. Misely take a crack at it?"

Robert was back to merely grasping his riding crop. Art's gentle tone had soothed the wild beast.

"Okay Mr. Miserly. If you succeed you'll get your money. Now, let's see just what kind of a detective you are."

Roderick shook hands with Robert, then Brendan. He was a little worried about the comment about being a detective. He certainly was not one, but figured he might be able to find the stolen stuff in the usual hot spots.

Before anyone else could speak, Robert re-took center stage.

"All right. You are trying to figure out how the burglars got into a locked room without a key. Let's think about that." Robert bit his lip and crossed his arms in an exaggerated display of concentration.

"Brendan, when we were here last Friday, had you opened any of the windows or the sliding door to the balcony?"

Brendan looked puzzled. His tiny white mustache twitched slightly.

"Well it was hot. Didn't we both start opening windows?"

Robert snapped his fingers for dramatic effect. "Yes - you opened the balcony door and those two windows and I was going into father's bedroom to open that one - but we started a discussion. You closed and locked all of those before we left, right?"

Brendan looked on blankly.

"I would think so."

"Well did you? Do you remember sliding the balcony door closed?"

Brendan prepared for the onslaught. "Well, I don't remember, exactly, Robert. We had gotten into another tiff about those swords and we left in a hurry, right after Mrs. O'Brien had finished the appraisal."

Robert rapped the riding crop against his right thigh. The sound frightened Salathiel who retreated two steps.

"Damnation! You left the place wide open!"

As Brendan tried to compose himself to answer, Robert fired a volley over at Roderick.

"See Mr. Miserly, this is called 'detective work.' This is what a real investigator would be doing."

Roderick was caught a bit off-guard. He would certainly be asking the same questions of the two had Robert not taken over the show. He was rallying to speak when Robert charged ahead.

"No comment? Okay. Now we have to figure that the burglars used a ladder to gain entrance right through the open balcony door, right Sherlock? Do you want to test that hypothesis?" Robert glowered at Roderick who felt positively under siege.

"You're saying you want to check outside?"

Robert rolled his eyes back and sighed theatrically. "Elementary my dear Miserly."

The group left the unit and headed down the hallway to the elevators. As they walked, Roderick began to notice a loud clacking sound. The sole of his shoe was coming unglued and was slapping against the linoleum flooring in the corridor. He tried desperately to disguise the problem by walking forward normally with his left foot and sliding the right along behind. But as the pace quickened, Roderick fell behind. Robert looked back in time to catch Misely in the rear, holding up his foot, inspecting the situation.

"What's going on there, detective? Having a little trouble?" The others stopped in their tracks and looked back at Misely. Nearly half the sole was hanging limply off his right shoe.

"Does this make you the 'gum shoe' who needs a little gum on his shoe?"

Robert then gave out a loud guffaw, which nearly knocked Salathiel over. He glanced over to Brendan, seeking approval for his clever pun and Brendan joined in, chuckling.

"That was good Robert, but let's leave the poor man to tend to his problem." But the two continued to laugh.

Roderick stamped a few time on his right foot, which didn't do much good. He felt about as embarrassed as he ever had been. Flopping around with a busted shoe was not the professional demeanor he intended to convey to "clients."

They took the elevator down to the ground floor. Ground level was one flight below the lobby and gave access to the quadrangle courtyard in the rear of the building on which the balconies of the Sorrento Mews buildings faced. A fountain, looking like an oversized birdbath, sat in the center of the quad. But the fountain was bone dry. Nary a single drop of water had ever splashed forth. The permit to bring in the required underground water line had been held up. Seems the developers had 'jumped the gun' and had begun selling-off units before certain amenities, like the fountain, had been completed. To punish the developers for this transgression against the bureaucratic machine, the County Council suspended all ongoing permit applications, including the one for the water line. Regrettably for the owners, the developers had no present interest in pursuing completion of the permit. All of the co-op units had already been sold.

The group walked around to the area just below the balconies underneath the Baird unit. A wilted rose bush sat among a healthy population of dandelions. The group instinctively looked up to the top balcony. Roderick was thinking that an ordinary ladder would not be able to reach the top floor balcony - even a telescoping one. It looked about 50 or 60 feet up. Workers would use scaffolding for that kind of height. But he kept his opinions to himself.

Robert pointed to the ground with his riding crop. "Here - look here."

He drew two careful lines in the air with the riding crop, tracing above two parallel impressions visible in the garden soil. The impressions were about a foot apart and would roughly correspond to impressions made by the feet of a ladder.

"A ladder was here, right under father's balcony. So Sherlock, does this answer the question as to means of access?"

Misely looked on, humbled. "Certainly seems feasible, Mr. Baird."

"Feasible? Come on, man, admit it. I've done most of your work for you. Maybe you should be paying me the $350.00?"

Misely got down on one knee and examined the impressions in the soil. He also quietly pushed his hand into the soil near the marks, getting a sense of how firm the soil stood.

"It's as clear as the nose on your face. This is how the thieves entered and exited the building."

"You're right Mr. Baird. I think you've solved the puzzle. Now let me get to the task of tracking down the stolen property."

After polite farewells, Roderick left the group at the courtyard.

Back at 7 North Central, Roderick sat at his desk in his office anteroom. He was recovering from a severe bout of humiliation. He liked to think of himself as a quick-witted, but somehow Baird had put him on the defensive before he even had a chance to think for himself.

But he took solace in knowing that he was on to a few things that Baird had not yet figured out. Even accepting the wild surmise that the thieves used an enormous extension ladder to enter through the balcony, they certainly did not exit that way. The windows and balcony were locked up tight when Salathiel returned on Monday. The windows and balcony locked from the inside, only. Which meant that the thieves must have locked the place up behind themselves, traveled through the hallway and down the stairs or elevator.

More importantly, Misely thought, the alleged impressions made by the feet of the ladder in the garden soil, were barely anything. A ladder seeking purchase in the soft ground and carrying the weight of one or more persons would have left severe gouges behind. There were no such gouges. And the impressions of the ladder feet were too close to the building. The ladder would have leaned at about a five-degree incline relative to the balconies - not very safe and not practical. The thieves stood the risk of a fifty-foot drop had the ladder fallen back from the wall. A safer angle would have been about 15 or 20 degrees, which meant the feet should have been planted about two or three yards farther away from the building.

Roderick unconsciously opened and clenched the top drawer of his desk.

And it was ridiculous to picture a crew of thieves banging their way through the courtyard in the dead of night with an enormous ladder, without someone noticing or hearing. Someone always saw or heard something.

He felt certain that the ladder marks in the flowerbed were a misdirection designed to fool the Bairds or anyone else investigating the theft. Someone had a spare key and that "someone" did not want that fact known. Misely was back to thinking about the concierge and locksmith. He was going to do some more thinking.

He still had some time to kill so he thought about grabbing a late lunch - a hot dog from the vendor at the Courthouse would do. And then he'd walk back over to the Sorrento Mews to take a closer look at the exit and entry points. But he had to change his shoes. He hated to do it, but he would have to wear the oddly colored, dark blue-green wing tip shoes that he purchased from the Dime A' Dozen thrift shop for 50 cents. They were extraordinarily comfortable shoes, but the color was odd - almost luminescent - and made him self-conscious about wearing them. He only wore the shoes at night, when the blue-green color was less obvious.

After wolfing down a hot dog, Misely decided to stop back at the Register of Wills Office to see if Art had any further observations. But as he approached down the long corridor, he saw Tip waving him down, two arms doing a windmill.

"Hey Buck-O, don't forget Harry Buscomb - with the stolen car - said he might stop by?"

Roderick had forgotten. "Oh - you bet. I'm going to see Art. Just give me a yell if he shows up."

But Art's office was dark, so Misely figured that he was still out with Persky or had maybe gone off on a job. Just then Meg O'Callanan spied Misely.

"Hey Roderick. Did you have any luck with that radio?"

Meg had given Misely the task of fixing the tubes in her table radio. But there was a particular tube giving him trouble. It was not going to be impossible to replace. He just needed to stumble across one.

"Ah, Meg. I'm close to finished, but I'm short one tube that's a little hard to find. Give me just a little more time and I think you will be pleased with the results."

"Should I just get a new radio?" Meg was getting a little exasperated.

But, as if on cue, Tip waved Misely down from the entranceway.

"Have to run, Meg." And he was off, leaving Meg behind, shaking her head and muttering to herself.

Harry Buscomb had arrived. Like a lot of the retired men of Elk Neck, Harry was dressed for golfing, wearing a polo shirt and casual slacks - but without the golf shoes. And with no possibility of being anywhere near a golf course, due to the present Elk Neck heat wave.

Tip introduced the two.

"Call me Harry, please. Tip says you're a one-man lost and found department. Ever tried to find a stolen car?"

"Well, that's a new one for me, but I would enjoy the opportunity to give it a whirl. What exactly happened?"

"Well I bought a very nice 1950 Ford Crestliner, used, a couple years ago. Low mileage. Beautiful car, two-tone, gold and black with a vinyl roof. I actually brought some pictures."

Buscomb took 2 snapshots out of his pants pocket.

"Kind of funny walking around with pictures of your car. Don't tell my wife!"

Buscomb chuckled and passed around the pictures. "There she is."

One was a side view with Buscomb looking on, proudly. The second was a shot of the grill with a woman and boy standing proudly on each side.

"That is my long-suffering wife, Brendy, and my delinquent son, Schuyler." He chuckled some more, and then became serious.

"Actually, in all seriousness, my son is the whiz kid of the group. He's a senior at Elk Neck, but he's already taking advanced English at the Normal College. That picture is a couple years old. He's an honor student. He was founding member of the German Language Club at the high school. We're very proud of him."

Hearing about the German Language Club sparked a momentary recollection, but Roderick put it aside to listen to the rest of the narrative.

"So, everything was fine and dandy and suddenly about 2 months ago, we go out one morning and the car's gone. Just vanished. And, no, I didn't leave the key in the ignition. So, if someone got in, they must have hotwired the car."

Buscomb pointed to the pictures, again.

"You know, my wife and I have been happily married for 20 years?"

Roderick glanced up. "That's great."

"Problem is, we got married 30 years ago!"

Tip had already begun laughing before Buscomb's joke crossed the finish line.

"What do you think Rod, is this guy a cut-up?"

Roderick smiled, but he was already distracted, thinking about his fee. Tip finished-up his laughing jag and asked: "That's one of Plinky's, right?"

Buscomb confessed. "Yeah that was not an original but I couldn't help myself."

The two settled down and Roderick got back to business.

"So, Harry, you said that the car was stolen about three months ago?"

"Correct."

"Did you bring the key?"

Buscomb fumbled around in his pants pocket and produced a single car key.

"Here 'tis."

"How are you getting around without a car?"

"My wife has her own car which I can use, too, if I behave myself. We're right on the streetcar line, too, so that helps. And Sky just rides his bike everywhere. Schuyler's the one missing-out. I hadn't let him use the car except for special occasions but told him that once he was 21 it would be his free and clear. I feel bad about that, but maybe you'll be able to track it down? So, what do you charge for this kind of thing?"

Determining the fee was always a delicate balancing act, but Misely was up to the task. He figured that the used, low mileage Ford Crestliner would be worth about $400. A 25% recovery fee would be nice.

"Well, I work on a contingency fee basis. You only pay me if I return your car. So how does $100 sound?"

Buscomb produced a ham actor's recoil, then cupped his hand to his ear. "I couldn't hear you. What did you say?" He was grinning, wryly.

Roderick adjusted accordingly. "How does $75 sound?"

Buscomb slapped his knee. "Loud and clear, Mr. Rod, that's a deal!"

The two shook hands. Buscomb held out the snapshots. "Do you need these?"

"No thanks. I know exactly what the 1950 Crestliner looks like - gold, black and that vinyl top."

He took down contact information for Buscomb and left the two to continue their joking.

Roderick still had some time to kill before dinner, so he headed back over to the Sorrento Mews. He avoided the front door and lobby. He walked around the courtyard in the rear to check out the ground-level entrance. He looked over the courtyard to the building opposite the Bairds' and saw that some of the residents were gathering in the patio gardens that opened from their terrace apartments below the rows of balconies. From a distance it looked like they were sitting around their patio tables, probably playing cards. Roderick made a mental note to stop back and chat with the group once he finished up.

The back entrance consisted of a single large door. Swung open, a small piano could fit through the entrance. The back door was unlocked and open, but Misely presumed that the door would be locked up at night. He was thinking that the thieves likely entered in the rear at ground level to avoid the prying eyes of the attendant manning the desk on the first floor lobby. He took a closer look at the door handle and lock assembly and saw that the lock utilized a spring latch - which could be easily defeated by use of a few strands of cellophane tape. He noticed that the spring latch was free and was not taped-over. But he ran his raccoon fingers, tactilely, over the bolt assembly and felt a distinct stickiness - the unmistakable sign of a previous tape-over. So, there was the least the possibility that the thieves had entered and exited through the back door and not with the use of a ladder.

But then there was still the problem of that key. Getting inside the building was one thing; getting into the apartment was another.

He entered the building and noticed the stairwell located a few feet from the elevator. The stairwell door had no lock. He entered the stairwell and walked up the one flight of stairs to the lobby.

Sid Stempel was not at the post; a middle-aged man sat reading the paper. He glanced-up and gave Misely a "Can I help you?" Misely fired back a "Just passing through" and left through the main lobby doors. But the experiment proved that the lobby attendant was not asleep at the switch and that the thieves would likely have bypassed the lobby.

Roderick circled around the building back to the courtyard and walked though the scorched grass surrounding the "fountain." The sun was moving closer towards the horizon and the blast of the day's heat was finally beginning to subside. As he approached, he saw that there were two pairs of residents playing checkers at their patio tables. Others were sitting on lounge chairs sipping on cold drinks. A few were wandering around between patios, socializing and sharing a pitcher of iced tea.

The brown-suited man wandered over to the first set of retirees playing checkers. "Good afternoon, folks. I was wondering if any of you could help me?" He spoke the words loud enough to be heard by most of the group - the others were filled-in by their neighbors, bucket brigade style.

"I'm trying to help out some people across the way, there, at Sorrento Mews." He pointed up to the building.

"They had a break-in there over the weekend and I wanted to know if anyone saw or heard anything unusual." On hearing of a break-in, the group began mumbling and he heard a delayed gasp from one of the terrace dwellers at the end of the line. He had gotten their attention.

"The unit is just across the courtyard, up on the top floor, the corner unit - so does anyone remember seeing anything suspicious - like workmen on a ladder, or someone hanging around below the balconies, maybe looking up to the 4th floor?"

"Like a peeping tom?" One of the old guys playing checkers chuckled.

"Well - maybe - or how about anyone wandering around outside the building carrying a large sack? Or someone with a ladder or rope?"

The group spoke among themselves with most shaking their heads in the negative.

"How about anything suspicious or unusual in the courtyard? Anything out of the ordinary - anyone you did not recognize?"

The checkers crowd grumbled some more and the rest yelled back and forth repeating Misely's question to one another. A frail looking man in a reclining lawn chair in the terrace unit where the second group played checkers spoke up gently. Despite the temperature, he had covered his legs with a red plaid blanket. "I saw a man mowing the lawn with his dog." He wagged his finger back and forth pointing towards the courtyard.

But the description of a pet-loving gardener didn't quite fit the bill, so Misely moved about the various groups at their patios, just to make sure he did not miss any useful information. One man beckoned him over.

"If you're in charge, can you find out when they're going to fix our fountain?"

The group had not seen anything. They had nothing useful to offer. He was not surprised and in fact was glad because it buttressed his belief that the thieves had entered through the back door without the drama of a balcony break-in.

Misely was now ready for dinner and decided to grace County Restaurant with his presence. His wristwatch read 5 PM and the usual dinner crowd had not yet populated the booths.

He took up his usual station in the rear booth and sat facing the payphone on the blank rear wall, with his back to the entrance.

Eleni had seen the brown-suited man enter. The well-groomed man was something of a mystery to the Georgelus family. He had been dining there, regularly, for the past six months or so. But Eleni noticed something different about the man this time. There was a certain sparkle to his step - she couldn't quite put her finger on it. But she delivered the silverware, napkin and menu to the booth and went about her business.

Misely enjoyed the tyro pita with hummus and dolmades. He was thinking about the loot. Stealing the gold coins, silver dollars and stamp collection made sense. But why bother with the little table radios and the two Manet copies? No one would have mistaken the small oils for originals. The two larger lithographs were numbered and at least had some value. And, although the swords were likely collectible, why bother with the cumbersome mahogany mounting plaque? The swords would have to be removed from the plaque, anyway, for transport, so why not leave the heavy mahogany plaque behind? It had no value. Carting it around made no sense.

He thought some more about the lobby attendants at the concierge desk and their access to the passkey. A lobby attendant could be bribed or possibly distracted - perhaps giving access to the key. He wondered just how effective security measures had been. On the other hand, according to Sid Stempel, there had never been a break-in before. He would have to quiz Stempel some more, but he was not overly enthused over the prospects. And Misely was thinking about the possibility of the key being copied. But, as much as he disliked admitting it, Garland Greer was not likely the type of locksmith to accept bribes in return for duplicating restricted keys.

He was hitting a mental dead end. Feeling weary, he headed around the corner to 7 North Central and made the long trudge up the two flights of wooden stairs to his quarters.

Wednesday morning found Misely fast asleep on his cot. The summer's heat was stifling and he had kicked the olive drab horse blanket onto the worn linoleum floor in his sleep. But the blanket had rolled-off onto a pile of books towering dangerously at the foot of his cot. The books were now scattered about the floor. A hardcover's jacket ripped underneath Roderick's foot nearly sending him flying, but he caught himself in time to avert further calamity.

He decided to spend a little time on the stolen car case. It was only worth $75, but that was $75 that Misely could desperately use. He hadn't had a chance to log-in his two new cases, so he grabbed the bound copy book that served as a ledger from the top drawer of his desk. For the time being, he was using the anteroom as his office. But the bottom, side drawer of the desk was becoming cluttered with case files. He would eventually need a proper filing cabinet but he wasn't sure how it could fit in the anteroom office.

He made two new entries into the copy book: C-56-21 Baird Burglary and C-56-22 Buscomb - Stolen Car. Across from each name, he penciled-in the proposed fees of $700 and $75, respectively. He used pencil, because experience taught that fees sometimes did not materialize, or perhaps not quite in the agreed-upon amount. And, of course, with his "contingency fee" basis, oftentimes not at all. The last column indicated payment status: "P" for "paid," "D" for "desperate" and "S for "sperate," adopting the ancient terminology still used in estate administration accounts.

He looked over the cases logged-in so far since beginning his consulting practice earlier that year. Initially, he logged-in virtually every odd job, including typing jobs and surveyors' assistant jobs with Tack. But he soon decided to dedicate the case file ledger to "real" consulting cases, not the routine stuff. Besides a series of "O" files, he hadn't been all too busy during summer and the new cases were a welcome distraction.

Harry Buscomb's mention of his son's involvement in the German language club gave Misely his first clue - or more accurately a hunch. He thought he remembered young Schuyler as being one of the ne'er-do-wells who had signed-on to the library's "rare book" project. Back in the spring, Misely had happened upon the group of high school students touring the library in assigned lab coats. Curious, Misely followed behind to learn that the group was comprised mostly of students from the German Language Club who had volunteered for an archiving and preservation project for the library's rare book collection. The project was funded through a grant by the Graham family, which had donated most of the rare books. The volunteers received a stipend that would have been modest for most, but was positively excessive for the average high schooler.

Misely learned that part of the training involved use of the photographic reproduction equipment in the glassed-in area of the library's Rare Book room. So he ran across the street to his own quarters and returned dressed in his own, personal lab coat, with clipboard in tow. He joined the others without missing a beat and not an eyebrow was raised.

The gambit worked. Over the weeks that followed, Roderick learned a great deal about the photographic reproduction equipment.

The head librarian, Mrs. Marsh, was receiving her own education on the deficiencies of the students under her charge. A great deal of her time was spent riding herd on the delinquents of the German Language Club or "Umlaut gang," as they called themselves. Cutting-up and cursing at each other and German seemed to be their major preoccupation.

Regrettably for the Umlaut gang, a schism within the Graham family oligarchy led to the plug being abruptly pulled on the project. No more funds would be drained for Wylands Wainscott Graham's rare book sinecure. Stripped of their cozy stipends, many Umlaut gang members ventured off to private enterprise. The fortunate ones found work busing tables and washing dishes at the Omelet House. This unfortunate coincidence led their rivals to rechristen the group as the "Omelet gang" - a bitterly humbling appellation - and fighting words for any "gang" member.

Roderick remembered Schuyler and figured he would not be above stealing his own father's car on a lark or a dare from his friends. Perhaps Schuyler decided that waiting for his 21st birthday was just not convenient?

Roderick walked over to the library building to make use of the pay phone and phone book. He figured that Schuyler was probably working during the summer. He looked up the Omelet House, swung around into the phone booth and dialed the number. It rang nearly a dozen times.

"I'd like to speak with Schuyler Buscomb - is he working today?"

"He doesn't get in here 'til 10. Call back later." Which was followed, immediately, by a click and a dial tone.

Misely decided to do a little reconnaissance work. It wouldn't be that hard to follow Schuyler around before or after work to see if his paths intersected with the Crestliner. Going incognito made sense because young Schuyler was likely to recognize him.

Had a disinterested third party witnessed the goings-on at 7 North Central, such person would have certainly noted a black-mustachioed man in a blue seersucker suit and black lunch pail, making his way over to the No. 6 streetcar line, which ran through the outskirts of "Old" Elk Neck and north to Carlton Highway. The man in the seersucker would have been seen waiting at the stop just prior to the stop located virtually in front of the Buscomb residence.

The streetcar ran like clockwork on weekdays during the rush hour and Misely was planning to time his travels with the appearance of Schuyler Buscomb. He knew that Schuyler would be heading towards Carlton, because the Omelet House was located just a couple blocks to the east, at Celeste Avenue.

He figured the fake mustache was not the most convincing, but at least sufficient to avoid detection should he come face to face with Schuyler.

Schuyler would remember him from the library. The teenagers were remarkably badly behaved for children of solid Elk Neck families. And Schulyler was the worst of the worst. Besides annoying the few well-intended students, Schuyler and his band had taken to harassing innocent members of the public. While Head Librarian Marsh and Technical Advisor, Mrs. Pumpel, demonstrated dewy decimal cataloging and operation of the photographic reproduction equipment, the rats slithered around behind library patrons seated at their tables, quickly slamming the patrons' books closed - sometimes slapping the book shut on their hands. And before the victim recovered from the shock, the perpetrator quickly slid away, adopting an innocent pose.

Roderick witnessed the nonsense but saw that Schuyler was about to go too far when he had snuck up behind "Dad" Graham, seated at the partners' desk in the Rare Book room. Schuyler was about to flick Graham's earlobe with his thumb and forefinger, when a forcefully delivered "Cut the crap" sounded from behind.

Schuyler froze but quickly regrouped to confront the intermeddler. He turned about face, but saw it was the man in the brown suit with the clipboard and instantly calculated that that this man likely had something to do with his paycheck. So he slunk away, meekly, back to his gang, uttering German epithets under his breath.

Mrs. Marsh was glad to see that the man that she had surmised to be a Graham family member was able to restore some order and discipline. She would commend him later, privately, for looking out for his father or uncle or whomever, as the case may be.

"And sometimes there's good luck," Misely thought to himself, because just as Schuyler departed from the back yard of the

Buscomb house with his bike, the streetcar came along to pick Misely up.

The streetcar was packed with mostly business people and workers carrying satchels and lunch boxes. The seating was standing room only, which didn't bother Misely one bit. Standing around gave him the option of moving anywhere he pleased within the car. This was far preferable to being trapped in a seat next to a fellow citizen.

The streetcar and Schuyler played a lazy leapfrog along the route. Schuyler would bike along the sidewalk, ahead of the streetcar, and then the streetcar would stop and Schuyler would catch up and pass. And then the streetcar would move ahead of Schuyler, with Schuyler eventually overtaking the car when it stopped - and on and on for several blocks.

Eventually, Roderick saw Schuyler turn the corner onto Celeste Avenue. Misely disembarked at the next stop and quickly followed on foot from behind. Surprisingly, Schuyler did not go directly to the Omelet House. He stayed on Celeste and rode to Jaffe's Paint and Body Shop and peered deeply into the open garage door, looking for accomplices. Misely stayed a safe distance behind and watched Schuyler enter the garage. Misely acted as an ordinary pedestrian, passing by and glancing into the large garage in time to hear Buscomb and a couple other Omelet gang members cutting up. It seemed to Misely that at least one had found employment in the garage and that the rest must have used it as a hangout or rendezvous point.

Misely turned the corner down the gasoline alley to the rear. It would be the perfect place to stash a stolen car. He saw a couple other quasi-abandoned cars, in various states of fix-up - but no Ford Crestliner. He was looking over the weed-covered field in the rear when he heard the sound of a car turning the corner heading in his direction. He quickly ran into the field and crouched down in the tall grass and weeds. Sure enough, the vehicle rounding the sharp turn into the alley happened to be a Crestliner. But this was not quite the car described by Harry Buscomb. This car was an all black Ford Crestliner. He retrieved his binoculars from their safekeeping in his lunch pail. He watched the Crestliner pull in back, behind the paint shop. The driver moved out of the driver's side and got back in as a passenger. In a few moments, the bicycling Schuyler reappeared, stopped and leaned his bike across a rusted chain link fence. Schuyler greeted his friend in German, slid into the drivers seat, shut the door and rolled down the window.

A few moments later Misely saw the flash of a cigarette lighter and wisps of blue gray smoke, oozing out of the window. Schuyler was enjoying a cigar break. Misely laughed to himself knowing that Schuyler's private smoking lounge would soon be whisked away and returned to his father - who would be paying a fat $75.00 for the easy effort.

Schuyler eventually bored of his cigar and conversation and rode his bike over to the Omelet House. His fellow Omelet gang member removed the license plate from the back of the car and went back to work at the body shop. Once the coast was clear, Misely walked over to take a look at the car. Schuyler and his gang had painted over the gold sections of the car with black paint - and a lousy paint job it was. But, in an obvious affirmation of artistic integrity, Schuyler or his friends had hand-painted a depiction of bared fangs, in white, along the front sides of the car. Smaller red paint droplets, representing blood, dripped down from the white fangs. Two sets of dots, presumably representing the umlaut, were painted in white on each of the driver's and passenger's side doors.

Misely looked inside and saw that a screwdriver had been jammed into the ignition in lieu of a key. He opened the driver's side and pulled-out the screwdriver. The blade had been roughly machine-tooled to approximate the teeth of a car key. At some point, Schuyler must have borrowed his father's key to bootleg a surrogate. He figured the gang must be sharing the car for joy-riding. Misely chuckled to himself. It was nice to see that shop class at Elk Neck High could provide such a useful outlet for the students.

He left the car where he found it. It wasn't time to turn it in, yet. He headed back to the streetcar line. He had a lot more to accomplish that day. He could have walked back to his quarters, but he figured he would take the streetcar back; the temperature was already climbing into the eighties and it was barely 10:00 o'clock.

He climbed onto the next streetcar. It was virtually deserted. The rush hour had subsided. He took a seat halfway down that had the window already opened. He unbuttoned the seersucker suit jacket and relaxed.

Amelia Prentiss was concerned about the effects of the heat on her garden. She had forgotten to water last evening. She enjoyed her daily trip to the market but was usually disappointed by the ride back. She wanted so desperately to make new acquaintances and learn about the wonderful people in her own community. She got on the streetcar and was surprised to see a "new" visitor. She had never seen the mustachioed man before.

Misely glanced up. He was awfully glad that the streetcar was practically empty. There would be plenty of wide open spaces between himself and the diminutive, elderly lady that had just embarked. He didn't dislike humanity; he simply preferred his own company.

But something troubling was happening. The short woman was ignoring a sea of empty seats and was looking straight at him. He quickly averted his eyes and crossed his arms, feigning a "napping" position. But for naught. Mrs. Prentiss strolled down the aisle and plopped herself down, right next to Misely. He shuddered, involuntarily

"Hello kind sir! My name is Amelia. What is yours?" She held out her tiny hand.

Misely pretended to wake from his slumber. "R.T. Mossley." He reluctantly shook her hand and quickly re-crossed his arms.

He stared out the window and wondered how he had earned such purgatory.

"I always like to meet my kinsmen and learn about their histories - their likes and dislikes - their hobbies, their careers…"

Misely continued to look away.

"So tell me Mossley, what makes you tick?"

Misely was about to make the excuse that he had been working all night and needed to nap - but Amelia continued the monologue.

"I'll tell you a little story about Elk Neck back about a hundred years ago…" and Roderick was able to tune out the drone. There were only five or six stops to go and he could always jump off early.

But Amelia beat him to the punch. She saw her stop come up and excused herself with great apologies; she had deprived "Mossley" of the more recent history of Elk Neck, but she hoped to see him again, soon.

His discomfort averted, he sat back and thought about Schuyler's folly. The car was his to own. He just needed to hang on for a couple years. Instead, he had stolen his own inheritance. Soon, car and owner would be reunited. And Roderick would be $75 richer.

Schuyler would have a lot to learn about life. Misely saw Schuyler as the typical, young rebel destined for a lifetime of conformity. He would go to college and succumb to each and every required social convention. Before long he would be saddled to a desk and chained to a country club. The sharp edges of his youth would be sanded-down, smoothed-over and slowly and steadily polished-out under the microscope of social acceptance. The process of socialization and "maturity" would transform him into a bank clerk.

Just thinking about Schuyler's fate made Roderick feel uneasy - even a little threatened. He had already embarked on a course far divergent from that of Schuyler's. He had refused, and would continue to refuse, each and every effort by the world to constrain his freedom. He would not be shaped into a socially compliant, paint by numbers suburbanite. He would not waste his lifetime serving the process of conformity. He would join no clubs, groups or other forms of artificial friendship. "Friends" were not necessary to Roderick; only business acquaintances and clients. Freedom and self-reliance were his comforts and the only friends he needed.

He looked out the window and saw the Buscomb residence pass by. He thought some more about how silly it was for Schuyler to have, essentially, stolen his own property. His need to fit-in with the other Omelet gang members had driven him to stupidity. What sort of fool steals his own property?

And then it struck him - and he immediately knew and unequivocally understood - that Robert Baird had stolen the swords. How had he not seen it before? He hadn't had a chance to think it through on his own. Baird's bullying demeanor and aggressive assertions about the break-in were the smoke screen designed to send Misely off to an inevitable dead-end. But it now seemed very obvious. A real thief would have taken the more valuable lithographs, the television and hi fi sets. A real thief would not have bothered with the worthless oil paintings or with the heavy mahogany plaque mounting for the swords. Robert Baird wanted to keep the swords intact and keep them for himself. He staged the break-in. He pilfered the smaller, portable, items along with the swords to make the burglary appear legitimate. The ladder imprints below the balcony were a plant; a ham-fisted misdirection.

But that meant that there had to be a third key. How had he managed it?

Roderick realized that he had missed his stop, so he grabbed the bell cord, disembarked, and headed back to 7 North Central.

At the Register of Wills office, Meg O'Callanan was adding up a column of numbers from one of last week's appraisals. Her phone rang, and she marked off her place in the column with her pencil.

"Meg, it's Roderick Misely. Did you know I'm working on the Baird case?"

"Sure Roderick." She cradled in handset between her neck and left shoulder and looked back at the column of numbers.

"This is really important - do you remember when you handled the Baird appraisal last Friday?"

"Yes Roderick."

"So, you remember Robert Baird - the bigger guy - did you notice whether he had any tattoos on his arms?"

Meg was about to ask what possible connection Baird's tattoos could have to the burglary but she stopped herself. She thought it best not to ask.

"Yes, he had one on each upper arm - I think one was an anchor in the other maybe a battleship? Does that help?"

Roderick slumped back in his seat, disappointed. He was sitting in the phone booth on the first floor of the Graham Independent Free Library.

"Well that does help Meg - but doesn't solve my problem - but thanks anyway." She responded with a "You're welcome," but was answered back by a dial tone.

Eleanor McRae, of Summit, Utah, sat sipping her coffee. She had just finished re-reading one of her favorite mystery novels - a Dorothy Sayers. She had no patience for lawbreakers, yet she secretly longed for some small amount of excitement in her life. If only she could be like one of her mystery story detectives, off in spectacular cities, rubbing elbows with police and clever perpetrators.

At that very moment, Eleanor McRae's closest nexus to crime was occurring without her knowledge. Misely was carefully attaching Mrs. McRae's expired Utah license plate to the Ford Crestliner. It was after 11:00 PM and joy riding for the day had concluded an hour before. The Omelet gang had stashed the car back in the alley behind the paint shop. Although Misely had come armed with Buscomb's key, he didn't need it. The last driver had thoughtfully left the screwdriver in place in the ignition for the next pilot.

He worked by the dim glow of the streetlamp up at the corner. After attaching the plate, he jimmied open the lid of an ancient paint can. He had checked the paint back at his suite. Although intended for barbecue grills and metal railings, it would do. He just needed something to obliterate the fangs and markings on the car. The used paint was one of many amenities provided with his suite.

Within a few minutes, he had slathered-over the high art with gritty black primer. "Good enough" he thought. He now had some wheels with which to undertake some much needed surveillance.

Within a few days, Misely had figured-out Robert Baird. Baird was retired, but maintained fairly predictable hours and routines. In the evenings he frequented the Hog's Ear pub, just 2 blocks south of the Courthouse, where a plate of wiener schnitzel, sauerkraut and a schooner of beer could be obtained for less than a dollar. He often closed-down the establishment, following an evening of beer, darts and loud conversation.

Baird was no early riser. Eventually, by 10:00 AM, he would make his way to Veteran's Park with his small pug at his side. The dog was obviously long suffering - and noisy. Misely cringed watching Baird march along with an old brown cane in one hand and dog leash in the other. His omnipresent riding crop was stuffed through a belt loop. He held his leash hand stiffly before him, manipulating the dog's behavior with a series of tugs on the leash. If the dog dared to ignore the yank at his collar and veer off for a sniff, it received a swift smack in the rump, courtesy of the cane. Loud yipping would follow. More serious transgressions were met with the sharp sting of the riding crop. Misely watched the suffering animal strain the length of the leash to distance itself from Baird, who marched along behind with a military gait.

Misely chuckled to himself. With his exaggerated, militaristic movements, Baird probably saw himself as a modern day Roman charioteer with the reins in one hand and Javelin in the other. But to the world, he looked like a highly domesticated retiree pushing a shopping cart with a tiny dog straining ahead in advance.

Misely thought some more about the comic sight and the eccentricities of dogs and their owners. He had recently read or heard about a man who mowed his lawn with his dog. And then he remembered that he hadn't read it - the man in the lounge chair in the plaid blanket had mentioned about such a man.

And then, just like that, he had it. He finally understood how Baird had gained access to the locked room.

Later that afternoon, the group of retirees noticed the approach across the courtyard of that same brown-suited man, this time holding a clipboard. The brown-suited man waved a cheery hello to all, but advanced directly to the gentleman in his lounge chair, covered up in his plaid blanket.

"Sir, do you remember me? I came back to ask you another question."

There was a little room, so Misely sat gently on the edge of the lounge chair, careful not to tip it over.

"About what?"

"Remember, I was here about the break-in over in that building?"

Misely pointed backwards to the Sorrento Mews building.

"Yes."

"Do you remember saying that you saw a man who was mowing the lawn with his dog?"

"No." But he paused a bit. "I said the man looked like he was mowing the lawn the way he was walking his dog."

"Of course. Did the man have a cane?"

"The man had a cane."

"Did he have a mustache-bald-headed?"

"Yes."

"Do you remember the dog?"

"Like a little bulldog?"

And Misely knew he had it for sure.

"Thank you."

The man looked puzzled. "What does it mean?"

The rest of the lounge chair community were straining to overhear the conversation, but messing up, drowning out the dialogue by asking one another "What did he say?"

"It means very helpful information. Thank you."

And with that, the brown-suited man headed-off across the courtyard.

The man who, previously, had been concerned about the courtyard fountain yelled out, "Will we get a reward?"

But it was too late. Misely was out of earshot.

Knowing, with certainty, that Robert Baird was the culprit, Misely set about on a plan to separate Baird from the stolen loot.

A few days later found Baird taking his usual parade march through Veterans Park with his unfortunate animal. Baird had not noticed the man in the rumpled seersucker jacket sitting alone on the park bench gently waving an open and outstretched hand towards the dog. A trail of meat morsels had been placed along the sidewalk. The trail led to the man. The dog caught the scent of the meat along the pavement and gobbled-up each piece, straining frantically to get to the next. Ground sirloin was not the sort of treat that frequently appeared in his diet. He sniffed and sniffed and saw the ball of raw meat in the stranger's hand.

The little dog pushed harder towards the man's outstretched hands extending the leash to its full length and eventually yanking so hard as to cause Baird to lose his grip on the reins. Before Baird could react, the dog had hopped onto the lap of the stranger and devoured the ball of meat, oblivious to the barking commands of his master: "Billy-Billy Budd - come back here! Stop that, Billy!"

Billy Budd licked the man's palm and the man deftly retrieved a second meatball from his jacket pocket and fed it to the happy dog, which devoured the meat enthusiastically.

Moments later, a winded Baird approached the middle-aged man in the seersucker jacket. He wasn't sure why Billy Budd had gone haywire. He had not observed that the man had lured the dog over with meat. He avoided eye contact with the man in the seersucker, choosing to direct his attention to his dog.

"Billy. Billy Budd! Get over here, you rotten beast!"

And without so much as a hello, he grabbed Billy Budd from the man's lap and walked the dog back to the pavement, smacking it on the rump with the riding crop. And Billy let loose with howling and yapping appropriate for the punishment suffered.

Having a set of wheels always helped. It was 10 PM on the following Tuesday evening. The moon was not quite full, but was a little too bright for Misely's tastes. Despite the summer night's heat, Misely was wearing his black turtleneck sweater and dark navy pants. Not to mention the fake black mustache. It was his best effort at camouflage - but certainly not conducive to comfort in the stiflingly humid evening.

He was prepared. He had his trusty putty knife, flashlight and bleached white canvas duffle bag. His pants pocket held three balls of chopped sirloin each wrapped separately in tinfoil.

He had pulled the Crestliner into the alley behind Baird's row house. He had parked it tightly up against the chain link fence that ran along the rear of the backyard lot. He didn't want to cause a disturbance by blocking the alley. Either way, he wasn't planning on staying there all that long.

He was a little concerned over the legality of his efforts but had decided that he was not breaking any law by entering Robert Baird's home under the cover of darkness. Both Robert and Brendan had expressly authorized him to take the necessary steps to recover the stolen property. And that was exactly what he was doing.

He approached the back of the home gently. He didn't want to send Billy Budd into a yapping jag. He quietly unlatched the gate. He walked up the stairs to the back porch and listened for Billy Budd. So far, so good.

He put his flashlight away; it wasn't necessary. The moonlight was a mixed blessing. He knelt down by the door and removed a meatball from the tinfoil. He slid the putty knife between the door and the doorframe, working his way down to the bolt assembly. Misely had had a fair amount of experience with the putty knife. His Uncle Tack had educated him in the technique years before. Seems that Tack had experienced his fair share of lost house keys and changed locks during his lifetime.

Misely wriggled the putty knife between the latch and strike to success. As he pulled open the back door, he saw Billy Budd charging through the kitchen. The dog let out a couple of quick yelps, but quickly sensed the aroma of raw meat and recognized that wonderful man. Within seconds, Billy Budd snuggled onto the lap of Misely, who sat cross-legged on the kitchen floor feeding the hungry animal. Henceforth, the two friends were inseparable.

Misely began searching through the first floor, but didn't expect to find any of the property stashed there in plain view. He took a look around the living room and chuckled to himself. The "parlor" looked as though it had been decorated by someone's grandmother. Small serving tables, lace doilies and throw rugs were everywhere. Misely wondered how a bull in a china shop like Baird had acquired such sensitive tastes.

But there was one corner of the living room that surprised Misely. Baird had put together an absolutely ace short wave and ham radio setup. He took a close look at the rig, which was scattered over a desk and adjoining set of metal shelves. There were a couple well-built Heathkit receivers, broadcast microphones and a stack of Allied Radio catalogs. And, incredibly, there was a virtually brand-new Hammarlund short wave radio, covered with a piece of cheesecloth used as a dust protector. It was a gem.

He looked around some more and happened upon the infamous riding crop. It had been laid politely on top of a lace doily sitting on a tiny tea table. Unable to resist, he picked up the riding crop and marched around the living room sticking out his gut and doing his best impression of Robert Baird. As he admired his performance in the floor length mirror, Billy Budd looked on in seeming appreciation. But he quickly felt stupid and stuck the riding crop into his rear pants pocket. He had work to do.

He had to move things along. He knew from trailing Baird, that Baird should be out playing darts for about another hour, but he preferred postponing any face-to-face meeting with the beast, indefinitely.

He figured the basement would be fertile grounds, so he flicked on the light switch just inside the basement door and clambered down the wooden stairs, carefully, with the pug falling in behind. He immediately saw a dark corner next to an oil burner. He clicked on his flashlight, illuminating a dark green tarpaulin. He pulled back the tarpaulin and saw everything that he had come for: the swords, leaning up against the corner next to the mahogany plaque. The oil paintings, table radios, stamp collection and coin books sat on the cold basement floor. Everything was there. He quickly jammed the swords, plaque, coins and a table radio into his white canvas laundry bag. Billy Budd looked on, enthusiastically.

He tossed the tarp aside, emulating the haphazard movements of an amateur crook. He had decided to grab only part of the stash. Taking it all would have seemed suspicious, as though the thief had targeted only the estate items. Misely thought to himself - "just as Baird had done."

He headed back upstairs to grab more items. He noticed the silverware chest sitting atop the dining room bureau. He grabbed handfuls of silverware, straightening and wrapping the silverware in a fat rubber band. He left the chest open, revealing a random soup tureen, left behind. He rifled through the drawers of the bureau, leaving them partly open.

He saw the china closet in the dining room. He grabbed three decorative porcelain plates that were displayed on small easels inside the closet. He needed to protect the plates from breakage, so he took a look around in the small clothes closet situated near the front entrance door. He found a large sized sports coat and wrapped the plates with the coat.

He took a quick tour upstairs to Baird's bedroom, leaving the canvas bag behind. He nearly tripped over Billy Budd's water bowl but rallied. Billy followed, earnestly.

Below the watchful eyes of Baird's Varga Girl pinups - cellophane taped to the walls - he removed each of the clothing drawers in the dresser and placed them on top of the bed. The top drawer held some tie clasps and ties. He opened a small jewelry box containing what appeared to be a diamond tie tack, grabbed the box and headed back downstairs. He left the drawers askew on the bed, in a ransacked condition.

He took one last look through the living room and, on a final whim, swiped a few more items, securing them, carefully, in the canvas bag to prevent damage. After all, damaged property would not represent marketable "collateral."

He used his final moments to feed Billy Budd his last meatball from the tinfoil. He sat cross-legged on the living room floor, while feeding and gently petting the grateful animal.

He picked up the canvas bag, which was something of a struggle. It weighed a ton. But he gently walked it out through the kitchen to the back entrance door. He gave Billy Budd a final affectionate rub and allowed the back door to close and lock behind him. He was working his way back to the Crestliner - walking a few paces and resetting the bag; regrouping and working his way down the backyard walkway to the gated fence. About halfway down the walk, he felt something in his back pants pocket and realized that he still had Robert's riding crop. He had forgotten to put it back.

On impulse, he grabbed at the riding crop and flung it with all of this might into the moonlit sky. He was aiming for the roof of the row house across the alley. The riding crop hit the roof, caromed-off of a stubby vent pipe and rolled down towards the rain gutter. There, it hit a loose shingle and performed a 2 ½ flip onto the asphalt roof of the adjoining carport, where it braked and came to an abrupt halt.

Misely barked out a wild, involuntary laugh. The sound reverberated against the banks of row houses across the alley. He couldn't help himself; watching the riding crop bounce around on the roof, pinball style was just too much. But he instantly regretted his folly. Out of the corner of his eye he saw a back porch light illuminate from a home, two doors down.

Misely quickly grabbed his canvas bag and struggled forward for the final few paces down the walkway. He cleared the gate and pushed the sack onto the back seat of the Crestliner and motored away. He had made his escape.

Two mornings later, Salathiel received the phone call he had been waiting for. "Yes" he was available that afternoon and would call the Bairds immediately and arrange to have them meet at American Eagle Pawn at 2 PM.

American Eagle Pawn was one of the grimier pawnshops drawn from among a collection similarly questionable establishments found in the City's Eastside. Pawnshops were heavily regulated - the risk of taking in stolen goods by 'mistake' was omnipresent. But strong regulations were not necessarily accompanied by strong deterrents and the profit motive often superseded concern over legal fine points in the City's Eastside.

Persky and Misely had gathered together at the front counter, waiting on the arrival of the Bairds. The front counter was a "cage" set-up featuring steel bars and a limited exchange area, designed to prevent an unhappy patron from throwing a punch or assaulting the clerk with a baseball bat. Salathiel wandered around taking a look at the dirty place. He felt surrounded by the collateral of human misery - a grotesque selection of items delivered up in poverty or through thievery for quick cash. The jewelry counter's inclusion of a selection of pulled gold teeth set his stomach turning.

But Misely directed Persky's attention to the long metal shelves behind the main counter and to the right. There, in plain sight, were the two sabers, side by side, on one of the shelves. The mahogany plaque was directly below on the floor, leaning up against two umbrellas and a jeweled walking stick. The shelf immediately to the right held the oil paintings, table radio and coin collection books.

Robert and Brendan arrived at the shop together. As Persky triumphantly pointed out the soon-to-be recovered items to the two, Robert's eyes darted around the shop. He had spied his silverware in the rubber band and the porcelain pieces laid unceremoniously just one shelf below. But he breathed a sigh of relief. There was no sign of his stolen riding crop. If anyone had seen the riding crop among the other items, the coincidence would have been very difficult to explain away. Feeling confident, he resumed his ordinary belligerent demeanor.

Misely was suggesting quietly to Persky that Misely be allowed to "do the talking." Persky was only too grateful to step into the background. He handed over the copy of the police report on the theft.

Misely assembled the group at the front counter making every effort to quell the dissension in the ranks. Brendan was trying to calm Robert down, grateful for the opportunity to retrieve the family heirlooms. Robert simply stood there arguing and demanding to speak to the management. There was no particular management to speak of. The gaunt looking man in a green visor sat on a stool behind the cage taking it all in stride, barely noticing Robert Baird's accusations and protestations.

"This is an outrage." He sneered. "Your "company" has received stolen property and will be prosecuted!"

Brendan continued to try to settle Robert down telling them "It's okay," and "Let's just get our property back."

Misely turned away from the cashier, hands held high, motioning them to step back and quiet down. "Let me handle this."

He turned and addressed the man in the green visor. "Sir, I'm sorry to report that you've taken in a few items stolen from the estate of Robert Baird, Senior."

There was a lengthy pause. "What items?" The man did not look up. Misely saw that he was actually playing a game of solitaire on the counter below.

"Over there, behind you - those two sabers, that plaque below. And just to the right of the sabers - see those oil paintings, the coin books and that little table radio?"

The man in the green visor finally looked up. "I can't release anything without the police. You have to fill out forms and then the police come over, check it out, and then you can get your stuff back when they're done."

From behind, Misely heard Robert bellow "Outrageous!" But Misely waved him back down with a backwards hand motion.

"I think I can help with that." Misely pulled out the carbon copy of the police report from his suit pocket. He unfolded the form and laid it on the counter.

"Here's the police report - Elk Neck Township."

The visored man was shaking his head and waving his hands in idle rejection. But before he could verbalize his position, Misely made a counteroffer.

"How about we call Officer Duckworthy and see if he can approve the release over the phone?"

This was a new one, and the man in a green visor mulled it over. Misely continued.

"Here, pass me the telephone and I'll get the officer on the line." The man in the visor felt a little uncertain but saw Misely beckoning for the phone. And then he spied the folded $10 bill that Misely was palming with his thumb, unseen by the others.

The telephone was slid over across the counter and as Misely reached for the phone, he subtly slid the $10 bill into the grasping fingers of the man behind the counter. The man in a green visor was quite pleased. Besides the receipt of the quick cash, he was enjoying Misely's performance. It was just slightly more engaging than his solitaire game.

Misely dialed the phone and turned to face the others, giving them a quick thumbs up.

"Officer Duckworthy, please." A few seconds went by. "Ah, yes. Officer Duckworthy - it's Roderick Misely here with Salathiel Persky and Robert and Brendan Baird." He paused again.

"That's right, the Baird estate theft. The police report number is 1872-C." He re-folded the paper and paused, giving the officer time to retrieve his file.

"Yes, look, we are at the American Eagle Pawn in the City? Yes. Good news, we've located some of the stolen items."

Back at County Restaurant, Eleni Georgelus was cleaning-off the formica tabletops. The lunch crowd had been and gone. She enjoyed the quiet time following the lunchtime rush; she liked putting the place back in order while her parents cleaned the grill and dishes in the kitchen. It was odd hearing the pay phone ring at the back booth. Every once in a while, someone would dial a wrong number, but her curiosity got the better of her. So she walked over and picked up the phone. Before she could answer "Hello, County Restaurant," she heard a man's voice already in the middle of a conversation. She said "Hello" but the voice ignored her and continued speaking.

"Yes officer, the proprietor has been extraordinarily helpful and has offered to authorize our retrieving the items on your verbal say-so. Yes, and I did produce the police report for him.

Yes? Excellent! That will please the heirs and the estate executor very much."

Eleni thought that this was the oddest thing. It was a lot like the party line that she and her parents had at home. But this was a pay phone and she thought it would be different and that strangers would not be able to listen in on a conversation from a pay phone.

She said "Hello?" again and listened some more. She felt the voice sounded familiar - like that man in the brown suit - but she wasn't sure. She didn't want to intrude on the conversation so she said: "Sir - just to let you know, we will be having the lamb stew special this evening. Thank you." She gently returned the handset of the phone back onto the cradle and went back to work.

Misely heard the dial tone, but pressed his ear hard against the handset. "Hang on officer, let me see if the proprietor needs to speak to you."

Misely beckoned to the man in the visor, inviting him to the phone. But the man shook his head in the negative, rejecting the offer to communicate with the authorities. The deal was already done.

The man in the green visor found a cardboard box and began gathering up the "collateral." Brendan was taking a good look around the place and walking over to the wall of pawned radios and other electronic items. He noticed a particular item. It was a virtually new Hammarlund short wave radio. A cheesecloth cover had been pulled back, exposing the extraordinary set of dials and controls. Brendan beckoned Robert over.

"Look at that, Robert. Some poor sap had to pawn a brand new Hammarlund. It's almost exactly like yours!"

Robert's face grew red. "No - no - mine is newer - that one is ok, though."

And Robert quickly distracted Brendan with a diatribe against the filthy environment of the pawnshop.

Persky had signed the man's paperwork and the four headed out the door with the loot. The Bairds insisted on meeting with Persky back at his office, to assure themselves that the property would be safely secured. Persky invited Misely back, too, figuring that it might provide an opportunity for the Bairds to pay Misely's fee.

Misely arrived last, about twenty minutes later than the others. They had driven their cars, but Misely was relegated to the streetcar, which required two transfers. None of the others had thought to offer him a lift. They had presumed that Misely had driven, too. But it didn't matter. Riding along with the argumentative Bairds or subjecting himself to the hair trigger reflexes of Cyclone Sal behind the wheel were both equally unsupportable travel propositions.

Misely arrived in time to witness yet another verbal battle over the swords. Persky was at his wits end and glad to see the arrival of his new hero, Roderick Misely.

"Roderick - you did it. Congratulations! You got back the swords!"

Brendan joined in. "Yes, congratulations, Mr. Misely. We are deeply grateful!" He gave Misely an enthusiastic handshake.

"Let's pay the man, Robert." Brendan had been prepared. He pulled his checkbook out of the breast pocket of his blazer.

Robert sniffed and crossed his arms. He was smoldering, angry that through plain, dumb luck, Misely, the dim wit, would be credited with finding the swords. He wasn't sure how a burglar could have gotten past his locked doors and attentive watchdog. He was angry that the rotten little beast had not earned its keep. But he was going to have the last laugh.

"Under no circumstance will I pay. And I advise you to put that checkbook away."

Brendan groaned loudly. "Aw - now what Robert - what are you talking about?"

"He didn't fulfill his part of the bargain. He has not yet retrieved all of father's stolen property. We have not received the stamp collection and the other little table radio that had been in father's bedroom."

Persky cleared his throat. "Now, Robert, Mr. Misely was hired to find the swords - do you remember?"

"That's right." Brendan rejoined. "The swords were the important thing to us!"

"That is not my recollection. He agreed to retrieve all of our stolen property within 30 days, or he received no payment. Those were his own words. And with less than two weeks left, I dare say Miserly, by his own terms, will have agreed to recover the swords for us, gratis, just as Persky should have done from the get go!"

To emphasize, Baird had involuntarily attempted to smack the open palm of his left hand with his riding crop. But mid-motion, he realized that the riding crop was nowhere near.

Brendan wailed. "That is not fair, Robert!"

Misely quickly stepped in to calm Brendan down. "No - no, Mr. Baird is correct. Those were my terms. You gentlemen owe me nothing and as your brother suggests, the chance of my stumbling upon the other few items is remote. But I'm still glad to have helped you with this. Perhaps you will keep me in mind for future consulting jobs? I'll be a little more careful in how I word the deal, though." He chuckled good-naturedly.

Robert looked on, smugly.

Persky looked confused. "Are you sure?"

"Yes, Mr. Persky - I always stick to my terms."

Brendan jumped in. "Look, not so fast Mr. Misely. I really appreciate what you did, including getting that policeman to help us. Father's will can be done, now. That plaque will be burned and the swords distributed. For that, I'm happy to pay you my $350.00. Here it is."

And, quickly, Brendan scribbled out a check payable to "Roderick Miserly, Consultant." Misely inspected the check. It was close enough.

"Thank you, Mr. Baird. I appreciate your generous gesture." The two shook hands, again.

The following Friday morning found Misely in the driver's seat of the Crestliner, motoring over to Buscomb's house. He had kept the Crestliner stashed in the street behind the library, safe from prying eyes. Without an economic incentive, no self-respecting Omelet gang member would be caught dead near the library. The stale Utah license plate had been removed.

Misely had called ahead to a delighted Harry Buscomb - the car had been recovered! Misely had chosen to return the car at a time when Schuyler would be busy burning scrapple at the Omelet House. He didn't want "Sky" to get a good look at the villain who had separated car from rebel.

Harry stood in the front yard as Misely tooled the Crestliner into the driveway.

"Oh my, Mr. Misely - what have they done to my girl?"

Misely braked and handed Buscomb his key.

"It's hard to believe that some fool would paint over that beautiful gold paint."

Buscomb shook his head. "Wow! That's nuts. It looks like an entirely different car. But that's my girl. I can see right here from the front bumper!"

Buscomb got down on one knee. "Now, I'm not proposing to my car, Mr. Misely but look right over here!"

Harry was pointing to two tiny initials scratched into the driver's side of the chrome bumper. The initials were "B.B." Misely hadn't noticed it before.

"Who is B.B. - Mrs. Buscomb?"

Harry blushed. "No - actually, it's a little silly Mr. Rod and you probably won't understand until you are a father someday, but it stands for "beloved boy." That's our Schuyler. Brendy and

I had Sky a little late in our lives and he means everything to us. We meant for this car to be his one day, so we scratched that into the bumper as a tribute. But we could never show him the initials. He would die of embarrassment. Schuyler is a "cool cat" and our parental doting is best kept our little secret."

Buscomb paid. He turned over $75 as agreed, in cash. Misely quietly breathed a sigh of relief. He had been running precariously short of funds and the $75 came along just in time.

A few days of calm followed. Roderick had been working in the Register of Wills office, handling a few odd typing jobs. Art Green had been quite busy. There had been a lot of decedents, lately, and a lot of appraisals. The summer had not been kind.

Misely notice that Art Green was now back in his office so he took a break from his typing. He rapped politely on the outside doorframe of Art's office.

Art looked up from his work. "Come in, Rod come in! I've been running around like a chicken with my head cut off the last few days. Take a seat!" Art's genuine welcome sounded barely louder than an enthusiastic whisper.

Roderick took to one of the high-backed stools facing Art's desk. There were several piles of hand-written appraisals and valuation books splayed open on Art's cramped desktop.

"I was very sorry to hear about Robert Baird's welching on his agreement. Salathiel told me what happened." Art was secretly proud that Roderick had handled the situation so graciously.

"Oh, that was no big deal, Art. Brendan came through and paid his share. Robert's decision to withhold payment is just one of the hazards of the trade. Besides, running down stolen goods in a crooked pawnshop is not all that taxing. I figured that's where the better stuff would wind up, ultimately."

"Well you're a good sport, Rod. Needless to say Salathiel is absolutely ecstatic."

"I'm happy for him. Sometimes things do work out the way they should. And it helps to be lucky."

"Well, don't sell yourself short Rod. Trawling around in the Eastside is real work. There must be a dozen pawnshops over there. Despite the fact that Robert solved part of the mystery on how the thieves broke into the apartment, it still took time and effort on your part to track down the property."

"Thanks, Art. I appreciate the vote of confidence."

Art looked at the mess on his desk. He had a pile of work to do. Roderick sat back in the stool and clasped his hands behind his head.

"Well, Art, you know I had been thinking about Robert's theory on the break-in. And I think I came up with an alternate theory."

Art looked up, puzzled. "Really? What do you mean?"

Misely quickly leaned forward, drawing closer to Art Green for effect. "Well, listen to this idea and tell me what you think. First, let me place this in the hypothetical mode, only, because anything else would be unbelievable."

Art looked on, interested. "Sure?"

"Okay. Suppose, hypothetically, that one of the Baird brothers - we'll call him "Mr. X."- had been behind the theft."

Art gave Roderick a pained expression. "Rod, that's kind of crazy. Why would either one of them steal their own property?"

"Well, remember that the two had been fighting over the swords - dividing the set or keeping them together. Suppose - just hypothetically - that Mr. X. had decided to steal the swords to settle the controversy."

Art shook his head from side to side indicating grave doubt. "Hmmm... sounds like a stretch Rod."

"Well, hear me out. Suppose Mr. X found a way back into the apartment without using a ladder and without having to enter through the balcony, which - let's face it - presents some difficulty. What if Mr. X. found a way to make the shared key available to himself and not his brother?"

Art grimaced, communicating continuing doubt. "Okay, Rod, but how? Robert threw that key into the living room and slammed the door shut behind him. And we both saw the key sitting there on the living room floor." Art looked down at his desk. Real work was beckoning.

"Well, I thought initially that perhaps Mr. X had not actually thrown the key into the apartment. Maybe he palmed the key or hid it up a shirt sleeve. But he was wearing a short sleeve shirt and Persky saw him whisk his hands together after slamming the door closed, so that wouldn't work."

"Sure - okay."

"Well, what if rather than throwing the key onto the carpet, Mr. X. flung the key across the room, through the open balcony door and down to the garden area below?" Roderick looked on, proudly.

Art shook his head and rejection. "Rod, come on - that's really far-fetched. Could a person do that?"

"Well, think back, Art. The balcony is only about five paces from the front door. It had been left wide open. The open balcony door would be a pretty good sized target, especially to someone who's a dart player, like Mr. X. It would be a pretty easy toss."

"But how would someone find that tiny key out in that enormous courtyard? It's a needle in a haystack."

"Well, a lot of the grass has dried-up due to the drought, but either way, a person could simply search parallel, adjoining swaths of turf, much like someone mowing a lawn. You would just go one row after the other. And, with a little luck, you might just find the key."

Art was shaking his head in general disagreement. But he let Roderick finish.

"So, Mr. X. would retrieve the key from the lawn, enter the building from ground level to avoid the concierge and simply reenter the apartment through the front door, courtesy of the key. No need for a ladder or balcony entrance. Once in, Mr. X would swipe the swords, the plaque and some of the more portable items like the coins and the radios, to divert suspicion and to make it look like a true burglary. And when finished, Mr. X would simply toss the key back onto the carpet on the way out, where it would be found by Salathiel."

Art was mulling it over, looking up at the ceiling. "No, no Rod that doesn't work because the stuff was found in the pawn-shop. How did it get there? Under your theory, it would have to have been stolen, a second time from Mr. X., right?"

"Well it's not inconceivable. It would require a certain amount of coincidence, but a real burglar could have happened to break into Mr. X's house and steal the stuff?" Roderick was quietly smiling to himself, watching Art's reactions. But Art had had enough.

"Now, Rod, isn't that just kind of ridiculous? I mean, seri-ously, your theory requires two separate break-ins by two differ-ent thieves. Robert's theory requires just one thief. Can you see the flaw?"

Art was getting a little anxious. He had a lot to do and as much as the liked Roderick, he really had to get onto his next task. He figured that Roderick was probably a little sore about the treatment he had received at Robert's hands and was trying to demonize him. Not that Robert needed it.

"You're right, Art. That is kind of far-fetched and a bit ri-diculous. I shouldn't be wasting your time with idle theories." Roderick was smiling broadly.

"That's okay, Rod you have a creative mind and that alone will keep you going." Art couldn't think of anything better to say.

With that, Misely quickly slid off the high-backed stool and headed for the door. "Thanks for listening to me Art!"

Art was about to say "goodbye" but Roderick was off.

But Art's subconscious had already begun toying with the crazy idea of a second break-in. It was an uncomfortable feeling, somehow. Just then, Art's phone rang - and rang again - and Art was back to business. The thought evaporated.

Later that evening, Roderick returned home from County Restaurant with a casebook on criminal law in tow. He settled into his leather chair in his office anteroom.

He was thinking about the Baird case. He had made some stupid mistakes. He had been careless in breaking into Baird's home. He hadn't taken it seriously enough. The casebook he had been reading mentioned that the victim of a burglary had the legal right to use force - even deadly force in some instances - to protect life and home. He was picturing what would have happened if Baird had come home, unexpectedly. He was imagining Baird grabbing a sword and jabbing him - an apparent stranger - in the gut, which might have been legally justified.

And he should never have hurled the riding crop onto the roof - it was childish. But he couldn't help but chuckle to himself, again, as he replayed the scene over in his mind's eye. He had dodged a bullet. Whatever noise he had made had not been enough to trigger a call to the police. He had been lucky.

And he was feeling a little bad about torturing Art Green, his biggest fan, with the "hypothesis" of the second break-in. Even if Art had taken the hint and realized that his pupil was responsible for retrieving the swords and delivering them up as collateral to the pawnshop - what did that make Art - his Fagin? No. Art really should not be informed about such things. He didn't need to know.

It was time to close out the Baird Burglary file. He had closed-out the Buscomb file, C-56-22, earlier that morning. Thinking about the Buscomb case, he noticed the screwdriver still sitting on the corner of his desk. It was the ersatz key for the Ford Crestliner. He walked the screwdriver back into his chaotic living quarters and tossed it gently into the box of rusted tools. He was thinking that one never knew when one might need a set of wheels, in an emergency.

He re-entered his office and grabbed the copybook ledger from his top desk drawer. He was struggling with whether to mark the Baird file "paid in full" or as a "sperate," or more likely "desperate," debt. He was mulling it over and glanced back into his living quarters. He couldn't help but notice the nearly new Hammarlund short wave radio. It was sitting on the linoleum floor at the foot of his cot, covered with a piece of cheesecloth, used as a dust protector. Redeeming the pawned item was a simple matter at American Eagle. Questions were so seldom asked there.

He thought it would only be fair to mark the case "paid in full," as the radio was easily worth the $350.

Files C-56-21 and C-56-22, once found in the lower right hand desk drawer of the desk located in the office anteroom, can now be found in the metal filing cabinet located in the living quarters of Roderick Misely, Consultant, at 7 North Central, just up the street from northeast corner of Iroquois and Central.

CHAPTER SIX
SERVING THE PROCESS

"Call Mrs. Blane." Roderick could barely make out the words. The phone number was no clearer. He was staring down at what appeared to be a piece of a papier-mâché bowl - the kind usually found holding pretzels or potato chips at a delicatessen or tavern. Someone had torn off a piece of the bowl to use as makeshift writing paper. That 'someone' had to be Tack.

Just moments before, Roderick had walked through his doorway at 7 N. Central, his brown oxford crushing the rounded papier-mâché chunk underfoot. For a second he believed he had stepped on a dried leaf. He had stooped down to see what the wind had blown in.

Inside his office anteroom, he held the papier-mâché up to the light. Tack's pen must have run out of ink half way through the task, but Roderick could still make out the impressions of the ballpoint in the paper. He pulled the small notebook from his breast pocket and jotted down the phone number. He wasn't sure who "Mrs. Blane" was, but messages from Tack pitched under the door, although rare, usually turned into money-making ventures. And, as usual, Misely was running seriously low on cash and would welcome a new job. The Panama Exposition gold piece was sitting safely in his file cabinet. He had convinced himself that he could "cash-out" and sell the coin any time he wanted. But he simply couldn't bring himself to do it.

Roderick clomped down the two sets of wooden steps that ran along the outside of the building. He soon found himself across the street at the library payphone located on the first floor next to the rear stairwell.

"Law offices of Kent and McCullough, good morning."

"Good morning. Is there a Mrs. 'Blane' there?"

"This is Honora Blaine speaking. May I help you?"

"Mrs. Blaine? This is Roderick Misely. My uncle, Tack Misely, asked me to call you?"

"Yes, Mr. Misely. Do you remember me? I was Mr. Friedman's secretary."

"Ah - yes of course, Mrs. Blaine." He did remember - but barely.

"I'm working for Mr. Kent's firm in Elk Neck, now. They have a case they might need you for - that is, if you still serve process? Mr. Friedman gave me his list of contacts before he retired and he had your name under 'elisor.'"

She didn't mention that the entry for his name also stated "title searching, odd jobs, special projects - anything."

"Yes, I'm still authorized by the Elk Neck Superior Court to serve process, here, or in any state court with reciprocity. Where's the case filed?"

"Well, the case is here in Elk Neck, but the man they want is in the City. Mr. Kent can fill you in. They're both here, now. Could you drop by this morning - 10:30 or so?

By the way - you're a tough man to track down. Mr. Friedman didn't have your phone number on the list, but I saw your uncle's name and a phone number so I called him. Did you know your uncle's phone number rings over to a pay phone at a stable? A jockey answered."

Misely took down the information on the firm's location. It was not much of a hike. Their office was on the south end of Chancery, not far from the Courthouse. It was one of the many offices along the street that had once served as homes and were now converted to offices.

"Just take a seat, Mr. Misely. They'll be ready for you in a minute."

Roderick stationed himself on the maroon, Victorian-styled loveseat just across from Mrs. Blaine's reception desk by the front door. Honora Blaine leaned forward on her desk and craned her neck around the corner to get a view of the conference room. Old man McCullough was already seated in his favorite chair in the corner of the room near the entry door, his back to the bank of windows. By stationing himself away from the conference room table he made it clear that he was a virtual observer, only, such being one of the benefits of "semi-retirement."

Misely amused himself by reading the sports pages of the Star Sentinel stashed on the side table next to the love seat. He glanced up to see two men descend the stairs from the second floor, a taller, well-dressed man in a three-piece charcoal grey business suit and a shorter, rotund man in a blue sports coat and grey slacks sporting a club tie. The taller man was carrying a thick manila file folder. They entered the conference room, closing the door behind them. Five minutes later the door opened and the taller man gestured to Mrs. Blaine with a nod, to bring Misely into the room.

"Mr. Misely, I'm Roger Kent and seated over there is my partner, Mr. James McCullough."

Roderick moved from man to man, shaking hands before taking a seat. McCullough, dressed in a bruised-looking banana yellow linen suit, offered a particularly damp limp fish. The poor man's hand was downright icy, even though it was only late summer. No mention was made of the smiling, much younger round man in the blazer who remained seated, cattycorner, from McCullough. Misely looked over, waiting for an introduction. There was none, just the beaming face of the odd little man in the corner. His bright eyes and tiny white teeth gave him the look of a happy cherub, smiling down from a chapel ceiling at a flawed congregation.

Misely was about to journey back to the corner to make acquaintance when Roger Kent's "Let's get down to business" forced Misely to do an about-face and take a seat at the table, across from Kent.

"So, you are an elisor?" There was some doubt in his voice.

"Yes, Mrs. Blaine said you needed process served on someone in the City?"

Kent looked over at McCullough who seemed to have fallen asleep. He then glanced back at the round-faced man who smiled sheepishly from the rear of the room.

"Well, here's the scoop. Everything here is confidential, so please keep that in mind."

Misely nodded in the affirmative while Kent continued.

"We have filed suit on behalf of our client, Mrs. Sarah Gilvane, against one Arthur Slake. Slake is a con man. He's swindled Mrs. Gilvane out of nearly $37,000. He's some kind of securities sharpie. He sold Mrs. Gilvane a bunch of worthless stock and insurance."

Kent glanced back to the round-faced man and continued.

"Anyway, according to Sarah - Mrs. Gilvane - she was introduced to Slake through a friend. She's never told us who that friend is, but that is not relevant. You see, Mrs. Gilvane is... well, an elderly lady ... um, without a spouse."

Kent looked over again to the round-faced man. He was trying to communicate that Mrs. Gilvane was a gullible old maid without sounding insulting.

"She met Slake a few times in his swank downtown office and corresponded with him on several occasions. She started out with a few small investments and after a couple of appointments and friendly luncheons, Slake managed to extract a few thousand dollars more, followed by another few thousand dollars until, at the last luncheon he took Mrs. Gilvane for a $20,000 hit."

Mr. McCullough piped up from his corner chair. "Roger, I think the total is now $37,000." He then rested his chin on his chest and appeared to go back to his nap.

"Slake is a manipulator. His correspondence with Mrs. Gilvane is a textbook demonstration of how a conscienceless con man can prey upon a susceptible personality."

He unconsciously tapped his fingers on the closed manila file folder before him.

"Ollie, do you want to chime in here?"

The round-faced man stood up. "Mr. Misely, I'm Oliver Choate - the new guy here." He smiled, humbly, giving the appearance of a bashful kitten.

"Sarah Gilvane is my aunt. That's why this firm has the case."

Misely hopped out of his chair and shook hands with Choate. Choate grinned, his white skin turning a bashful pink.

"Aunt Sarah was taken in by Slake. He's a crass Svengali. First, it was business - some worthless stock - some fake insurance - and then came the lunches and the love letters. Before you know it, my aunt had been swindled out of $37,000. And she would've gone back for more if my cousins hadn't discovered the losses and intervened."

Ollie chuckled and gave a sheepish grin. "My cousins check in with her constantly, now. Aunt Sarah doesn't drive anymore but she is quite adept at getting out and about using the streetcar system - to the surprise of my cousins." He chuckled some more. "No one had any idea she was leaving her apartment and taking the streetcar down to the City of all places."

Misely interjected. "So you filed suit and the constable hasn't been able to serve this Arthur Slake?"

Roger Kent took back the reins. "That's correct. It's the strangest thing. We know where this Slake is holed up. He's got a nice office in the Towers Building, downtown. Jeffrey Stock, the Chief Constable, has been over there himself trying to serve the process. Stock says that they can hear him in his office and can see that the lights are on. But of course, as soon as they knock on the door he clams-up and the lights go out. He plays possum, refusing to answer the door and receive the process."

Misely was about to speak, but Kent cut him off.

"And, yes, the constables have stationed themselves in the lobby by the elevator in the mornings and late afternoons, waiting to catch him as he comes or goes from his office. They never see him. And they are no fools. They deal with these kinds of characters all the time. Somehow, Slake is able to get past the constables without them recognizing him."

"Is there another way to get to the office - back stairs - a fire escape - anything like that?"

"Well, I've been over to the building myself, just to figure out why the constables can't serve my papers, so I know the lay of the land. There are stairs that empty directly into the lobby, so anyone using the stairs would have to get through the lobby past the constable. There's no fire escape because the building is surrounded on three sides by adjoining buildings. Unless your office fronts on the street, you don't have a window. And, unless Slake is scaling the front of the building with a rope every day like a mountaineer, he's got to be waltzing right past the constable in some sort of disguise."

"Why doesn't the constable just perch himself in front of Slake's office every day. Why try to intercept him in the lobby? Wouldn't that work?"

Kent looked pained. "Well, of course that would work, Mr. Misely, if the building manager allowed it. But he doesn't. He makes the constables stay in the lobby, only allowing them up to Slake's floor twice a day. Such are the rules. Apparently the management does not allow the public at large to wander around inside the building. They patrol periodically, trying to catch door-to-door salesmen and other undesirables. Stock told me that the building manager is ex-military and has sympathy for the constables' situation, but that the owner does not like having uniformed constables wandering around inside the building as it might indicate some sort of trouble - which would reduce the appeal of the building to prospective tenants. But the constables are allowed a few quick trips up per day and then they have to lay low in the lobby."

"Is there a back entrance to the building - a way to avoid the lobby?"

"No. There is no alley in the rear or sides of the building. Everything comes in through the front lobby. That's why I figured he's been heavily disguised."

"You must have a photo of Slake?"

Kent chuckled. "Oh he's given us a wonderful photograph." Kent opened the file folder and removed a glossy, four-color pamphlet, handing over to Misely.

"This is his 'prospectus' I guess you'd call it."

A smiling face looked out from the front page of the pamphlet emblazoned with the words, "Amalgamated Commodities." The text was placed behind the head for dramatic effect. The words "Arthur L. Slake, Investment Advisor," were placed below the face in a starkly formal typeface, giving an impression of great seriousness. The face belonged to a mid-30's model of corporate exuberance and confidence. Blonde-haired and with smooth features, the face's sole, apparent physical flaw was a chipped front tooth which blazed forth, brightly, from a mouth full of otherwise perfect white teeth, courtesy of some obvious retouching.

Misely checked-out the brochure. There were some small charts and graphs, each indicating unabated earnings growth over an unspecified time period. The text seemed to be a pastiche of accounting gobbledygook that barely formed sentences.

"May I hang onto this?"

"Of course." Kent reached into the file and produced an envelope. "This is the process - the Bill of Complaint and trial notification." He held up the fat business envelope, which was addressed to no one. "Stock's men exhausted two service periods without luck and we have about 14 days left on this third set."

Misely understood the system and was thinking quickly about his favorite topic, his consulting fees. He knew that a process server was given only 21 days to serve before the process issuance expired. A fresh issue date would then have to be set by the court clerk - at an additional expense of $22.00. The constable's fees cost an additional $35.00 per issuance. They had already wasted over a hundred dollars with no results.

Kent looked over at Choate and began the delicate discussion of Misely's fees.

"So Mr. Misely, what sort of fees do you charge for serving process and signing the 'return' for the Clerk? Do they regulate that kind of thing?" Kent knew that the fees of a private process server were not regulated, but wanted to convey his earnest interest in keeping the fee as low as possible.

Misely glanced over at Choate. He saw possibilities. 'Ollie,' being a new associate, was probably not that important to the firm at the moment, but could become an invaluable contact for Misely in the future. McCullough was virtually furloughed for good and he gauged that Kent would not be far behind. They would - Ollie would - need an associate in the not too distant future. He noticed that McCullough was definitely sleeping, now.

"Well, I sympathize with Mrs. Gilvane's plight. And I have to say that I would very much enjoy the opportunity of working with your firm on this case."

He sat back in his chair and looked up at the ceiling, resting his fingertips together on his chest in a demonstration of great mental concentration. The trance broke seconds later and he hunched forward in the chair, looking over at Choate and then directly into the eyes of Kent.

"Mrs. Gilvane is obviously in a bad way, financially, so I propose simply collecting the same $35.00 fee that you would have paid to the constable's office, plus any small, additional expenses for things like car fare."

Kent nearly fell out of his chair with relief. His firm had been fronting the money for the attempts at service and this was a boon. He would have been willing to go as high as $100.

"That's just fine Mr. Misely, we all appreciate your being so reasonable. No wonder Honora spoke so highly of you!" He stood up and reached over the desk shaking Misely's hand in affirmation.

"Now - is there anything else you need?"

"You had said that there was correspondence. May I take a look at a sample?"

Kent would have been a little uncomfortable in having a mere process server review confidential client correspondence, but he figured that it was a minor concession when weighed against the value of Misely's dedication to his task - and reasonable pricing. He looked over at Choate, who nodded in the affirmative, and plucked three sheets of letter-sized notepaper from the folder.

"Here's the correspondence from Slake. You see, we'll have him dead to rights once we get him served. He hand-wrote these letters on his notepaper. He's a bold character."

Misely quickly read through the letters. The paper was of top quality and had the same "Amalgamated Commodities" typeface at the top of the paper, with Slake's office address and phone number: "Suite 804, Towers Building, RO5–2241." Slake understood the value of proper penmanship. His very deliberate hand delivered his florid text firmly and accurately into the pages.

The letters were saccharine affirmations of devotion, beginning with the inappropriately personal salutation: "My Dearest Sarah" and continuing with prose of wholesale flattery: "Since our last wonderful lunch together I have had time to dwell upon my good fortune in making your acquaintance, as a man seldom encounters a woman of both rare beauty and bounteous intelligence ..." The letters were are all similar; eely efforts to goad Mrs. Gilvane to continue investing, followed by the promise of another afternoon's luncheon at "their" favorite French restaurant, "L' Amour du Coeur."

Misely was more interested in the notepaper. He was thinking about his efforts earlier that day in deciphering his uncle's papier-mâché bowl note. He turned around in his chair and held the pages up to the window behind him, turning the pages, one by one, gently at several angles, trying to catch the light. He could see impressions of text from previous notes, thanks to Slakes's very strong hand. Most of the impressions were obliterated by the text on the page, except for on one page. He could make something out in the upper left-hand corner - perhaps an addressee's name? Kent and Choate watched Misely with great interest; spellbound suckers at a séance.

"What do you see, Mr. Misely?"

"Well there's an impression of something up in the corner, probably part of one of Slake's earlier notes. Would you mind if I lightly trace a pencil over the corner? We can erase it once I'm done?"

Kent looked over at Choate who was already nodding in the affirmative. "Yes, go right ahead."

He grabbed a lead pencil from the conference room table and began to softly rub the lead over the lettering, massaging every gentle crease, forcing out some truncated text, which appeared as white script against a charcoal grey background. Choate left his seat and stood behind Misely, watching with great interest.

The effort had produced part of a date at the top: "August 21, 1959" and the text:

"Star Se...

Class..."

Choate squinted his eyes at the page, disappointed. "Not much to write home about, pardon the pun." He giggled, his cherub's face turning a light pink.

Roger Kent reached over the table. "Here, let me have a look."

Kent removed his glasses and held the paper up to the light. "A date from last month and 'Stars and Class?' Doesn't help us too much? What do you make of it Mr. Misely?"

Misely actually understood what he saw, but did not want to give up the tiny clue at this point – at least not yet.

"It's hard to say Mr. Kent. Best not to speculate." He handed the page over to Kent. "Have you brought the police in?"

"Well, we tried. We spoke with the State's Securities Division, but, not surprisingly, they told us that, for the time being, this is a civil matter. Mrs. Gilvane made the 'investments' of her own free will. We need to provide evidence that Slake knowingly pawned off worthless stock with the intent to defraud. Hopefully our civil suit will generate the necessary evidence to bring him to justice. But for now, we need to get him into court to get back Sarah Gilvane's money."

Misely nodded. "Understood. Well, I've taken up enough of your time. Let me get to this task."

Hands were shaken all around, causing McCullough to rouse himself back to attention. Arrangements were made. Misely would stay in phone contact with Ollie Choate and give daily progress reports. Kent handed over the process and gave Misely a friendly slap on the back. "Go get 'em, tiger!" And Misely was off.

Walking on his way back to 7 North Central, he thought that the job couldn't be all that difficult? The constables were bright men but probably didn't devote themselves as fully to the task as a private process server would. They couldn't be expected to divine Slake's presence through a successful disguise. There were limits. And the $35 could still be a good fee - if he were only able to serve Slake, quickly, without a lot of time spent hanging around the Towers Building.

Coincidently, at that very moment, Arthur Slake was seated at his desk in Suite 804, looking at a copy of his 'prospectus.' He was admiring his own photograph. He knew he was a handsome man. He gently rubbed his left hand along the sides of his face. Yes, very handsome and it was paying off. He continued stroking his face, feeling the depression just above the left jaw line caused by the scar tissue - but that incident was from a time long ago. He had learned his lesson…and the scar was barely noticeable in ordinary light and completely invisible in the photograph. No wonder his 'clients' felt him irresistible. He looked at his neatly groomed blonde hair in the photograph. Unconsciously, he tugged at the nape of his neck and adjusted the blonde hairpiece He didn't like wearing it, but sacrifices had to be made.

He held the prospectus before him, again, gently turning it, allowing the overhead fluorescent light to dance against the glossy paper. He liked the fact that the photo revealed his chipped tooth - it presented his rugged side - a too perfect face would make it difficult for male clientele to relate to him. Not that he presently served a single male customer.

Slake plucked a small notepad from the breast pocket his suit coat. He prided himself on his ability to avoid capture by never leaving a trail. The tiny notebook was his ledger, address book and appointment calendar, all in one. He had no further office appointments, today, but was satisfied with the list of phone prospects.

Suite 804 suited him perfectly. It was one of the furnished units. It came with desk, chairs, small sofa end tables, a small file cabinet and a telephone. It was all he needed. There was no window - always useful should the need for a hasty exit arise - but the lack of a window kept the office affordable. And he had found a way to enter and exit that mooted any need for a window. He chuckled to himself over his good fortune. And it helped that he had found the perfect partner and just in the nick of time. Things had gotten a little hot in the Big Apple. But there were sufficient fish in the sea down here. He had a steady catch of routine rubes - and he didn't mind sharing those, once the monthly accounting was done. But holding Mrs. Gilvane out for himself was the right thing to do. Even partners had secrets.

Roderick was ecstatic over the new job. He considered having an early lunch over at County Restaurant, but decided to patronize the hot dog vendor stationed outside on the manicured park grounds of the courthouse. He purchased two dogs and double-wrapped each carefully in paper napkins. He squeezed them together into the left breast pocket of his suit coat. The right pocket held the process, in the fat business envelope, and the prospectus. He didn't want to take a chance at having mustard seep into the papers.

The Friday was stunningly beautiful and Roderick decided to take a walk towards the railroad trestle over Minebank Run. Even though the bridge was on the outskirts of old Elk Neck, it took him less than ten minutes to get there and to find a comfortable, grassy spot on the bank of the run. He unbuttoned his suit coat and carefully removed his brown oxfords and socks. He rolled his pants legs up, nearly to his knees, and dipped his feet into the chilly fresh water. The cold sensation temporarily cramped his left big toe, but he shook it off and relaxed, swirling his feet around in the flowing water. A light breeze, mixed with first warm, then cool air cascaded across his face. Breathing in, he felt the warm promise of spring balanced against the cool foreboding of fall. He was alone and was half-tempted to roll over onto his side for a nap - but he rallied.

He enjoyed his hot dogs and felt glad. The opportunity to work with Kent and McCullough was a break. He would make the most of it.

He eventually made his way back to 7 North Central. He pulled the copybook that served as his file ledger and a fresh manila folder from the filing cabinet crammed into his living quarters. He entered "C-59-31 Gilvane - Process" into the ledger and marked the file folder, accordingly. There was nothing yet to file, though. He had to hang onto the 'prospectus' to help identify his target. And he needed a better way to cart around the fat process envelope. He didn't want the envelope to give out through wear and tear in his suit coat pocket.

He remembered the pink pencil case that he had come across among the boxes of salvageable junk left behind by the former tenant. He sat himself at his desk in the office anteroom and pulled open the top drawer. There it was, sitting below a clutch of pencils and pens. He pulled it forward, causing the pencils and pens to scatter into the drawer like pickup sticks. He held it up and felt the rubbery material. It would do perfectly, despite the purple ink stain permanently tattooed on its surface. He stuffed the process into the pencil case and pulled the reluctant zipper across. He simply needed Slake to voluntarily receive that pencil case and its contents. How difficult could it be?

Had a disinterested observer viewed the scene at 7 North Central, later in the afternoon, such an observer may have noticed a nicely dressed, middle aged gentleman in a light blue seersucker suit, ambling down the two stories of wooden steps to the pavement below. The man would have been seen standing at the corner at Franklin and embarking the streetcar leading to the City. The streetcar may have been seen stopping on Prince Street, directly across the street from the Towers Building.

3:30 in the afternoon found the lobby of the Towers Building facing the inevitable mid-day lull. The lunchtime crowd had abated and it was too early for the even the earliest participants of the rush hour ritual. The revolving doors were at rest. The grey-haired man in the seersucker suit walked unnoticed past the building manager stationed at the front desk of the lobby, across from the bank of elevators and stairs.

Misely took the elevator to the eighth floor and walked quietly to room 804. He pressed his ear gently to the wooden door and listened. He thought heard a chair being pulled across the floor, but it was difficult to tell. He dropped down to the floor. The slit between the doorframe and floor was minute - at best he could tell that a light was on inside the office. He figured the door would be locked. He stood up and gingerly grasped the lever-styled door handle, moving it ever so gently. It moved only slightly in the catch. The door was locked. Not that he could have simply walked through an unlocked door of a private office, unannounced. The rules for serving process were strict. An elisor could not barge into a home or office. The process could not be dropped at the door. The process had to reach the hand of the recipient - and the report or "return" of the process server had to attest to such. A failure in serving the process meant that the court had no jurisdiction over the individual - and that ongoing efforts in a case could be for naught.

He rapped at the door. "Delivery for Arthur Slake." He rapped fiercely a few more times. "Mr. Arthur Slake? Are you there, sir? I have a delivery for you!"

But there was no answer - and no discernible movement behind the thick door. Misely rapped again, even harder, and felt a sharp twinge of discomfort in his knuckles. "Mr. Slake - I have a delivery for you. Would you please open up, sir?" He had barked the request. A fellow tenant down the hall opened his door out of curiosity and peeped down the hallway, retreating quickly with disinterest.

Misely dropped back down to the floor and saw that the office light had been turned off. Slake was playing possum.

He took the elevator back to the lobby and decided to wait there for his prey. Stationed directly below and along side the manager's desk were three overstuffed armchairs, used for building visitors. He took the middle seat right below the desk that most directly faced the elevators. He pulled the prospectus from his breast pocket for one more look.

The afternoon wore on. Deliverymen and couriers came and went - some, with larger deliveries, first announcing themselves to the man at the manager's desk. A few tenants or customers came and went, but Misely could not see Slake's face in any of theirs. He was able to manage the surveillance while still seated in the chair.

Finally, the Friday afternoon rush hour broke, starting as trickle of people and soon building to a flood of humanity, pouring out of either of the two elevators or through the stairway that emptied into the lobby. Misely had to stand and face the crowd heading towards the building doors for any chance of finding Slake. Looking for Slake's features among the onslaught seemed nearly impossible task. He soon realized why the constables had not succeeded.

By 6:30 PM, the cascade had resolved back to a trickle. Misely decided to visit 804, again, to see if Slake was still in the office; he certainly had not spied him among the exiting crowd. He walked gently over to the office and dropped to the hallway floor. He saw no light through the tiny crack. He stood and placed his ear, gently, against the door. He heard no sound. It was not possible to tell whether Slake was still playing possum or had left the office. Eventually, the man would have to dine and sleep. He was human.

Misely was feeling tired and hungry, himself. He got back on the elevator and fumbled looking for the "L" button for "lobby" nearly hitting "B" by mistake. As much as he wanted to take the streetcar back home, he knew he had to wait things out for at least another hour. It was misery - but certainly a misery he was well used to, by now.

He could no longer perch himself in the lobby. The building manager would become suspicious of the omnipresent man loitering after normal business hours, so he stood in front of the building waiting for the departure of the latecomers. He could not find Slake's face among those of the stragglers. Finally, at 7:30 PM he walked around the corner to catch the streetcar back home.

"Globokar - where's the doggy bag?" Slake shook his head in disgust. "I wanted that corn bread for breakfast tomorrow." He was angry.

"Stop calling me that. I told you before - I will not converse with you if you insist on using an inaccurate appellation." Goodley's face went beet red.

Slake smiled to himself. He enjoyed riling-up "Doctor A. T. Goodley." Whenever Goodley got mad, his "English" accent eroded, exposing his distinctly Hungarian lilt. And he genuinely enjoyed hearing Goodley's 'all too proper' English vocabulary.

"O.K., 'Goodley' - are you going to run back around the corner to get me my food or are you going to make me do it - presuming it hasn't been tossed out already."

"Get it yourself if it's that important. I can live without my chicken wing…"

Slake decided to drop it. There were other things to discuss. "Never mind." He saw that Goodley was getting ready to turn in.

"Let's cut to the chase, Doctor. I don't mind paying for the meals. But your little pill-pushing operation has not been bringing home the bacon - at least not the pork I thought I'd see. I've held-up my end. I've been reeling in idiots right and left. But the arrangement is getting a little unbalanced. What are you doing here all day? Sitting around in this hell hole waiting for the phone to ring?"

The attack surprised "Goodley," putting him off-balance.

"What do you mean? We split my $800 last week! Do you remember that?" He was sitting on the edge of his cot dressed in his undershirt and suit pants. He still had the suspenders over his shoulders. He had loosened the bindings of the male girdle worn beneath his undershirt and pants. His flabby gut stretched the undershirt and folds of the girdle over his waistband.

"Of course, but did you forget my $900 from last month - and the fact that I am paying for all of my office, half of yours and both of our ads? Your operation has not grown at all, while mine has. If we stick to the 50-50 split I will soon be supporting you. Maybe I could take you off my taxes as a dependent?" Slake shook his head in disgust and chuckled at his own joke. He thought it all the more humorous because he hadn't filed a tax return in a dozen years.

Goodley rallied. "Hold on, Slake - we have a deal. Look, my practice is the medical arts. It's not like the sales job you have. You can't treat patients like mere rubes purchasing watered stock. Each patient's needs are unique; each prescriptive regimen individualized. There is no way to predict income with absolute certainty, unlike your securities sales."

Goodley had retreated back to the file cabinet behind the cot to complete changing into his pajamas. He rolled his pants and shirt together and put them in the second drawer of the cabinet, on top of a dirty carpet bag.

Slake's jaw had dropped. He looked to the grimy ceiling and bellowed out a laugh.

"Doctor - you've been popping too many of your own pills! You've become delusional! You're believing your own hyperbole! 'Medical arts?'" Slake then made a quacking sound, imitating a duck.

Goodley refused to respond.

"Okay - look let's drop this for now, but you have to do what I suggested. Unglue yourself from that phone. Get out and do something. Try some 'customer outreach.' I hold investment seminars. It's easy to rent a hall and drum up audience with ads and flyers. Just put the word 'free' in the ad. My seminars made me a lot of money in New York."

Goodley mumbled something. He was under the covers of his cot.

"Come again?"

"I said, if things were so good in New York, why are you here?"

Misely considered dropping into County Restaurant for dinner, but the hour was late and he was more tired than hungry. He trudged up the two long flights of wooden stairs along the side of 7 North Central and retreated into his quarters. He carefully hung the blue seersucker suit back into its assigned spot in the metal wardrobe. The door initially refused to close and he absent-mindedly kicked the door at a spot on the bottom; another victory notched for the laws of physics.

He sat on the edge of his cot, waiting for the can of beef stew to warm on the hot plate. He hoped he had not bitten off more than he could chew. How had Slake managed to get past him at the end of the day? He must have been well disguised and planned his departure to coincide with the worst of the rush. And whatever disguise was getting him in and out of the building must be sitting somewhere in that office during the day, while Slake was trussed-up in normal business attire. If he could get into the office on some pretense, he could look for the disguise. He couldn't serve the process on Slake based upon an entry by false pretense - but just knowing what disguise to look for would be invaluable. And finding a clue as to where the man laid his head at night would be perfectly fine, too. It didn't matter where he served him.

Misely took a break from the case over the weekend. Most offices did not maintain Saturday hours and he would stick out like a sore thumb if he hung around a quiet lobby. Instead, he had decided to clean his living quarters. If he waited too long, winter would arrive making it difficult to bleach out the walls and floor of his shower stall. He would have to open the nearly never opened windows to accomplish the task. Although the place had been delivered in an alleged "broom clean" condition years earlier, Roderick had come to understand that it did not stay in that condition, irrespective of how carefully one wiped one's feet.

8:00 AM the following Monday morning found the Towers Building slowly absorbing the trickle of weary office workers. The man in the black suit and dark tie leaned against the outside of the building scanning the sports section of a day old Star

Sentinel. The man had greasy black hair and odd-looking eyebrows - burnt umber brown and a little powdery looking, at that. But he was virtually invisible to the steadily increasing stream of office workers, all of whom were too absorbed in their own concerns to care very much about a fellow drone.

Misely had been stationed outside the building since 7:00 AM, when the doors were unlocked for the day's business. The throng increased over the next hour, exponentially. Misely struggled but felt certain that every face was viewed sufficiently for him to identify Slake. He could not divine the face of Slake from among those of the incoming crowd.

At a little after 9:00 AM, Misely decided it was safe to take a seat among the chairs in the lobby. One came free as he entered and he turned his attention to the final stragglers of the morning rush. He was getting bored. As the flood turned to a trickle, he amused himself by guessing which floor a given person would exit, by watching the dial indicator above each elevator.

By 10:00 AM, he decided to visit Slake's office and confirm that Slake had not entered the building. He stooped down in front of the door to 804. Unbelievably, the lights were on in the office. He stood and gently pressed his ear against the door. Yes, he heard a man's voice probably speaking on the telephone! Slake had gotten past him, somehow. But how?

He waited until he could no longer hear the voice and took another stab at serving the process. He rapped sharply against the door, three times. "Mr. Slake - I have a delivery for you. Could you open the door, please?"

The request was met with silence. He knocked harder, three more times. "Arthur Slake - open the door please for a delivery!"

More silence.

Misely got back down to floor level and saw that the lights had been turned off. He felt defeated. He gave three more distinct raps. "Mr. Slake - I'm not going to give up. I just need you to open the door and receive my delivery."

More silence.

He timed himself to wait for three long minutes, hoping Slake would stick his head out the door. Slake did not. He rapped again three more times.

"Mr. Slake, please open up for a delivery."

He had barked out the command, but there was no movement. Misely gave up for the time being. As he walked down the hall towards the elevator, coincidently, the elevator arrived and coughed up the building manager, who appeared to be in a state of agitation. He looked directly at Misely, who had lowered his head to pass.

"You - you there. What are you doing up here?"

Misely stalled. "Pardon - are you addressing me?"

"Yes, I'm 'addressing' you. We've had a complaint about noise on this floor and that a salesman was up here bothering people. Would you now anything about that?"

"I am not a salesman, sir. I am on business. In fact my business here this morning is completed, thank you."

Misely hit the "down" button and the doors opened, ending the uncomfortable standoff and leaving the building manager to continue his patrol of the eighth floor.

'That rat.' Misely figured that Slake must have phoned down to the manager's desk. Well, why not return the favor?

Misely walked up to the manager's desk, now unattended, and picked up the nameplate. "Wm. Pyvak, Building Manager." He replaced the object and spied the payphone in the lobby in the corner near the entry doors. He pulled the prospectus out of his jacket pocket and dialed the phone number. Slake picked up on the third ring.

"Amalgamated Commodities, Arthur Slake, here. It's a beautiful day to make your financial dreams come true! How may I assist you?"

"Yes, Mr. Slake. This is Pyvak, your building manager. I believe you had called earlier with a complaint about noise? It was a false alarm, Mr. Slake. There was no one up there. I just wasted part of my morning on your false alarm." He spat out the terse response with venom, leaving no room for a reply. "Please be careful about filing false alarms in the future. It is not appreciated."

Slake sat shell-shocked at his desk, holding the phone to his ear, hearing only the ringing sound of a dial tone. He placed the handset back in the cradle. How had the manager figured out who had placed the call? He had disguised his voice and the request to "please get to the eighth floor to toss-out a salesman banging on doors" was so short...

He would have to be more careful. He couldn't afford to get on the wrong side of the building manager...especially with process servers hot on his trail - a little detail he dared not share with Globokar at this time...

Misely racked the handset back into the payphone cradle. He figured the call would give Slake a little food for thought for the next time. But he was done for now. Thanks to Slake, he would not be able to hang around the premises. He'd have to adopt a different disguise and come back later.

As Misely was about to head out the revolving door, he saw the glassed-in notice board, just next to the building directory near the phone booth. Several formal announcements relating to building safety, hours of operation and building regulations were neatly organized and tacked onto the board. He studied the papers. In each case, the directives were neatly typed-up on the very expensive looking letterhead of the building owner, "Dynamic Realty Resources, Ltd." The letterhead featured a color engraving of an impressive office building standing next to the company's name. Each missive was signed by a "Christopher A. Caples, Assistant Vice-President."

Misely retrieved the small note pad from his pocket and made some quick notes. He slapped the pad shut and departed through the revolving doors - just in time, as the manager had disembarked from the elevator and was heading back to his station.

Marguerite Laidlaw was happy to assist the man. He was only the second customer that morning; things had been fairly slow so far. "R.T. Mossley," like a lot of the other Dalrymple Stationers customers, had come via 'word of mouth.' And of course it did not hurt that Dalrymple's was the premier stationer in the metropolitan area. She had never heard of Mossley's company, though. And Mossley seemed like a nice enough man, although she couldn't help but notice that he was definitely using some kind of makeup to darken his eyebrows. And the greasy black hairpiece was a ludicrous fraud. 'Male pride!' she thought.

"Yes Mr. Mossley. I know exactly the letterhead you are describing. It really is a fine specimen! I think the color engraving of the building is spectacular!" She strutted over to an olive green filing cabinet behind her desk and thumbed through the neatly organized folders in the second drawer. The "D's" were not too far back.

The customer nodded agreeably. "Our art department is working on the color graphic for the watch and having a sample of the other company's letterhead and envelope will really help sell them on placing the order, here!"

"Well that sounds like a good idea to us," she beamed. She handed over two sample pages of the letterhead and accompanying envelopes.

"Just look at the quality of the engraving. We really do the best work!"

And, moments later, "R.T. Mossley" could be seen exiting the building at Claypoole Street with a crisp, white Dalrymple Stationers paper bag in tow.

Misely was not done for the day. After taking the streetcar back to 7 North Central, he shed the black suit and disguise for his always comfortable brown suit, button down shirt and dull necktie. He left the stationary in the bag on his desk and elected an early lunch, just around the corner, at County Restaurant.

Mrs. Georgelus, standing next to the wooden podium in the entry alcove, fell into a virtual fit of exuberance upon seeing her faithful customer. Misely felt that her shriek of welcome, although substantial, had caused no further damage to his hearing and decided to take a seat at the counter. He spied an abandoned copy of the morning's Star Sentinel and paged back to the classified ads.

And there it was: the advertisement for "Amalgamated Commodities, Arthur L. Slake Investment Advisor." The ad featured a reproduction of the prospectus photo, but due to the reduced quality of the bulky newspaper print, Slake's chipped tooth was exaggerated, giving Slake's feature s a decidedly 'rustic' appearance.

The 'pitch' encouraged those interested in "turning the tables on the Wall Street insiders," to pick up the phone for a free consultation with Arthur L. Slake, a seasoned Wall Street veteran and preeminent investment advisor who had "seen the light" and wanted nothing more, now, than to help the "average hard-working American" achieve the same success as their wealthy, far less hard-working cosmopolitan counterparts.

Roderick enjoyed shrimp haloumi and iced tea. He polished-off several packet of saltine crackers before paying the bill and working his way back around the corner with the discarded Star Sentinel under his arm.

He checked his pocket. He had enough change to make a phone call so he went directly over to the Graham Independent Free Public Library and perched himself in the phone booth on the first floor near the rear stairs - his favorite. He looked up the number for the Star Sentinel's Classified Department in the paper and reviewed his notes from his note pad. Based on the revelations of the one love letter, he believed that Slake had written a letter to the "Star Sentinel Classified," dated August 21. He was curious about its contents.

"Classifieds - Nell Burton speaking."

"Good afternoon Miss Burton. This is Arthur Slake of Amalgamated Commodities. I was hoping you could assist me with my account?"

"Of course Mr. Slake."

"Could you check my account to make sure that you received my correspondence of this past August 21st?"

"Hang on Mr. Slake." Misely could hear the sounds of the creaky wheels of a desk chair moving out from behind a desk. Within a few moments, Miss Burton returned to the line.

"I've got your file, here, Mr. Slake, and I see that we did get your payment back in August."

"Ah excellent."

"Did you want any change made to your account?

Misely decided to improvise. "Yes, unfortunately I need to cancel my ad, immediately and would like the appropriate refund for the ads not yet run."

There was a puzzled pause.

"Of course, Mr. Slake. We're sorry to lose your business, though. Is this a temporary development? If you're revamping your ad, you can keep the account open and you can just send us the new copy and new publication dates?" Miss Burton figured the answer would be 'no,' but was giving it everything she had...

"Well, unfortunately, at this time I'll just need to cancel - but one never knows what the future will bring!" Slake sounded positively cheery.

"Understood - did you mean to cancel both ads?"

"Excuse me?"

"Did you mean to cancel Dr. Goodley's ad, too?"

Improvising again Roderick responded enthusiastically. "Yes, please, Dr. Goodley's ad too!"

Roderick was wondering exactly who Dr. Goodley was, but figured any friend of Slake deserved whatever he got.

"Okay Mr. Slake. I'll take care of that. Oh, wait a minute. Dr. Goodley had also placed a secured credit deposit of $20.00 with us back in December when he started the account. Did you want us to send that to him separately?"

"Uh... no, if you send it to me, I will adjust with Dr. Goodley. As for the address, please send the refund to my home address and not my office. Do you have that address?"

"No sir - just your office address, but if you give it to me I can do that."

"Ah, never mind - thanks. The office address is probably better anyway. Do you have an up to date address for Dr. Goodley?"

She was wondering why it mattered as the account was obviously being closed. And she chuckled to herself, remembering that they had required the $20.00 advance from Goodley because he would only give out his post office box.

"Well it's the same as in the ad, Mr. Slake. The post office box. It's all we have on him currently." She was wondering just what sort of partners these two were. It sounded like Slake barely knew anything about Goodley. But then again, the Classifieds always brought out the kooks...

"Ah yes - understood. Thank you so much for the assistance!"

Misely sat in the booth and anxiously flipped the pages of his Star Sentinel back to the Classifieds again. He quickly scanned up and down the columns until he found the ad:

Dr. A.T. Goodly, Master of Medical Arts, announces his "Reduce Now" dietary compound. Lose weight quickly and simply. Let the science of nutrition and art of metabolic synergy help you achieve the thinner you." Enquire Box 1127 Suite 1600 Rickenhoefer Building for your complementary informational package. Discretion assured.

Misely was ecstatic. There was some sort of connection between the two charlatans. If he could find Goodley, he could find Slake. He knew from past cases that the 16th floor of the Rickenhoefer building was a notorious mail drop service. A person could take out a box there and arrange to pick up or have the mail forwarded as directed. Visiting the building was a waste of time, but he could send away for the brochure. It might just have an office address or phone number for Goodley.

Later that evening, had a disinterested person viewed the scene at 7 North Central, such an observer may have noted a brown-suited man busily working at his office desk, first composing and then carefully typing a letter on the beautifully pressed, high rag content letterhead of Dynamic Realty Resources, Ltd. Later, the same brown-suited man would have been seen typing a second letter on entirely unremarkable and slightly yellowed plain bond paper. The second letter described the writer's lifetime discomfort over his weight. His "undeserved and unwarranted obesity" was said to be caused by "the misfortunes of heredity." The man would later have been seen bounding down the wooden stairs outside of the office and over to the mailbox at the corner of Franklin and Iroquois, where he deposited the two letters.

Tuesday morning found Misely at the Towers building. He had donned the blue seersucker outfit and powdered his hair with white baby powder, approximating the look of a graying retiree. He was standing outside the building, again, at 7:00 AM, clutching a cup of coffee in a paper cup, with yesterday's Star Sentinel under his arm. He was ready to sift through another series of hard working faces.

But just like the day before, try as he could, he could not discern the face of Slake from among the faces in the crowd.

By 9:30 AM, the incoming stream of office workers was back to a trickle. Misely entered the building and took a seat in the lobby chair just below the manager's desk and pretended to read the paper. Pyvak was on the phone, reviewing a clipboard, occupied with coordinating an office furniture delivery for a tenant.

Just after 9:30, Misely noticed a particularly well-dressed, older woman enter the building. Her fox stole and expensive turquoise dress, alone, would have set her apart from every other ordinary office worker. But the diamond bracelet on her left wrist was positively other-worldly. As she walked confidently through the lobby towards the elevators, the sunlight played against the diamonds in the bracelet setting off beautiful fireworks of white light and colors, dazzling the walls of the otherwise spartan lobby. The bracelet appeared to be a white gold mesh at least two inches in width, stuffed with an array of diamonds. The diamonds seem to nearly overtake the bracelet as though overflowing from the wearer's wrist. Misely stared at the bracelet. It twinkled back a spellbinding retort of brilliance, communicating extraordinary wealth.

Curious, Misely watched the elevator dial and saw that the diminutive woman had taken the elevator to the 8th floor. He sat back and wondered if the lady was going to meet with Slake, presuming Slake had gotten up to his office somehow? He walked over to the building's directory and saw that, beside's Slake's office, most of the 8th floor was taken up with what appeared to be an import business. But there were a few single offices there for a trade union, a charitable foundation and an architect. He hoped for the lady's sake that she was on her way to one of the other offices.

By 10:00 AM, Misely felt it was time to make another trek up to Slake's office to see if Slake had somehow managed to sneak past his sentry. He had the pink pencil case in his breast pocket, but figured he would not even bother to try to serve Slake. He just wanted to confirm that Slake had gotten past him, again. As he was about to get out of the overstuffed chair, he saw the same lady in the fox stole exiting the elevator. But this time, there was little fanfare as she made her way across the lobby. She was no longer accompanied by the diamond bracelet.

Misely had a sick feeling. If the woman had met with Slake, she had likely just been cheated out of a king's ransom. He thought back to what Kent and Choate had said during their conference earlier in the week. Mrs. Gilvane had become adept at getting around and had been visiting Slake's office! He had a bad feeling that the lady walking to the front doors could be Mrs. Gilvane.

As she passed by, Misely pretended to read the paper, but barked out, "Mrs. Gilvane," watching to see if the woman reacted. She did. She slowed down and looked around to see who had spoken. And recognizing no one, she continued on her way out the front door.

Misely immediately headed over to the phone booth. He pulled his notepad out of his breast pocket and dialed the number for Kent and McCullough.

Ollie Choate had been occupied with the Nettlestone brief, due in just two days. He had asked not to be disturbed, but Honora had said that Misely had important news, so he thought he'd better take the call.

"Yes - Misely, what's the word? Did you serve Slake?"

"No, not yet. But I saw something over at the building I thought you would want to know about."

Choate was disappointed. He had a lot of work to do and did not want to waste his time chatting with a process server. "Okay Mr. Misely - but could you please make it quick?"

"Yes - my apologies. Listen, I saw an obviously well-to-do lady head up to the 8th floor - that's where Slake's office is located." Misely heard Choate breathe impatiently on the other end of the line.

"Anyway, the lady was wearing a lot of jewelry. At least, she was wearing it on the way in but not on the way out. Whoever she met with on the 8th floor must now have the jewelry."

Choate let out another sigh of frustration. "And how does this concern me?" He sounded annoyed.

"Well, I know you had said that Sarah Gilvane was able to manage her way downtown and I was afraid that she had made another visit to Slake."

"Describe the woman." Choate practically barked the command.

"Short, gray hair, well dressed. Had a fox stole on..."

"Short? Well that's not Sarah. Aunt Sarah is practically five feet, seven inches. And very thin. Was this woman thin?"

"No - she was probably a little chubby, actually."

"Well that's not Sarah. Look, Misely, my cousins have had Sarah under virtual lock and key since this happened. The odds of her slipping away and finding her way downtown are astronomical."

Misely persisted. "But when she walked by I called out loud, 'Mrs. Gilvane,' to see if she would react, and she did. She stopped and looked around. I just hid behind my newspaper."

"Well, that can't be Sa..." Choate stopped mid-syllable.

"Describe the woman again! No! The jewelry. Describe the jewelry!"

"A diamond bracelet. An incredible looking thing - a silver looking mesh band about two inches wide filled with diamonds."

Roderick could hear Choate moaning over the phone line.

"No - no - no!" He groaned some more.

"Mr. Choate?"

"That was Mother! Oh no, Mother, what have you done!! Those were the Choate Diamonds, Misely!! Oh no, no!!"

Roderick had to pull the phone away from his ear, due to the volume of Choate's wailing.

"Your mother?"

Choate continued to moan and mumble to himself.

"Yes, Misely. My mother. Mother's maiden name was Gilvane. She married a Choate. That's why she answered to Gilvane!" And Choate was back to moaning some more...

"Get over here right away Misely. We've got to get those diamonds back! Right now!"

And the directive was followed by the clack of a receiver being slammed back to rest and a dial tone.

Misely jumped out of the phone booth. He had worked some odd cases that took some strange turns, but he thought that this could top them all. He collected himself and began a dignified jog back over to the streetcar line around the corner on Holiday a block over.

He sat towards the front of the streetcar, mildly winded from his sprint, and wondered what Choate would have him do? He saw his reflection in the window and remembered that he was still in costume. He decided that, notwithstanding Choate's directive to come immediately, he needed to get back into his normal clothes. He didn't want his clients to know too much about his business techniques.

Within forty minutes, Misely was back in the waiting room of Kent and McCullough. Choate was already in the conference room, the door ajar, waiting for Misely's arrival. He heard the front door open and beckoned. "I see him Honora. Mr. Misely please come in." He smiled sweetly for Honora's benefit and then clicked the conference door closed behind the two.

"Dammit Misely, how could you let this happen!"

Misely was only mildly surprised. He hadn't even sat down, yet. He decided to sit down and let Choate continue.

"I can't believe you let a defenseless lady go up on the elevator to see Slake!" He pulled out a chair, sat, and rubbed his face with his hands. The silence went on for several uncomfortable moments.

"Well, that was stupid, wasn't it?" He looked over at Misely, exposing his beet red face. "I'm sorry for that Mr. Misely. I'm just very upset. Those jewels mean everything to our family. It is our legacy. The Choate Diamonds have been handed down through the generations through the Hohenzollern line. Father was always too generous with the bracelet, allowing mother to wear it out for special occasions. It belongs in a bank vault, Mr. Misely. And now it's gone!"

Misely thought that Choate was beginning to weep.

"Mr. Choate, are you sure it was your mother? I could have been wrong?"

Ollie stopped rubbing his face long enough to look up. "Oh, no that was Mother. I phoned her all morning waiting for her to get back. She finally picked up and told all. Aunt Sarah had recommended Slake to her. Isn't that nice? Slake promised to use the bracelet purely as collateral for a series of investments that he personally guaranteed would make the Choate family wealthy for all ages! Unbelievable! The diamonds, alone, had guaranteed our wealth for all ages! And now they are gone!" Choate seemed to be crying, again.

Misely couldn't think of much to say. "Is your mother okay?"

Choate looked up, angrily. "Mother? Oh yes, Mother is on cloud nine! She's ecstatic over her investment decision - Slake even gave her a hand-written receipt for the 'collateral!' She's doing just wonderfully, thank you! I'm the one in trouble, here, Misely!"

"Yes, of course, sorry. How would you like me to help you?"

"Hmm… well, what do you think?" Choate's cynicism was positively venomous. "How about getting that bracelet back for starters! Look, I wasn't born yesterday. I know how you and your kind work. You can accomplish things that the police cannot. Get me back that bracelet Misely and you will be well rewarded! I mean it - I, and everyone in this firm, will be eternally indebted to you. Can you do it?"

Misely was shocked. A golden ring had been extended for his grasp. The reward for returning the diamonds could be substantial. And the opportunity to gain an apprenticeship from Choate would be priceless.

"Yes, Mr. Choate. I would like to undertake to retrieve your bracelet."

The two shook hands and Misely reiterated his promise to check-in with Choate, daily, on both matters.

Misely was back at 7 North Central sitting at his desk in his neat office anteroom. He had just entered the new case into the copybook ledger and had prepared the accompanying file folder: "C-59-32 Choate Bracelet."

Misely considered his next move. Serving process was subject to many rules designed to engender fair play. A process server could not use a ruse or artifice to trick a target into receiving service. The days of delivering process disguised in a gift box were long past. But retrieving stolen property had far fewer rules - and taking back something like the Choate Diamonds - perhaps none? He knew that it would be more important than ever to gain entry to Slake's office. Slake would have to stash the bracelet somewhere - and keeping it close at hand would be the natural human instinct.

Misely unconsciously opened the top drawer of his desk and grasped the lip of the front panel with his left hand. He had really bitten off a lot. But he was determined to make the most of the opportunity. He didn't want to bother returning to the Towers Building that afternoon. Waiting around to look for Slake was a dead end. He could occupy himself the rest of the day cleaning up a few older cases. He had wanted to track down Dusty Blackwell about that property deed he had come across that could interest the church. But he secretly couldn't wait until tomorrow when he just might find himself face to face with Slake.

Wednesday morning's mail was delivered to the Towers Building by 10:00 AM. But Bill Pyvak was puzzled. The letter was from Chris Caples, all right - but not one single tenant had ever complained about electrical outages. Orders were orders, though, and these orders instructed him to turn over the passkey to the electrical engineer upon arrival. That smarted, a little. He should be accompanying the guy - Matsley or whatever his name was - to the particular office to let him in himself. That was his job. Why on earth would Caples have him give up the key to a stranger? And why didn't Caples just call him first. It didn't make sense.

He had considered making a call over to Chris ever since receiving the letter. Several times during the morning he found himself dialing the first few numbers of the exchange and then hanging up.

Later in the morning he looked at the letter again. As he put the letter aside, he saw the man in the white lab coat enter the building. He was holding a clipboard and carrying a catalog case. He proceeded in a deliberate fashion to Pyvak's desk.

"Mr. Pyvak, I'm Robert Matsley. Hopefully, Mr. Caples forwarded his instruction to provide me with the office master key in order to complete my electrical inspection? Here is my card."

Pyvak took a close look at the business card. The man had several letters after his name. The title "Master Electrical Engineer" was impressive.

"Yes, Mr. Caples informed me that you would be here to do your work. Now, can I suggest that you allow me to provide you with an escort to the offices you need to work on? It would be no trouble?"

Matsley winced and moved closer to Pyvak, making certain that no eavesdroppers were near. Dropping his voice he said: "I'm sorry Mr. Pyvak. He specifically instructed me to handle the inspections, solo. I just follow orders."

Pyvak was wounded, but understood how the chain of command worked. Reluctantly, he handed over the passkey to Matsley.

'Matsley' took the elevator directly to the 8th floor. He knocked on the door to suite 804 twice.

"Mr. Slake, this is Robert Matsley, electrical engineer. I'm here to do an inspection. Could you open up so that I can proceed with my work? Mr. Slake?" He knocked again.

Misely was not surprised. He figured that Slake had turned off the lights and was laying low again. He put the key into the lock and turned the handle. The lights were out, so he cautiously entered the room and flipped the switch.

He looked around. There was no one there. That was disappointing. He wanted to get a close look at Slake even if he couldn't serve the process. He figured that Slake must have left at some point, presuming he had even bothered to arrive today. After all, why bother fishing for minnows when you had already caught the prize marlin?

He put on a pair of rubber gloves and began hunting for anything useful. The gloves were a necessary precaution. He felt certain that it was only a matter of time before Slake's crimes earned the attention of the police. He didn't want to confuse a crime scene by leaving his own prints.

The desk drawers had no locks. Nor did the small filing cabinet. He figured that constantly reproducing keys for the furnished offices used by the more transient business customers must have been a bad deal, hence the non-locking drawers.

He opened up the drawers of the desk. Besides the usual smattering of pens and pencils, there was nothing exciting. No past correspondence, no ledgers no invoices. He did find a healthy supply of the infamous "prospectus" and several notepads and envelopes, just like those used for the 'love letters.' He pulled off the top two sheets of notepaper and grabbed a couple envelopes and placed them in his catalog case.

The file cabinet drawers held two thick files. One had a variety of old stock certificates, mostly from abandoned mining and livestock companies. The certificates were quite beautiful - full color engravings on high quality linen paper. Misely figured that the old certificates had no actual value beyond their artistic beauty: "wallpaper." The other file held about two dozen insurance policy forms - all uniform and all likewise economically meaningless. He grabbed two stock certificates and two insurance policy forms and placed them carefully in the catalog case.

Misely was looking for something else: a false beard or mustache or a hat or some other article of clothing. He found a couple of empty paper shopping bags stashed on top of the filing cabinet. Nothing. It was just about lunch time and presuming Slake was out at one of his romantic luncheons, Slake would have had to stash his disguise somewhere. He was greatly disappointed. The whole effort had yielded not a single clue - and certainly not the Choate Diamonds.

He left, relocking the door to 804 behind him. He decided to walk down the stairs to see if there was a way to secrete himself, there, for any length of time. Surprisingly, the stairs seemed fairly busy. He heard several people using the stairs on the floors below. A person could probably hide in the stairwell for a short time, but sooner or later it would look suspicious.

He got on the elevator on the 6th floor and accidently pressed the "B" button. He hit the "L" button, but reconsidered and figured there was no harm in taking advantage of his 'inspector' status to take a quick tour of the basement. He ignored the elevator opening to the lobby. It continued to the basement where Misely disembarked.

Once the doors closed behind him he realized it was virtually pitch black. He had no idea where the light switch was located, presuming there was one. The elevator call button, wherever it was located, was not illuminated. He stood squinting, waiting for his eyes to become adjusted to whatever residual light was present. Finally, after a few minutes, he could see the grey outlines of the strange basement. Directly before him were a series of large squared-off rooms, with dividing walls constructed of wire mesh. The wire walls ran upward from the floor to a length of about 10 feet. The walls never reached the ceiling though. The ceiling must have been at least 20 feet high.

The spaces appeared to Misely to be storage and file rooms, most likely for the tenants. Most of the makeshift storage areas had a wood framed entry doors made of metal mesh, usually with padlocks in place to protect the contents.

As his eyes became further accustomed to the light, Misely looked around in all directions. The basement was cavernous.

Ersatz corridors were formed everywhere and in all directions by the oddly sized storage areas. He was overwhelmed by the enormity of the space. He could now see the outline of the call button. He also saw that directly next to the elevator was a series of concrete stairs that must have once led to the lobby, but were now obviously walled-off. He wished he had brought a flashlight.

He didn't want to stray too far from his exit point, but he decided to explore the corridor immediately adjacent to the building elevator. He left his catalog case and clipboard by the elevator door and gingerly made his way along the makeshift corridor. The floor was rough concrete and very uneven. It looked like some parts were painted gunship grey, while further down the corridor, the cement was unpainted and dirty. Dust and grime were everywhere. Many of the storage areas had exceeded their capacities and tenants had begun storing excess boxes, drums and furnishings outside the areas and into the corridors. Misely found himself maneuvering a virtual obstacle course in the weak illumination.

The corridor wound around to the left for about 20 yards to intersect with another messy passageway also formed by the walls of storage areas. The intersecting passageway revealed a light source, about 30 yards down, so he quietly made his way down the corridor in that direction. The faint light allowed him to see the extreme variety of stuff kept in the storage rooms. Many had filing cabinets and office furnishings in various states of disrepair. Some areas had industrial supplies, large pipes, machinery, cables. Almost all had a variety of cardboard boxes, large and small, stacked one on top of the other. The boxes were often jammed to the brink and overflowing with junk. Some of the box towers had fallen over, the boxes split open, their contents spilling out into the dust and grime. Abandoned files and papers littered the corridors. Some of the storage areas were stuffed so full as to cause the mesh walls to bulge out, creating freakish shapes.

Misely grew closer and saw that the light was from a bare bulb hanging above one of the storage areas. He approached cautiously. The area was used as an office of sorts. Besides filing cabinets, a small desk sat facing away from the corridor. The desk was jammed with files, a radio, a walkie-talkie and a hot plate. Roderick sensed the telltale aroma of heated canned food. A filthy sofa sat along side the mesh wall. The sofa was leaking fuzzy upholstery in several places. Someone was actually working or living there. He shuddered.

As he moved along further down the makeshift corridor, he heard sounds and saw another light source. After passing along more storage areas, he cautiously approached the lighted area. He could then tell that the sound was tinny music bleating from a small transistor radio. He looked into the area and saw a man sitting at a metal desk with his back to the corridor. He was reading a book and eating a sandwich. Misely's jaw dropped when he saw that the room, inexplicably, also held an electronic organ. Sheet music was propped up in front of the keyboard. Misely quickly and quietly retreated. He wondered what sort of job - no, what sort of life the man had?

He wandered away and realized that he had lost track of which way he had come. Behind him were more intersections of storage areas and corridors. He felt a twinge of panic. He needed to get back to his catalog case and back upstairs. But he was not sure how he had gotten where he was.

He stopped and calmed down. He would find his way out. He steeled himself and continued exploring, trying to backtrack.

He heard voices in the distance and decided to turn in that direction. He wandered down the lengthy corridor and saw flashes of light coinciding with a swinging door being opened. And every time the door opened, the volume of the sound of the voices increased. He crept his way along the wall, avoiding collisions with cardboard boxes and abandoned storage drums, staying out of the direct sight of anyone behind the door. He saw that a man in a butcher's smock was loading frozen meats into a white meat locker located in the corridor, just outside of the swinging door. He was in conversation with another man in a smock, who was bringing the cuts of meat down the stairs, handing the meat off to the other, bucket brigade style. He could tell they were talking about college football.

Within a few minutes they had completed the task and went back upstairs. When the coast was clear, Misely walked over and lifted the door of the freezer and looked at the cuts of meat. It seemed strange that the locker was sitting there, exposed to thieves. He shut the lid and walked over to the swinging door. He gently pushed the door open and listened. He could now hear several voices at the top of the stairs. He worked his way up the stairs to the door, which held a round window. He peaked through and saw that he was now looking into a kitchen. Several men in chef's hats and smocks were working frantically over enormous grills, yelling to each other and other kitchen workers. Two were carrying a large vat over to an industrial sized sink. Another set of swinging doors must have led to a dining area. Misely observed a middle-aged woman in a light blue smock occasionally entering the kitchen to bark orders to the team. He calculated that there must have been about eight kitchen workers involved in the fast-paced production.

Dressed in his white lab coat, he figured he could be taken for a health inspector, so he decided to make his move. He strolled unnoticed through the kitchen doors and walked right by the busy cooks and workers who paid him absolutely no mind. He then passed into the dining area. He realized that he was in Blickenstaff's Cafeteria on Holiday Street. It seemed impossible. Holiday Street ran parallel to Prince. Somehow the maze of corridors in the enormous basement led all the way to Blickenstaff's, which was nearly at the end of Holiday. The Towers Building was close to the center of the square block. That meant that the basement cavern must have taken up the entire square block.

Misely simply walked past the hostess at the cash register and out the front door. No one noticed anything unusual.

Misely got his bearings and walked back along Holiday to Carlton and around the corner to Prince. As he approached the Towers Building, he realized that he had solved the puzzle about Slake's access to and from the building. Slake was almost certainly entering some other building with basement access and finding his way over to the elevator for the Towers Building. That would explain everything. There was never a change out of a disguise.

Misely entered the Towers Building and strolled past Pyvak. He waved Pyvak a casual salute and continued to the elevators. Pyvak did a double take, wondering how and when Matsley had left the building. He had been stationed at the desk all afternoon and would not have missed him. He did not like it.

Pyvak spoke in a near yell, loud enough for the passing Matsley to hear: "Are you through with the key, yet?" But it was too late. The elevator doors had closed.

Misely took the elevator back to the basement and grabbed his things. He returned the master key to the scowling Pyvak, thanking him, graciously, and advising that he would inform Mr. Caples about his excellent level of cooperation.

Misely made his way to the streetcar line on Holiday and stashed his rolled-up lab coat in the catalog case. On the way back to Elk Neck, he considered what he had learned. He could easily serve Slake by lying in wait in the shadowy basement near the elevator. Serving the process seemed a simple side task, now. But the real task was retrieving the diamonds. He figured that the bracelet was likely with Slake or locked up somewhere on Slake's other premises. Or perhaps Slake had the good sense to open a safe deposit box account at a bank? If he confronted Slake with process, Slake could be spooked and Misely might never see him again. He would be much better off following Slake through the basement maze to see where he called "home."

It was nearly mid-afternoon by the time Roderick worked his way over to County Restaurant for a late lunch. The place was virtually empty. He showed himself over to the counter and grabbed a copy of a leftover Star Sentinel.

Eleni and Sam Georgelus heard the door open from the kitchen. Sam craned his neck around to see if the noise was someone entering or leaving. He was dearly hoping for the former, as none of the remaining patrons had paid their bills yet. Delighted to see his favorite customer, he wiped his hands on his apron and entered the dining room grumbling a hoarse "welcome" and sliding a menu over to Roderick.

Roderick glanced up to see Sam's back in retreat to the kitchen. He had been distracted reading an interesting piece that sounded just a little too familiar. The story was under the "Across the Nation" heading. Authorities in New York City were seeking the arrest of one "Jacques Capri," known to have defrauded several wealthy dowagers out of considerable sums. Capri had sold the victims worthless securities. He met the women by leaving colorful flyers and brochures in their brownstone mailboxes. The brochures touted the individualized attention that Mr. Capri provided to his clients, handpicking just the right investments deemed worthy of his clients' unique interests. The "Wall Street Casanova," as the article referred to him, had made subsequent contacts with other targets through recommendations of victimized friends. He had built a network gullible lunch partners, each believing themselves to be the sole recipient of Capri's steadfast devotion. Eventually, the frauds were discovered and Capri disappeared, leaving neither hide nor hair behind.

The piece included commentary from C. Allan Aimes. Aimes, of Oxford Investigations, had been engaged by two of the families to track down Capri. "Don't let the 'Casanova' nonsense fool you. The man is dangerous. He will strip a family of its fortune quicker than hell scorches a feather."

Aimes warned that, "Capri is on the move and likely operating in other states. We are following all leads and are absolutely confident that we will bring this scorpion to justice. Otho Pramm is personally involved in the case and requested that I report to you that 'no stone will remain unturned.' Additionally, the families have authorized a reward of $2,500. for anyone providing information leading to the arrest and conviction of Capri. Persons with such information should contact Oxford Investigations on 5th Avenue, Manhattan."

The piece concluded with Aimes' comment that "Capri uses aliases and has struck in other areas before. Capri is believed to have gone by the names 'Peter Billington' and 'Adolpho Fostini' in the past."

Grainy photographs of Capri's face were published along with the article. One, purportedly of 'Peter Billington,' showed a serious looking, middle-aged, bald man wearing wire-rimmed glasses. There was no photo of Fostini, but the photo of Capri was of a much younger looking man with a thick head of hair and a nicely groomed mustache. His somewhat sly looking smirk showed just enough of his teeth to reveal what appeared to be a chipped front tooth.

Misely stared at the photos. That was him.

Misely put the paper down and ordered a bowl of seafood soup with pita and hummus. Eleni had been hovering, patiently waiting for the brown-suited man to order.

'This could ruin everything,' he thought. The last thing he needed was interference from other parties on the hunt. If they got to Slake and the bracelet, first, Misely's opportunity would be lost forever - not to mention Ollie Choate's reward. He sipped his soup, glumly. Oxford Investigations had resources, police contacts and manpower. Misely had himself and his wits. He did not relish going up against Goliath.

But the more he thought about it, the more encouraged he became. At least he had a head start. He was on the verge of tracking Slake back to his lair - so very close to retrieving the diamonds... Aimes could not be that close, yet. The article made no mention of the name 'Slake.'

And the idea of the New York reward began to play upon his mind. After all, he might just be able to obtain and deliver evidence that could lead to 'Capri's' arrest and conviction. Owing to his past interaction with Pramm, Misely wouldn't dare come forward to provide such evidence to Oxford Investigations, himself. He needed to stay in the background; way, way in the background. But Ollie Choate could. Presuming he succeeded in tracking down Slake and the bracelet, he would also let Ollie know what he had learned about Capri and New York. Ollie could then provide whatever information the two would have developed, to Oxford Investigations. The two would split the reward...

Now that was an incentive. His spirits raised, he paid his bill and returned to 7 North Central, newspaper in hand.

It was nearly 4 PM when the man in the black suit with the black mustache entered the Towers Building and headed to the elevator. He made his way up to the 8th floor. He walked quietly over to Suite 804 and knelt down to the ground, looking for the telltale signs of occupancy. Light gleamed through the tiny crack between the doorframe and the hallway floor. Slake was there!

Misely headed back to the elevator and pressed "B." This time he was prepared. He clicked on the flashlight and peered around looking for a safe place to stage his surveillance. He decided on a group of stray boxes stashed at a boundary between two storage areas, just a few yards way from the elevator doors. He searched around and found an abandoned heavy cardboard drum, turned it over and created a makeshift stool for himself.

Surveillance was always the worst part of his job. Waiting around caused the clock to move very slowly. He entertained himself with thoughts of his potential apprenticeship with Choate. Yes, Choate could be a difficult person, but the "cherub" was a lawyer. That was enough.

Just then, he heard the elevator make its way down to the basement level. He clicked off his flashlight and waited in the dark. The doors opened and Roderick saw Slake disembark, holding a small, illuminated, penlight.

Slake began by taking the same course as Roderick had earlier that day. Misely tried to follow behind, carefully avoiding the basement obstacles. He was at a disadvantage because he could not turn on his flashlight without revealing himself. He soon found himself falling behind Slake, who had peeled-off and was heading down a corridor that Roderick had not yet travelled.

Misely tried to pick up the pace. He moved a little too quickly and brushed against a large wooden spool, causing it to rock noisily against the floor. In the distance, Misely saw Slake come to a dead halt, turn, and shine the tiny penlight beam down the corridor in the direction of the sound.

Misely froze, knowing that the light beam would not be able to pierce the shadows where he stood - unless he moved. Slake turned back around and headed quickly down the corridor making a left turn at the intersection. Misely gingerly continued down to the end of the corridor. But when he made the left turn he could no longer make out the figure of Slake and his penlight. It was pitch black.

Misely stopped and listened. He heard no sound but feared that Slake could be lying in wait, hoping for Misely to make a false move. Misely stood in the darkness, knowing that turning on his flashlight could expose him to the trap. He had been sucker punched before under similar circumstances and wanted to forego that experience indefinitely. He hated to do it, but he decided to wait for at least five minutes before clicking on his flashlight and continuing.

The eternity eventually passed and Roderick clicked on the light and continued in Slake's last direction. Within seconds he felt and heard the sound of an object clatter against the corridor floor. It had whizzed by, just missing his face. He immediately cut the light and crouched down. He then heard Slake's footfall moving quickly away, the sound diminishing as Slake moved through the corridor. Misely rallied and followed the sounds to the best of his abilities. He heard footsteps as on stairs in the distance. Slake was exiting the basement through his rat hole, somewhere fairly close by.

Eventually Roderick found a metal door, surrounded by stacks of empty liquor boxes. He extinguished the flashlight and gently opened the door, revealing an illuminated metal stairway. He clambered up the long metal stairs, which led to a second door. He gently pushed open the door by a crack and listened. He heard the muffled sounds of a gathering. Pushing open the door, he found himself in a short hallway. He saw the doors for public restrooms and realized he was in a restaurant or bar. He pushed through the next set of doors and walked into a noisy barroom. He thought he must have wound up in Ware's Den - just down the street from Blickenstaff's. He squeezed past the crowd keeping a lookout for Slake. At the front entrance he saw that, as he suspected, he was in Ware's.

Out on the street, he looked around, again, for any sign of Slake. Slake was long gone. Dejected, he headed down to the corner to pick up the streetcar back to Elk Neck.

It was nearly 7 PM when Misely arrived back home. He changed out of the disguise and into his long johns. He sat on the edge of his cot eating chicken noodle soup warmed by his hot plate. Exhausted, he stretched out on the cot listening to his transistor radio. Tomorrow would be a better day. It would have to be.

Medyev Globokar looked around the grim office suite. If he could just stick it out for a few more months he'd pack it in and head back to Bradenton. He ran his fingers through his fluffy white hair. He was sitting in his white lab coat at the barely functional desk that came with the office. He had opened the large window directly behind his desk chair, desperate for some circulation.

He was worried about Slake. He did not trust the man. Slake was rash. He took a lot of chances. Peanut James, from his circus days, had put the two together. Slake needed a place to crash and, according to James, "Slake had made a lot of money for a lot of people." A partnership was born.

But Goodley had seen the two men, again, today in the hallway. They were about the same size, 6 feet tall and tough looking. They both wore the same kind of dark blue suits, white shirts and blue ties - almost like a uniform. He had spotted them two days ago in the lobby, where they were just waiting, biding time. Yesterday he saw one in the hallway. When he said 'hello,' the man turned away, as thought to ignore the greeting or avoid further identification. Today, he had heard footsteps outside of the office and when he opened the office door, he saw them leaving by the stairwell. Why would anyone use the stairwell with the elevator, there? It was unsettling. They were lawmen or process servers and they were just a little too interested in the doings on the eighth floor for comfort.

He looked over to the right to the two large portable screens that separated the two banged-up, green filing cabinets and 2 army cots from the rest of the "examination room" and office. It was not an ideal setup for a medical man. He didn't mind sleeping on a cot when he was by himself. It was bad enough taking his meals with Slake. But Slake was a snorer and he just didn't care for his company. They both knew the arrangement would not be permanent, but he felt stuck with Sake for as long as Slake wanted. The trick was in figuring out when Slake would want to dissolve the partnership - and when that day came - to 'light out for the territories.'

He glanced, proudly, over to his left at his neatly organized, stacked boxes holding his diet pill prescriptions - his inspiration. He had come up with three of the compounds himself. A lab outside of Sarasota made the prescriptions to order. Lacking a "traditional" medical license was no drawback because the compounds were made from non-prescription elements. He was particularly proud of his "Seafresh 1000," pill which was composed of equal parts rose hips, caffeine, sugar, acerola extract and fish oil.

He opened up the bottom drawer of his desk and pulled out his framed degree from Cambridge. He looked it over, proudly. He would have hung it in the office but for the fact that it listed his real name, which he had changed at various times over the years, purely as a concession to his patients. He was told that people in this country would find the name "Globokar" frightening.

And it was a lot easier to simply tell his patients that he received his degree from Cambridge. Explaining that the certificate was from the "College of Medical Arts and Industry" in Cambridge, Ohio, would only complicate things. But he was proud that his design for a "portable night table with flexible tray top" was the third runner up thesis project for his graduating class. He put the frame back in the drawer.

As he did, Slake unlocked the office door and entered.

"So what's the word, Doc., did you make us any money today?"

Before Goodley could answer, the phone rang. Goodley picked it up on the first ring. Slake pulled up one of the scarred aluminum office chairs close to the desk to eavesdrop on the conversation.

"Dr. A.T. Goodley, how may I help you?"

"Yes Mrs. Ratliff, I do recall that the 'Starbright 500' seemed most suited to your condition. No doubt you've experienced success. Refund?"

"Yes, of course, your satisfaction is guaranteed! However, we had not yet tried a combination of both the Seafresh and Starbright compounds and I would recommend that course of action before abandoning the regimen…"

Slake sat, smiling sarcastically, shaking his head.

"Indigestion? Well that could be caused by many other factors…"

Slake barked out a theatrical laugh, causing Goodley to grimace disapprovingly and cover over the mouthpiece.

"No, I understand. I will mail you the reimbursement form, immediately. Simply complete the questionnaire and return it to our offices, straightaway."

"No, regrettably, we do not have a cashier on premises and would be unable to process the remuneration in that fashion even if you were to pay us a visit. However, doubtless you will find the reimbursement process efficient and most satisfactory."

"Hello... hello?"

Goodley replaced the handset back into the base.

"Unappreciative. Some folks are just plain unappreciative."

Slake pointed to the phone. "I would have handled that entirely differently. 'Some folks' just need the proper kind of persuasion. You were falling all over yourself to give our earnings back to that idiot. Sometimes you have to use a little vinegar."

Goodley shook his head and smiled. "Really? Who has the money, right now? We do. By the time Mrs. Ratliff completes the various forms I will send her, accompanied by more pitches for more compounds, she will be sending me money. And, if at the end, a refund must be provided, I always do so in the form of a coupon redeemable solely through the offices of Doctor A. T. Goodley."

He looked on smugly at Slake. "What do you think, now?"

Slake shook his head and smiled wryly. "I think that's an awful lot of trouble to get rid of pest. I like my way, better."

Slake removed his blonde toupee and chucked it on his cot. The two reached enough of a truce to allow for dining together at Blickenstaff's.

On Thursday morning, Misely roused himself, dressed, and walked around to the library. He telephoned over to Kent and McCullough, but Honora Blaine told Misely that Choate was at a court hearing and to try again later.

Misely was certain that Slake had made his exit through Ware's. He would camp out near the cellar stairwell that led to Ware's that evening and wait for Slake to pass by. He would then pick up the trail.

On a long shot he decided to stop by at the Elk Neck Post Office to see if he had received his informational packet from Goodley. He turned his key in the post office box and was delighted to extract a thick envelope of information supplied courtesy of "Dr. A.T. Goodley, Master of Medical Arts."

Back at 7 North Central, Misely unraveled the papers from the bulging envelope. The package consisted of mostly mimeographed sheets comprising pseudo-scientific text and "patient testimonials." He looked through the sheets and finally hit pay dirt: a phone number. At the very least he could call the number and make an appointment. Possibly, the medical office could be the den of thieves.

He headed back to the library payphone and dialed.

"Dr. A. T. Goodley, here. Can I help you?"

"Hello Doctor. This is Ron Mizer. I just received your informational packet and would like to schedule an appointment."

Goodley remembered sending out the information just the day before. He liked the anxious ones. They were always easiest to prescribe for.

"Of course Mr. Mizer. I was very troubled to learn of your hereditary obesity. Genes are not fair are they? I have only a few openings in my schedule but could try to squeeze you in?"

"Yes please, Doctor. Just tell me where and when. I am very desperate."

"Of course. How about tomorrow afternoon at 1 PM? My medical office is located at Suite 703 in the Muncie Building. Do you know where that is?"

Misely nearly fell off of the phone booth seat. What a hellhole. "Yes Doctor. Thank you so much for agreeing to see me so promptly! Good day!"

He tapped the handset into the cradle. That made sense. The Muncie Building was on Holiday Street, a few doors up and across the street from Ware's Den. There was a good chance that both of the thieves were holing up there.

The Muncie was notorious for being one of the worst, but cheapest, office buildings in the City. It was rumored that half of the tenants actually lived in their offices - illegally, of course, because the zoning didn't allow it. But when there is no management to speak of, who would be there to stop it - and who would be heard to complain?

Playing a hunch, Misely decided that it would be easier staking out 703 of the Muncie Building than sitting around in the dark basement. By 11:00 AM he had made his way to the Muncie by streetcar.

He walked into grim lobby. The reception desk was unmanned. A homemade cardboard sign in green crayon stated "Manager at Equitable." The Equitable Building was a couple doors up the street but several notches in quality above the filthy Muncie Building. Misely figured that if he were asked to manage both, he certainly would do so from the Equitable, too.

He took a look at the office directory, just above the vacant reception desk. There were very few names on the board. Apparently, many of the tenants of the Muncie were content to remain unbothered by the potential onslaught of clamoring customers. For several, the white peg letters had become dislodged revealing only parts of the tenant's name. A few of the firms had cellophane taped their own makeshift lettering onto the board. Roderick looked throughout and saw no listing for Goodley.

Misely waited a seeming eternity for the single elevator and clicked-in the stubby Bakelite button for 7. He had to look at the button a couple times. The top part of the "7" was worn away, giving the appearance of there being two "1's" in the building.

He walked, quietly, down the hall to the door marked 703. The door had no sign or other indicia of office use - just the number "703." He stooped down to the skeleton keyhole and peered through. The florescent lights were on. He could see a messy desk in the rear of the room in front of an open window. He also spied what appeared to be two cots and a medical scale, but a screen was obscuring part of the view into the back of the room. He couldn't see anyone, but he could hear the sounds of someone shuffling around the room. He heard a file drawer being opened.

"Good," he thought. He looked across the hall at two other offices having doors most directly opposite the door to 703. There was work of some sort going on in 708. He could hear voices and saw light from underneath the door. But the keyhole for 706 answered back with only darkness. The vacancy encouraged Misely to become a short-term tenant.

Roderick waited another eternity for the elevator back down to the lobby. Rather than walk the four doors up the street along Holiday to get to the Equitable Building, he decided to check out the rear of the Muncie by walking up the parallel alley.

He traversed an obstacle course of trashcans, scarred wooden pallets and rusted containers interspersed with piles of trash. He looked up to the fire escape serving the Muncie. Not surprisingly, he saw that at least two sections of fire escape stairs had collapsed; the stairs hung limply and uselessly below the two sets of landings, offering no means by which a tenant above could hope to escape from a fire. An old mattress had been stuffed onto one of the landings. He pitied the soul having to lay his head on the filthy mattress at night.

He realized that the alley dead-ended ten yards further and backtracked to Holiday.

Gordon Lucketts was sitting at the manager's station at the Equitable Building reviewing the list of tenant complaints on his clipboard. It never ceased to amaze him that almost all of the complaints were from the Equitable tenants; not the Muncie ones. Yet the Muncie was nearly falling apart at the seams. The phone rang. Another call about an office furniture delivery.

Misely entered the Equitable Building and saw that the manager was occupied. He took a walk over towards the desk and, with nothing better to do, glanced up at the building directory. Now, that was a proper directory. Each name was clearly indicated; larger firms had individual listings of key employees below the company name. Most of the floors were well accounted for. He was surprised to see a particular name that he recognized from the past and made a mental note.

The phone call concluded, Lucketts looked up to face the neatly groomed brown-suited man.

"Good morning. Can help you?"

Misely extended his hand in greeting. "Yes, my name is Ron Mizel. I would like to rent an unfurnished suite in the Muncie. I am looking for a short term rental - just two weeks should do."

Lucketts was mildly puzzled. The man looked like he could certainly do a lot better. But he had long ago learned that, when it came to the Muncie, curiosity was a definite liability.

"Well, our minimum tenancy is actually a month. We have some nice suites available on the third floor. I could take a break in five minutes and show you a few?"

"Thanks, but I'm interested in the 7th floor, in particular number 706. Is it available?"

Lucketts did not want to know why. He grabbed the dog-eared spiral notebook that served as the tenant list for the Muncie. Some loose pages fell out. Lucketts stooped down and stuffed the pages back into the book. He found his way to the current hieroglyphs for the 7th floor.

"Let's see. Yes, here's 706. But it is a furnished suite. Let me see what else we have on 7."

"Furnished will do, after all. What's the rent for 706?"

Sizing up Mizel as a particularly interested potential client, Lucketts decided to offer a quote "on the high side." After all, rents at the Muncie were fluid and ultimately "market driven."

"One month would be $52.00."

Mizel winced. "Ah that's a bit too much. Thank you, anyway, for your time." He extended his hand to signal a friendly conclusion to the conversation.

"Now, wait - we do have special rates for corporate customers and vets. Would $38.00 sound better?"

"$30.00 would sound even better."

Lucketts extended his hand and the two shook, sealing the deal. But Lucketts was not quite finished.

"There is the matter of the security deposit. We do require $25.00, cash, in advance." He smiled exposing a deeply nicotine stained set of teeth.

Mizel smiled back. "Of course. By the way, is it considered customary to provide management with gratuities for services rendered?"

Lucketts felt a wave of happiness flow throughout his very being. "Of course, sir!"

"Excellent. Now at present I have limited cash resources and I would propose that management's waiver of the security deposit for a corporate customer would constitute a goodwill gesture well worthy of this $10.00 gratuity." He withdrew a $10.00 bill from his wallet and placed it on the mangers desk.

"Why thank you, sir, and yes that certainly makes sense to me!"

The deal was finalized by Mizel's payment of the additional $30.00 in cash. The lease was a photostatic copy of a virtually unreadable mimeograph, but Lucketts verbalized the key terms, quickly and efficiently; an auctioneer at a hog auction. He pointed out, in particular, the clauses that prohibited sleeping and dining on the premises. He had Mizel initial those clauses. He then mentioned that hotplate rentals were also available from management, for a separate fee, but Mizel declined. Mizel also declined a preliminary inspection of his new corporate suite so Lucketts simply handed over the skeleton key and wished the new tenant "Best of luck!"

Back at the Muncie, Roderick turned the key and flipped over the light switch. There was an audible buzzing sound from the fluorescent lights overhead. He touched the surface of the metal desk. It was both dusty and sticky. Someone had spilled a soft drink and left the clean-up to the processes of nature. The office chair behind the desk was leaking foam upholstery.

He pulled out the chair and sat down, gingerly. He tested the spring in the backrest, leaning back ever so slightly. The tiny effort caused the backrest of the chair to collapse back violently, nearly toppling over chair and Misely, together.

But, it would do.

Misely gently opened the office door and peeped across the hall. By keeping the door just slightly ajar, he would be able to get a decent view of the goings on at 703.

Slake had worked his way back through the basement and up through Ware's Den. He had just ordered the two BLT sandwiches and two iced teas, extra sweet. He had gotten in the habit of having lunch with Goodley on the days when he had no lunchtime appointments. He did it for self-preservation. He did not trust Goodley. And he hated being by himself. He enjoyed the company of others, even a bump on a log like Goodley. Slake had a lot of useful ideas and opinions that others enjoyed hearing. He did not want to be responsible for depriving others of such pleasure.

As he stood at the bar, he fondled the diamond bracelet in his left pants pocket. That bracelet made him a rich man. He could leave right that minute and head out for a new town, a retired man. He was sick of holing-up in the Muncie. But he had not fully played his mark, yet. Mrs. Choate had cash and he would extract as much as possible. Then he would up and leave. Goodley would be on his own. Big deal. He'd be fine pushing his pills without him.

Roderick was sitting in the foul office chair scribbling notes in his breast pocket notebook. Provisions would be required for the stakeout. As he went through the list again, he heard movement across the hallway.

Cracking the door open, slightly, he saw the figure of Slake fumbling with his key and juggling two white paper bags. Misely figured that, being nearly Noon, Slake had brought in lunch for the two.

"Here's today's rations." Slake dropped the bags on the desk in front of Goodley. He walked back to the door, removed the blonde wig and hung it on the door handle. Slake reached down and picked up a manila envelope that had been pushed underneath the door. It was from the mail drop service. He placed it on the corner of the desk.

"Mail call."

Godley had been packaging several bottles of brightly colored pills in cardboard boxes for mailing.

"That for a new patient?"

"No, a couple old faithfuls." He carefully brushed the packaging materials and manila envelope aside to make room for lunch.

Slake ran his fingers through his stringy brown hair. He looked over at the door. He had learned, early on, to stash the hairpiece at the door during the day so that he did not leave the office without it. "Wearing that thing is a sacrifice - I hope you appreciate it."

Goodley bit into his sandwich. He was about to complain back that he had his own cross to bear: the girdle he had to wear on days when patients visited the office - but he realized that Slake would turn it into a means of ridicule so he shut up.

Once the door was closed, Misely walked quietly to the door of 703. He bent over to look through the keyhole, but it was dark. Slake had probably hung his suit jacket over the doorknob.

Instead, he leaned his ear gently against the doorframe and listened. The two were conversing, but he could not make out the dialog. There was no question that the louder voice was doing most of the talking. He retreated back to 706.

"You ought to get out a little more, Doc." Slake sniffed. "And you might want to consider showering at the 'Y' more than once a week."

A little over an hour later, Slake left 703 and headed down the hall to the elevator. Misely heard the skeleton key turn in the door. Goodley had locked himself in.

Misely needed to get into that office. He decided that Slake was either carrying around the bracelet on his person or had locked it somewhere in Goodley's office. It seemed likely that the two were using 703 as living quarters - there would be no other good reason for the cots. He had mentally discounted a safe deposit box. He figured Slake had to be prepared to bolt at a moment's notice. The bracelet would have to be close at hand.

A moment later he thought he heard movement in the hallway near his door. He froze. He worked his way over to his door, quietly. He stooped down to the floor and looked through the crack between the floor and doorframe. He could see two sets of black shoes, across the hall. Others were checking up on Goodley. He heard no knock on the door.

Misely opened his own door, just by a crack. He saw the two men in blue suits. One was stooped over, peering through the keyhole of 703. The other stood guard, looking up and down the hallway.

Misely gently clicked his door closed. This was not good. Someone else was out to collect Goodley or Slake. A few minutes later, he heard the gentle footfall of the men as they left the hallway and exited by the stairwell.

He was going to have to move quickly. He needed to get inside of 703, pronto. And if he didn't find the bracelet there, he needed to be in a position to take the diamonds from Slake, directly. Precisely how was the problem. He couldn't threaten Slake with violence. He had never owned a weapon and the notion of gaining a criminal record and losing any chance for a career as a lawyer eliminated any thought in that direction. He was going to have to think of a way to bluff Slake out of the diamonds - to have Slake hand them over, voluntarily.

But for now, why not "divide and conquer?" He locked up his office and slipped out to the stairwell. He figured it might be quicker to walk down 7 flights than wait for the ancient elevator. The phone booth in the lobby was vacant. He dropped a dime into the pay phone and dialed Goodley's number.

"Dr. A.T. Goodley, here. How may I help you?"

"Ah yes, Dr. Goodley, I'm calling from the Star Sentinel Classifieds. I was closing out your account and just wanted to make sure that you knew that your $20. deposit has been sent to Mr. Slake. He confirmed that he would handle it for you, but we wanted to make sure that you knew, should you have any questions."

Goodley was stunned.

"Did you say close the account? Why?"

"Well Doctor, as you know, Mr. Slake pulled both of your ads. They've ceased running as of the end of this week. Had he not informed you of such?"

"No. There must be a mistake. Slake paid for 3 months' worth of ads. They're supposed to be running." Goodley sounded flustered.

"Well, I'm sorry Doctor. We tried to encourage him to let the ads run, but he said to send the balance of the money to him - including your deposit. I'm sorry that he hadn't informed you. But I'm glad to have called you to let you know. Thanks again for your patronage Doctor. Just let us know if you'd like to re-establish the account. Of course we will need another $20 deposit in such event. Good day."

Goodley placed the handset back into the cradle. 'That cur!' Slake was planning to dissolve the partnership and head for the hills. Not surprisingly, he was cheating him out of every available dollar. He did not like it. Not one bit.

He walked over to his desk. He opened the right side drawer and lifted the cigar box lid. He withdrew his revolver and held the grip, tightly. After a few minutes of pacing around the office, gun in hand, he dropped it back into the cigar box, along side of the single bullet, which rolled around in the box. He had calmed down. The gun was not loaded and he wasn't planning on using it, but perhaps it was time to place it out of Slake's reach?

Misely was on the streetcar heading back to Elk Neck. He was deep in thought. Others were closing in on Goodley and Slake. He would have to bring the case to a close, immediately. Tomorrow at the latest, presuming he even had the luxury of a tomorrow. He needed at least a half hour for a minimal search of 703. But he hadn't had a sufficient opportunity to scout out 703 to see when a search would be safe. The alternative was to free-up 703 for a search by frightening Goodley away, permanently.

He looked up at the bell cord absentmindedly, touching his fingertips together, deep in concentration. Within a few minutes he had figured out a simple plan. It would take a couple of phone calls and some paperwork. With any luck, Goodley would be gone by 11:00 AM, tomorrow. Misely would have about an hour in which to search 703 and, if necessary, prepare to confront Slake upon his return at the lunch hour or later.

He thought some more about the plan and then remembered his appointment with Goodley for 1:00 PM the next day. He laughed to himself. He had never intended to keep the appointment. He hoped that his plan would be good enough to drive away Goodley, despite Godley's pending opportunity to sell more pills to a new mark.

Back at 7 North Central, Misely sat at his desk in his office anteroom. It was nearly 3:00 PM. He had racked his brain for a plan to bluff Slake out of the bracelet for nearly an hour. And he had a plan. He just didn't particularly like it. But it was the best he could come up with. Resigned, he rallied and began to organize. There was an awful lot to accomplish in a very short time. But he could do it.

Had a disinterested party witnessed the activities of the brown-suited man, such a person may have observed the man loading up four large paper shopping bags with: a crow bar, umbrella, masking tape, bandages, a variety of clothing, a flashlight, putty knife and 2 hot water bottles. Some of the clothing would have been seen retrieved from one of the two metal wardrobes in the man's living quarters. The man may have also been observed retrieving and opening the low-slung footlocker from beneath the cot, examining hairpieces and mustaches.

Later, the man would have been observed in the Constable's Office of Elk Neck Superior Court obtaining certain carbon copy forms. The same forms would have been seen in the office typewriter of the man, who, later, would have been observed completing the forms. The man would have also been observed writing a short message onto notepaper, addressing a corresponding envelope and later posting the correspondence at the mailbox at Franklin and Iroquois in Elk Neck.

By late afternoon the brown-suited man would have been seen on the streetcar, with bags in tow, and later, dropping-off the bags to Suite 706 of the Muncie Building.

Finally, towards 6:00 PM, the man would have been observed riding the elevator of the Towers Building to the basement level, carrying a shopping bag and with a flashlight stuffed into his breast pocket.

Slake had stashed his hairpiece onto the pillow of his cot. The "Doc" had been grumpy and not too talkative. But it was time for dinner. He was fed to the teeth with Blickenstaff's and Ware's, but, there weren't many other options in the immediate vicinity. And they could keep a low profile at Blickenstaff's. None of his clientele would be caught dead in a cafeteria. And he figured most would be too dumb to recognize him without the toupee.

"My treat as usual Doc." Slake smirked. He had the kitchen worker fill his plate with generous portions of chicken drumsticks, mashed potatoes and green beans. Goodley followed behind, solemnly. He was not particularly hungry. He was being betrayed and it left a foul taste in his mouth. He had the worker spoon him a small bowl of applesauce. He grabbed a diner roll with his fingers.

"Hey Doc, you're a medical man - that was not hygienic! That's why they have those tongs!" He smirked, hoping to get a rise out of his dour companion. There was no retort.

Slake gnawed through his dinner. "Cat got your tongue? What's wrong with you?"

Goodley looked ahead, stoically.

"Is that all you're eating? You must be sick, huh?"

"Yes, I am a little sick. Sick of a lot of things."

"What's that supposed to mean?" Slake's tone had become harsh.

"Nothing, partner, nothing." Goodley leaned back in his chair and stared into the eyes of Slake, without expression.

"Well you're not much of a dinner companion. I'm the one paying for this so maybe you could show some gratitude and lighten up a little. These meals cost."

Goodley continued peering. "How much - twenty dollars?"

"Twenty dollars? What's gotten into you? I'm going back for desert."

Friday morning found Misely back at suite 706. He had placed another call to Ollie Choate from the phone booth in the Muncie, but again, Choate was in court. He had asked Honora

Blaine to pass along the message. "Making some progress, but no results, yet." He knew that Ollie the "cherub" would not be thrilled with the message, but by day's end, he believed he would have a lot more to report.

Slake had worked his way over to the Towers Building via his established route. In the mornings, he passed through the basement exit of the Santa Maria Coffee House, through the underground maze, to the Towers elevator. He had been extremely cautious of late. He knew he had been followed, once, while in the basement. No big deal. He had gotten pretty good at avoiding the local constables and process servers. They were a petty nuisance. But the two men in the blue suits were another matter. They had to be from New York.

He had read the news columns. He knew that his nemesis, Oxford Investigations, was hot on the trail of "Jacques Capri." If he were picked-up by the blue suits or their obnoxious boss, he would go to prison. And he could not allow that to happen. He touched the outside of his left pants pocket. His career "catch" was sitting safely there. The bracelet represented permanent financial freedom. But he could extract more and would. Mrs. Helena Choate had booked the follow-up appointment to meet on Saturday for lunch during the initial "consultation" three days ago. She had been encouraged to bring her checkbook. She said she would. The thought actually caused Slake to salivate.

Slake took the elevator up to the seventh floor. He no longer dared to disembark on eight. He walked cautiously to the stairway door and peered up and down. The coast was clear. He walked up to eight and ever so gently opened the stairwell door, just enough to check out the hallway.

And there they were - the blue suits. One was standing directly in front of 804. The other was standing along side of the elevator doors, waiting to pounce.

Slake gently closed the stairwell door and instinctively headed back down to 7. He wasn't safe loitering in the hallway so he took a chance and pressed the elevator call button, hoping the blue suits would not be there. They were not, so he took the elevator back to the basement and headed back over to the Santa Maria. He didn't think Ware's would even be open yet. It was barely 9:30 AM.

He killed some time sipping coffee, but got bored and decided he'd be better off laying low at the Muncie for the time being. But going back so quickly before lunch would make Goodley suspicious, so he came up with a workable alibi. He decided to come back with breakfast for both because Goodley had eaten so poorly the night before and the dinner roll was not much of a breakfast for him. That would do. He ordered two pastry buns, two turnovers and coffees and headed, cautiously, over to the Muncie.

Roderick was sitting in the phone booth of the Muncie lobby. He had two simple calls to make. The first would be from a petulant, disgruntled customer. The customer would threaten police intervention. The second call, a few minutes later, would be the police. They had the warrant and would be effecting Goodley's arrest, momentarily. If that didn't send Goodley off in a panic, Misely would slap the "seized property" paper onto the door and bang a few times, announcing that the authorities were there for Slake. He figured that if he didn't run on his own account, he would likely run to avoid arrest in connection with Slake. Then he could work his way into 703 to look for the bracelet - and be ready for Slake's later arrival.

But Roderick could not have seen Slake reenter the Muncie from his position in the phone booth in the lobby.

Goodley heard the skeleton key turning in the keyhole. He looked up from the desk to see the smiling Slake with bags in tow. He looked on, puzzled as Slake performed his song and dance about why he was back before lunch.

Goodley was not entirely buying the story about breakfast. Slake had never lifted a finger on his behalf. Slake seemed agitated. Something was up. The two sat down at the desk to enjoy the "brunch."

Goodley had bitten through half of his pastry bun. He had a sweet tooth all his life and could not resist the treat. The phone rang and he picked it up.

"Doctor A.T. Goodley. Can I help you?"

"Refund? Well of course. Who is this?"

Slake was scowling - agitated at Goodley's weak business practices.

"I do not recall having a patient by that name sir. Are you certain you are calling the correct establishment?"

The voice on the other end of the line exploded. Slake could hear the angry monologue of the caller from where he was sitting. He thought he heard something about the police. Goodley seemed helpless.

"Sir? Sir?" But the angry discourse continued.

Slake grabbed the phone out of Goodley's hand.

"Listen you worthless vermin, just who do you think you are? Do you know who you're dealing with?" Slake had hurled the retort into the phone with maximum volume. The office walls seemed to shake.

Sitting in the phone booth, Misely knew that something had just gone wrong. Slake was inexplicably in the building, somehow. He had seen him leave earlier. Why was he back?

Improvising, Misely continued the diatribe. "Listen whoever you are - you and your quack friend are in serious trouble! You sound like the stupid one. Loud and stupid. There's always a stupid one!"

Slake screamed back: "Stupid? Do you think so? I'll show you who's stupid. Why don't you come by for an appointment? I'll straighten you out, but good!"

Goodley was beside himself, trying to calm the mad dog down. "Shh shhh…forget it… give me back the phone… please! Please!"

Slake ignored his pleas. He held his hand over the mouthpiece and shouted at Goodley: "Shut up!"

Then he heard the voice, taunting: "Look idiot, I don't have time to visit your rat's nest in the Muncie, but if you have any spine, why don't you come by and pay me a visit? I'm just down the street in the Equitable Building. The name is Terence Whitelake. That's Terence 'Buck' Whitelake, room 502 in the Equitable. I'm with American Bonding. Come see me if you have any guts!"

And with that Slake heard the phone slam sharply into the base, followed by a dull dial tone.

Slake's hands were shaking with anger. He reached around to the side desk drawer and fumbling, opened the cigar box, extracting both the revolver and the single bullet.

"What are you doing! Have you lost your mind?" Goodley was breathing rapidly, panicked.

Slake loaded the bullet into an empty chamber. "What am I doing? I'm taking care of business the way I like to! Once I am done with that loudmouth, we'll have one less thing to worry about. Whitelake is in for a big surprise!"

And with that Slake charged out the door with the gun stuffed into his breast pocket.

Goodley looked around, dazed. 'Who was Whitelake?' The caller said he was Anderson… he knew the time had now come to 'light out'…

He pulled his carpetbag from the bottom filing cabinet drawer and began to pack. Minutes later, he heard a loud bang at the door. He nearly jumped out of his skin. Trembling, he stood alongside the wall by the filing cabinets, hoping that the door would not be kicked in.

"Slake, by order of Court this premises is seized! Come out with your hands up!"

He waited but soon heard no more sounds. He pressed his ear gently against the door and listened. There was silence.

He quickly packed up his display cases of prescriptions and finished with the carpetbag. He could leave the rest behind.

He ever so carefully opened the office door and peeked. There was no one there. He left, closing the door behind him. He glanced at the outside of the door and saw legal papers - forms of some kind. The papers said, "Warning – Seized Chattels – Levy Made – Attachment." The papers said something about "People versus Jacque Capri, alias Arthur Slake." He scurried away, bags in hand.

As he approached the elevator, he saw the obese man with the funny hat and umbrella heading quietly in his direction. He remembered that he had an office appointment scheduled for later and assumed that the man must have come early.

"I'm sorry sir, but I've been called away on an emergency and have cancelled all office appointments."

The heavy-set man looked mildly puzzled and peered at Goodley as though a curiosity. But he said nothing as Goodley passed and caught the elevator, which, for the first time since Goodley had taken the office, was actually waiting for him when he pressed the call button. The large man had a change of heart, though. He turned around and followed after Goodly, arriving at the elevator just seconds too late. He pressed the call button and waited patiently.

Within the dingy walls of suite 706, Misely moved at lightning speed. He had filled the water bottles earlier and began attaching the masking tape to the outsides. The clothes were laid out on the desktop. He heard Goodley make the predicted hasty departure. He peeked outside to see that the hallway was clear. Wearing latex gloves, he grabbed the crowbar and walked across the hall. He was ready to fiddle with lock using his rusted set of skeleton keys and putty knife in his pocket, but on a hunch, he tried turning the doorknob. It opened. Goodley had not even bothered to lock the door behind him.

Inside he looked around, frantically, for any locked drawers. He inspected the filing cabinets and pulled out the drawers. None were locked. He didn't need the crowbar. The drawers were filled with a variety of men's clothing. He rifled through the dirty clothes. The two had been using the file drawers as dressers.

He ran to the desk. Although the top desk drawer had a lock, it was not locked. He opened the door and saw the usual variety of pencils, pens and lint.

The three side drawers had no locks. He pulled out the top drawer: just an empty cigar box sitting amidst handfuls of paper clips and file fasteners. The second drawer was stuffed with Goodley's stationary: letterhead and envelopes and rolls of postage stamps. The third was stuffed to the brim with brochures and forms, much like the stuff sent to 'Ron Mizel.'

To the side of the desk he saw abandoned boxes of the diet pills - there must have been thousands of pills. But he discounted such as the repository for the Choate Diamonds. He had seen enough. He knew Slake had to be carrying the bracelet on his person.

Misely retreated to 706, crowbar in hand. He sat on the edge of the desk and prepared for the next phase of his plan.

Terence "Buck" Whitelake sat at his desk chair, shaking. His vision was blurred by the tears in his eyes. His heart raced, pounding nearly out of his chest. What had just happened? The lunatic had barged into his office, gun drawn. He had ranted and raved about his brand of 'customer service.' He had waved the gun in his face and yelled something about introducing him to the 'complaint department," which he took to mean the gun.

After being further verbally abused, he realized that he was about to be pistol whipped by the screaming man, so he had begged for mercy, apologizing frantically for whatever wrong had been committed. That calmed the madman down. The madman left yelling something about 'try not stuffing your face.'

Shakily, he reached down to open the bottom drawer of his desk. He saw the bottle of Pike's Rye Whiskey topped with the overturned shot glass. The shot glass rattled against the neck as he placed the works on his desk. He wiped the dusty shot glass out with his trembling thumb.

Slake returned to suite 703 feeling fulfilled. He couldn't wait to describe the idiot's look on his face when he saw the gun. The smile left his face. He stared at the legal notice taped to the door. What did it mean? The premises were seized? He then saw the mention of "Jacque Capri, alias Arthur L. Slake." What had happened?

He placed the skeleton key in the lock but realized that the door was not locked. He opened the door and looked around. Goodley was nowhere to be found. Had he taken off for good? He walked over to the desk and fished through the drawers. It didn't look as though Goodley had taken any of his stuff. He removed the gun from his jacket pocket and tossed the loaded gun into the top desk drawer.

He tried the filing cabinet drawers. They were still filled with Goodley's less than sweet smelling clothing. Maybe some were missing? He then noticed the pill collection on the side of the room. He couldn't tell if Goodley had taken any - there were so many boxes of the crap.

He sat down behind the desk to think. He picked up a partially eaten turnover.

Suddenly, he heard the office door slam open, smashing against the wall. He thought the wood must have splintered.

In walked a heavy-set man with bowler hat and stringy mustache. He was carrying an umbrella. He faced Slake directly and bellowed: "I am Otho Pramm!"

Slake sat steadfast in his chair, feigning a cool demeanor. "Well hello sir. Can I help you with something?"

Pramm smiled, malevolently. "Why I think so Mr. Capri. There's the small matter of the warrant for your arrest issued out of New York City. You could help me with that."

Slake squirmed. "My name is not Capri, mister. You've got the wrong man. And I'm going to call the cops to have you arrested. You just broke down my door."

Pramm bellowed out a thick laugh. "Oh, splendid! We both want the same thing! Please do pick up that phone and call the authorities. Alternatively, it may gratify you to know that the police are already here, on the premises. Shall I summon them?"

Slake thought about the gun in the drawer. Why in the world had he put it there? If only it were still in his coat pocket. He stood up and pretended to stretch. He yawned as though the interaction with Pramm bored him. His eyes darted behind him to the wall and open window. He was feeling trapped. He faced Pramm.

"You're boring me big fellow. You've got the wrong man so please move on! Get out of here, right now!"

Pramm took a step forward and held out his hand in a conciliatory manner.

"Look Mr. Slake - yes, we know you are known as Slake down here - make it easy on yourself. Turn yourself in. There's no place to run. You are surrounded. Now, I can't make any promises, but I can assure you that things will go a lot easier for you if you cooperate. For example, we must retrieve that diamond bracelet, now. Yes, we know about the little racket you've been running here with the locals. The Choate family has also engaged my services. I will make it easy on you. Hand me the bracelet and I will arrange for your civil treatment while in custody here. You will be treated with the utmost courtesy and comfort."

Slake unconsciously fumbled with the bracelet in his left pants pocket.

Pramm held out his hand to receive the treasure, humbly. He purred, "Isn't it time to put this to an end?"

But then, Pramm watched in horror as Slake turned and grabbed at the already open window behind the desk. It creaked, loudly, as he forced it open to its physical limits.

"Arrivederci, Mr. Pramm!"

A split second later he saw Slake whip his legs out over the window ledge and jump.

Misely couldn't believe what he was seeing. He ran over to the window. He looked down and saw the figure of Slake crumpled in a heap two stories below.

But then, the figure began moving, unscathed by the fall. Slake had landed on the mattress stuffed onto the fire escape landing. It was the mattress he had seen the other day when he had made his tour of the back alley. Slake looked up and waved. He got to his feet and began running at full bore down the fire escape stairs to the alley below.

Misely watched him flee, in horror. The bluff had failed. Slake, like all good criminals, had figured out an escape route. Had Misely realized the function of the mattress, he could have yanked it down that morning. Why hadn't he figured it out?

Misely pulled his head back into the office room and looked around. He had failed to retrieve the bracelet, but there was still the New York reward. He sat at the desk and looked around. Slake was doing something at the desk and may have left something behind. He saw the remnants of the breakfast and a stack of unopened mail sitting on the corner of the desk. As he stuffed the envelopes into his breast pocket, he looked up to see the two visitors that had quietly entered the room.

One was a police officer in a deep blue serge uniform. The other was a large, mustachioed man dressed in a black suit, wearing a bowler hat and carrying an umbrella.

Misely began to tremble. It was the real Pramm and Lieutenant O'Hanrahan of the Metropolitan Police, who Misely recognized from previous interactions.

"Well, Officer, look what we have here! My twin! Or shall I say my nemesis. This is undoubtedly the clever creature that caused me great discomfort during my last trek to these putrid wastelands. Arrest this man, immediately!"

O'Hanrahan looked from the one to the other. He drew his gun from his holster and began to approach Misely.

Misely took a deep breath and stood up from the desk chair and bellowed: "Lieutenant O'Hanrahan, I am Otho Pramm! Please arrest that imposter!" He pointed an accusatory finger towards Pramm.

O'Hanrahan noticed that this new Pramm knew his name and rank. And he wondered what his Pramm meant by "putrid wastelands?"

Misely continued his performance to a dramatic crescendo. "Yes, Officer, that man is the fake. Do not be confused by the ingenuity of a crass reward-seeker. He is your false prophet!"

Pramm clapped his hands in mock appreciation. "Oh, chee-rio! Bravo, 'Mr. Pramm!' 'Handy-dandy, which is the justice, which is the thief?' like that? Now, officer, arrest this imposter at once!"

O'Hanrahan, again looked from one to the other. As he turned to take a better look at his Pramm, his pointed gun followed, aimed at Pramm.

"Moron! Do not point that weapon at me! There's the fraud - arrest him!" Pramm's bellow shook the flimsy office walls.

Misely stood his ground and adopted a demeanor of reason and patience. "Lieutenant O'Hanrahan, I have been on the trail of Jacques Capri for months. My efforts in this town have been fully sanctioned by your superiors and performed through all appropriate legal process." He pointed again at Pramm. "That man is a mere bounty hunter, a simple reward-seeker who is now interfering with the work that you and I are doing to protect the public from a vicious thief. Again, I respectfully request that you please arrest that man."

O'Hanrahan looked, again, from one to the other. He thought that the man at the desk looked more like Otho Pramm than Otho Pramm did! And he liked the Pramm at the desk more. He seemed reasonable. His Pramm seemed arrogant.

Pramm went red in the face: "Buffoon! Are you blind? Look at that fake mustache! It's practically falling off of his face! Arrest him immediately!" He pointed his umbrella, angrily.

Misely had been sweating profusely during his performance and felt some of the masking tape and bandage around his torso begin to slip, causing a slow movement of his stuffing towards the tug of gravity. He sat back down at the desk to prevent disaster and continued his improvisation.

"Officer O'Hanrahan, let's review the facts, simply." He smiled calmly and pleasantly. Absent mindedly, he opened the top desk drawer by just a crack and grabbed onto the lip of the drawer with his left hand. Pramm stood, arms folded, observing all. He saw Misely's move for the desk drawer and instinctively felt for the tiny silver pistol he maintained at all times in his breast pocket. But he did not draw.

"One of us is the real Otho Pramm. I posit to you: would the real Otho Pramm insult a fellow lawman as this man has done, several times already? Would the real Pramm lose his cool under pressure?"

Misely stood up and pointed past the two to the office door, holding his slipping girth back with the other arm. "I have entered these premises under force of law and have seized this office. Did you see your Pramm affix the seizure notice to the door before you entered? No? Please take a look."

Both looked towards the door and in a split second Misely made the decision he had hoped he would not have to make. He grabbed his failing stuffing and swung his legs around the window frame. He jumped.

The trip down to the mattress, two stories below, was not pleasant. As he fell, his left ear slammed against the rusty metal of the fire escape causing a stinging pain. He landed partly against the rusty structure of the fire escape and partly on the mattress, wedged between the two. His ribs and side were racked with pain. The impact of the fall caused one of the hot water bottles to burst at the neck. The water gushed out, soaking his torso. His pants and part of his suit coat were drenched in water. Dazed, he looked up to see the mustachioed visage of Pramm, leering out from the open window. He heard Pramm's voice yelling, "Get over here, idiot!" A split second later he saw Pramm holding a British Bobbie's whistle to his lips and blowing out a shrill call to his henchmen below.

Misely knew he had to get up and make a run for it. He rolled over to right himself and nearly passed out. But he breathed in deeply and struggled to his knees. And then, as in a dream, he encountered a thing of unimaginable beauty. He saw the sparkling of a thousand stars on a clear dark night, a beautiful and wonderful object. He couldn't believe his eyes. The Choate Diamond bracelet was hanging from the perforated metal of the fire escape landing by its clasp! It must have fallen out of Slake's pocket when he made his own freefall, minutes earlier.

With trembling, raccoon fingers, Misely carefully fished the bracelet from its snare and stuffed the object into his pants pocket. He righted himself and began running down the fire escape stairs to the alley below. He endured the agony of his badly bruised ribs, but pushed forward to the bottom. Pramm was now back again at the window, blowing the whistle, over and over.

Once free of the fire escape, he grabbed the pillows and the other hot water bottle from beneath his shirt, ripping the now soaked mess free from the masking tape truss. He chucked the assemblage onto the ground. He began a mad dash to the mouth of the alley at Holiday Street. As he ran, he held up the wet saggy trousers with his left hand. His oversized pants, no longer filled out with the false girth, were slipping badly. Somewhere in the fall he had lost the bowler hat. Only half of the stringy mustache remained glued to his face.

He made it to the intersection at Holiday and looked each way. A mere 20 yards away stood a man in a blue suit. The man spied Misely and began a fierce sprint along Holiday. Misely could hear the man screaming: "You there! Stop now! Freeze!" But Misely kept running along Holiday, away from the man.

Misely didn't think he could outrun the man - but he would try. His ears were filled with the sounds of his own panting and his heart throbbing at full bore. Why hadn't he tried to stay in better shape? As he breathed deeply, his ribs throbbed in agony. He looked behind to see the man in the blue suit gaining ground. He had to make it across the street. He saw a chance - a possibility of getting across the street and away from the man.

The streetcar in the road was beginning to accelerate away from its stop, scraping faster and faster along in its metal tracks. Misely ran out into the street, in front of the streetcar, just avoiding a fatal collision. The engineer yelled and Misely heard the blast of the streetcar horn, stabbing his ears with its sound.

But he had made it across the street; the man in the blue suit was stuck on the other side, temporarily blocked by the streetcar and the swell of early afternoon traffic.

Misely was almost there. Near collapse, he summoned his last strength and pushed his way through the front doors of Blickenstaff's. He stumbled past the line of patrons waiting for tables and headed straight for the kitchen.

The kitchen crew saw the odd man in the baggy, wet pants, but he passed by too quickly for anyone to react. And in another second, the man had pushed his way down the storeroom stairs and into the basement.

Once the door closed, Misely was cast into darkness. He felt his way down the stairwell grabbing onto the wall and banister to steady himself as he made his way to the basement floor. Once on the ground floor he felt his way forward, four paces until he brushed up against the round drum he had placed there the day before. He reached into the drum and withdrew his flashlight.

He clicked on the flashlight and looked around. He had made it to his escape route. He reached into the drum and pulled out a dry dress shirt and pair of pants. He quickly pulled off the wet pants and slipped on the dry trousers, securing the precious bracelet in the left pocket. He ditched the wet shirt, changed, and rolled the wet pants and shirt into a ball, chucking them into the barrel. He felt at the remains of the false mustache on his face, and pulled it off. He realized he was still wearing the greasy grey toupee, so he pulled the bobby pins from his hair to release the toupee and stuck the nasty mustache onto the wig, chucking them both into the drum.

He had no choice but to put the wet, black suit coat back on. He had not planned to change the jacket. It would be ok, even though a few sizes too large. But he hadn't planned on it becoming soaking wet. He put the lid on the drum, sealing away, forever, his final performance as Otho Pramm.

Still out of breath, he grabbed the flashlight and made his way through the basement towards the Towers Building elevator. He now knew the route well. With any luck he would soon be free. As he walked quickly through the corridors, he listened. He heard the sound of voices in the distance. His pursuers were coming into the maze. "Good luck," he thought.

He finally made it to the Towers elevator and pressed the call button, forcefully, several times. There was just one task left to perform.

Arthur Slake had just about finished up inside Suite 804. He had gathered his insurance forms, stock certificates, notepaper and envelopes and had chucked them into the paper shopping bag. He was now furiously wiping down the telephone handset with his handkerchief. He had wiped down the drawer handles of his desk and filing cabinet.

He felt, again, at his pants pocket, as though doing so would bring back his treasure. He cursed his bad luck in losing the bracelet. It must have fallen out somewhere back in the alley.

Not only was his bracelet gone, but also his opportunity to fleece the lamb again - if he had only made it to tomorrow? But it was too late for regrets.

As he opened his office door, bag in hand, he nearly ran into the blue-uniformed man that stood at the door, blocking his way. Slake retreated two paces back into his office, his heart pounding.

"I'm sorry, sir. Didn't mean to sneak up on you like that. Just one today."

It was the mailman. He handed Slake the one letter and left for the next office, leaving the door ajar.

Slake put the paper bag down by his desk and looked at the letter. It couldn't be. It was a letter from himself, addressed to him, in one of his own envelopes. He had never addressed an envelope to himself. He tore open the envelope and saw the one-word message written on his own notepaper. It said: "Caught!" and was signed, "Otho Pramm."

A split second later he became aware of the odd looking man standing at his doorway. Out of the corner of his eye he saw the blur of something flying through the air - it was pink - like a small pink football. It was headed straight for him. He heard the man cry out, loudly: "Arthur Slake - think fast!"

Slake instinctively grabbed and caught the flying object with his left hand. As he looked at the strange thing he heard the man yell: "You've been served!"

And with that, Misely made a mad dash to the stairwell. He emerged into the lobby and stood back looking to see if the coast was clear. He saw no tormentors, so he walked confidently through the lobby and out the front door. He quickly looked up and down Prince Street - just the usual pedestrian traffic. He saw the streetcar pulling up across the street.

He ran across the street without calamity and hopped onto the car, just as it was pulling away. He paid the fare and took a seat in the rear. The streetcar was going in the wrong direction - away from Elk Neck. But he didn't care. He needed to get off the street, quickly, and move as far away from the scene as possible. The streetcar line ended at the bus terminal, just a quarter mile or so from the taxi dispatch lot. He would simply pick up a taxi back to Elk Neck.

As the streetcar headed away, it passed O'Hanrahan who was engaged in animated conversation with the blue-suited man. The man began speaking into a walkie talkie. Neither man looked up to see Misely riding by.

The streetcar ride was uneventful. It gave Misely an opportunity to take stock of the situation. He had never felt happier in his entire adult life. He had hit the trifecta; pulled-off a hat trick. He had retrieved the bracelet, served the process and collected significant evidence against Slake. That meant a payday, Choate's reward, and the possibility of getting his hands on the New York reward, with Ollie Choate's assistance. More importantly, it meant he would have proven himself to Ollie Choate, the "cherub." The possibility of a legal apprenticeship seemed more real than ever.

The streetcar arrived at its terminus by the bus line. Coincidently, as Misely exited and walked past the terminal, he came within a few yards of Goodley, who sat in the bus terminal with his carpetbag and sample case of pills. Goodley had managed his own escape and was heading south.

During the cab ride home, he thought back on the day's events. His ear and ribs were still sore. But he would survive. He was glad he had come up with the idea of using the trumped-up legal forms to post at the door. He knew that the forms were actually meant for landlords to claim liens on a tenant's possessions. They had nothing to do with "seizing" a premises. But they looked authoritative and gave him the split second he needed to jump from the window.

Luck was on his side, he had to admit. Diverting Slake over to Whitelake bought him just enough time to check-out the office. And finding Slake standing in his own office with the door wide open was a minor miracle. He wondered if Slake had received his "Pramm" letter, designed to smoke-out Slake and drive him back over to the Muncie, in the event Slake had made other luncheon plans?

Once back in Elk Neck he phoned for Ollie Choate. Honora Blaine said that he had gone for the day, but encouraged Misely to stop in first thing Saturday morning to give Mr. Choate the good news about serving Slake. She would prepare the service return for him and get the check cut for his fee.

Arthur Slake had been holing-up at Ware's that afternoon. He had abandoned the blonde toupee. As the sun began to set and dusk settled, he put his plan into effect. He had decided to let a few hours slip by to let things cool down. He would wait for twilight and backtrack to the alley to search for the bracelet.

He approached the alley with extreme caution. He looked carefully up and down but saw and heard no movement. He worked his way back towards the fire escape, peering down at the ground for any glittering object. He came across two inexplicable hot water bottles, both mottled with strands of bandage and masking tape. He kicked them aside out of curiosity and continued towards the fire escape.

Once in front of the stairs, he bent over looking throughout the vicinity. If the bracelet had fallen, that's where it should be. Somewhere near the intersection of the stairway and ground. But he saw nothing.

He hadn't planned on climbing back up the fire escape stairs, but he was driven to find the bracelet. It could be sitting on the mattress, waiting to be snagged.

He cautiously climbed back up, first trying to look into the windows located at the given landing. It was warm and most offices had windows open. He finally approached the landing with the mattress. He looked up two stories towards the seventh floor window, his jumping point. He saw nothing suspicious. He saw the open window at the mattress landing. A stained chiffon curtain was blowing gently in and out of the open window. But he saw and heard no movement, so he advanced up to the mattress.

As he was beginning to inspect the mattress, he felt something touch his neck. And then he felt his head being pulled, and then slammed, violently, against the window frame. His neck had been snared by an umbrella handle.

"Come here my slippery eel!" The umbrella held Slake's head firmly against the frame. He could not move. And a second later he felt the officer's service revolver press against his temple.

Misely slept well that evening, despite his injuries. In the morning light, he inspected his face in the bathroom mirror. His ear was red - a little roughed up. But otherwise he would survive. He enjoyed his dry cereal, clothed in his long john pajamas. He knew the day would be extraordinary.

By 10:00 AM he had found his way over to the law office of Kent and McCullough. Honora Blaine did not work Saturdays, but she had left the service return paperwork to be signed along with an envelope addressed to Misely, at her desk.

Moments later, he was greeted enthusiastically by Ollie Choate, who bounded down the stairs.

"Ah - there you are! Let's finalize things in my office, shall we?"

Misely followed Choate back up the stairs and took a seat across from Choate, who sat at his desk.

"Honora left a message saying you had good news, Misely! Do you have the bracelet?"

With that, Misely reached into his pants pocket and extracted the gleaming marvel. He handed it over to Choate, proudly.

Choate held the bracelet up to the light of the window. He squinted, turning the bracelet over in his hand and sniffed. "I'm sorry Misely, but this is not the bracelet. These are not the Choate diamonds."

Misely felt as though he had just been punched in the gut.

"What? Did you say that isn't the bracelet?"

Choate quickly turned the tiny key sitting in the lock of his top desk drawer. He opened the drawer and, in an instant, placed the bracelet into the drawer and turned the key.

"That's correct, Misely - that was a costume piece - just glass, but you wouldn't be expected to know the difference. Regrettably, I am not in a position to provide a reward for retrieving such, but I do want to tell you how much I appreciate your efforts - even though not successful."

Choate smiled, bashfully, exposing his tiny white teeth. Misely was speechless.

"Now, as to the matter of the Choate Diamonds, the family has decided to turn the search over to the professionals - we're going to let the police handle everything from here on out. But, I encourage you to keep a lookout in the 'Lost and Founds.' Perhaps someone will want to reclaim that costume piece? It will be here in safekeeping should the owner come forward. Please feel free to keep me apprised."

Misely sat back in the chair, thunderstruck. He had been unconsciously feeling at the newspaper clipping in his jacket pocket - about Capri and the New York reward. It was moot.

Choate looked up from his desk, no longer smiling. "Not to be rude, Misely, but I believe our business is now concluded and I do have other matters to attend to. Please stop down to sign the return at Honora's station. Your check for serving the process will be found there as well. Good day." Choate waved his hand, dismissively.

"Yes Mr. Choate. Thank you."

Misely found his way down the stairs, defeated. He signed the paperwork and opened the envelope with his check for $35.00. He had forgotten to add-in the carfare.

Dejected, Misely walked back to 7 North Central. His physical discomfort had been temporarily staunched by his optimism over the day's prospects. Now, his side began to ache and his left ear throbbed. Ollie Choate, the "cherub" had done him in. It was bad enough that Misely would never receive the reward he had so dearly earned; worse was the likelihood that Misely had been cast off, for good. Choate would never be comfortable having Misely as his apprentice. Misely's presence would be a constant reminder of Choate's betrayal.

Back at 7 North Central, Misely sat at his desk and looked at the pile of correspondence that he had grabbed from the top of Slake's desk just prior to Pramm's arrival. He hadn't had the chance to go through the envelopes and did so, now.

He realized that the envelopes had become partly soaked by the exploded hot water bottle. They were still damp. He opened them up. They were all intended for Goodley - there was absolutely nothing relating to Slake. Two were forms for refunds. A few more appeared to be complaints; a typewritten letter threatened legal action. A handwritten letter mentioned something about the police. Roderick could not figure out the entire letter because the ink had run.

Several more were orders for more pills. He tore the checks into pieces and chucked them into his metal waste paper basket. He counted the still damp cash: $26.00. He decided to place the $26.00 "in escrow" pending any published requests by the police for information on Goodley. He would give it a couple months and then would allow the funds to "escheat" to the finder, based on legal principles presumed by Misely but not yet fully explored.

Two days later found Misely sitting at his favorite booth at County Restaurant, reading a discarded Star Sentinel. The headline read: "Wall Street Casanova Captured, Here!"

The photo showed Slake in handcuffs being ushered into police headquarters by a solemn looking Lieutenant O'Hanrahan of the Metropolitan force. Behind him, the enormous man in the black suit and bowler hat looked on, smugly.

The story detailed the capture of Jacques Capri through the efforts of Oxford Investigation's own Otho Pramm. Police Commissioner Brantley heaped praise upon Otho Pramm and gushed about the incredible cooperation between the Department and Oxford Investigations. Captain Wilmer Claxton, asked about the Department's opportunity to work with the famous Otho Pramm was quoted as saying, "After our initial meeting with Mr. Pramm, the men said it would only be fair to draw straws to see who would get the assignment."

No mention was made regarding a Pramm double. And the story never mentioned the name "Arthur Slake." Looking at the photo of the wig-less Capri on the front page, Roderick guessed that Kent and Choate would never realize that their prey had been snared and would soon be hauled off to New York City - and definitely unavailable for a civil trial in Elk Neck Township.

Misely returned to his quarters with the abandoned newspaper. He tore out the article and dropped it into file "C-59-31 Gilvane-Process." He looked at file "C-59-32 Choate Bracelet." The folder was completely empty. He pulled his copybook ledger from out of his filing cabinet and sat back down at his desk. He entered the Gilvane case "paid in full." The Choate case was marked "D" for "desperate."

He rescued his portable typewriter from among the books heaped onto the tiny pupil's desk stuffed into his living quarters. He typed out a letter addressed to Oliver Choate, Esquire:

Dear Mr. Choate:
I wanted to thank you, again, for the opportunity to work with you and Mr. Kent on Mrs. Gilvane's case. Although I regret that I was not able to accomplish every goal assigned, I am happy to have, at least, assisted by serving the process on

Arthur Slake. I hope that you are successful in bringing Slake to justice and I wish you continued good fortune in your efforts to retrieve the Choate Diamonds. Please keep me in mind should process serving or other opportunities arise in connection with your practice.
  Sincerely,
  Roderick Misely.

Misely held no ill will towards Choate. He felt that Choate had simply acted as any rational businessman, weighing the costs and benefits of his deal with Misely. Breaching the agreement made good sense for Choate, economically. The verbal agreement would be unenforceable. And Choate had presumed that Misely and his services were non-factors; disposable. It was Roderick's job to convince Choate that a future business relationship with Misely had value. Misely didn't care which attorney apprenticed him. He just needed one and Choate would certainly do. And next time he would get the fee, plus relevant surcharge, set out in writing.

Months passed. The uncertainty of fall slipped into the bitterness of a cold winter. Quietly, in a government office in Elk Neck, thirty pieces of silver were proffered by a giving hand and accepted by a receiving hand. The receiving hand had discussed the transaction, preliminarily, by phone. "Yes," he knew the man and knew him well. And "Yes," he could certainly arrange an introduction. But it would not be a typical introduction. Far from it.
  The compact was sealed by receipt of the check made payable by Oxford Investigations to Grayson Porter. An instruction letter followed, detailing and confirming the matters discussed by phone. Grayson Porter set about to follow the instructions.
  And so it was that Roderick Misely had been invited to the office of Grayson Porter on a bleak January day of the new decade. Porter, near retirement, had been elevated to position

of Ombudsman to the County Council. He was the "ears" for Council Executive Jim Bynam - one of Bynam's inner circle, a confidante. His rank carried with it the necessary trappings, including a spacious executive office on the fourth floor of the County Council Office Building.

The office held a substantial desk, thick carpeting and a plush sofa on which Porter often napped in the late afternoons. A coat closet was built into the wall, just behind the desk. But Porter's coats, galoshes, coat hangers and boxed-up Christmas decorations had been removed from the closet over the prior weekend. The closet now held only a large person in a black suit, one black bowler hat and a black umbrella. The hat sat atop the handle of a black umbrella, which leaned against the back wall of the closet. The door was kept slightly ajar and the man peered out through the slender crack between door and frame.

Porter's desk had been re-positioned 180 degrees by Pramm and his associate so as to provide a person peeking through the door crack with a perfect view of the individual sitting behind the desk. Porter had mildly protested the re-positioning of his desk. He thought it wouldn't make sense for a visitor to take the seat behind the desk with the office occupant sitting where the visitor normally would - and that no one would position the desk so as to face the blank wall or closet. But Pramm dismissed the objections and suggested that Porter attend to his own responsibilities.

Pramm had never given up on his search for the dangerous imposter. Following his success in the Capri case, Pramm had assigned two of his best men to develop a list of private investigators and flimflam men known to work the City and environs. The men were instructed to pay particular attention to those known to use costumes and disguises. Pramm had gotten a decent look at his doppelganger back at the Muncie. The faulty mustache, grey wig and bowler hat had not disguised the man's eyes, nose and complexion. And Pramm had invented Oxford Investigation's system for observing and recalling a subject's facial features, despite disguises and imperfect environmental conditions.

Pramm had been disappointed, so far. He had eliminated each of the losers dredged-up by his men from among the muck of the City. He was down to one, final long shot; a small time yokel on the City outskirts by the name of Roderick Misely.

He would put the imposter away for a long time. Back at the Muncie Building, the imposter had sat at the desk and fiddled with the top drawer. Pramm believed that the man was either displaying a nervous affectation or, more likely, fishing for the loaded gun that was later found in the drawer and booked into evidence. The fidgety attempt to grab at the gun had put Pramm on his guard and qualified as an assault - a felony - as far as Pramm was concerned.

The assignation had been set for 10:00 AM that morning. Pramm had arrived at 8:00 AM with his driver and lieutenant to set the scene and run through the 'script' with Porter, several more times. The assistants now waited below in the black sedan parked in the rear alley. Finally, at 10:00 AM, the brown-suited man was ushered into Porter's office by the receptionist.

"Mr. Misely - thank you for coming by today!" the two shook hands, warmly.

"My pleasure, Mr. Porter!" Misely was offered the seat behind the desk. Pramm looked directly into the face of Misely from his vantage point in the closet.

"Now, I've asked you here today for two matters that may interest you. One is routine, but the other represents, in my view, a unique opportunity."

Misely looked on, eagerly. "Sounds great Mr. Porter. What is it?"

Porter leaned forward towards Misely, dropping his voice to communicate secrecy. "Well young man, inquiries are being made about you!"

Misely looked on, cautiously. "Really? Do you have a lead for a new client?"

"Well, perhaps much better than that. Let's just say that a very important man would like to make your acquaintance!"

"I am all ears!" He placed his right hand to his ear to dramatize the statement.

"Good, good," chortled Porter. "It is the one and only Otho Pramm of New York fame!"

Misely appeared shocked. "'The' Otho Pramm? Really? Wow!" He sat back in his chair and glanced up at the ceiling in disbelief, letting out a small whistle. He looked eagerly to Porter. "That would be tremendous, Mr. Porter. What an opportunity! Does he want to hire me for a case?"

"Well that would be up to Mr. Pramm. I don't have the details. I only know that he contacted me to track you down because, quite frankly, you're a little difficult to get a hold of! You're still not in the phone book!"

Misely looked on, earnestly. "Oh - well I've never gotten around to bothering with a phone because there are so many payphones around - but people know how to get hold of me. They just drop a note right under my door." Misely pantomimed a person scribbling out a note and slipping it under the door. He produced an accompanying whistle as a sound effect.

Porter shook his head in mock disbelief. "You haven't changed a bit!" He then looked solemnly towards Misely. "Now, to reiterate, if I could arrange a meeting between you and Mr. Pramm, you would be willing?"

Misely beamed. "Oh absolutely! The man is a genius and a legend! Did he want me to call him to set it up?"

"No, no - I can get hold of you with a note." Porter imitated Misely's earlier pantomime of slipping a note under the door, minus the whistle.

Porter then looked on, blankly at Misely. He had been going off the script, slightly, improvising to adjust to Misely's responses. He had lost his place and had almost forgotten the next part.

"Oh - the other matter was my sister, Ellie. Her dog - a little poodle - went missing last week. Could you give her a call? I told her I would track you down for her." He scribbled out a note with his sister's name and phone number and handed it over to Misely.

"Absolutely! Thank you for both leads! This has been a banner day!"

And with that, Porter and Misely both rose. Porter hobbled from around the desk and shook hands, vigorously, with Misely. He was relieved that his performance was over.

"Very good, Mr. Misely. Don't be a stranger - and Happy New Year!"

Misely brushed back his thick red-blonde hair with his hand and smiled back, his broad smile revealing a missing molar. "Yes! You too, Mr. Porter, you too!"

Moments later, Pramm forced his frame from out of the cramped closet. He was gravely disappointed. That was not the man he observed at the Muncie building. The ruddy complexion - the hair - the missing tooth - and the mannerisms. Not him. There was a vague similarity in the eyes - but the rest was all wrong. And this man did not flinch when confronted with the possibility of meeting with Pramm. There were no desk drawer fiddlings. This man seemed genuinely enthused at the prospect of meeting him. 'Poor buffoon! To think that Otho Pramm would ever seek out an association with a mere dogcatcher!'

He peered down his nose at Porter. "And that was Misely? You're certain?"

Porter pulled himself up, proudly. "Yes, sir. Unequivocally, that was Misely!"

The black suit, bowler and bumbershoot exited the County Council Office Building. Porter watched from his window as the black sedan rolled away down the alley.

Christmas and New Year's had passed, but the festivities were well underway for the three men seated in the private dining room of the lodge of the Beneficent Cavaliers, Elk Neck

Chapter. The room was seldom booked. It adjoined the regular dining room of the lodge, which, on a cold Thursday night in January, was now virtually deserted.

Grayson Porter had been holding court for hours with his two guests, Roderick and Tack Misely. A virtual banquet had been prepared for the private party, courtesy of Porter. French Onion soup, a garden salad, mashed potatoes, peas and sirloin steaks had all been completely consumed hours before. Misely had passed up the madeleine and ice cream desert 50 minutes ago. He was full and not used to eating so much. Tack had plowed through every course, including half of Roderick's abandoned steak and multiple helpings of potatoes.

Porter had ordered wine for the table - and there had been multiple bottles, so far. But Tack had inquired about the availability of beer. To his great relief, there had been plenty. Roderick had been nursing a single glass of the chosen cabernet all evening. Porter was telling 'the story' for the fourth time that evening.

"It was a phone call out of the blue! Pramm's henchmen contacted Jim Bynam, asking just who within the community understood the 'pulse' of Elk Neck - knew her citizens and her 'goings on'! Jim said, 'Why that would be my right hand man, Grayson Porter - he knows everyone and everything about Elk Neck!' And that's because I have served successfully though five administrations here - but anyway - when Pramm's man asked specifically about you, Roderick, that's when I got a little suspicious. I decided to go along with things and sniff things out."

Roderick nodded as he had been for half of the evening.

Tack chimed in. "Tell the part about when you talked to Pramm!" Tack's voice boomed, ricocheting around the dining area but disturbing no one. All other diners had since left for cozy homes and beds.

Tack had begun the evening in his brown suit outfit, the same one used for the meeting with Pramm. Suit coats and ties were required in the dining room. Roderick had assisted his uncle in assembling the suit and tie disguise for the gambit, courtesy of the Dime A' Dozen thrift shop. The coat was a little tight, but did the trick. Tack had slowly disassembled the outfit throughout the evening. The tie was loosely hanging from his now unbuttoned neck collar. The suit coat sat crumpled in a heap next to him on an unused chair.

Porter lowered his head and drew forward as though telling a secret for the first time. "Well, I called the number and was put through directly to Mr. Pramm. But I did not like Mr. Pramm's attitude - not one bit! He was very smug and sounded like he thought himself some kind of big shot, so when he offered me $150.00 to set up a meeting in my office, I said 'yes' because I knew he was up to no good!" Porter banged the table with his open hand for emphasis.

"And when he said that he wanted to hide out of sight and just get a look at you and that there'd be a script to say to draw you into conversation, I knew it was time to help a friend in need - the man who saved my bacon just a few years ago, my good friend, Roderick Misely!" Tears began to well up in Porter's eyes.

"I told him, 'Yes, you betcha, Mr. Pramm! Glad to help you!' And then I drove straight over to Roderick's and left that note saying to call me pronto! And the rest was history!"

Porter practically bellowed the last part.

Tack was shaking his head in admiration. Roderick was embarrassed, again.

"So tell me again which one had the idea to take advantage of my acting skills?" Tack was coughing out a laugh.

"Why, that was me, after consultation with Roderick, of course. Roderick and I had pulled the old 'switcheroo' in another case on which I am bound to secrecy, except to say that my hide was saved - and well, thanks to your consummate acting skills, Tack, we pulled it off! We pulled it off, indeed!" Porter slapped his knee, loudly, as Tack laughed.

Roderick smiled to himself. He knew, then, that Pramm was hunting him and he had come up with the idea of having his uncle stand in as a substitute. Porter could honestly identify Misely for Pramm - it would just be a slightly different Misely. And Roderick knew that Tack would come through for him. They were family - of the same stock - they would always look out for each other.

But Roderick was troubled greatly as to Porter's motivation. Why had Porter decided to blow the whistle on Pramm? Throughout the long, never-ending, evening, Porter had declared his steadfast friendship for Roderick and appreciation for the services Misely provided on the one matter in which they were involved. Roderick did not fully understand why. He and Porter had a business arrangement that was concluded satisfactorily by Misely. He had barely thought of Porter over the ensuing years. Yet Porter had declared earlier that "Seldom a week goes by that I do not thank my lucky stars for the help I received from my dear friend, Roderick Misely!"

Misely had never felt comfortable in accepting kindness from strangers, let alone, former customers. He didn't want to be part of the social fabric - the community. He relished his independence and freedom from society's whims and obligations. He did not want to waste a lifetime serving the process of conformity. But he had to admit it; having Porter's friendship had probably saved his life. He was beginning to accept the notion that having a friend or two was not such a bad thing. It would take some getting used to.

Tack had changed the subject back to horse racing and the two regaled each other with stories of the great Elk Neck thoroughbreds of yesteryear. Tack spiced up Porter's understanding of the local scene by supplying tidbits of insider gossip and lore about jockeys, trainers and tracks.

The evening wore on. Eventually, the kitchen shut down and the wait staff were cut loose. Only Stanley, the lodge's groundskeeper and occasional bus boy, stayed behind to mop up.

Misely was dying. The two were now on their fifth round of stories about the Wrens, most of which had already been discussed hours before. Misely sat, miserably, wishing that he were comfortably back at 7 North Central, asleep on his cot. He thought about the last time he found himself under similar circumstances with Porter. He was thinking back fondly to his hot plate. He excused himself and left the table, ostensibly to visit the restroom.

Had a disinterested observer viewed the scene at the lodge, such an observer may have noticed the brown-suited man detouring away from the restroom and into the deserted kitchen area. The man would have been seen examining the stove's burners and dials and then moments later, rummaging through the pantry and rifling through the variety of canned goods.

Files C-59-31 "Gilvane-Process" and C-59-32 "Choate Bracelet" and can still be found in the file cabinet located inside of the living quarters of Roderick Misely, Consultant, at 7 North Central, just up the street from the northeast corner of Iroquois and Central.